THE CHALAM FÆRYTALES BOOK III

THE PARALLAX

MORGAN G FARRIS

For all those times I watched The Princess Bride.
I'm pretty sure I built my life on the theory that
happily ever after is inevitable.

THE PARALLAX (THE CHALAM FÆRYTALES, BOOK III)

3

A paperback edition of this book was published in 2019 by Minor 5 Publishing.

FIRST MINOR 5 PUBLISHING PAPERBACK EDITION PUBLISHED 2019.

Designed by Morgan G Farris.

ISBN 978-1-7331668-1-2

TABLE OF CONTENTS

Map

MAJESTIC MOUNTAINS
CHESEDELLE CASTLE
HARAVELLE
MIDVAR
N
W
E
S
to the Western Continent
Har Omer
the Northern Pass
Ramleh
TSAFONE
Province
Adina's House
BENALLE
Province
GAV
Province
NAVAH
WILD WOOD
Gaevast
BENALLE PALACE
QADIM
Province
Benalle City
Army Encampment
Hazelnut Forest
TEMAN
Province
Teman City
to Goleath
the Secret Place
Fount Barakah
THE GREAT SEA

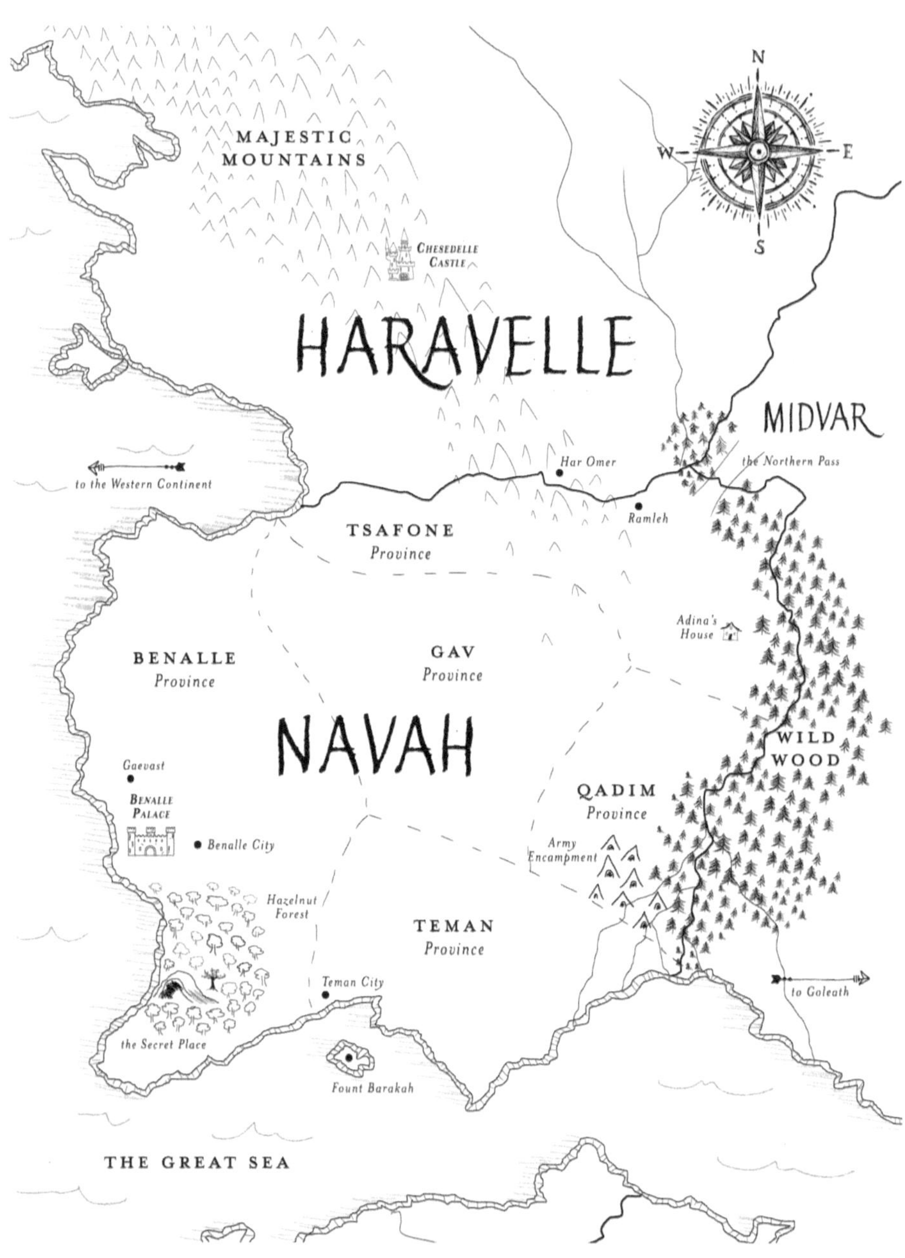

Chapter I

The snow bit through his gloves, burning his trembling knuckles as they ground into the white expanse. His breath came in gusts, puffing clouds around his beloved's face as she lay trembling beneath him. He kept his head low, below the fray, his body covering hers as best he could as arrow after arrow whizzed over them. The last one had been too close for comfort, the dribble of blood on her cheek already drying on her skin.

"Through the trees!"

"Don't let them get away!"

The Haravellian soldiers shouted their commands as the king and queen of Navah lay sprawled in the snow, hiding from the sudden attack. Ferryl could feel Adelaide's heart pounding in time with his, not in the embrace of lovers but rather the desperate grip of two people dodging the arrows of the enemy.

The icy ground was taking its toll on Ferryl's hands as he pinned his wife beneath him, the skin of his palms freezing though sweat beaded his brow. He dared to lift his head just enough to see exactly what was happening.

"Rebels," he spat, catching sight of the attackers as they jumped from one tree to the next, hiding behind the fat, snow-covered trunks, firing their arrows with dizzying perfection.

Beside him, a Haravellian soldier fell with a thud, his eyes frozen in shock, his blood staining the snow, a crimson pool slowly growing beneath his throat. And around him in a pillar of black…those were…

Moths.

Black moths.

By the hundreds.

His eyes grew wide as he took in the sight of the minuscule beasts that had once plagued and tormented him. The sunlight glinted off their wings, which were iridescent despite their sheer blackness. So similar to the moths he had seen that morning not so long ago on the mountain in Haravelle, despite their darkness. More than moths. More than insects, they were…

I don't think they're really moths, he heard his wife say in his mind. He turned his attention back to her, only to narrowly dodge another arrow as it whizzed just above his head.

Ferryl gritted his teeth, took the risk, and grabbed the fallen soldier's bow before jumping to his feet, pulling Adelaide into a sprint with him.

This way, he said for only her benefit. She followed without hesitation, letting him shield her with his body as they sped through the icy forest.

She landed by a fat sycamore, her breast rising and falling rapidly, her back to the fat trunk. Ferryl covered her body with his own, peering around the tree as her hot breaths caressed his neck. Just one shot…if he could just get in one shot…

Ferryl, she said, her words breathless even in her mind. There were ten rebels that he could see, their black arrows meeting their targets much too easily. Perhaps these were Midvarish wraith beasts. Or perhaps they were just boys. They moved too rapidly to tell. Either way, Ferryl and Derwin had met one of them in Ramleh only a few months ago. Met and killed him. Today would be no different.

Ferryl, he heard again, turning to meet her eyes. But Adelaide was not looking at her husband. And when he realized her gaze was fixed behind him, the hairs on the back of his neck stood on end.

He whirled, facing his enemy whilst simultaneously pressing Adelaide against the sycamore. For as long as he could, Providence save him, he would protect her. Because the world did not yet know that she lived. It did not yet know that the lost princess Adelaide of Haravelle had been found.

And Providence help them all when that fact was no longer a secret.

No, this was just a random rebel attack as they journeyed south to Navah. It had to be.

"Hiding something, Princeling?" said the man. No, not a man. A beast. A wraith. A devil incarnate. A demon made flesh with teeth as black as obsidian and skin as rough as boot hide. He grinned—if you could call it a grin—and his eyes glittered with the promise of a swift death.

"How rude of me," the man went on, and Ferryl used the moment to press Adelaide more closely behind him. He dropped the soldier's bow, inching his hand toward his side for the hilt of his sword. Adelaide's breath was steady at his neck.

"I suppose you're not a princeling anymore. Daddy's dead."

Ferryl bared his teeth, unsheathing his blade, the metal singing as it extended before him, the steel glinting off of the sun-kissed snow, momentarily blinding them both.

"What is that you're hiding so fiercely?" the beast asked, cocking his black head to one side, unfazed by Ferryl's sword. Blood dripped from his thick hands, a shock of crimson against his charred skin. The blood of Haravellian soldiers, no doubt. Ferryl took a moment to thank Providence that King Aaron and Queen Avigail's carriage was far down the road towards Benalle—hopefully out of danger.

The beast-man bore no weapons. At least not any that Ferryl could see. He was not sure whether to be relieved or terrified. But he let the bastard speak. Let the beast buy him some time while he made a plan and figured out how in Sheol to keep Adelaide safe while he killed a nearly invincible foe.

"What a pity that you should lose your whore so soon after losing your dear father," the man purred.

Ferryl lunged. Whether it was prompted by blind instinct or vengeful rage, he couldn't be sure, but he would be damned if he let this beast get the better of him. And he sure as Sheol wasn't about to let him take his wife.

So Ferryl lunged. And parried. He whirled and spun. He called on every skill which had been trained into him and every ounce of the strength in his bones.

But it was not enough. Not against a man who was more than a man. Not against a demon.

Ferryl cried out as the beast whipped a sword from his back, slicing through the air with deadly accuracy, aiming right for his heart. It missed, but only just. And when Ferryl whirled to parry, that's when he realized—

"Adelaide!" he called out, panicking that she was not there at the tree. He realized his mistake the moment the beast started laughing.

"Not doing a very good job of hiding your precious princess," he said. And then he lunged. The beast moved so fast Ferryl hardly had a split-second to react. He lifted his sword but it was too late.

No, it *should* have been too late.

The beast should have killed him. Skewered him like a stuck pig.

Instead the beast fell, toppling to the ground like a sack of potatoes. And from behind his gargantuan form, Ferryl saw the reason for his foe's sudden demise.

"I am not a princess," Adelaide growled, ripping a dagger from the beast's back. "I am the queen of Navah."

The beast groaned, clutching his side from where the black blood pumped in thick rivers across the snow. Ferryl wasted no time lifting his sword, and the beast's head was severed with one fatal blow.

Black, oily blood sprayed her face, neck, and hands, yet Adelaide stood resolute, eye to eye with the king of Navah. Her breaths came heavily but steadily, the tremble of the dagger in her hand the only glimmer of any fear in her veins.

A moth—no, a butterfly landed on her shoulder, its wings glowing fiercely and radiantly ruby against the backdrop of fallen snow. And Ferryl could have sworn it bowed. *Bowed.* But he couldn't be sure before it flitted away.

"Where did you learn—"

"Your Majesties!" cried a soldier, cutting Ferryl off. "Here, John! They're over here!"

Though she surely knew what question he'd started to ask, Adelaide said nothing as she let the soldiers guide her back to the road and the carriage that awaited them.

~

Steam billowed around her bare shoulders, curling the rogue midnight locks that spilled from the pile of hair atop her head. She poured a basin of water over her arm as Ferryl made his way into the tiny inn privy somewhere inside of Navah's northern borders.

Wordlessly, he took the cloth from the side of her small tub and set about washing her. Adelaide let out a soft moan as he began working a handful of lavender oil into her shoulders.

"Are you going to tell me where in the world you got that dagger, or are you going to leave me guessing?" he asked.

She breathed a laugh, her black lashes resting on her cheeks as she relaxed into his touch. Sixteen years. Sixteen years he had known her, and yet Adelaide of Haravelle never ceased to surprise him. And terrify him.

"Mother gave it to me when we were in Chesedelle. She said it was no good for a queen to be unarmed. Or unskilled."

"You learned to brandish a blade in our time in Haravelle?" he chuckled, unable to resist pressing a kiss to her bare, oil-slicked shoulder.

"No. But I did learn a few tricks on exactly where to stick it should the need arise."

"I see," he said. "And you never thought to tell me?"

She cocked her head to one side, meeting his eyes. "Would you have approved?"

"Absolutely not," he said.

She kissed him soundly and with so much passion that Ferryl's interest in his wife's weapon-wielding soon began to wane.

"Which is why I didn't tell you," she said when at last she took her lips from his.

"Adelaide, I will protect you."

"I know, Ferryl. But you may not always be able to."

"Don't be silly," he said. "You're not allowed to leave my side."

"If you think that now that I'm your wife you're going to put me in a cage and pull me out to pet me now and then, you married the wrong woman."

He laughed, pulling her hair down and running his fingers through it. "There is no cage that could hold you, my love. Or I would have already tried."

She turned, resting her chin on her arms where they perched on the side of the tub.

"Ferryl, I know you're joking. But I also know that if you could, you would hide me away from the world until all this business with Midvar is over."

He looked down, fiddling with the thread of her washcloth, knowing it was true, knowing she was right. The woman saw straight through him. She always had.

She drew his attention back to her, running her fingers through his hair. "We face war, my love. You cannot protect me from everything."

"I can try, can't I?"

"Providence has brought us both this far. Do not take the credit from him so soon."

He pressed his brow to hers, the steam from her bath billowing around them both. "Are you always right about everything?"

"Yes," she said.

He kissed her once, swiftly, reaching so that he might lift her out of the tub. The water sloshed around her, dousing his gauzy white shirt and breeches. But he did not care. Holding his wife to his chest like a newborn babe, he carried her out of the privy and into their tiny attached bedchamber, laying her down on the paltry excuse for a bed.

He climbed over her, devouring the sight of her beneath him as he said, "Well, you were certainly right about one thing."

"And what is that?" she asked, a smile threatening her mouth as he moved to remove his sodden clothes.

"It is good for a queen to be armed," he said, settling himself over her once more. He bent and pressed a kiss to her neck, still slick from her bath. "It gives her people peace of mind," he said as he let his lips make their way down, down, down… "It gives her husband peace of mind," he went on. When she let out a little breath of delight, he smiled against her skin and continued his exploration. "And it is certainly a turn on."

"You, husband, are hopeless," she said, and he could hear the smile in her voice as he moved to worship the queen of Navah.

CHAPTER II

he room was dark. Too dark for the middle of the day. Michael walked gingerly down the small hall that spilled into the sitting room before him. The windows that boasted views of the hazelnut forest beyond the castle were hidden behind thick velvet curtains, allowing not a single ray of sunlight to penetrate the space. Instead, ghostly orbs of candlelight hovered in the room like the souls of the dead. A candle on a table. A single candle by the chair. Hardly enough light to see the next step in front of him.

But Michael walked on.

"Your Majesty?" he said hesitantly. There was no answer. He tried again and was greeted only with eerie silence. So he decided to call her by her name, in the hope it would offend her enough to answer.

"Meria?"

Still, the queen said not a word.

But he could see her, sitting solemn and still in the chair that faced the drawn curtains. He could make out her slender silhouette in the candlelight. She was a statue, holding vigil over a loved one. A monument to a kingdom marred by death. A queen of dark magic, frozen in time by her own transgressions, her own sins.

"Meria, can you hear me?"

Michael walked the remaining steps to face the queen, but she remained motionless. Her hair was piled in matted knots atop her head, the gray that she usually so painstakingly hid with intricate braids and curls now frizzing out in knots and tangles. Her skin hung limp and pallid from her face, ashen even in the golden candlelight. She wore a dove-gray gown that bore not a single embellishment or adornment.

The queen of Navah, Michael thought mockingly.

The Queen Mother. Regent in Ferryl's absence, but no longer the ruling monarch of this kingdom. She might as well have been a sarcophagus. A pillar of salt. For she bore no signs of life or of the fire that once burned brightly in her black eyes.

Michael knelt before his queen, an odd sense of fealty at the sight of her. For more than a decade, he had given his life to protect her and her husband. But he had failed the latter. Failed that fateful day he had taken Delaney from the castle that he might woo the prince's betrothed. Like a lying, traitorous bastard.

And he would pay for that day. With the guilt that plagued his very soul, he would pay every day from now on for not being there when the king of Navah was murdered right under the noses of the entire castle.

"It was supposed to be you." That's what Sir Thomas Nachash had said, his last words before he took his own life like a coward.

It was supposed to be you. Michael. *He* was supposed to be the one who had killed the king. Because he was supposed to be the one who had been cursed that day. Not Amos, his friend, the guard who had been caught in the crossfire of a wicked scheme. Him. Michael.

Michael had been set up to take the blame for the death of the king.

By whatever mercies, he had been spared such a fate, but seemingly only to face a much worse one. Guilt, it turned out, was much worse than being falsely accused of murder.

"Meria, talk to me," Michael tried again. Her cold eyes met his, but she made no sound, no other movement.

"You must speak to your people. They need you," he tried. The court was getting antsier by the day, the courtiers buzzing with rumors, questions, and worries because no formal announcement had been made. Nothing had been said about the strange events of the previous month. The king had been murdered in his own chambers, but the queen had not said one word to her subjects, just as if all was well. As if the king was still alive.

But the court and the people knew the king was not alive. And they knew all was not well. They knew the queen hid in her chambers like a coward.

Maybe she hadn't directly murdered her husband. But no one believed she hadn't been behind it, Michael included.

"Meria, can you hear me?"

The queen's black gaze held Michael still like a spider lurking from her web. Queen Meria, the Black Widow of Navah.

"You must convince him," she said, her voice hoarse from disuse. Or screaming. Michael couldn't be sure.

"Convince him? Convince who?" Michael asked.

The queen seized Michael's hands so suddenly that he nearly yelped, his heart a sudden war drum in his throat. Her grip was like iron on his hands, but it was not cold, as Ferryl had once described it. It was clammy. Lifeless. Numb.

"He will not believe me. Not after this. But you must help me, Michael. You must convince him."

"Convince who? Your Majesty, what are you talking about?"

Her grip tightened, his hands going numb at her vice-like strength. "It was not supposed to be this way," she said. "He was not supposed to die."

Michael's eyes shot to the queen's. "Who? The king? The king was not supposed to die?"

"Convince him, Michael. Please. Convince him of my innocence. You are the only one he will believe."

~

The air reeked of excrement and vomit, a stale, untouched foulness that permeated every crevice of the dungeons. A slow dripping sound haunted every step as Michael made his way farther and farther down this forsaken place. But for his friend and for the sake of his duty, he would endure it. For Amos, he could brave almost anything.

Michael gagged at the reek as he walked past cell after cell, some occupants passed out in the darkness, some clinging to the bars, begging.

"Please, sir!" one of the prisoners cried as Michael walked by. "I'm innocent, I swear it!"

Every one of them had sworn their innocence at one time or another. Michael hated the sickening sounds of their cries. For half of these men, he had no idea why they were here. And considering the vengeance of the queen of Navah, there was no accounting for the legitimacy of the verdicts of their guilt.

He could not get her words out of his head. *Convince him, Michael. Convince him of my innocence.* They sounded in his mind like the caw of an eagle echoing off the cliffs of Navah. Meria, the queen regent of Navah, had looked terrified. And Michael had no idea what to think of that.

But he could not think on the queen just now. Nor could he listen to the cries of these prisoners as he rounded the last corner. Michael was here for one reason.

Amos.

Amos, whom he could not release. Not without the king's permission. Amos whom he knew damn well to be innocent of his crimes. Amos hadn't killed Captain Samuel. Not intentionally, anyway. He had been cursed. Michael knew it in his bones.

And he knew who was responsible for the curses that seemed to abound at Benalle these days.

"Michael," Amos breathed, grabbing hold of the bars that separated him from his freedom. "Tell me you've made progress."

"I'm sorry. The king has not returned yet. And I sent letters, but I would imagine he's on the road."

"You swore my innocence, right? You swore it?"

"Yes. Yes, Amos, I swore it." Michael reached into his pocket, retrieving the contraband he had procured from his breakfast.

Amos devoured the biscuit in two bites.

"I'm sorry it's not more," Michael said, and he meant it. If there was one thing he would take up with Ferryl upon his return, it was the state of the dungeons. And the treatment of the prisoners. One meal of questionable gray mush a day was hardly enough to keep a man alive. But right now, he could not risk bringing anything down here that someone might see. If the other prisoners caught wind that a guard was sneaking food in…

Everything about this place bore the signature of the vengeful queen who once ruled the palace, the same woman who now sat alone and quiet in her chambers like a prisoner awaiting her own death sentence.

"How much longer, Michael? How much longer must I bear this?" Amos asked, a crumb from the biscuit clinging to the red beard that had grown in his time down in this Sheol-hole.

"He will he home soon, Amos. King Ferryl will be home soon."

~

King Ferryl will be home soon, Michael reminded himself as he stared into his fire, his arm resting on the mantle. King Ferryl. Not Prince Ferryl. King. Ferryl was now the king of Navah. The king whose former betrothed would greet him with another man on her arm. The king whose most trusted guard had betrayed him with one kiss.

King Ferryl would be home soon to see all of the mess Michael had made in his absence.

A knock at his door tore his attention from the licking flames, and Michael answered to find the source of his problems and the answer to every question standing before him in a cerulean skirt tied over a round belly. He had always been a damned fool where Duchess Delaney was concerned. Former duchess, that is.

But when she was near him, when he looked at her, all his worries, all his scruples fell by the wayside. And the only thing he could think of was her—the one person in the world who truly understood him. One look at Delaney Dupree, and Michael Aman didn't give a damn what the king of Navah thought. Or anyone else, for that matter.

"Done with your rounds?" she asked, and it was concern in her eyes.

Michael merely nodded before he pulled her into his chambers and slid into her arms, breathing against the skin of her shoulder as he held her tightly. Her rounding belly pressed against his own stomach, and when he felt a tiny thump, he pulled away just enough to look down, a smile curving his mouth from ear to ear. Delaney pressed his hand firmly into the side of her belly.

"Feel her?" she asked, her attention on her belly as well.

Michael laughed at the notion that Delaney had decided her baby was a girl. Laughed more at the notion that the baby seemed to move—dance, really—anytime he was near, according to Delaney. He laughed in delight and with a deep breath before he pulled the love of his life back into his arms and kissed her thoroughly.

It was stupid to wish for something so impossible. But every time he thought about it, every time his mind wandered to that day when her time would finally come, Michael wished he could be there. Wished he could be a part of it.

But it was stupid, and she would never allow it. Men, as a rule, were not welcome and certainly not *allowed* to witness the birth of their children. How much less the birth of another man's child?

Her cheeks were flushed, her lips glistening as Delaney snaked her arms around his shoulders. "Michael, what happened?" she asked.

"What do you mean?" he asked.

"I can tell something is on your mind. It is written all over your face."

He wondered if she could read him so well all the time.

"It was an unsettling day, that's all."

"Did you see the queen?" she asked, making her way farther into his chambers. He eased down onto the settee beside her before he answered.

"She begged me to plead for her."

"Plead for her? In what regard?" Delaney asked.

Michael took hold of her hand, playing with her fingers as he spoke. "Her innocence," he finally managed.

"What?" Delaney scoffed. "After all that she's done, she wants you to plead her innocence? What—to Ferryl?"

Michael merely nodded, running his fingers along Delaney's left hand, along the finger that would have already been wearing his mother's ring, if not for the king, the friend who was owed an explanation, at the very least. He pulled her hand to his mouth by way of distraction.

"She is a fool if she thinks anyone believes her to be innocent."

But Michael said nothing, absently weaving his fingers between hers, tasting the tip of every finger.

"Michael, what's really on your mind?" Delaney asked.

But that was the one thing he could not tell her. He could not be the source of even one moment of worry or burden for her. Providence knew she had already been through enough.

So he mustered a smile and said, "Nothing, beautiful. Nothing at all."

25

Chapter III

eneral Titus Melamed made his way down the busy streets of the little village near his home. Cobblestones and dirt combined to make a mess of the roads during the wet, cold winter that had settled in northern Midvar. He passed by the apothecary he had visited frequently in the last few weeks, procuring tonics for his wife's aches and pains. All part of a normal pregnancy, she had promised.

He prayed to the gods every day that it was true.

But today was not for a trek to the apothecary. Today, he had a very different but no less important mission.

The mist stung his eyes as he rode his steed through the mud and muck, the passersby hunched over, blocking their faces from the biting wind and cold, icy rain. They seemed rather in a hurry today, bustling to and from shop to shop as if they couldn't move fast enough. Considering the biting rain, Titus understood the sentiment. He pulled his cloak tighter over his chest and rode on.

He reached his destination soon: the bank, a formidable building of tall stone pillars and veined green marble, a stark contrast to the simplicity of the rest of the village. Just how King Derrick liked it. Money. The pillar of a thriving society. Every financial institution from here to Goleath Palace was a testament to that end: money and power and little else mattered in this kingdom.

Which was precisely why Titus hated every single bank in Midvar.

But his visit was a necessity today, so he lobbed himself off of his mount, tied it to a post, and went inside the colossal building.

This was no simple visit to withdraw a few bekas or invest a few talents. No, this was a visit that required speaking with his banker face-to-face, in his office, doors closed. Which is where he found himself rather quickly—being the king's dog had a few perks, after all.

"Ah! General Titus!" said Gidon, his banker for so many years. The man was tall—typical of most with Midvarish blood in their veins. But he was also gangly and spindly, his mantis-like limbs only accentuated by the tiny pinstripe of his trousers. He preferred clothing of the more flamboyant variety—vibrant colors, ruffled cuffs, gold-tipped walking canes. He looked more suited for a traveling carnival than a bank.

"How nice to see you, my friend. Come in, come in!" Gidon ushered him inside his ostentatious office, offering him a plush leather seat and a hot cup of tea, his mustache curling with his toothy smile. Titus took the seat but refused the tea.

"It's rather busy today, wouldn't you say?"

"I would," said Titus. "Any reason?"

"Everyone is preparing to leave our little village, I suppose."

"Leave? Why?"

"You haven't heard?"

"Heard what?" Titus asked, annoyed at the small satisfaction Gidon took from his ignorance. The man always loved intrigues. Much like a woman. For some reason, it annoyed the Sheol out of Titus. But from the look on Gidon's face, this was no trivial intrigue or gossip.

"The Navarian soldiers. They're advancing farther into the kingdom every day. It seems Commander Derwin is not nearly as peace-loving as their former commander."

Navah's *former* commander. Titus wondered what blissfully ignorant Gidon would think if he knew that *Titus* was their former commander. The traitor in disguise.

"Does that really come as a surprise to you? Our diplomat killed their king. I hardly see why that's a reason to leave. It's not as if they're going to attack civilians."

"That's just it. That's exactly what they're doing," Gidon said.

Civilians? Titus knew the hot-headed Prince Derwin quite well. And while he was eager and perhaps a bit ill-tempered, the young commander was by no means a monster. Titus had trained him, for the gods' sake! Why in Sheol would he order the attack of civilians? And what could they possibly be doing that would give people cause to abandon their homes? Their lives?

Gods, wasn't that what Titus himself was here to do? But for such very different reasons.

"I didn't mean to set off the meeting on such a dark note, my friend," said Gidon with a flippant flick of his hand. "What can I help you with?"

Titus cleared his head and looked back at the banker across the desk. "I need to consolidate my assets."

"So you're leaving, too, then," Gidon said, but it wasn't a question.

Titus only shrugged. The less the man knew, the better. Of course he wasn't leaving to run from Navarian monsters. He was leaving to run from the true monster of this war: his own king. And he intended to leave nothing behind. Today's visit to the bank was the first step in the process of starting a new life with Penelope. Somewhere far, far away from Midvar. And Navah.

A new continent sounded like the right idea. And thank the gods, Penelope agreed.

"Isn't consolidation of assets a bit drastic?" Gidon asked, in his typical intrusive style. "Perhaps just take out a few hundred talents to tide you over for a few months until all of this settles down."

"I'm taking everything, Gidon. And I need it ready to leave in one week."

"One week? So soon?" Gidon asked, a flash of abject horror on his face.

"I am counting on you to keep this as discreet as possible. No one can know."

Gidon sighed, pulling out paperwork and a pen. "I can't say I blame you. I'd probably want to leave if I had a wife as beautiful as yours."

What in Sheol did that mean? "I'm sorry?"

"What with the soldiers," Gidon said casually as he scribbled on the parchment before him. "I wouldn't want my wife—if I had one—anywhere near them, either. Not with what they're doing to the women."

"Gidon, what are they doing to the women?" Titus asked, his heart hammering in his throat.

Gidon looked up, his face grave. "You really don't know?"

Damn this man and his intrigues. "Just say it."

"The Navarian soldiers, they're taking all the women in Midvar.

Well, at least all the women of childbearing age."

"For what? What in Sheol would they need women of childbearing age for?"

"Slaves, Titus. They're abducting women for their pleasure."

~

Oh gods. Oh damn. Oh shit. This was much worse than he thought. What in Sheol had gotten into Derwin that he would allow his soldiers to behave so abominably? That was *not* the kind of training he had received. And no matter the sins he had committed over the years, Titus would have sooner been condemned straight to Sheol than approve of such brazen evil. Such atrocities. And against women, no less. They were innocent, damn it. What right had Derwin to give such an order? Sexual slavery? Gods above, the depravity in this world was reaching a new low.

He tried to clear his mind as he paced about his sitting room. The last thing he wanted was to give Penelope any more reason to worry. Not in her condition. His head shot up when she walked inside, her head tilting to one side at the sight of him.

"What's wrong?" she asked.

He strode to her, placing his hands on her shoulders. "Do you think you can be ready to leave sooner than we had planned?"

She nodded quietly, her eyes colored with concern. "What's happened, Titus?"

"Nothing yet. But we need to leave. And we need to do it quickly."

"Why? What's going on? I thought the plan was to leave in a week."

He let go of her so that he might resume his pacing. "It's going to need to be sooner than that."

"Titus, what's going on?"

"Gidon told me that he thinks he can have everything ready in as soon as three days. Let's pray it doesn't even take that long. I'll have the servants pack our trunks. We'll have to just take whatever we can fit, whatever we have time to—"

"Titus," Penelope said, stopping him with a hand on his arm. He whirled to face her, and at the worry he saw on her beautiful face, he rushed to take her in his arms.

"Don't fret, Lopee. It's going to be all right, but we need to be ready to leave as soon as possible. Are you prepared? Prepared to leave everything behind, start over? I know it's away from everyone we know. From your family, but—"

"Titus," she said, placing her hands on his face and looking him deeply in the eyes. "I don't care where we live. I don't care if we leave everything behind and start over. All I care about is *our* family," she said, taking a moment to place one of his hands on her rounded belly. "Because where you go, I go. Where you live, I live. We're a family. And we're going to stay that way."

He kissed her brow. Then he kissed her lips. And then he pulled her into his arms and held her as tightly as he could. And he prayed to every god he could name that she was right.

Chapter IV

The carriage bumped and jolted down the gravel drive, but Adelaide's hand rested firmly in her husband's. The dreary clouds hung low, a blanket of gray over the city of Benalle, casting silvery light through the window and onto Ferryl's unruly locks. The castle loomed before them, great white stone halls flanked by towering turrets that looked as if they staked the castle to the edge of the cliffs. The black-and-white flag of Navah flew proudly at each corner of the castle, greeting Ferryl's return. Hailing the return of the king.

And the queen they did not know they were getting.

Adelaide swallowed once. Twice.

They will love you, Lizybet, Ferryl said to her mind, squeezing her hand for emphasis.

It's not them *I'm worried about,* Adelaide admitted to him. And Ferryl met her eyes, pulling her hand to his mouth.

But he gave her no words of reassurance, for what could he say? His mother had despised Adelaide—Elizabeth—as long as they had known each other. How much more so now that she had gone and married Ferryl? Never mind that they had been betrothed since they were children—Meria herself had signed the betrothal contract to the

Haravellian princess when Ferryl was only a boy. Would the queen of Navah believe them? Would any of the courtiers or people of the kingdom believe that she really was the princess of Haravelle?

"Yes," said Ferryl out loud. "I will make sure of it."

"It looks an awful lot like a prince who ran off to marry the woman he wanted instead of living up to his duties," she said.

Ferryl took her face in his hands and kissed her once. Twice. "Yes, I did. How convenient that she should be my betrothed to boot."

Adelaide huffed a laugh before Ferryl kissed her once more. But even in his confidence, she could see the worry that plagued him and slumped his shoulders slightly. It limned his brow, narrowed his eyes, and played in his nervous fingers as they tapped along her hand.

For Ferryl would not return to his kingdom as the hero prince with a legion of allied soldiers in tow.

He would return to his kingdom as their leader, with war on his doorstep and a murder lingering in every whisper, every stare. He would return to his kingdom with a queen they did not know they were getting.

A dead princess, come to life again.

For an absurd moment, Adelaide imagined they were in a circus caravan, pulling into the next town they would entertain.

Ladies and gentlemen! Step right up to see greatest show in Navah! Elephants! Lions! Beasts of all sizes! A terrified prince, poised to take the throne of the greatest kingdom in the realm. And if that's not enough, you won't want to miss the mysterious Dead Princess of Haravelle!

It was Ferryl's turn to breathe a laugh. "Don't forget the cretin cousin, the brooding half-wit passed over for the throne!"

"You shouldn't joke like that," Adelaide warned, though a laugh bubbled in her own throat. "Lord Adam won't tolerate it forever."

"I still don't see why he had to come along."

"And miss all the drama? Not a chance in Sheol," she said. "I'm sure he is convinced no one will believe my heritage."

"And like a spider, he can lurk in the darkness, waiting to claim his rightful throne once more," Ferryl said, a scowl on his face like he had just swallowed sour milk.

"Ignore him, Ferryl. He is no real threat."

"Let's hope you're right," Ferryl said cryptically.

The carriage came to a halt, and Ferryl turned his attention out the window once more. Benalle Palace did not gleam in the endless sunlight of the Navarian coast. No, the blanket of clouds made the glorious castle appear gray. Sad. As if the weather itself understood the darkness, the curse that loomed over the people of Navah.

Ferryl took a deep breath. "This is it," he said.

"Are you ready, King Ferryl?" she asked, the first time she had said his title out loud.

His attention returned to his wife. "I don't think I'll ever be ready, my love. But as long as I have you, I know I can face all of this."

"You're stuck with me now, sir," she said.

Ferryl only waggled his brows as the page boy opened the carriage door. "Your Majesty," he said, his prepubescent voice squeaking. He took a deep bow before pulling the door open all the way, calling out, "His Majesty, the king of Navah!" when Ferryl stepped foot on the gravel.

Ferryl looked around at the small crowd that had gathered at the castle entrance, all of them courtiers come to greet their king. Then he turned and extended his hand to his wife. "Come, Queen Adelaide. Your court awaits."

He could hear the whispers as they passed. They crawled along his skin, and he ground his teeth to keep his retorts to himself.

It looks like the king has made her his official mistress.

She was always his whore, wasn't she?

Quite the jewels for a paramour.

Adelaide walked beside him, arm in arm, her shoulders back, her chin high. She looked every bit a queen in that emerald-and-gold gown. He had given her the jewels before they departed Chesedelle, but it was her mother who had given her the circlet that currently sat atop her head. An intricate weaving of gold and silver made to look like the needles of a conifer, it shone from the top of her black tresses, even in the muted light. Princess Adelaide of Haravelle, Queen of Navah. Today—today these courtiers would gain a new queen. A queen in mind and bearing, not just in name. So Ferryl ignored their insults and walked proudly beside his wife.

It was Delaney he spotted first, and a flash of guilt soon followed. She stood at the top of the stairs, her belly protruding rather prominently from her skirts, but she, too, held her shoulders back, her chin resolute. And Michael stood steadily beside her, their faces expressionless as the king and queen approached.

Ferryl decided to swallow his pride. "Your Grace," he said, bowing his head to the former duchess.

"Your Majesty," she responded, dipping into a low curtsey. Michael bowed, too. So did all of the gathered courtiers.

Delaney's attention went to Adelaide. "Elizabeth," she said, bowing her head. "You look beautiful."

And Adelaide only smiled, bowing in return. Ferryl caught his wife's eye and winked for her benefit.

The king and queen of Haravelle soon followed behind them, along with Leala and Lord Adam. Talia and the rest of the servants lingered behind at the caravan, though Talia beamed as if Adelaide were her own daughter.

"Michael," Ferryl said, acknowledging his friend.

"Your Majesty," Michael said with a dip of his chin. "We are glad of your return."

Ferryl looked around at the courtiers that peppered the top of the steps —and noticed which ones did not. "Where is my mother?"

Michael did not answer immediately. No one did. When Ferryl met Michael's eyes again, the guard only said, "There is much we need to discuss."

King Ferryl sat with Elizabeth by his side, holding her hand as if she were an anchor and he a ship adrift on a raging sea. He listened intently as Michael recalled the events of the last few months: the death of the king, a court riddled with rumor and gossip, a queen who hid in her chambers away from it all. An invisible burden rested on the king's shoulders—something Michael couldn't quite place. He privately wondered what had happened on the road home to Navah.

"And my mother has not emerged? Not once?" Ferryl asked, appalled by what Michael conveyed. The muted light lit the king's receiving room in a wash of silver sun—a real winter, unlike any Michael could remember in Navah. The chill seemed to have settled into his bones and blood.

"She is…not herself, Your Majesty," said Michael.

"What does that mean?" asked Elizabeth, her face drawn in concern.

"Something is different," Michael admitted. "She is much altered."

"In what way?" Ferryl prodded, leaning forward, his arms resting on his knees.

"I think you'll understand when you see her," was all Michael could think to say.

Elizabeth looked to Ferryl for a moment, their eyes locked on one another as if in a silent conversation. It had always been that way with them—an understanding between them which the rest of the world was not privy to. They were in love, yes. But it was so much more than that. A bond, deep and true. Impenetrable.

Elizabeth patted Ferryl's hand, and that's when Michael spotted a ring…on her *left* hand.

Oh Providence.

"I will deal with my mother later," Ferryl said, worry tainting his words. Not even home an hour, and Michael had already dropped the weight of the world on the shoulders of his king. Not to mention he had yet to tell him about what had happened with Delaney…

"Michael," Ferryl said, turning his attention back to the guard.

Michael wondered if the king would still consider him a friend when he learned the truth. "We need to discuss castle security."

Ah. There it was. Something *had* happened on the road home. Michael sat upright.

But the rest of the story seemed lost on Ferryl, who fidgeted with his fingers and instead suddenly turned his attention to Delaney.

"Delaney, I am glad you are here. I need to apologize to you," said Ferryl. Delaney only furrowed her brows. "I was unfair to you before I left for Haravelle. I said some things… things I should not have said, and—"

"Your High—Your *Majesty*, I mean—you do not owe me an apology," Delaney interrupted.

"My name is Ferryl," said the king warmly. "My friends call me Ferryl. And I do owe you an apology. My behavior was atrocious, not to mention unfair." He looked to Elizabeth by his side. She merely squeezed his hand, a small smile on her mouth. It seemed to be enough to give Ferryl the gumption to continue. "I was wrong to accuse you as I did, when I was guilty of the same." Infidelity—that's what he meant. He had called her a whore for conceiving another man's child while still betrothed to Ferryl. And here was Ferryl, admitting to her that he was just as guilty for loving another all the while. Michael wondered if his king would have the same grace when he learned the rest of the story—when he learned of his betraying friend who had stolen a duchess the moment he turned his back.

Absently, Ferryl rubbed a thumb along Elizabeth's hand as he continued his speech. "Delaney, I am truly sorry for hurting you."

Michael knew Ferryl. The prince was like a brother to him. And he could see in Ferryl's eyes that he meant it. Every word. That he was truly, genuinely sorry for how he had treated Delaney and for the things he had said. Michael stole a glance at the woman he loved, only to find her lip quivering as she fiddled with her fingers in her lap. Michael took the risk and rested his hand on her back.

Ferryl placed a hand over Delaney's, waiting until she met his eyes again. "I am so sorry, Delaney. You became a true friend to me in those weeks when I thought Elizabeth to be dead. I am truly sorry that I threw all of that in your face."

"You became my friend, too," Delaney finally managed. And despite himself, Michael ran his hand down her back once. Only once. He dared not touch her more, though the urge to comfort her, to take her in his arms and hold her tightly nearly consumed him.

"Then it is settled," said Elizabeth, a kind smile in her eyes. "We will be friends."

Delaney's gaze danced between the king and queen for a moment. "You do not know how thankful I am for it."

"I meant what I said in my letter, Delaney," Ferryl added. "You have a home here. For as long as you like, Benalle Palace is yours to call home."

Delaney looked to Michael, tears brimming in her eyes. Michael gave her a soft smile, clasping her hand in his for good measure, taking no small amount of pleasure from the way she held on tightly. He ran a thumb along her palm as Ferryl went on, tracing idle patterns on the soft skin—a clover, an evergreen, an eight-pointed star.

"There is something I must tell you both," Ferryl continued. He looked to Elizabeth beside him, and she nodded once before he spoke again. "I need your support. More than ever, I need you both."

"Increasing castle security..." Michael said, curious why Ferryl had dropped the subject a moment ago. Delaney noticed the ring on Elizabeth's hand, and she squeezed Michael's hand once as if to tell him something.

Ferryl held his chin high when he finally said, "While we were still in Haravelle, we married."

"I noticed," Michael said, a small laugh escaping despite himself.

"That is not all," Ferryl said, and at the worry, at the fear Michael saw... *Why in the world would marrying Elizabeth merit increasing castle security?*

"She is not... Her name is not Elizabeth," the king stammered.

Michael furrowed his brows as he observed his king and the queen beside him.

Ferryl breathed once, clearing his throat. "Her name is Adelaide. The lost princess of Haravelle."

The room went deadly silent, not a sound to be heard. Not even a breath. Michael took a moment to absorb the words, the sheer concept...

Adelaide of Haravelle. The lost princess. Supposedly dead. Alive again.

Married to the king of Navah.

"Say something," Ferryl finally interjected through the silence. "Tell me you believe me."

"How?" Delaney asked. "How did this happen?"

"I was cursed," Adelaide said. "The same way Ferryl was last summer. I was cursed to forget who I am, from where I came. Only I was cursed as a little girl. And I did not remember. Not until we went to Haravelle."

"And now you remember?" Michael asked.

"Magic. Magic gave me back my past. Just as it gave Ferryl back to me."

The room went silent again.

"I know this is…a lot to take in," Ferryl tried.

"If this is true," Delaney said, speaking up. "If this is really true, it changes everything."

"I know," Elizabeth—Adelaide said, her voice small.

"And castle security…" Michael tried.

"We wanted to keep it a secret. As long as possible," Ferryl said, his grip on Elizabeth—Adelaide's hand a vice. "But they know. Midvar knows. And on the way home we were attacked."

Michael could barely take it in. The idea. The sheer concept. Princess Adelaide of Haravelle, Queen of Navah.

The world would be forever changed by such a revelation.

"We must protect her," Ferryl said, and it was desperation that colored his every word. Michael wondered how he would feel, what he would do if it were Delaney in those shoes. If it were Delaney that needed to be protected from the world… Then again, in some ways, she did.

"My uncle," Delaney said, but it was clear she could not bring herself to say more. It was a damning, palpable worry that settled on the four of them.

"I know," said Ferryl solemnly.

"On my life," Michael said, straightening his back. "I will protect you, Ferryl. I will protect you both. My king," he said, taking Ferryl's hand and bowing low to press a loyal kiss to his knuckles. "And my queen," he went on, pressing the same kiss to her hand. "I will protect you both with my life." At his side, Delaney shifted slightly.

"You believe us?" Ferryl said. It wasn't his king asking the question, it was his friend looking for solidarity.

Before Michael could answer, Delaney said, "Yes, we do." And when all eyes met hers, she said, "Only a fool would make up such a story at such a time. And I have never known you to be a fool."

CHAPTER V

here is she?" the king asked Michael. After sharing the news with his friends and taking a few moments to let them reel, he had asked Michael to call a council meeting so he could meet with the people who helped run this kingdom. To tell them that damning truth, too.

"She said she would be here," Michael responded, standing shoulder to shoulder with Ferryl. The king's council room buzzed with advisors—lords and dukes from around the kingdom who had been granted lands, powers, and a place on the council in exchange for loyalty to the throne. In exchange for running the day-to-day affairs of Navah. Some Ferryl knew well—had known since boyhood. Some he hardly knew at all. But now he was not the prince who attended the king's council meetings. Now he was the king who would run the meeting. The king who would rule the kingdom.

Ferryl swallowed and made his way to his seat at the end of the long, heavily-carved table. The blanket of clouds muted the glaring winter light to silver as it spilled across the polished wood. Ferryl took the queen's chair—usually pushed back against the wall behind them—and pulled it up to the table beside him. Two monarchs at the end of the table now, not one.

He would not rule this kingdom without his wife. His equal.

A few of the lords at the table watched wide-eyed, appalled as Adelaide took a seat beside Ferryl. One in particular seemed keenly shocked, watching Adelaide's every move as if she would sprout horns and a forked tail. Lord Adam took a seat near the opposite end, his face nearly obscured by a shadow, but a threatening smirk showed enough that Ferryl wanted to spit. King Aaron and Queen Avigail took seats at the council table, too, but their eyes were neither leery nor appraising. Avigail gave a small nod to her daughter, a glimmer of kindness in her gold eyes.

"Thank you all for coming on such short notice," said Ferryl, adjusting his jerkin. For some reason, it seemed uncomfortably tight at the moment.

"Did we have a choice?" asked the particularly appalled nobleman.

"Sir Westerly, is it?" asked Ferryl, cocking his head to one side. "I had forgotten you were on the council."

Lie. He hadn't forgotten at all. How could Ferryl forget the man who had thrown his atrocious daughter at him last summer? Lady Anna Maria Nanette Denae Westerly of Teman. Her father had been given a lordship after Ferryl had refused to marry her. A lordship, and a place on the council as a consolation prize.

"It's *Lord* Westerly now, Your Majesty," said the yellow-toothed man, an oily smile on his dry lips.

"Ah yes, *Lord* Westerly. I had forgotten. And how is your daughter?" asked Ferryl.

Lord Westerly eyed Adelaide for a split second—the girl who had usurped what Lord Westerly surely considered his daughter's *rightful* place on the throne. "She is well, Majesty. Married and expecting her first child."

Expecting her first child which led to her hasty marriage, if rumor serves me correctly, Ferryl said for only Adelaide's benefit.

His wife laughed in her mind, squeezing her husband's hand under the table. *Be nice, Ferryl.*

When am I not? he quipped.

"How delightful," said Ferryl, even as he held the private conversation with his wife, and Lord Westerly dipped his head with a mocking grin.

"We shall get started, then, I think," the king went on, bobbing his knee under the table.

"Are we not to wait for the queen, then?" asked Lord Adam, sitting with his arms crossed at the end of the table.

"The Queen *Mother,*" Ferryl corrected, willing himself not to roll his eyes at his wife's cousin, "will be along shortly."

The king did not miss the multiple pairs of eyes that glanced Adelaide's way, not daring to linger on her for too long.

"I know that many of you were under the impression that my trip to Ramleh was to assess the damage from the rebels, and while that is true," said Ferryl, "it is not the complete story. In case the presence of the king and queen is not evident, we also went to Haravelle to forge an alliance with our sister kingdom. I am glad to report to you today that Haravelle has provided a hundred thousand men to join with ours in our efforts against Midvar."

"So we are to war, then?" Lord Westerly asked, crossing his slender arms.

"We are preparing for potential war, yes," said Ferryl, swallowing.

"All due respect, Your Majesty, but that is not how this looks," said Westerly. A few of the other lords around the table nodded in silent agreement.

"Pray, how does it look?" Ferryl asked through his teeth.

"Like you are launching an attack on the kingdom whose bride you set aside," said Westerly. Another, older lord—Mistar, if Ferryl remembered correctly—eyed Westerly with a warning stare. But the haughty lord ignored the old man and went on. "May I ask what you plan to do with her?"

From the corner of his eye, Ferryl spotted Michael standing along the wall near the door, his shoulders suddenly tense, his hand gripping the pommel of his sword.

"I have offered her a home here in Navah,"said Ferryl, lifting his chin. Some of the advisors nodded, some looked around in wide-eyed shock.

"That seems a bit risky at such a time as this, Your Majesty," said one of the lords.

"She is a friend to this kingdom. And to me. I will not put her aside," said Ferryl.

He realized his mistake the moment Lord Westerly spoke again. "But you have, haven't you?" The lord nodded toward Adelaide without even looking at her, and Ferryl could have crawled across the table and throttled the bastard for it. "It seems you have put aside your duty for the sake of bedding your mistress."

Ferryl sucked in a breath, ready to retort, but was cut off by his wife.

They do not know, Ferryl. You cannot blame them for what they do not know.

Ferryl breathed in and out once. Twice. Assuring himself that he was calm again, he finally said, "That is another matter we need to discuss today."

"Clearly," said Lord Westerly under his breath—just loud enough that it could not be missed.

Ferryl ignored him, though his heart began to pound. Adelaide squeezed his hand under the table. *There is no easy way to tell them, my love,* she said. *It just has to be said.*

So Ferryl said it.

"While we were in Haravelle, it came to our attention that Adelaide, the lost princess, was alive."

Around the long table, almost every pair of eyes widened in shock. Whispers bounced back and forth across the polished wood. Ferryl swallowed past a thick throat. Then he swallowed again.

"And so I married her."

"Married her?" blurted Lord Westerly.

"Remember your place, Lord Westerly," said Lord Mistar from the other end of the table. Ferryl nodded in silent thanks to the old lord.

"We have been betrothed since her birth nearly twenty years ago. By fulfilling the marriage contract—"

"Forgive me, Majesty, but this all seems a bit convenient, don't you think?" asked Lord Adam.

"Convenient?" asked King Aaron, his brow raised warningly at his nephew. Lord Adam crossed his arms and sat farther back into his chair.

"Of course anyone can see the resemblance between you, but I find it a bit odd that your daughter has been under our nose for fifteen years and none of us were the wiser," scoffed Westerly, his attention on the king of Haravelle.

"She was cursed," said Ferryl, his heart a war drum pounding in his chest.

"Cursed?" balked one of the lords at the other end of the table.

"So now not only is the princess miraculously alive, but magic is the reason?" laughed Lord Westerly.

Just then, the meeting room doors opened. All eyes turned to see who was intruding on the uncomfortable meeting as Michael announced, "The Queen Mother."

The queen entered the room like a ghost, wearing a drab-gray gown that fell loosely from her thinning frame. She hadn't bothered with kohl on her eyes or jewels on her neck, either. This woman…she was not the queen of Navah. She was a skeleton in wool with a simple graying plait down her back, walking with her shoulders back and her gaunt chin high.

As everyone stood, she floated across the room, her eyes hauntingly distant, and took a seat next to Ferryl. It was only once the advisors had all bowed and taken their seats again that she inclined her head to Aaron and Avigail, nodding silently to them before saying, "Your Majesties, it is an honor that you have come at such a time, and my kingdom thanks you for your show of loyalty and friendship."

It was King Aaron who responded. "The honor is ours," he said, his words sincere. Even Avigail's eyes shone with a mixture of pity and worry. Ferryl's in-laws knew the taste of unexpected loss and heartache quite well.

Then Queen Meria turned her attention to Adelaide—the girl who to her was still Elizabeth, the nuisance stable girl. But now there was none of the signature hatred in Meria's eyes. No disdain. Just something else Ferryl couldn't quite place. As if she were putting the pieces of the puzzle together even without realizing it. Finally, she turned her attention to Ferryl, her face a blank slate all the while.

"Welcome, Mother," Ferryl said. "The council is glad of your presence." He wasn't sure if he sounded perturbed or sincere. And he was equally unsure which of the two he meant.

"We are so sorry for your loss," said Queen Avigail. "King Aiken was a good man and a good king."

Silence. Uncomfortable, haunting silence. Then, "He was indeed both," said Meria, to Ferryl's shock.

Well.

What in Sheol was he to make of that?

Her response—uncharacteristically sincere and honest—threw him off course so violently that it took Ferryl a moment to recover his train of thought. He stumbled headlong into his mental list of discussion points, as if pushed off of one of the cliffs of Navah straight into the breakers of the Great Sea below.

"As I was saying—" said Ferryl.

"Yes, in case you missed it, Your Majesty, your son was just regaling us with the tale of his surprise marriage to the miraculous princess of Haravelle," said Lord Westerly.

Ferryl ground his teeth, but Meria's eyes slowly landed on Adelaide, appraising her for an uncomfortable moment.

"I know how this looks," said Adelaide, looking the Queen Mother in the eye.

"Is it true?" Meria asked. Everyone around them seemed to be holding their breath. Then again, so was Ferryl.

"Yes," Adelaide breathed as she nodded softly.

Queen Meria said nothing even as her black gaze held Adelaide's.

"I am sorry, but we are going to need more than just your word, dear Elizabeth," said Lord Westerly.

"Her name is not Elizabeth," chided Ferryl. "Her name is Adelaide, Queen of Navah, and you will address her as such."

"You do recognize the danger you put our kingdom in by making such a claim?" asked Westerly. "No one would have balked," he went on. "No one would have even batted an eye at you taking her as your mistress. But for some reason—perhaps some insatiable need to think yourself noble—you've married her instead. Which would have been ridiculous enough without adding the pathetic farce that she is the dead princess come to life again!"

Ferryl looked to Lord Mistar and then to King Aaron, neither of whom seemed to have anything to say.

"It is true. She is Adelaide of Haravelle. I swear it on my life," said Ferryl, drumming his fingers wildly on his knee. To his right, Queen Meria said nothing.

"I am sorry, but I find this absurd," said Westerly. "You leave our kingdom for months without a word of your whereabouts. And in your absence, your father is murdered—an act of war. An act of treason at the very least. You return to us a *month* after his death to let us know that you've miraculously found the lost princess of Haravelle and ask what? That we should support this tomfoolery? That we should believe you?"

"Lord Westerly," chided Lord Mistar from the other end of the table.

"Does not our presence here confirm his claims?" asked King

Aaron. "Do you think we would go along with a brazen lie about our beloved daughter?"

Lord Westerly puffed a scornful laugh. "Forgive me, Majesty, but even kings can be bought."

"For what purpose?" asked Queen Avigail. "For what purpose would Ferryl buy us off?"

"To marry his whore, of course," said Westerly.

Michael advanced across the room in all of three steps, unsheathing his sword a few inches from the scabbard, a look of murderous contempt in his silver eyes. King Aaron also looked ready to plunge his sword right through Westerly's throat. Lord Adam, conveniently, sat silently at the other end of the room, that smirk no longer just a threat to his narrow mouth, as smug as if he couldn't have planned this any better. But to Ferryl's eternal shock, it was Queen Meria who spoke up.

"Can you prove it?" she asked, her words shattering the tension. "Can you prove who you say you are?"

Ferryl practically growled at his mother. "She owes no proof. To any of you."

Ferryl, Adelaide said to only him. *We can prove it to them.*

He looked over to find the amulet of Haravelle in her palm, her emerald eyes alight with determination. She turned to her father, his eyes meeting hers as if he knew what she was asking. He reached within his own jacket, pulling out his half of the stone.

"This is the amulet of Haravelle," said King Aaron, standing. Adelaide stood as well. "It has belonged to the royal family in my kingdom for generations. It was divided into two stones many centuries ago, a relic that cannot be worn by any but the reigning monarch and his heir. I gave this stone to my daughter when she was a child."

"Forgive me, Your Majesty," said one of the lords at the table. "But anyone could forge such a thing."

"Perhaps," said King Aaron. "But none can forge the magic of Providence."

More silence succeeded his statement. More wide-eyed shock as King Aaron lifted his half of the amulet, as Adelaide lifted hers as well and joined the two, just as they had in Haravelle. The miraculous display that had restored a lifetime of memories to a lost princess.

But today—

There was not even a flicker of light. Not a hint of magic in the joining of the two stones.

Nothing.

Nothing but a king claiming to have found a miracle and a council who would not have the proof.

"You will destroy the entire kingdom with your lies, Ferryl," said Westerly as he stood. He pushed his chair away from the table. "And I will be damned if I stand by and watch."

CHAPTER VI

Ferryl lay in a bed that was much too large, one arm behind his head, staring at the ceiling, his mind reeling. The sun had long-since set, the black ocean visible from the walls of windows as endless as the burdens that lay before him. Adelaide—even her thoughts—had been silent all day. That or he was so wrapped up in his own thoughts that he couldn't hear hers.

She emerged now from the attached bathing chamber, untying the robe from her slender waist as she climbed into the vast bed beside him. Unbound, her raven hair fell in a curtain of loose waves around her face, her eyes conveying nothing of her thoughts, either.

"What a day," Ferryl sighed. But Adelaide said nothing, pulling the blankets up as she settled into the bed.

"I am thinking of appointing Michael as captain of the guard. What do you think?" Ferryl asked.

"He is well suited," she said, but there was little in the way of enthusiasm in her voice. There was little of anything there.

"I agree with him. I believe Amos to be innocent, and despite what the council thinks, I am going to let him out tomorrow," Ferryl went on.

Adelaide only nodded.

"I cannot imagine all that Michael has had to deal with while we were gone," he said. "That man is a rock. He should have his own kingdom," he laughed.

Still, Adelaide was silent beside him.

"Can you believe my mother?" he asked, hoping to find some subject in which she was interested. "I don't think I've ever seen her wear gray, much less wool. What sort of game is she playing at?"

"I don't know," she said.

"Do you think she believes us?"

Only silence answered him at first, the moonlight spilling across them in the bed. Then, "Yes. Though I cannot think of any good reason why."

Nor could Ferryl, which was perhaps what made his mother's wordless stares today all the more worrisome.

There was too much silence coming from his wife. Too much space between them in this bed that was made for a king. In this chamber that was his father's and was now his. A room that he had hardly visited more than a handful of times his whole life.

It was all his now. Theirs.

The king and queen of Navah.

"The king, anyway," said Adelaide, having heard what he was thinking.

Ferryl rolled over, facing his wife and pulling her shoulder until she was facing him, too.

"And the queen," he said.

She raised her brows in mockery.

"They will come around," Ferryl said, but it did not sound as helpful as he had hoped.

"I knew it would be surprising. Even difficult. But I never thought—"

"They will believe us," he said, kneading her shoulders. "Just give it time, my love."

"Time, yes," she said. "But not magic, apparently."

"Maybe…maybe the magic needs time, too," he said. It was stupid. But what else could he say? There was no logical reason why the amulets did not confirm their story today. No reason he could think for why Providence would not have wanted the haughty Lord Westerly and the rest of his cronies to believe that Adelaide was indeed who she said she was.

"Maybe it was a mistake," she said.

"What was a mistake?" Ferryl asked, stopping the shoulder massage for a moment.

"Marrying the way we did. Westerly is not wrong, you know. It looks exactly as he says—like an impetuous prince marrying the woman of his choice."

"I did marry the woman of my choice," he said, inching closer to her. He rested a hand at her waist, tracing a finger along her hip. "But she also happened to be my intended. Do not forget that we were betrothed. Our parents signed the contract when we were children."

"It hardly matters when no one believes who I am," she said. She fiddled with the laces on his shirt, not bothering to meet his eyes.

"Michael and Delaney believe us," he said.

"Yes, a guard and the niece of the enemy king. We're off to a solid start."

Ferryl pulled his wife closer, leaving no more space between them as they faced each other on the vast bed. "Ignore them all, my love.

They will believe us in time. I will make sure of it."

"You're always sure of the impossible," she said.

"I am sure of Providence. And I am sure of us. I do not need anything else."

"I feel like an impostor," Adelaide admitted, nibbling at her bottom lip, a sure sign that she was worried.

He kissed her brow. "You are my wife. And the love of my life. Whenever things feel like they're falling apart, I remind myself that I have you. And that's all I really need."

She breathed a small smile, touching his cheek.

He cupped her chin, running a finger along her lips, never having gotten over just how soft, how supple they were. He took in the sight of her as she lay beside him, the wan moonlight obscured by the wintry clouds floating by the massive windows, bathing her in the palest silver light. Radiant, that's what she was. Resplendent. The kind of beauty about which legends were written and wars were fought. And she was his. A benediction. Providence above, he knew he didn't deserve her.

"I read once in the ancient texts about the very beginning of time. About the beginning of all things. Of when Providence made the stars. And the seas. And the creatures that roam about. And all the life that flourishes around us.

"He looked at everything he made—every creature of the sea, beast of the land, every flower, every tree—and after inspecting it all, there was only one thing he said was not good. Do you know what it was?"

Adelaide shook her head under his fingers as he trailed them along her cheek, her jaw, through her hair.

"He looked at man and said, 'It is not good that he should be alone.' And so he gave him a wife." He took the opportunity to kiss her—to taste of her soft lips, to run his hands along her back until he had her wrapped around him. Until he had eliminated any remnant of space between them. Then he relinquished her lips and captured her gaze.

"When I look at you, Adelaide, when I look at our life and all the years we've had together, I understand him. I understand Providence in that moment." He tucked a strand of hair behind her ear, relishing in the little sigh she breathed at his ministrations.

"He was right, my love. A man is not whole without a woman at his side. Hand in hand, that they might walk through this life as one. As companions. As lovers. As man and wife."

A warm tear fell down her cheek and across his fingers. He held her body against his—this woman, this love of his life—and she wrapped her arms around him, tilting her head that she might give him better access to her neck. He obliged her silent request by trailing impassioned kisses down her soft cheeks, her delicate chin, her lithe neck. And the way she fit into his arms, as if she had been custom-made for only him, Ferryl found himself lost in her softness. He a vessel adrift at sea, and she the lighthouse guiding him home. It had always been so between them. He would always need her, always *want* her.

He pulled at the laces of her gauzy shift, lifting it over her head, then removing his own braies with a few economical movements. His fingers trailed delicate paths along the dips and curves of her body. And he delighted in the little sounds she made as he kissed her secrets from her, as he lingered in the places only he had ever explored, as the tension left her body with every new kiss, her body melding into his.

There was one pure and simple truth he knew with every fiber of his being. Adelaide of Haravelle, Sovereign Queen of Navah, was a miracle—to her husband and to her kingdom. He would make sure they knew it. He would make sure the world knew it.

He rolled her onto her back, holding her eyes as he moved with her. She wove her fingers into the hair at the nape of his neck, her own splayed in wild, inky tresses on her pillow. But he did not kiss her—no, he watched her. He delighted in every flicker of her eyes, every intake of breath, every contented sigh as he gave her all of him over and over again—lapping waves upon the cliffs of Navah.

Wife.

Lover.

Friend.

Gift.

Yes, as he held her and whispered his desire for her as they made love in the silver moonlight overlooking the Great Sea, King Ferryl knew he would go to any lengths necessary to protect this miracle in his arms.

Chapter VII

elaney paced her chambers, cupping her heavy belly as she walked. She simply would not let her pregnancy give her an excuse to sit and grow fat. Well, any fatter than necessary, that is. She hated her belly. She hated how she lost a little more of her figure every day. She hated how nothing seemed to fit anymore except skirts that could have passed for circus tents.

She hated the fact that the usually sunny province of Benalle was now in a perpetual state of gray, as if the sun had forgotten how to shine. Delaney paced and paced some more, hating the foreboding sense of helplessness that had settled in her heart ever since King Ferryl had returned.

She was a helpless, useless, fat nobody.

No wonder Michael kept himself so busy these days.

It had been two weeks since the king had returned, his perfect, perfect wife on his arm. Two weeks since the feeling that she was becoming little more than a waste of everyone's time had begun to grow. Now it was starting to fester until she could do nothing but pace. And worry.

Delaney paused before the vast windows that overlooked the

ocean. The sea churned beneath the cliffs, agitated. Even the weather seemed to understand.

And Michael—he was always gone these days. Helping Ferryl with this or that. Working, working, working. He seemed eager to please Ferryl, like he couldn't wait to be at the king's beck and call. As if he owed him penance. Or as if he could not kiss the king's ass enough.

And Delaney knew why. In her soul, she knew.

Michael felt guilty.

Guilty for a lot of things, but guilty for loving Delaney perhaps most of all. She huffed, grabbing a lock of her auburn curls and wrapping it around her finger. Tears stung her eyes, a lump threatening the back of her throat.

She had never imagined that she would be left here in Navah, abandoned and helpless, a bastard on the way. Growing up in Midvar, she had always expected the dull life of a duchess—the usual life as the female heir of a king's ransom. A life she had never wanted, but one she had spent years preparing for. Perhaps Michael's attention had given her a glimpse of hope that life in Navah wouldn't be so bad. But that hope had dissipated the moment Ferryl returned and Michael had conveniently named himself the king's very own lapdog. She should have known it was too good to be true.

Nothing good in her life ever lasted.

She shouldn't really have been surprised, after all.

She huffed and marched across her sitting room, plopping down on her settee, taking up a cold cup of tea and a book she had read at least a thousand times. That's when she heard a knock at her door.

"It's just me," said the familiar voice, and as if in answer, the little one in her womb began to dance. She looked down, smiling despite herself, reminded of one thing: the baby was hers. Hers and no one else's. And no one could ever take that away.

No one.

That familiar voice was soon an equally familiar kiss at her temple. Michael sat down beside Delaney, settled an arm around her shoulder, a heavy hand on her belly, and sighed deeply.

"How was your day, beautiful?" he asked, rubbing her belly.

"Useless, as usual," she sneered. "And yours?"

Michael met her eyes in silent reprimand before he said, "Busy. There is so much to do to get ready for the funeral and the coronation later. It's hard to believe we're about to say goodbye to King Aiken once and for all."

Delaney could see the genuine sorrow in his eyes—sorrow for the king he had loved, grief for his part in that king's death. No matter the truth, Delaney knew Michael would never forgive himself for the way King Aiken had died. That regret had played a huge part in Michael's penance of late. And his absence from Delaney's side. Perhaps it made her the most selfish person on the planet, but Delaney very much wished she could mean as much to Michael as Ferryl and the royal family.

"There is a rumor your uncle will be in attendance," Michael went on.

"Really?" Delaney asked, surprised. "Why in the world would he come? Doesn't he know everyone thinks he's responsible?"

"Of course he knows," Michael practically growled. "He's taunting Ferryl, that's what. He's playing a dirty game."

She sighed, knowing Michael was probably right and hating the fact that the man was blood. That he was her late mother's brother. That his blood flowed through her veins as well. She wished absurdly that she had been born here in Navah, perhaps to a simple family—farmers or merchants. She wished she could have met Michael without all the complications that came with her life, her very blood. She wished they could simply love each other, that the child in her womb was his. That he was her husband—a simple farmer or something.

That none of this mess she called life was hers to deal with.

But it *was* hers to deal with. And her uncle would soon be here. She would have to face him after failing him. The child in her womb that was supposed to be the next prince or princess of Navah. Instead it was a bastard, without any marriage to even give it a name.

Michael chuckled, catching Delaney off guard. She looked down to see his hand on her belly, the baby kicking with vigor.

"I cannot tell if she's telling me she's glad I'm here or ready for me to move my hand," Michael laughed.

Delaney couldn't help it; she laughed, too, resting her head on Michael's shoulder. He pulled her deeper into his arm, kissing the top of her head.

"If she's anything like me, she's probably telling you to move your hand," said Delaney.

Michael lifted her chin, grinning as he said, "Providence help me if I must live with two of you." Then he kissed her—soft and sweet. And kissed her again for good measure.

"What? In separate rooms in this castle?" she quipped, immediately hating herself for the comment. But for all the times Michael had said he loved her, he had never once mentioned anything more. Especially not since Ferryl had returned.

Maybe he didn't *want* anything more.

Michael sighed, resting his head on hers. "I will be glad when all of this mess with Lord Westerly is over."

"What mess?" she asked, lifting her head. The baby in her womb stilled.

Michael seemed to regret his words, looking for something to say. Anything other than what he had meant. "Nothing, beautiful."

"What mess, Michael? What are you talking about?"

Michael fiddled with a ruffle on her sleeve, not meeting her eyes.

"Michael?" she tried again.

"Delaney, it's nothing, I promise."

"Then why is there worry in your eyes?"

Michael finally looked at her, still fiddling with the ruffle on her sleeve. "Ferryl doesn't agree, of course. But Lord Westerly—he's a mouthy sort of fellow. His opinion hardly matters."

"Michael."

He finally met her eyes, lingering for a moment before he mustered himself to say, "He doesn't think you should be at court here at Benalle."

"Because I am Derrick's niece."

"Because you made Ferryl a cuckold." He let silence fall before he said, "And because you are Derrick's niece."

She puffed a sigh. "I suppose I cannot disagree with him."

"I can," Michael said swiftly. "And anyway, nothing will come of it, I'm sure. He's just mouthy and opinionated. He doesn't like having to answer to a king half his age."

They were excuses, and Delaney knew it. But she nodded anyway, conjuring a weak smile as she rested her head on Michael's shoulder once more, wishing she was a different person indeed.

Chapter VIII

"Why isn't he back yet?" Ferryl asked, pacing the dressing room. "Something is not right."

"Perhaps he was delayed," Adelaide offered, brushing her hair, despite the fact that Talia had gone to painstaking measures to brush every tangle away this morning. The servant had left only moments ago, wise enough to know that Ferryl wanted a private audience with his wife but was too distracted to ask for it.

Adelaide caught a glimpse of her reflection in the looking glass. Her skin was brighter somehow. Smoother. Perhaps Talia's homemade lotions and oils were working more miraculously than Adelaide realized.

"He should have sent word if he was so delayed. He cannot miss this," Ferryl went on, his harried steps wearing a trail in the plush carpet.

Adelaide turned on her tufted stool, facing her husband fully. "You sent your men, Ferryl. They will report back anything they find."

"What if something happened to him?" Ferryl asked, at last meeting his wife's eyes. "How could I ever tell Leala?"

"Let's not jump to any conclusions yet. Perhaps Derwin truly is just delayed."

Ferryl crossed the small space between them, kneeling before his wife and taking her hands in his. She rubbed her thumbs across the new callouses in his palms—gifts from his extra practices of late. Ferryl was determined to be prepared for anything, and early morning sword fights with the guards seemed to be the only thing that gave him any peace of mind.

The heaviness of the day before them settled in her husband's shoulders as he bent his head to press a kiss to each of her palms. Today was King Aiken's funeral. Worry for the reason Derwin was absent was perhaps exaggerated by the greater burden of the day: it was time to finally say goodbye to his father.

Adelaide ran a hand down her husband's head, and he used it as an excuse to rest his head against her breast like a child comforted by his mother's touch.

"This doesn't seem real," he finally said, his words clipped with emotion.

"I know," she admitted, her own tears threatening and closing her throat.

"I should have been here," Ferryl went on. "I should have stopped this from—"

"Don't do this, Ferryl," she said, lifting his head. "It won't do you any good."

A solemn tear fell down his cheek as he nodded once. He was the king of Navah now—a king much too soon thanks to the games of a king from the east. The same king who was due to their castle any moment.

Ferryl, able to read her thoughts, stiffened at the reminder. "Who does he think he is? What does he think he will accomplish by showing up here?"

"I don't know," Adelaide admitted. "It seems like a slap in the face." Nausea churned in her belly. What would she say to King Derrick when he arrived? How was she to act? Was she to pretend that she was oblivious to the fact that he had orchestrated her father-in-law's death?

"It's a game," Ferryl said, interrupting her thoughts. "He's playing a game with us. So we shall play one with him."

"What?"

Ferryl stood, taking his wife's hands and pulling her to her feet with him. "No mention of Derwin's search for Derrick's armies. No mention of the Haravellian army encampment in Gaevast. He probably already knows, but we will play it off if he mentions it, say that your parents insisted on the extra precautions. We must let him believe that we are lying low out of fear. That we think we have no chance against him and we know it. We must let him think we wouldn't dare to provoke him. And then, like an insidious disease, when we find his armies, we will destroy him."

The king sat on the dais, his proud, thick shoulders back, his heavy crown resting on his head, a scepter perched in his mighty hand. A warrior king, valiant and brave and true. Ferryl watched in awe, wondering if he'd ever be half the man his father was. Wondering if his father was as uncomfortable as he was. Wonder-

ing if he, like Ferryl, would rather be atop his mount, riding across the plains that separated the castle at Benalle from the city beyond.

Ferryl grinned to himself, wishing Elizabeth were sitting beside him right now instead of Derwin, if for no other reason than that they could make fun of these obnoxious courtiers together. But he'd join her soon enough; they had plans to ride out later. She turned fourteen today, and Ferryl had promised her a day together to celebrate. But not until this audience was finished.

This was just a formality—a time for the nobles to kiss the king's ass, beg for favors, vie for positions in his court. But King Aiken never wavered, never so much as flicked a brow as courtier after courtier bowed before him, kissed his rings, and filled his head with syrupy words. Yes, Ferryl hoped he'd be just like his father someday.

But for every bit of spine his father showed against these sniveling courtiers, he was equally as shocked when from the left of his throne, the door to a small antechamber opened to reveal the queen of Navah.

Ferryl thought his mother looked a lot like a storm in that black gown. It trailed behind her like a black-bellied cloud. And the ridiculous circlet on top of her head didn't help, the onyx glittering in the candlelight, feathers bobbing with every step she took, the small veil of lace covering her kohl-lined eyes. She loved to scare the ever-loving shit out of the courtiers when it came time for audience. It seemed to him lately that she scared the king even more.

No. No, that wasn't fear in his father's eyes.

That was…that was need.

Ferryl nearly fell out of his chair as he registered the look in his father's eyes. It was not a look he was used to seeing. It was not anything normal for his father to show even hint of desire for his wife.

The queen practically floated in that gown, finally perching on the edge of her throne next to the king, never even batting an eye when the king took her hand. He brought it to his mouth, kissing it once and with a possession Ferryl had never witnessed before. Then Ferryl watched his father lean across the space between the thrones, heard his father whisper to his mother words that sounded a lot like, "You look good enough to eat."

It was his mother's eyes that flashed this time. And Ferryl could not be sure if the surprise was because of her husband's sudden show of affection or because she hadn't expected him to reveal it here. But for the rest of the audience with the court, the king did not let go of the queen's hand. Nor did she let go of his.

~

Ferryl sat now on the very same throne, his wife beside him, clad in black to mourn the king whose memory had stolen over Ferryl's thoughts like a tidal wave. He supposed it was the same heavy crown perched atop his head that had spurred the memory, and he knew that his adolescent musings had likely been correct—Aiken had probably been just as uncomfortable wearing it as Ferryl was now.

A few of the courtiers watched him but they watched Adelaide more, looks of skepticism and doubt in their eyes. Some even sneered when Ferryl reached across the small space and took her hand in his. But Ferryl held on tightly and silently thanked Providence for the woman beside him as he ignored their doubtful glares, as he looked out across the sea of courtiers who had gathered—not to kiss a king's ass, but to pay homage to a man who had led them well for the better part of two decades.

The man who had been a king to these people, but a father to Ferryl. A father to Derwin, who had still not returned from his search for King Derrick's clandestine army. Ferryl knew it was more than just mourning for the death of the king that had settled on Leala's shoulders today. She was worried for her husband. They all were.

It was the queen mother who caught his eye next. She was wearing black, of course. But it wasn't her dress that surprised him so much as it was the circlet atop her head: the very same circlet from his memory of the only time he had ever seen his father show any sign of affection toward her. She wore it today in the very same way. Even her dress was similar—not quite as garish, but a similar cut and style. As if she wanted to remember that moment, too. Perhaps it was as etched in her heart as it was in Ferryl's.

She met Ferryl's stare, her black eyes betraying nothing of her thoughts. He was just far enough away that he could not tell if there was a tear in her eye or if it was just a trick of the candlelight.

Michael shouldered his way through the crowd, stepping up near the dais, clad in black from head to toe—a jarring departure from his usual black-and-white uniform. A man of Navah through and through, it was so rare to see him in anything but the colors of his kingdom. The former duchess stood by his side, her belly protruding so far that Ferryl wondered how she could stand for any amount of time. Michael rested a hand at her waist, a gesture that looked as comfortable, as normal as if they had known each other a lifetime.

When he realized Adelaide had spotted Michael's hand, too, he mused for her benefit, *They've grown quite close since we've been gone.*

It would appear so, she thought, but a brief flicker of pain in her eyes tore his attention from his guard.

What's wrong? he asked.

She met his worried gaze. *I'm fine, Ferryl,* she said with a small smile that he knew she was attempting for his benefit.

Are you in pain?

No, not pain. Relax.

Ade—

A collective gasp from the courtiers stole Ferryl's attention. He and Adelaide looked up to see the reason for that outburst.

If Meria had once been a storm in a black gown, King Derrick of Midvar was thunder and lightning itself. As he strolled into the throne room, flanked by several Midvarish guards, Ferryl knew that the black the foreign king wore was not for mourning, but because it was the only color he ever wore. It was the only color fitting.

Death. Darkness. Terror.

King Derrick was a nightmare made flesh, his tight auburn locks spilling across his tanned brow, the lines in his face a little deeper since the last time Ferryl had seen him. A heavy black brocade cloak trailed behind him, the fine threads catching candlelight now and then, revealing the ornate weave. Gaudy rings rested on every meaty finger, the stones as black as his eyes. But it wasn't the make of his clothes or the shimmer of his jewels that gave Ferryl pause—it was the moths. By the hundreds, the black moths swarmed the king in a cloud as he swept across the marble floors.

Ferryl stole a glance at Adelaide, who returned the look with wide-eyed horror.

Those aren't moths, Ferryl, she said for only his benefit.

No, he was beginning to realize they weren't. Months ago, he had been plagued by those dastardly pests for weeks on end, when Adelaide—Elizabeth—had disappeared, and in the wake of that tragedy, the moths had consumed him.

Except they weren't moths.

Færies, Adelaide breathed, even in her thoughts.

Dark færies.

Ferryl swallowed once. Twice.

Færies. They only existed in fables. Legends. Not here. Not now.

But he could see them. In the flesh, swarming around his greatest enemy. Adelaide could see them, too.

He wondered who else could…

A smarmy curl to King Derrick's mouth redirected Ferryl's attention. It was enough to set Ferryl so much on edge that Adelaide squeezed his hand and said to only him, *It's a game, Ferryl. Don't forget that.*

Oh, he wouldn't forget it. He was playing a game today—walking a tightrope. He would not let this king think for one minute that he was losing. He would let him think of Ferryl as a terrified, shivering prince turned king. Never mind that he practically was.

You are not, Adelaide scolded.

Perhaps not. But only by a degree, at best. And as this storm made flesh slithered across the polished marble of the throne room, parting the wide-eyed courtiers like the sea during a storm, Ferryl took to playing his part well, even if it didn't require much acting. His heart pounded mercilessly in his chest, and his palms sweated. He gave the dark king a curt nod, which Derrick returned before taking a place near the front of the crowd. Ferryl stole a glance at Michael, who looked ready to flay the Midvarish king's skin from his bones, his hand having absently pulled Delaney a little closer to his side. She seemed terrified of her uncle.

Then again, *she* was supposed to be sitting on this throne beside

Ferryl. Not Adelaide, the lost princess whom Derrick had tried to extinguish so many years ago.

All the worry of the past few months rushed over Ferryl in an instant. The sweat at his brow might help him look like a fledgling prince, but playacting aside, the truth was that he was terrified.

Terrified to the marrow of his bones.

This king held him—held Ferryl's entire kingdom—in the palm of his hand. And Derrick knew it. He had Ferryl by the balls. There was not a damn thing Ferryl could do until Derwin found those armies of Midvar, wherever the Sheol they were.

Derwin will find the armies, Ferryl. He will.

Providence-willing.

Music began, soft and mournful, a choir of young boys singing a melody in unison. A song for the king they had lost. A song for the kingdom he had loved.

Ferryl did not have to fake the tear that fell down his cheek as the notes washed over him and the reality of his loss threatened to swallow him whole. He shouldn't have been king until he was an old man himself. He shouldn't have inherited this throne for several more decades, at least. Instead he was a few weeks away from turning twenty-two and scared witless, missing Aiken. Not missing his king. Missing his *father*. The man he had loved, trusted, and even idolized.

Ferryl wept.

Adelaide let go of his hand that she might slip an arm around his slumped shoulders, rubbing her hand up and down his back. Her warmth seeped into the marrow of his bones, her calm assurance a balm to his shredded soul.

So much. He had lost so much. Too much.

But he had her.

He had this friend, this love by his side.

He knew he could only face this, only sit in a room with his ene-my, surrounded by his court because she was by his side. Because she was his rock in the storm. His anchor in the waves.

The hallowed song ended, and a priest—the very priest Ferryl had commissioned last summer to marry him to Elizabeth—began his eulogy.

From the dais, Ferryl watched the king of Midvar smile.

In his youth, he wouldn't have had such patience. In his youth, if Derrick—then only a prince—had dared to look at Aaron's father the way he now looked at his son-in-law, he would have brandished a blade and drawn blood, just to make sure the son of a bitch knew his place.

Instead, from beside the dais on which his precious daughter and proud son-in-law sat, King Aaron of Haravelle fidgeted like a schoolgirl, seething. Avigail breathed a small chuckle, taking hold of his hand. When he looked over, she gave him a look that let him know he was being a bit too obvious. But he didn't care. Not really. Let them see. Let them know that Derrick was pissing him off.

How dare he show up here! When he knew—when he knew that everyone here did, too—that he was the reason this funeral was hap-pening at all. What a brazen, arrogant, asshole move he had made to dare show himself.

Aaron wanted to shove it all in his face. Yes, it was foolish of him. Perhaps even immature. Years of training and running his court at Chesedelle had taught him to school his emotions, to hone them into a blade he could use on the battlefield. But war was still a ways away for them—unless Commander Derwin returned soon with news of the Midvarish army's whereabouts.

But he doubted it very much. Derrick was nobody's fool. He never had been. He would not let his army be easily found. He would not show his hand until he had to. So Aaron seethed as he watched the bastard silently gloat, and he itched to put Derrick in his place.

As if in answer, the rock around his neck—the other half to the one hanging from his daughter's neck—seemed to pulse. Again. It had been doing that a lot lately. Ever since they had arrived here in Navah with Ferryl and Adelaide. It was as if the stone around his neck had something to tell him.

That had only happened once before: on the night they had discovered that the woman Ferryl had brought with him—the one who looked so much like his wife—was not just some stable girl. She was the lost princess of Haravelle. His daughter.

From the moment Adelaide, then called Elizabeth, had arrived at his castle, that rock had pulsed at his chest, pounding like his heartbeat. He hadn't dared tell Avigail then, too afraid of what it meant.

But when he discovered that his daughter lived, when he discovered that she was a breathing miracle before him, he had understood that pulsing in his amulet.

And now, sitting in the throne room at Benalle, he understood the pulsing once more.

Avigail was looking at him again—that way she had of knowing his thoughts without saying a word. Providence, he loved that about her. So when the audience stood for the benediction, he stole a kiss, ignored the skeptical furrow in her brows, and marched up to the dais, his shoulders back, his heart pounding like a drum in time with the pulse of the amulet at his chest.

Ferryl was the first to realize that Aaron meant to join them on the dais. His eyes held a question, but he moved to make room for the king of Haravelle nonetheless. Aaron nodded once to his son-in-law, kissed his daughter on the cheek, and then turned to face the throngs of mourners before them.

The room had gone silent, the funeral almost over now. But all eyes were rapt on him and his interruption—including King Derrick's. Good. Aaron looked Derrick in the eye as he removed the amulet around his neck.

He held it aloft, the sun glinting off the rough-cut crystalline center. He could have sworn it was glowing as he said, "The Amulet of Haravelle—a symbol of my power in the north, gifted with the magic of *Providence,*" he emphasized that little tidbit with a pointed look at Derrick before he continued "and now a gift to my new son, the king of Navah. A twin to the amulet my daughter, the heir of Haravelle, has worn her whole life. May their reign be long and blessed."

Perhaps he should have waited until the coronation for such a gift. But as he watched Derrick's eyes widen and then narrow again, as he watched the people's attention remain rapt on their king, Aaron knew he had made the right choice to bestow the amulet on his new son now. Here. Before everyone.

Because he knew something else, too. Something the world would soon understand. Soon see for themselves.

So he grinned like a caracal and clasped the chain around Ferryl's neck.

"Long live King Ferryl!" Aaron cried.

The audience repeated the shout.

And then, like he knew they would, the twin amulets ignited, blanketing the room in a deluge of impossible light. The magic of Providence.

Power. Providence's magic was power, pure and undiluted.

And Aaron had just made sure the world knew—that they'd seen with their own eyes just exactly *where* Providence had bestowed the blessing of that power.

Aaron slid his eyes to his enemy, still seated in the audience, his black cloak gobbling up the light.

The king of Midvar was seething.

Chapter IX

hat a charming little display that was," purred King Derrick from the other end of the long banquet table. "Positively quaint." He cut into his venison with deadly precision—a master with a blade.

Ferryl resisted the urge to snarl at Derrick's arrogance.

The Midvarish king went on, oblivious to Ferryl on the other end of the table. "Why, I haven't seen tricks like that since I was a little boy. It reminds me of the days of yore when court jesters were the fashion." At that, he chuckled.

Ferryl gripped his goblet and ground his teeth. How dare the bastard speak of the amulets as if they were some sort of sleight of hand! How dare he brush off the very magic of Providence as tricks and games! The rock around his neck seemed to pulse in response.

Easy, Adelaide said for his benefit. He let her take hold of his hand under the table. Let her stroke her thumb along the back of his hand, her touch soothing him. He let his eyes roam around the table, registering the reactions of his dinner guests. Lord Westerly seemed positively giddy to be at the table tonight. Ferryl had only invited him to placate the mouthy lord. But it was Michael who caught Ferryl's eye; standing by the door; the guard's gaze had not left Delaney, his shoulders tight, his hand resting on the pommel of his sword, as if he were just daring anyone to make a move against her—her own uncle included.

"Indeed, the magic of Providence has been neglected in this realm for too long, hasn't it?" said King Aaron with equal oiliness, a feline grin on his mouth as he sipped his wine.

A chuckle. "I had forgotten that you still pray to the ancient spirit," said King Derrick. "How charming. Your cultures are steeped in delightful little traditions."

"You are too kind, Majesty," said Lord Westerly with an overtly humble bow of his head. Derrick all but ignored him; Westerly was a pebble in his shoe, at best.

"The service was beautiful, Ferryl. You should be proud," King Derrick went on. "Your father was a great man, and he will be greatly missed."

"Indeed. He *was* a great man. One of the greatest I've known," said Adelaide, her shoulders back. Not an ounce of fear shone in her blazing eyes.

"And all three kings of the realm in one room? Why we are the picture of peace!" said Derrick, his glass raised. "It is a red-letter day, indeed. Although I cannot help but wonder as to the absence of some of your family, King Ferryl."

"Oh?" Ferryl asked despite himself.

"I cannot ignore that your dear mother and brother are missing from this table."

"You will excuse my mother. She has been ill since my father's death," Ferryl said, holding Derrick's gaze.

"Tragic," he finally said. "And your brother? Is he ill, too?"

"No," was all Ferryl could think to say.

"Dear me. What on earth could have kept him from his own father's funeral?"

Ferryl stole a glance at Leala, who eyes shone with muted worry. "Duty," he finally said.

"The life of a war commander is never dull, is it?" the dark king asked, a cloying tone to his voice.

Ferryl said nothing, never taking his eyes off of Derrick as he took another sip from his goblet.

Relax, Ferryl. He's trying to get under your skin.

It's working, Ferryl said to his wife.

She squeezed his hand, and even at so small a gesture, Ferryl took a breath and reminded himself of who he was.

From the other end of the vast table, Derrick cocked his head to one side, observing the royal couple's every movement. "Silly me," he eventually said. "I almost forgot to congratulate you, Ferryl. Though I confess I was stung that you did not invite me to your wedding."

"It was a hasty affair," Ferryl said.

"So it would seem," said Derrick, slicing into another piece of venison. "Though I cannot imagine why." He popped the meat into his mouth unceremoniously, chewing silently as his eyes fixed on Ferryl. But it was Adelaide who answered.

"We needed to return to Navah," she said. "And I insisted on marrying in my homeland."

"Of course," Derrick drawled. "The *miraculous* lost princess of Haravelle should indeed marry in her home kingdom."

It was the way he said it—the way he emphasized the word *miraculous*—that set Ferryl's teeth on edge. The king had long been suspected of killing Princess Adelaide. That's what everyone had believed, even though, just like with Ferryl's own father, there was no solid evidence. Somehow, the king had gotten away with too much without a shred of evidence to taint his name. So Ferryl supposed that look of amused interest on Derrick's face was all part of whatever game he was playing tonight here in Ferryl's own kingdom. Feigning mourning for a king he all but murdered. And now feigning his own delight in the miracle sitting across from him.

Ferryl only realized he was clenching his napkin so hard that his knuckles were white when Adelaide laid a hand over his on the table. He tore his gaze from the Midvarish king and met his wife's eyes, lacing his fingers through hers and sucking in a deep breath.

The Midvarish king appraised those clasped hands for a moment before he said, "She is the light of your life, isn't she, King Ferryl? You draw your strength from her." Ferryl wasn't sure he liked the king's observation, regardless of how true it was.

"What a happy little miracle that your little princess was right here under your nose all this time," Derrick went on. "Why, it's not every day a king gets to marry his whore and call her his queen."

Ferryl was going to rip his throat out. But it was Michael who moved—Michael who unsheathed his sword, standing unflinching at the edge of the table. "You will not speak of my queen in such a manner," the guard breathed through his teeth.

"Apologies," Derrick purred, slicing through more venison. "I only meant that Ferryl is lucky to have a queen he loves. That is a rare gift." He met Ferryl's eyes at that—met them and held them, a secret in the depthless onyx that Ferryl couldn't read, couldn't fathom.

Michael held his sword before him, the room having gone so taut it might have shattered with one thought. But Derrick finally broke the silence.

"It is painfully evident that my presence here is problematic. I do apologize. My little niece and I will be out of your hair by morning."

"What?" Delaney asked, looking up from her plate.

Ferryl could have sworn Michael had asked the same question, even as he sheathed his sword once more.

Derrick sipped from his goblet before he spoke. "You did not think I would abandon you, Delaney, darling?" When she did not answer, he went on. "It is time you come home. You are the only family I have left, after all."

"I have sisters," Delaney said, her voice small, trembling.

"Yes, well, they are bit young, aren't they?"

Young? Young for what? Ferryl wondered.

"And besides, I'd hate for you to be a burden to dear King Ferryl. He's done enough for you, hasn't he? We are most thankful for his graciousness in not throwing you out when he discovered it was not his heir in your belly."

Delaney looked to Ferryl and then to Adelaide before her pleading eyes finally landed on Michael. The guard seemed ready to leap out of his skin as he watched the duchess fidget with her napkin.

"Have you asked her whether or not she wants to leave?" Adelaide asked.

But Derrick did not deign to reply, a serpentine smile curling his mouth. Instead, he looked to Ferryl. "I did not realize it was also part of Navarian culture to allow a woman to have an opinion."

"I would hazard there is a great deal about Navarian culture that would shock you, King Derrick," said Ferryl.

"Indeed," Derrick said, that smirk still on his face.

"I… I would like to stay here, Uncle," said Delaney from down the long table, her voice smaller, more timid than Ferryl had ever heard it.

"It is not an option, darling," said Derrick. "I think you've bedded enough Navarian men as it is," he added with a chuckle.

Michael's hand was gripping the pommel of his sword again in the span of a heartbeat. He had taken a step forward when Lord Westerly spoke up, his attention on King Derrick. "It would seem she has a taste for Navarians, doesn't she, Majesty? First the prince, then the guard. The gods know who else she has bedded in her time here."

"The guard?" Ferryl asked, jutting his chin backward. But when he turned his attention to Michael, his friend's eyes were wide. And that closeness he had observed…the easy comfort Michael and Delaney seemed to take from each other…

"Dear me, Majesty," said Lord Westerly. "I did not realize that you did not know. Why, the whole court titters about it on a daily basis. He's in her chambers every night."

Ferryl looked to Delaney before turning his attention to his wife.

"Delaney, darling," King Derrick mockingly scolded. "Have I taught you nothing? You must learn to use some discretion."

"He is my friend," Delaney said, her words trembling as much as her hands.

"Forgive me, but I've never had a woman friend with whom I've frolicked about the beach in nothing but my underthings," said Lord Westerly with a chuckle. "You'll have to tell me what I'm doing wrong."

Michael turned a shade of red so deep that Ferryl thought he might burst. But Ferryl had no idea what to say, what to even think. Michael. Sleeping with Delaney. For how long? How long had it been going on? Could he be certain the child in her womb was truly her father's vassal's? Could it be Michael's instead? What else would the guard—his friend—hide from him?

The world seemed to tilt on its axis.

"She will remain in Navah until her time comes," said Adelaide. "She is far enough along in her pregnancy that any long journey could be dangerous."

"Yes," said Derrick. "It would be a tragedy for the world to lose a bastard."

"Enough," Michael dared to say, stepping forward. Rage burned in his eyes.

Derrick ignored him.

Adelaide went on. "She is welcome at the Navarian court as long as she would like to stay. As for the accusations against her—"

"You had better rein in your wife, Ferryl," said Derrick, interrupting Adelaide. "Or she will be a tyrant before she reaches her twentieth year."

Indignation boiled in his gut, and Ferryl squared his shoulders. "Considering that she is the queen of Navah and heir of Haravelle, she is, by my calculations, the most powerful person in this room. I would suggest heeding her advice."

Derrick raised incensed eyes to Ferryl, his mouth a thin line. Oh, he didn't like that. He didn't like that one bit.

Good.

The room went taut with silence, rage still emanating from the guard who might be the father of Delaney's child as well as from the young king who was trying to prove himself to a maniacal monster. Finally Derrick spoke again.

"I will be gone by first light," he said, standing to his feet, the scrape of his chair a shrill shock in the silence. "Delaney, you will return home to Midvar once you've given birth. You're no use to me in that condition anyway."

And with that, the king of Midvar disappeared from the dining hall.

Chapter X

The endless cloudy skies grew ever darker with the sunset that loomed before her. Meria stood alone at her windows, watching the minutes pass with each new eerie shade of gray and green. Today had been one of the most difficult days of her life. Saying goodbye had been much harder than she had anticipated.

The ache of his absence still stung. And the funeral that had come two months after Aiken's death had felt more like the opening of an old wound than the closing of a chapter. It had left her hollow. Like a cliff with no bottom. A sky with no sea.

So many regrets. So many mistakes she had made. She knew now that she would spend the rest of her life paying for them.

No need for the fires of Sheol; she was living them here and now.

Her sons would never forgive her for her transgressions. And why should they? They were too many to count and too treacherous to overlook.

No, she deserved the darkness in which she now dwelled. The darkness that swallowed her whole.

She deserved it. So she would abide in it. Make it home. Try to find some semblance of peace here in this lonely chasm she had inadvertently carved for herself.

There was a knock at her door. And while she wasn't up for visitors, she was equally disinterested in further hurting her children. So she called out, "Enter."

But it wasn't either of her sons at the door.

It was him.

And for a moment, the whole world stood still as his presence filled her chambers.

Derrick of Midvar had always been a storm. A mighty storm that had blown into her life when she was young and naïve and had had the world at her fingertips. One that had consumed and devoured her from the inside out. A storm that wouldn't cease.

And she had loved the storm so much that she hated him.

"My little Navarian dove," he said, sweeping through the room, his black cape billowing behind him as if he controlled the very winds.

She only looked at him.

He smiled that signature smile of his. The one that had burned her from within—burned and burned until there was nothing but cinders and ashes.

He tilted his head, his handsome face tight with a question. "What's wrong, Meria, darling?"

"You know exactly what's wrong," she said, turning her back to him.

He crept up behind her so quietly that she didn't know he was there until she felt his arms wrap around her, his spicy breath hot on her cheek. So tall. He had always been so tall that even now, as he pressed a kiss to her cheek, she could feel just how low he had to stoop. "Don't tell me you're missing him. Not after all of this."

She closed her eyes and steeled herself. He couldn't understand.

He never had. "It wasn't supposed to be this way."

"And what way is that, my dove?" His hands—all possession and passion—stroked idle paths up and down her arms.

"He wasn't supposed to die."

"You know I had nothing to do with that."

"I don't believe you."

His hand found her neck, his fingers slowly tracing her contours. Intimate, yet controlled. Always, *always* a calculated balance of passion and power. The weight of his massive body pressed against her like a burden. "Sir Thomas took it upon himself to right the wrongs that were done to me when your son rejected my darling niece."

"She's the one who rejected him," Meria retorted quietly, knowing that bringing up Delaney's infidelities would do nothing to further her cause.

"Semantics, darling," he said, wrapping his strong arms around her waist, pulling her more closely to him. He rested his chin on the top of her head even as his fingers resumed idle strokes, this time along her ribs and waist. "The point is, our kingdoms were to be united. But now that your son has married the little Haravellian whore, that cannot happen. Sir Thomas was merely defending his king. How was I to know he would take such drastic measures?"

"You swore to me he wouldn't die," she said, her voice hoarse and strained, unable to stop the tears that began to fall. "You swore to me that he would be safe this way."

"If I didn't know any better," he said, pulling away from her, "I would think you were mourning his loss, Meria. You, the woman who willingly cursed him for years. Don't tell me you've finally fallen in love with your husband now that he's dead!" The mockery in his tone was enough to send her into a fit of rage. But she quelled her temper, swallowing down the bile that stung her throat before she turned to face him.

She gripped his muscled arms, the sheer breadth of them so great that her hands barely covered half. "Promise me, Derrick. Promise me you will not harm my sons."

Disdain darkened his eyes still further. "There is no need to promise something I have already sworn."

She gripped him harder, barely making a dent in the solid rock of flesh beneath her fingers. "Promise again, Derrick. Promise me that you won't hurt them."

"Meria," he cooed, stepping closer, circling an arm around her waist. His other hand found her neck, his thumb grazing lazy circles on her throat, his grip a bit too tight for affection. She knew that just a little bit tighter and he could...

"My dove, my darling. I know how much they mean to you. And if my poor little wife hadn't died while giving birth to my own son, I might better understand your stricken fear. But just because I have not had the privilege of fatherhood does not mean I do not have a heart."

At this, his grip slackened just enough, his hand traveling down her neck, her collarbone, her chest. She shut her eyes as his hand lingered over her breast before finally settling on her ribs. Silent possession, fiery lust. Always the same with him. He leaned into her, his voice as sensuous as it was serpentine. "I swore to you that I would never lay a finger on them. And I always keep my promises. But Meria, we must finish this; we must finish what you and I started. And Ferryl must know who is the true king of Navah."

He pressed his lips to her neck, his tongue flicking ever so faintly across her skin, a wave of fiery lust building in him before he contin-ued, "He is so close, darling. So close now. He is scared. Scared to be king. Everything is coming together according to plan."

The plan. Gods, how many times had she heard about the plan? And how many times had she lain awake at night asking herself who was the greater traitor, the greater whore?

"Isn't that what you want, darling? For you and I to be togeth-er? To take the throne that should be ours? You once loved me. You once dreamt of a better world with me. Do you not still share in that dream?"

"I do, Derrick, I just—"

He straightened and gripped her chin in his hand.

"Then trust me. Trust me and love me as you once did."

And then he pulled her to him and kissed her, his lips, his arms a storm of possession and power and lust.

But Meria knew—deep in the pit of her soul, she knew—that despite all the promises, despite all the years between them, she could never truly trust him. If he ever hurt Ferryl or Derwin. If he ever…

"We're so close now, my dove," he crooned, running his hand over her hair as if consoling a crying child. "So very close to every-thing we ever wanted."

His hand found the hair at the nape of her neck, gathering it into his fist and pulling taut. She winced at the pain, looking up to find his eyes dark and menacing as he said distantly, "All that's left to do is break him."

Chapter XI

Ferryl's hand was trembling, the heavy scepter catching rogue rays of sunlight which glinted off of the jewels that encrusted it. But despite his nerves, the king of Navah stood on the dais with his shoulders back and his chin high. He looked positively glorious in his Navarian colors, the crisp black-and-white uniform that had been custom tailored just for him accentuating his taut, broad form. Adelaide couldn't help but think what a magnificent king he made as she stood beside him, hand in hand, reciting her vows to the kingdom of Navah: to protect, to serve, and to rule so long as there was breath in her body.

The emerald gown Ferryl had insisted she wear was heavy, the jewel-encrusted velvet stifling hot despite the wintry chill in the air. But her mother had also insisted she wear the colors of her birth kingdom. She had insisted she display her heritage for all of Navah to see, and when Ferryl hadn't protested, Adelaide had acquiesced to the odd demand. Despite the fact that she was being crowned as the queen of Navah, today she looked every bit the princess of Haravelle.

The priest before them recited the ancient words, and Adelaide smiled as she watched the old man. His cottony hair and papery-thin skin betrayed his age, but genuine honor underlaid his every word as he crowned his new king and queen. Phinehas—that was his name. He reminded her so much of Bedell, the man she had called father for most of her life.

Adelaide had laughed out loud when Ferryl told her that he had commissioned the same priest to crown them that he had tried to get to marry them last summer, a humble old man from the small village of Gaevast, just north of Benalle. She had laughed a little more when Ferryl told her he had also named him the very first High Priest of Navah and that his first act as king would be to declare his intention to build a temple in Benalle.

A twinge of nausea bit at her belly, but it was her parents who stole her attention—the funny way her father fidgeted as he stood on the dais, as if he had something on his mind, words on the tip of his tongue that he was biding his time to share with the kingdom. She furrowed her brow once when she caught him looking at her. But he only winked, a conspiratorial grin on his mouth. Her mother smiled with similar conspiracy, and Adelaide began to wonder what they were up to.

You noticed it, too, then? Ferryl asked only her.

What are they up to, Ferryl?

I don't know. But your father was acting strange all morning. As if he had something he wanted to tell me.

I wonder if it has something to do with Derrick's behavior at the feast last night?

Adelaide stole one more glance at her parents, but they gave nothing away.

The priest finished his words, and a page stepped forward with two heavy crowns on ornate pillows. But before the new king and queen of Navah could be crowned, King Aaron of Haravelle stepped forward.

"If you will forgive my interruption, Your Holiness," he said to Phinehas, "there is something I must say."

Ferryl furrowed his brow, throwing a glance at his wife before stepping aside to give his father-in-law more room.

But before Aaron could speak, the doors of the throne room opened, and all eyes turned to see who dared interrupt the coronation. Fortunately, it was the one man who could get away with it, the only man whose interruption would be welcome.

Leala stood from her seat at the end of the dais, a look of utter joy on her face as she leaned on the balls of her feet and took off into a sprint down the aisle toward the man who had interrupted.

Prince Derwin's smile could have been seen all the way from Haravelle as he watched his wife run to him. She threw herself into his arms so violently that a lesser man would have toppled to the ground. Instead, Derwin merely hugged his wife to himself so tightly that he lifted her off the ground, taking a moment to kiss her shamelessly before he managed to acknowledge the rest of the room.

"Sorry I'm late," was all the prince said. Ferryl laughed, bowing his head to Derwin and smiling from ear to ear. "Your timing is impeccable, brother."

Derwin bowed low, his head still down as he said, "Hail the king and queen of Navah."

The audience repeated his words in unison, sending a wave of gooseflesh along Adelaide's skin.

"About that," said King Aaron, and all attention returned to him. When he was certain every eye was on him, he went on, "Good people of Navah, I have learned something in my time here. When I discovered weeks ago that my beautiful daughter was still alive and that she had been kept safe in your kingdom all this time, I was overwhelmed with joy. I knew then that great things were in store for her—our most precious treasure, kept safe for so long. Great things for the daughter of a great kingdom.

"And while I had always known that some day, upon her marriage to your good prince, she would reunite my kingdom with yours, I had always assumed that reunification would happen upon my death.

"But it appears I was wrong.

"When I gave your king my half of the sacred Amulet of Haravelle, it was meant as a gift—a show of my good faith. But it was so much more than that, for in truth, the kingdom of Haravelle became his the moment he made my daughter his wife.

"And so today, before all of these witnesses, I, King Aaron of Haravelle, abdicate my crown to the true king of Haravelle and Navah. And my wife abdicates to the true queen of Haravelle and Navah.

"For today, before Providence, we crown the first king and queen of Har-Navah, the reunified kingdom."

In response, as if in delight, the twin stones around Ferryl and Adelaide's necks ignited once more. But unlike at his father's funeral, the light was not blinding. No, it was a warm, radiance that filled the throne room. It kissed every corner with a thousand colors and a thousand more too impossible to name. It swirled and eddied around pillars and up to the arched ceiling, filling every nook with magic, rendering every eye in the room wide with wonder and every mouth silent with shock.

From the great balcony beyond the throne room, the windows burst open, the silvery light of the muted day obscured by a cloud of more light. And wings. And…that was music.

Færies, Adelaide breathed in her mind.

Færies of the Light.

Not with black wings like those that had surrounded King Derrick but with bright, wondrous colors and patterns. Like the butterflies Ferryl had seen on the mountain in Haravelle not so very long ago.

Except those hadn't been butterflies, either.

Færies, Ferryl parroted in his mind.

The ancient beings left to legends and fireside stories were real. As real as the magic of Providence that his people had ignored for so long.

But they would ignore no longer.

Providence, it seemed, had something planned. Perhaps for the whole world.

The room was silent, as still as a winter morning as the færies filled the room, fluttering about and landing on every surface—windows and rails, shoulders and chairs. Some of the færies even landed on the thrones behind Ferryl and Adelaide. The room remained in shocked silence as the music—the sound of the færy wings—filled the air.

It was Derwin who broke the silence once more—Derwin who, with pride in his words, shouted from the back of the throne room, "All hail King Ferryl and Queen Adelaide! All hail the king and queen of Har-Navah!"

The entire room repeated the chant as the heavy crowns were placed atop their heads.

"All hail the king and queen of Har-Navah!"

Chapter XII

ell, if every bit of that ceremony wasn't a slap in King Derrick's face, I don't know what is," laughed Derwin, clapping his brother on the back. The crowd of tittering nobility swirled about the ballroom, drinking and dancing, smiling and nodding. The coronation ball had commenced.

"It's just too damn bad he had to leave before he could witness it," Derwin went on. A surge of nausea welled in Ferryl's gut. Yes, he had known full well that his coronation would do nothing but add fuel to his enemy's very secret and nowhere-to-be-found fire. But even so, hearing it out of his brother's mouth—his commander's—did nothing to put him at ease, if for no other reason than that of the woman standing beside him, arm in arm.

Despite the beauty of today, the ease with which it had all come together, Ferryl knew in his gut that it was only a matter of time before King Derrick did something about the princess who shouldn't be alive. The woman who had just become a queen of the most powerful kingdom in the realm. The *reunified* kingdom.

Providence above, the very idea of it terrified Ferryl.

So the fact that Derwin's return hadn't been a glorious one—that he had instead returned knowing nothing more of the Midvarish army's whereabouts than when he departed—left Ferryl reeling, wondering what in Sheol he should do now. Because now he wasn't just the king of Navah. Now he was the king of Har-Navah. Married to a woman who shouldn't be alive, the most wanted woman in the world.

That worry simmered, threatening to boil with every passing second, Ferryl knowing—feeling—that they were all on borrowed time as they searched in vain for the Midvarish army.

How in all the realms of Sheol was he supposed to defend a kingdom—much less his wife—from an enemy they'd yet to find?

Ferryl took a healthy swig of the mulled wine in his goblet, savoring the heat as it chased away the chill, raising it with a feigned smirk on his mouth as if in salute of his brother's gloating. In truth, he simply needed the beverage to numb the worry, if only for tonight.

"You look stunning, as always," said Leala to Adelaide, kissing her friend's cheek. Ferryl welcomed the chuckle that blossomed at the flat look on his wife's face. Since it was Leala who had picked out Adelaide's entire ensemble for the ball and second dress of the day, an emerald-encrusted gown that hugged every single curve as if she had been painted head to toe in evergreen stars, Leala's compliment was—

"Your humility, as always, is an example to us all," Adelaide quipped to the princess.

Feigning affront, Leala placed her hand on her heart. "Can I help it that I have impeccable taste? If left to you, I've no doubt you would have shown up in a homespun dress and a filthy apron."

"I happen to like that look," Ferryl retorted.

"There's no accounting for taste around here," Leala said.

"You look beautiful no matter what you're wearing," Ferryl said to Adelaide. *Or aren't wearing, if my memory serves me correctly,* he added for only her benefit.

Such scandalous thoughts, Your Majesty, she responded, giving him a look, *that* look.

So he pressed a kiss to the shell of her ear as he said, *Well then, I dare not share what else I'm thinking.*

When she met his eyes again, she bit her full lower lip, and Ferryl began counting down the minutes until he could slip away from this ball so that he might pay passionate homage to the newly crowned queen of Har-Navah.

"Am I missing something?" Leala asked, interrupting their silent flirtation.

"What's wrong?" Adelaide asked.

Leala's brow rose, a hand on her hip as she said, "You two. You always seem to be in some sort of conversation none of the rest of us are privy to."

"That's impossible," Ferryl said, realizing how stupid his response was when Adelaide chimed,

"Is there a couple in the world who don't have an understanding of one another that no one else shares?"

"Plenty," Derwin said, but when Leala shot her eyes to her husband, examining him with furrowed brows, Ferryl couldn't help but chuckle again.

Indeed, Ferryl and Adelaide shared an *understanding* that was unique, to say the very least.

"I'll let the two of you work out this argument," said Adelaide, taking Ferryl's hand. "I want to dance with my husband."

Ferryl gladly followed.

~

"You are trembling, my love. Is everything all right?"

Adelaide bit her lip as Ferryl whirled her about the dance floor, the emeralds of her gown catching the light of the chandeliers and peppering the floor, the walls, even the courtiers and guests with glittering fragments of light. She twirled under his hand, her hair flying behind her before Ferryl caught her slender waist in his hand and pulled her to him again.

He would never get enough of this love in his arms.

Her eyes sparkled despite the quiet thoughts that swirled behind them.

"What is it you're not telling me?" Ferryl tried to draw her out again. "I can tell something is on your mind. It's been on your mind for days. And I'm mildly terrified that I haven't even been able to steal it from your thoughts."

In fact, the more he thought about it, the more he wondered *why* he couldn't glean those thoughts from her as he usually could.

She chuckled and looked over their arms. Ferryl followed her gaze to find Michael standing in the shadows at the edge of the ballroom, leaning to whisper something to the person standing next to him. It was only when the crowd parted that Ferryl saw who that person was. And when Ferryl saw the way Michael's silver eyes affixed on

Delaney as if she were the sun and he a mere planet in her glorious orbit, a twinge of doubt punched him in the gut. Why hadn't he seen it before? Why hadn't he noticed the way Michael looked at Delaney? Had he been blind?

And worse, why hadn't Michael told him?

He hated it, the thought that one of the few people he trusted implicitly had been lying to him. For what looked like quite a long time. He hated the questions it planted in his mind, the doubt it bubbled in his soul.

"Will you defend her position? If it comes to it?" Adelaide asked, shattering his thoughts.

"What do you mean?" he asked, turning to see her gaze set upon the same tableau.

Adelaide met his eyes again. "If the council continues to push for her banishment, will you defend her position here at court?"

Ferryl searched his wife for a moment, searched his own soul for the answer to that question. If she had asked him even a few days ago, the answer would have been yes. Without a doubt.

But knowing Michael had lied to him…knowing his best friend had been hiding a damning truth…

"Ferryl," Adelaide said. He focused on her once more.

"Yes," he finally managed. "I will defend her."

"No matter the cost?"

"Why are you asking me this?"

She looked back to where Michael and Delaney had disappeared into the crowd. "Because there was a time when our love needed protection, too. When it needed allies in order to exist in this world. It still does. And it may very well come to that with Michael and Delaney. I want you to be prepared for whatever comes."

Ferryl followed her gaze to the place where Michael and Delaney had just been, staring absently as he asked, "Why didn't he tell me? Why didn't he feel he could trust me?"

"She was your betrothed, Ferryl. Can you blame him?"

"No," he admitted. "No, I do not. But it still feels…wrong."

"He should have told you," Adelaide agreed. "But I understand why he did not. And I think a time is coming when both of them will need our support. And it may be coming sooner rather than later."

Ferryl turned his attention back to his wife. "Do you know something I do not?"

"No," she said, and he could see she was sincere. "All I am saying is that Lord Westerly has made it clear where he stands regarding Delaney. And with his wealth and influence, I wouldn't be surprised if he made a play in some manner, using them as bait. I want you to be prepared because I know how much you love Michael. And I know how much you love your kingdom."

"I will not be manipulated by bullies."

"Of course not," she said, placing her hand on his chest. "I am only asking as a reminder that sometimes, the right decision is not the easy one."

"No," he agreed. "It most certainly is not."

Adelaide gave him a small smile as the song ended and the next one began. One song after another, they danced as if, just for tonight, no war loomed before them and no enemies threatened their doorsteps.

After only a moment or two, Adelaide closed her eyes, taking in a breath through her nose.

"What is it you're not telling me, Lizybet?" Ferryl asked softly, for even with her eyes closed, her thoughts still and quiet, he could see the words she wasn't saying. They were written all over her face.

"Are you purposely trying to torture me?" he asked, hoping to lighten the mood.

But she did not smile when she at last met his eyes. Worry. That's what was written all over her.

"My love, what's wrong?"

"Nothing is wrong, really. I suppose. I mean, I don't know. I just…"

Never in all his life had he known this woman to be at a loss for words. Not like this. And the sight of it—the very idea of it—sent a wave of panic over him.

My love? he tried again for only her to hear. *You can tell me anything, you know.*

"I know, Ferryl. Of course I know that. It's just…"

Ferryl stopped dancing, taking hold of his wife's chin, forcing her to look at him. "What is it that plagues you?"

Her eyes moved to the smattering of guards nearby, their broad shoulders straight, their gleaming swords at their sides. An ever-present reminder of who she was now. *And* the price on her head.

She swallowed, and that's when he spotted a thin line of tears in her eyes. *Ferryl, I think I might be with child.*

For a moment, the whole world just stopped.

No dancers.

No ball.

No glittering chandeliers and prattling court.

Just Lizybet and Ferryl. In their Secret Place, laughing and talking, two young dreamers with the world ahead of them. On that mountain, overlooking the world, the light of Providence swallowing them whole. But they were at neither place. Instead, they were facing the greatest joy they might ever know right on the brink of the foulest war their kingdom would ever face.

Ferryl swallowed, his focus returning to his wife. When he finally remembered to breathe, he spotted the tears waiting to fall. He kissed her softly and then rested his brow against hers. "Are you certain?" he asked.

"My linens have been clean for weeks. I don't know what else it could be. I'm sorry I haven't told you. I've been so afraid… The timing. I mean, I'm happy. I'm so happy. But the timing is…"

He pulled back to take her chin in his hand again. A baby. *Their* baby. He was going to be a father.

"I don't care about the timing," he said. "We'll deal with it." *A child,* he said mind to mind. Heart to heart. *Our child, Lizybet.*

Our child, she repeated.

And the cautious joy in her eyes was enough that he let his lips find hers. He kissed his wife—the mother of his child. And despite the timing, despite the what-ifs that loomed before them, a smile, a laugh came over him.

He deepened the kiss, even while the laugh threatened to disrupt it. But the sweet rapture only lasted a moment before Adelaide cried out, clutching her side and going limp in Ferryl's arms. He gripped her tightly, distracted by a woman who screamed nearby. Ferryl looked down to find a man lying on the ground beside them, blood dripping from the tip of the dagger he clutched in his hand, an arrow through his breast.

No one—no one around seemed to be the culprit of the arrow. The eyes of the courtiers surrounding him were just as confused as he knew his own must be. With growing panic, he scanned and scanned the room again. But where—?

The mezzanine. He looked up to see Michael's keen eyes fixed on them, a bow in his arms. Another whimper from his wife had Ferryl looking down to see blood on his hands. Her blood.

Understanding dawned slowly as his breath grew heavier and heavier. She had been stabbed.

And then there was chaos.

Chapter XIII

Fifteen Minutes Earlier

’ve never been up here," Delaney said, looking at the courtiers below.

"There are few who have. The mezzanine is mainly for guards. A perfect place to watch the festivities with a bird's-eye view. It was my favorite spot when I first became a guard. I think it might still be."

Her captivating smile brought one to Michael's own mouth. He kissed her cheek in response, standing behind her, his arms wrapped around her rounding belly, feeling for any sign of movement within.

Sure enough, the baby stirred, as if it knew his touch, anticipated it. A smile welled from deep within.

"She knows you, Michael," Delaney said quietly, her head resting on his shoulder, her breath warm on his neck. "She likes it when you're near."

He had no words for that. He could think of nothing that would suffice, nothing to convey what he was thinking.

"I suppose she's a lot like her mother in that regard," Delaney added.

Michael kissed Delaney's shoulder, pulling her closer to him, unfazed by the smattering of guards that stood on either side of them. They, too, were overlooking the ball. Guarding. Watching. Protecting. He had brought her up here just to get away. There were too many eyes on them. Too many questions. And even Ferryl…

Michael had not had a chance to speak to his king yet. To explain himself. And by the way Ferryl looked at him any time he spotted Michael next to Delaney, Michael wasn't sure what he would even say when that chance finally came.

Providence knew he needed to. And soon. He owed his king—his *friend*—as much.

But the way she looked tonight—the gown she had paired with the only jewels she had left of her past… Michael had been so damn distracted by it that he decided he needed her all to himself for a little while. The mezzanine seemed a perfect respite.

The warmth of her body pressed against his coursed through his soul, and he wondered if she would ever understand the depths of his need for her.

"Tell me why this is your favorite spot," Delaney said.

Michael chuckled. "When I first became a guard, the bow was my preferred weapon. Which was handy then, because most of the inferior ranks were assigned to be archers. But I had always loved it, even though guards of any rank were much better at the sword. I knew if I ever wanted to be captain, I would have to master the sword, too. But my first love was always the bow. And while I was training for the army with Commander Titus, he didn't seem to mind. In fact, he took a liking to me because of my skill with the bow. It was his weapon of choice as well."

"I didn't know the bow was your preferred weapon," she said.

He shrugged as he held her against him. "I don't often get to use it these days."

He looked at the guard to their right. A young man, no more than sixteen. He had just sworn his oath not two weeks ago. Michael didn't even know his name yet, but the young man stood proudly, his shoulders back, his bow at his side, poised to protect his king and queen should the need arise.

He understood that fealty, that inherent desire to protect, to serve, no matter what. He had felt that way from the moment he had sworn his own oath. Now, he felt it even more for the woman in his arms.

Delaney sighed, leaning back against him, resting her head on his shoulder as she, too, watched the crowd below. He wondered if she missed it—being one of them. Among them. He wondered if she regretted her choices, regretted that she hadn't ended up on a throne instead of standing among a bunch of common-born guards, overlooking a ball she would have once attended as a guest of honor.

Most importantly of all, did she regret choosing him? Providence knew he had regrets—for the way he had handled things, for his bad timing. But not her. Never her. Michael could never truly regret how it had all happened if it meant he had her.

And that was it, really. That was what it boiled down to for him. Yes, he had not been forthcoming with Ferryl. And he needed to fix that. He *would* fix that. But it did not change the fact that in Delaney, he had found something sweeter than he had ever imagined. It did not—*would* not—change the fact that he had found the love of his life.

And he was never going to let her go.

So he did something impetuous. Ill-timed. Something he might never have done even a few months ago.

"Have I told you the most scandalous story to ever hit Benalle Palace?" he asked.

She inclined her head to him, her brows raised in curiosity, her luxurious auburn hair falling down her breast in careful, glossy curls, her hands resting on her belly as she leaned against him. "What are you talking about?"

"There is a man here at court—a guard," Michael began. "He was quiet, kept his head down, did what he was told. Until one day, his closest friend became betrothed. It would have been a happy occasion except that the guard had fallen madly in love with his friend's intended."

A knowing smirk came across her face. "Oh really? And what happened?"

"He didn't tell anyone of his love for the girl. He decided he would never tell anyone. That is, until his friend called off the wedding."

"And what did he do then?"

"Oh, confessed his love to her."

"And what became of them?"

"They're married now. Many children. They're quite happy together."

Delaney's brows furrowed in confusion.

"Well, I should clarify," he said. "They *will* have many children someday. Right now they have one on the way, though. A girl, they're fairly certain. They're quite madly in love, you know. He's going to make a wonderful husband. She is very happy she agreed to marry him."

A smile slowly crept onto her lips, but she did her best to purse them. "Is this your way of proposing?" she asked.

And so Michael kissed her. Thoroughly. He placed his hands on either side of her face and let himself get lost in her lips, the taste of her tongue, the sweetness of her breath as it mingled with his, completely uninhibited by the guards on either side of them or any nobles who might glance up to see them. Nor did he fail to notice the fervor with which she kissed him back.

"Is this your way of saying yes?" he asked, breathing the question onto her lips, still glistening from their kiss.

She drew in a breath to answer, but Michael's gaze was suddenly yanked elsewhere, distracted by a movement below them.

A strange movement.

Predatory. Unnatural. Like an asp weaving through thick brush.

A nobleman he didn't recognize was slithering through the crowded dance floor. A flash of terror raced over him when he realized the stranger was headed straight for...

It was on instinct that he moved Delaney behind him, gesturing with one hand for the nearby guard as he breathed to her, "Don't move. And don't make a sound."

She obliged, though he could feel her breath warm on his neck as she peered over his shoulder. Michael motioned for the guard to hand him his bow, and the young, wide-eyed boy obliged, obviously unsure as to why. But Michael didn't have the time to explain. He readied the arrow but kept the bow lowered, waiting, breathing, making certain he would need it before anyone might notice a guard with an arrow nocked on the mezzanine. The closer the man got to his king and his queen, the harder Michael's heart pounded. The man seemed keen, focused, determined, his movements purposed and preternatural.

Then the stranger's eyes momentarily left the king and queen, looking out to someone else. Who, Michael didn't know, for he didn't dare take his eyes from the stranger. But when the man nodded, a subtle movement that would have been missed had Michael not been so keenly watching him, he knew—*knew*—he had no time to waste.

His instincts kicked in, years and years of training under his former commander. For war. For readiness against any enemy, foreign or domestic. And while that training was meant for a battlefield, it had instead been put to use guarding the king for all these years, the castle its own kind of battlefield, the safety of his king and queen its own kind of war.

And tonight, Michael would make sure the battle was won. So he lifted the bow, pulling back the string that he might rest his knuckle at the corner of his mouth, his eyes sharp and keen on the serpentine man below. On whatever it was he was about to attempt.

Calm flowed through him. The calm he had been trained for. The focus. *The killing calm,* as Commander Titus had called it. He didn't let his beating heart get the better of him. He didn't let worry cloud his judgment. He just narrowed in on the man below. An asp in black. A sharp face he didn't recognize, broad shoulders and unnatural height. Michael knew everyone at the court of Benalle. This man was a stranger.

The king and queen fell into each other's arms, and Ferryl kissed his wife, momentarily drawing Michael's focus away from the predator they were oblivious to. But when a glint of steel caught his eye again, there was not even a moment's hesitation. Michael let fly the arrow nocked in his bow.

The arrow found its mark. Sure. True. *A natural marksman,* that's what the commander had always called him.

But while the natural marksman had been fast, he had not been fast enough. For the stranger had sunk his dagger in Adelaide's side just before he fell.

And drawn her blood.

~

"Guard the doors," Michael called to the guards on the mezzanine. "Don't let anyone in or out of this palace. Understood?"

"Yes, my lord," said the young guard, taking back his bow from Michael with wide, awestruck eyes. And just like that, the guards scattered to their duties. Michael spotted Amos below, the newly released guard already springing to action, calling orders, ushering the king and queen out of the room behind a wall of armed guards. Michael nodded. His friend nodded back.

He turned to Delaney behind him, her eyes wide, her breath shallow.

"What happened, Michael? Who was that man?"

"I don't know. I don't know anything except that he was trying to get to my queen."

"Where are we going?" she asked as he took hold of her arm.

"Somewhere safe."

~

Michael ushered Delaney through the crowded, confused corridors of Benalle, the nobles and servants alike tittering and milling about, questions and concern on their faces.

What's happened?

Someone killed an innocent man!

Where are the king and queen?

Already the court was buzzing with rumors, but Michael ignored it all, ignored the tugs on his sleeve, the nobles who stepped in his path as he plowed through, intent to get Delaney to safety.

She stayed close to his side as they threaded like needles through the thickening crowd, her head down as she trembled on his arm. He would be damned if he let anything happen to her.

Not tonight.

So he pushed on, calling out, "Step aside!" and "Make way!" as they went.

Finally, he reached the stairs that led to the floor below—the floor that housed the dungeons and also the safe rooms, those designated for times such as this, when threats were unknown and the danger was too great to risk exposure of the court's most important people. If he knew Amos, the seasoned guard was already ushering the royal family here as well.

But when he opened the door, he realized that Amos had beaten him here, for waiting behind the door were the king, the queen, the queen mother, Derwin, Leala, and Adelaide's parents. Ferryl knelt beside Adelaide, who was lying on a chaise, conscious but in obvious pain.

"The wound is deep," said Derwin gravely as if reading Michael's mind. He stepped closer, lowering his voice before he continued, "It's obvious he was trying to kill her. He might have, too, if not for you."

"Who was he?" Michael asked.

"I have no idea."

"Is she…all right?"

Derwin did not answer, an unexplained worry limning his hardened features.

Michael exhaled a breath he didn't even realize he had been holding.

Delaney paused on the threshold, looking to him.

"It's all right. You'll be safe here," he said softly.

But he could see that wasn't her question. She was questioning whether she would be welcome. In here. With the royal family.

It was Leala who walked to her, put her hands on Delaney's arms, and said warmly, "Come in, come in. You can sit over here." The princess gestured to a seat nearby, taking Delaney by the arm so that she might usher her inside the plush, windowless room.

But Michael could still see Delaney's hesitation, her fear. So he took her hand in his. "It will be all right. Just wait here. I'll be back as soon as I can."

"Where are you going?" Delaney asked, suddenly gripping his forearm.

"I have to help. I know the man was not alone. I'm going to find who was helping him."

Michael looked up to Ferryl across the room. Ferryl only nodded, fear and ire shining like ice in his eyes before he returned his stricken attention to his wife. No words. No commands. Just ice. Michael wasn't sure if that ice was solely for the man who had harmed the queen or if some of that ice was for him, too. For the conversation they had yet to have. For the lies he had told his king—or at least the truth he had kept from him. He swallowed once and nodded in return.

"I'll be back as soon as I can," Michael said again, to everyone. To no one in particular.

Then he turned on his heel and headed back out the door.

"Michael."

At the sound of his name, he whirled again, only to see Delaney walking back to him. Without hesitation, without an ounce of trepidation for who might be watching or what they might think, she kissed him soundly before she said, "Be careful."

He only touched her cheek before he disappeared.

Chapter XIV

Derryl had taken to pacing—his favorite pastime when worry was his constant companion. Kneeling by Adelaide's side, gripping her hand until it was white and cold, he fussed over her incessantly for the first hour. Then he had started pacing, frustration over his own helplessness welling with every marching step he took in the underground chambers where they hid like mice from a prowling cat.

Adelaide tried to placate him, tried to assure him she was all right. But with every new wince and every new drop of blood, her husband grew more agitated, more worried.

She watched him from the dusty chaise at the bottom of the castle in the dark, windowless room in which the royal family, along with Delaney, waited.

And waited.

Waiting for someone—anyone—to tell them it was safe to emerge again, safe to go to their chambers. Her mother tended to the wound where the stranger had attempted to take her life—a gash on her waist that had likely been intended for her heart.

Had it not been for Michael's keen eyes and quick hand, it might have met its mark.

Adelaide finally stopped bleeding after the second hour, but she had not stopped shaking. And the shaking went straight to her core.

Never—never in all her days—had she felt so vulnerable. So fearful.

She did not care for her own life. She did not care if she died right here. All she could think of, all she could wonder was whether or not the wound had harmed the baby. Their baby.

And every time pain lanced her side, every time her mother replaced another bloodied strip of cloth, the worry settled in deeper.

Ferryl was a bundle of frustration, pacing the room, cursing the hour after hour that had passed in silence. He stopped occasionally, knelt by her side, and brushed sweat-dampened strands of hair from her brow. His salty tears dropped onto her cheek and brow as he kissed her and fussed over her and worried himself into a frenzy.

Then there was the silence.

Providence above, the silence.

If the pain and worry hadn't been enough, then Providence save them, the silence would have been enough to drive anyone to the brink of insanity.

Finally, mercifully, somewhere in the wee hours of the morning, Amos came back and escorted them all to their chambers.

Adelaide insisted that they see Delaney to her chambers first, worried for the former duchess in her current condition. Ferryl silently argued that Amos would see that she was fine, but Adelaide hadn't backed down, insisting that Ferryl personally escort Delaney to her chambers, making sure she was guarded safely behind closed doors before returning to their own chambers.

But even with the comfort of fresh bandages and her own bed, even after tucking into the warmth of Ferryl's arms, Adelaide couldn't stop the shaking. Or the worrying.

Not for herself, but for the child in her womb.

The child that she knew would be even more of a target than herself, once the world knew of it.

She covered her still flat belly with her hands, letting silent tears fall as she stared out the vast windows surrounding them. Again and again she turned in bed, trying to get comfortable. But it was to no avail.

"Can't sleep?" Ferryl asked in the darkness beside her.

"I can't get comfortable." The tincture Mary, the palace healer, had given her did wonders to numb the sharpest parts of the pain, but it left behind a dull, throbbing ache that seeped to her bones.

"Your mind is reeling."

"So is yours," she pointed out, pushing out more tears with every blink. They fell warmly down her temples as she stared at the beams on the ceiling.

"We are safe now, my love. We are all right."

"It's not us I'm concerned about."

She knew he knew what she meant. She could feel his worry like an underground river. In the weeks since she had been discovered as the princess of Haravelle, it had been carving out holes in that beautiful optimism that had always characterized her beloved.

"Come here," Ferryl said, pulling her close to him, careful, so careful, of the wound on her side. He wrapped her in his embrace, his chest warm against her back, resting his chin on her shoulder as he wrapped his arms around her waist.

Minutes passed in silence as she let his warmth comfort and soothe like a balm. The years between them had only heightened her need for his nearness, his strong arms, his gentle embrace. And now, the way his hands splayed over her stomach as if…as if he could hold her close and protect their child at the same time. So she pressed into him, relaxing into his encircling warmth despite the pain that throbbed at her side. He had always known exactly what she needed, exactly when she needed it. Tonight was no exception.

"Do you remember when we first found our Secret Place?" he asked, surprising her at the question.

She breathed a gentle laugh at the welcome distraction, the memory of that stormy day. "We were so young."

"I don't think I was more than ten or eleven," he agreed.

She nodded, picturing Ferryl mounting Erel that morning, she on Eagle as the two of them set off into the hazelnut forest for a little exploration. They hadn't expected the storm that had come upon them, seemingly out of nowhere. And it scared Adelaide—Elizabeth then. The booming thunder, the lightning that seemed as if it were hitting right before them. It had scared her to her very bones.

"I started crying," she mused. "And then you found that little cave and helped me get inside. I remember sitting down, wrapping my arms around my knees while you stood at the entrance like a fool, watching the storm like you had conquered it."

"Until that bolt of lightning hit so close." He laughed into her neck.

"I thought you would jump out of your skin." She laughed as well. "But then you sat down beside me. When you noticed I was crying, you put your arm around my shoulder and told me that I could be frightened and it was all right because you wouldn't tell anyone. You would keep it a secret."

"I think that's why we started calling it the Secret Place, isn't it?"

She nodded. "And then you said something I've never forgotten. You said, 'Even though you're afraid, I'll be brave for you, Lizybet. And then you can be brave for me, too. That way, as long as we're together, we won't ever have to worry.' "

He hugged her closer to him, kissing her neck and the shell of her ear before he said, "I didn't know it then, but in retrospect, I see now that was one of the first moments I knew I would do anything for you. It was the beginning of my falling in love with you. The beginning of something deeper, sweeter than I ever knew possible.

"And my love, you don't have to be afraid tonight, either. Because I'm here. And I'll hold you all night. I'll be brave for us both."

She knew he meant it, too. She knew that despite the worries that riddled his thoughts, somewhere—somewhere deep down, Ferryl believed it would be all right. It was a sort of peace that had always been a part of him, from the time they were children.

But ever since Haravelle, ever since Ferryl had ascended that mountain, something had fundamentally changed in her husband. Deepened. That optimism had morphed into something unflinching. Despite his fears, despite his worries, Ferryl's soul had settled on something. Something she couldn't quite define. She wondered if it could ever be defined.

His mind—it sometimes seemed as if it battled with his heart, his worries at war with that peace that had settled in his soul.

But tonight, just for tonight, he would be her rock. He would be her secret place. He would hold her, and she would let him, let that river wash over her—that river of faith that had shaped the man she loved. And just for tonight, she would close her eyes, she would wrap her arms tighter around his, breathe in the leather-and-saltwater scent of him, and let her soul find rest in the sweetness of their love, the peace of what they shared as merciful, restful sleep wrapped her in its cocoon and tugged her down into sweet oblivion.

Chapter XV

Such a fuss you're making, little one, Delaney thought as she lay in bed. The morning was dawning; she could see it even through her closed eyes, its warmth as welcome as it was refreshing. Perhaps the relentless winter chill was finally going to subside. It was spring now, after all. She placed her hands on her belly, cracking a smile as her baby moved some more, despite the fact that she had been awoken much sooner than she had hoped. *If I didn't know any better,* she thought, *I'd say you're acting as you do when Michael is near, dancing about like a court jester in there.*

There was a sigh and movement somewhere nearby, and Delaney's eyes shot open, her heart pounding suddenly at the sight of someone beside her bed.

Asleep.

His chestnut hair was mussed, and his head was slumped to the side as he sat with his back resting against the bed.

Michael.

What in the world?

Delaney shifted a little to get a better look, but her movement woke him. As his eyes slowly adjusted to the light, he, too, looked around as if confused. But then he spotted Delaney, and despite his tired eyes, he cracked a sweet, sleep-addled smile.

"Morning, beautiful," he said, before stretching his arms above his head and yawning loudly. His boots and jacket lay shucked to the side, his shirt untied to reveal a sliver of his golden chest.

"What are you doing here?" she asked with a laugh.

"I must have fallen asleep."

"Obviously. But why were you here in the first place?"

Michael turned to her as he knelt beside the bed, fiddling with her hands before focusing his attention on her very round belly. Had it gotten bigger just since last night? Any larger and she would have to be wheeled around the castle on a cart.

His hands on her stomach, he kissed it tenderly before resting his head against it as he said, "I couldn't sleep without knowing you were all right."

The baby leapt again in her womb, and even Michael felt it, for he slid his eyes to Delaney with a cocky grin. He kissed her belly again. "And good morning to you too," he said.

Delaney couldn't help but laugh. "Why didn't you wake me?"

"You were sleeping so sweetly that I didn't want to disturb you. I know you're having a hard time sleeping these days."

"You must have been so uncomfortable. How long have you been there on the floor?" she asked, running her hand through his hair and down his neck.

"Not sure," he shrugged. "I've no idea how long I was helping Amos. All I know is that it was dark when I got here. And had been for a long time."

He traced idle circles on her belly as she asked, "Why didn't you just lie down beside me?"

Michael slid his eyes to her before a roguish grin curled his mouth. "I didn't want to be presumptuous."

She felt her cheeks heat as he climbed into the bed beside her, wrapping himself around her where she lay. "Are you always so nauseatingly chivalrous?"

"It's one of my greater flaws," he said with a grin, and then he kissed her soundly.

When his lips found her neck, she said, "You know, I never got to answer your question last night."

His kisses stopped as he pulled back to look her in the eye. "Oh, I'm fairly certain you did."

"No, I distinctly remember we were rudely interrupted." *By an attempted murder of the queen.* Delaney shoved the thought aside.

His kisses resumed, and he spoke between them. "Even so, I already know your answer."

"Oh, you do?"

"Mmm," he said as his lips moved on her neck. He pulled at her shift to expose the skin of her shoulder and trailed kisses along it. She closed her eyes, trying to remember how to breathe.

"And how is it that you know my answer, Michael Aman?"

"Well, you see," he said, his voice husky. "I usually know exactly what you're thinking without you saying a word."

"Is that so?"

"Yes. For example, I knew you loved me long before you ever said it."

"How is that?" she asked, growing breathless from his touch, his kisses. Providence, this man.

"By the way your eyes light up whenever I am near you." His

words were warm on her skin, his lips soft as they traced her collarbone, her chest. "I also happen to know that you cannot resist me," he said.

"I cannot? And what brought you to such a conclusion?"

"The way your breath grows shallow when I am close to you."

Bastard. A laugh bubbled in her throat while his hands trailed down her back, his lips down, down, down her chest...

"And I know that you want to be my wife."

"Oh, I do, do I?"

"Mmm."

"And how is it you're so confident in that assessment?"

"By the way your pulse quickens when I press my lips to your heart." He wasn't wrong—her heart pounded mercilessly at the feel of his lips. Never—never in all her life—had she known something so deep. Profound. Relentless.

He pulled at the hem of her oversized shift, exposing her belly and running his fingers over it as if it were a lost treasure, a precious gem.

A laugh escaped her even as her skin prickled at his touch.

"What?" he asked as he slithered down to kiss the taut skin that stretched across her growing womb.

"I'll never understand how you can even be remotely attracted to me in such a state."

He looked up at her from behind the swell of her abdomen. "Then you have no idea how beautiful you are. And how much I desire you."

His belly kisses resumed—soft, tender affection. Gentle, unhurried. As if he were savoring a fine wine. There were no words for what this man did to her. She understood something which she never had before. This feeling—to be loved, to be wanted. To want and love in return. It was... It was...

"Michael, I love you."

He smiled as he continued his lazy kisses. "I know."

"And just so we're clear, I want to marry you."

Another lazy grin. "I know."

A laugh bubbled out, the kind that she could feel in her face, her chest, her soul. "Is there anything you don't know about me, then?"

"Plenty, actually." When his eyes met hers and she saw the sly grin on his handsome mouth, nearly every thought fell out of her head. "But I'm certainly enjoying the learning process."

She dropped her head to her pillow, closing her eyes and breathing deeply. But within the span of that breath, a sudden, intense tightening stretched over her belly as if a thousand hands had grabbed her all at once, squeezing and constricting, a pain deeper and sharper than any she had had before.

Keeping up his unhurried kisses on her belly, Michael seemed oblivious. But then he stopped, and she opened her squinted eyes enough to see a stricken look growing on his face.

"Are you all right?" he asked, pushing himself up closer to her.

She nodded, shutting her eyes again as the pain increased. She clutched her belly as if it would help.

It's normal, she reminded herself. This was normal, right?

"Is it... Is it your time? Is the baby—"

"No, no," she gritted through her teeth. "It's all right."

Michael didn't seem convinced.

"I'll go and get Mary," he said, moving to get up. But she put her hand on his arm.

"Please don't leave," she said, but the request sounded more like a plea, so she quickly added, "It's all right, I promise."

While the pain had started suddenly, it certainly took its sweet time about waning again. But eventually, when the tightening relaxed, she collapsed back onto her pillow, her shoulders, back, and her whole body releasing the tension she hadn't even realized had built.

"What happened, Delaney?" Michael finally asked.

"It's normal." At the look on his face, she laughed, hoping to push away his fears—and her own. "It's a tightening of the belly. It has happened before."

"But why? What does it mean?"

"It just means my time is coming. But it could still be weeks," she quickly added. "My mother used to say that it's just the body's way of preparing for birth."

"But how… How do you know it's not your time yet?"

"When it's my time, that will happen every few minutes."

"Every few *minutes?*" he said incredulously.

She only nodded, closing her eyes and recapturing her breath. This had been a hard one. The hardest so far, actually. And while she had been feeling these tightening fits more and more in the last few days, this one was particularly—

"And you're not afraid?" he asked.

"Not terribly, no," she lied. "Don't forget I'm the eldest of five girls. I saw my mother give birth many times. I know it will be hard. But I know it will be all right."

Except that her mother had died giving birth to Dysis. And whether it was because of complications with the birth or not, the image of her mother's sweat-glistening body lying on her bed danced in her mind. Ashen and wan, collapsed from the pain, her lips as blue as ice, a newborn baby crying in the nursemaid's arms… Delaney knew she was lying through her teeth when she said she wasn't frightened. In truth, she was scared out of her mind.

"When my time comes," she said, taking another breath to clear her head, "when my time comes, will you be there? Will you be with me?" An improper question, and she knew it. Men, as a rule, did not attend births. Not even fathers. It was considered impertinent for them to witness such a thing. But Delaney wasn't sure she could face giving birth without him by her side. She wasn't sure there was much in life she could face without him by her side, actually. Impropriety be damned.

He took her hand as he lay stretched out beside her, propped up on an elbow, brushing hair from her face with his other hand. "You want me there?" he asked.

She nodded, sliding her eyes to him. "I know it's not—"

"Then I'll be there."

She could have sworn she spotted tears shining in his eyes, but before she could decide for certain, his lips found her mouth, solid and sure, as if he were sealing his promise with a kiss.

"Did you figure anything out last night?" Delaney asked, deciding to change the subject before she came apart into a thousand pieces.

With her belly pressed against his side, he placed a protective hand over it as he shook his head, his eyes darkening with disappointment—and fear. "I know nothing more than when I shot that arrow.

And the only one who could possibly give us answers is dead. But I know, Delaney—I *know* he wasn't alone. I saw him. He nodded to someone before he attacked the queen. Someone else was there with him. I am sure of it. But whoever it was, he or she is nowhere to be found. We searched everywhere. Every possible place. No one came in or went out of the castle last night. No one, Delaney. But somehow, whoever else was involved just—vanished. Like—like a phantom. No one could find so much as a trace…"

"Nor would they, I would imagine, if they were from Midvar," she said.

His hand stopped rubbing idle circles on her belly. "What do you mean?"

"I mean if the attackers were from Midvar, which seems most likely, it doesn't surprise me that you didn't find them."

"Why?"

"Because Midvarish men—pure-blooded Midvarish men—are not… They are not like most men. They are—stronger. Faster. Stealthier. Even taller. They are bred to be monsters on the battlefield. And their blood is prized above all else in my kingdom. Pure-blooded Midvarish women are prized, too. But not like the men. While the men are trained from birth for battle and glory, the women are… The women are expected to do nothing more than—bed and breed." Delaney shut her eyes and breathed in deeply.

Bed and breed. Exactly what had been expected of her upon her arrival in Navah. Marry the prince. Bear the heir to the Navarian throne. No wonder her father hated her so. She had not lowered her head and done his bidding like a good girl.

"My father's sole wish was to sire a male. With the queen unable to give the king living children, he was certain that a male would have been named heir to the Midvarish throne as nephew to the king. I think that's why my mother and father had so many children. We were not born from love but from greed. Greed on my father's part.

"Sometimes I think my mother must have willed herself to only bear girls just to spite my father. Their marriage had been arranged by her brother, the king, without her consent. She was little more than a slave to her brother's whims. She didn't love my father. But she loved her daughters fiercely and taught us to stand up for ourselves. I have often wondered if she did not die of complications from giving birth to Dysis, but from the weariness of her own life. There is much shame brought upon pure-blooded Midvarish families who do not bear sons. Especially ours, considering we are one of the oldest families in Midvar on both my mother and my father's sides. It was expected that my mother would give birth to a mighty warrior son. When she did not, my father became desperate. He made the deal with my uncle to marry me off to Ferryl solely for his own wealth and dignity."

"Why? Why is it that Midvarish blood is so different?" Michael asked.

Delaney breathed a sigh, wondering what she should say, wondering what Michael would truly think if he knew of the blood that flowed through Midvarish veins. Through *her* veins. At last, she said, "Have you heard of the legend of the Fallen?"

"The fallen?"

"I believe your people call them the Nephilim."

Michael didn't speak for a moment, his eyes looking away, out of the window. But Delaney knew his mind was elsewhere as he breathed, "Giants."

Giants, indeed. Monsters. Blooded for brutality and bloodshed.

"The legend says that in ancient times there was a woman of unearthly beauty who walked the earth looking for one worthy to sire her children. She would not settle for just any man. She wanted someone who would combine her ruthless cunning with his power and strength. A generation to be wrought of the purest, strongest bloodlines.

"The legend says that she searched for years until she came across a group of strange men dwelling in the desert. They were tall, fast, and stronger than most. They moved like wraiths among the dunes, monsters from another realm. Demons. Angels fallen from the heavens to dwell amongst men and torture them. Perfect for her ambitions. So she selected the strongest and bravest amongst them and took him to her bed. And from his seed, she bore the first son, the father of Midvar, and the first king: Midian.

"Midian's strength and cunning were unsurpassed. From his superior blood, he birthed an entire kingdom. A kingdom to rival those he could not steal for himself. A kingdom he believed would one day rule the world.

"That is the agenda of Midvar—to have what we are taught from birth is rightfully ours. To take back the lands of Haravelle and Navah that were taken from us. To rule the world with superior might. And that is why the pure bloodlines are coveted. That is why I was sent here. Not to bear Ferryl's children. I didn't understand it then, but I do now. I was never meant to have Ferryl's child. I was set up to bear Ravid's child. Because he, too, is from an old Midvarish family: his bloodlines are pure. Our child was to sit on the throne and Ferryl was to be none the wiser. A Midvarish child ruling Navah. It was all arranged right under my nose, and I was too stupid, too naïve to see it."

"But Ravid, your father," Michael said. "They are not warriors. They are not strong or fast. Tall, yes. But easily bested."

"There are exceptions, of course. The bloodlines are not a failsafe. Then again, who knows? Perhaps both my father and Ravid lied about the purity of their blood. My uncle is arrogant enough to believe them just to accomplish his plans. I wouldn't put anything past him. I don't know him very well personally. But I know my mother did not trust him. She hated him. And I didn't see what he was doing before it was too late."

She could practically see the blood boiling in Michael's veins, that protective instinct that rose up in him whenever her father or Ravid were concerned. That instinct she had grown to love, to need, to curl up in the safety of like a cat might nestle in a pile of blankets. And she knew the question he was going to ask before it even escaped him.

"Delaney, did Ravid—"

"I wasn't forced, Michael. It was the only way it would have worked, you see. I was convinced Ravid loved me. That was the brilliance of the plan. Ravid convinced me of his love for me, took me to his bed with my consent. If it had been rape, it would never have worked, for one word from me would have blown the whole plan. Ravid said so himself. He was paid, Michael. Paid to manipulate me. To bed me. To sire a child that Ferryl would have thought was his. Except that the plan didn't work because no one expected that I would help Ferryl delay the wedding over and over again. No one expected that Ferryl and I would become friends. No one knew how deep his love for the stable girl was and how far he would go to get her back.

"And so by the time we would have married, I already knew I was carrying another man's child. The plan had already failed.

"But if I know my uncle, I know I was not the only card in his hand. I am not his only plan. He will retaliate. And last night was only the beginning. Probably nothing more than a taunting. A reminder of who he is. He will find a way to get the throne of Navah, especially now that it is united with Haravelle. He will not rest until it is his. No king of Midvar has ever relented in that agenda."

Nor would they. And while she knew it—had always known it—her fear no longer lay in what King Derrick of Midvar might do to get his way, for she knew nothing was too base, too evil for him. No, the fear rested somewhere else now. Somewhere much deeper, a place in her soul she never knew existed.

The fear, she knew, was of the darkness that stretched out before them, the knowing that for all the happiness they might plan, all the dreams she and Michael might dream together, none of it would matter once her uncle decided it was time to exact his plan, whatever it was. And knowing Michael, knowing the kind of loyalty he felt for his king and country, fear like she had never known steeped deep within her soul at the inevitability that at some point, that loyalty was going to be tested. At some point, Michael would have to decide which mattered more—the love of a woman or the love of a king.

And she did not want to know which he would choose.

Chapter XVI

Chapter **XVI**

"A message for you, my lord."

Titus looked up from his plate of lunch—day-old roasted chicken, bread, and fruits, the dregs of what was left in their cupboards—to his butler standing on the threshold of the dining chamber. The man handed Titus a parchment. Not addressed with slithering black scrawl, thank the gods, but a small paper, a note really, folded and sealed with green wax.

The bank.

"What is it, sweetheart?" Penelope asked, and Titus knew from her tone that she was thinking the same thing he was.

"Not the king," he answered quickly, opening the parchment to read its contents. "It's from Gidon. Thank the gods, everything is finally ready." He pushed away from the table, the heavy, carved chair scraping harshly on the floors. "I'll go to the bank at once."

"Don't you want to finish eating first?" Penelope asked, rising to her feet as well, her sky-blue gown a bright, cheerful contrast to the darkness that seemed to relentlessly hover over him as of late.

She didn't need to know they were already on borrowed time, considering it had taken Gidon much longer than the promised three days to consolidate their assets. She didn't need to worry about the wealth of unknowns and obstacles that lay before them and their departure. She didn't need to know of the Navarian soldiers who were no more than a half a day away from their village. The soldiers who were taking Midvarish women for their pleasure. In her condition, as much as it pained him, it was best if she knew as little as possible.

So he smiled and walked across the room, taking her hands in his, kissing them hard before meeting her eyes. He found only steely determination there, and the sight was so welcome, so beautiful that he clung to her, hugging her to him, relishing the way her rounding belly pressed into his own stomach. He breathed her in for a moment, just because he hadn't stopped to do so in days. Too frantic with preparations for their departure, he hadn't stopped to savor her, to just hold her.

So when she pulled back a bit from his embrace, he kissed her soundly, holding back the desire that had unexpectedly begun welling within him. There would be time enough to enjoy his wife after they were well and damn good out of this gods-forsaken place.

"What is it, Titus?" she asked, a bit breathless from the intensity of his kiss.

"I love you, that's all. I'm going to the bank. I will be back in no more than an hour. Do you think you can be ready to leave by the time I return?"

"It's midday. Shouldn't we wait until the morning before we depart? We'll hardly be on the road more than a few hours before we'll have to stop for the night."

Too perceptive, this wife of his. She would have made a good general. He huffed a laugh, feigning a humor and casualness he didn't feel.

"True, but I'm tired of looking at all the empty rooms and fishing through bags and trunks for our things. I'd rather just get on with it, wouldn't you?" It was the truth. At least partially. The other truth was that if they didn't get out of there—and get out *soon*—there was no telling what could happen. He would put nothing past the king of Midvar. Or the Navarian soldiers for that matter.

She didn't buy his lighthearted comments. Not for one minute. "Titus..."

He kissed her again, partly because he wanted to and partly because he had no more excuses and she was often as distracted by their affection as he was.

It worked, thank the gods.

When she looked to him again with those bedroom eyes of hers, he decided that half a day's travel was all he could abide anyway, for surely tonight, with the weight of waiting, waiting, *waiting* to leave this place finally off his shoulders, he could take solace in his gorgeous wife's arms.

Yes, that sounded like a winning proposition.

"I'll be back in an hour," he said.

Had he known how much he would come to regret it, he never would have walked out of that door.

~

The streets of the village were eerily quiet, like the calm before a raging storm. Nearly every shop and tavern was closed, leaving Titus with an even deeper sinking in his stomach than before. Why was he the only damned fool left in this town? And what in Sheol had taken Gidon so long? Three days, he had said. It would take no more than three days to gather all of his assets so that they might depart Midvar, perhaps forever. That was a week and a half ago. Titus had been nearly coming out of his skin for at least a week, worrying and waiting for something to happen.

So the letter at lunch today was a bit like being handed a trunk full of crown jewels with a note reading, "Thought you might enjoy this."

Enjoy it, indeed. Titus would enjoy getting the Sheol away from King Derrick. Away from the life he had made for himself as the king's lapdog. Going somewhere far, far away where he and Penelope could live and rear their miraculous child together in peace.

The gods knew he was ready.

The bank doors opened easily, no throngs of people to contend with as he walked through the vast, open foyer replete with green marble trimmings and ornately carved oak surfaces. There were no tellers at the counter or patrons in line.

Quiet. It was too damn quiet.

And that's when he knew something was terribly, terribly wrong.

He walked to Gidon's office, one hand instinctively resting on the hilt of the sword he now kept sheathed at his side at all times, figuring that it wasn't nearly as odd as it might have looked to carry a bow—his much-preferred weapon—slung across his back. Swords, thanks to the relentless thirst for blood in this damned kingdom, were something of a fashion statement. Well, ornate, jeweled rapiers anyway. But there was no damned way Titus would be caught dead carrying a rutting trinket-weapon at his side. As if the ego of the Midvarish male knew no bounds, they carried the useless things around, not to threaten, but to gloat. To let everyone around them know that their brute strength made weapons an accessory, not a necessity.

Asses. Every damned one of them.

Thank the gods he wasn't a full-blooded Midvarish male. And thank the gods no one knew it, either.

Gidon's office door was open, but as Titus peered around the jamb, it wasn't Gidon sitting in his chair, bedecked head to toe in some sort of circus-worthy getup.

It was a Navarian soldier, clad in that kingdom's signature black and white, a grin plastered across his dirty mouth.

"Looking for something, General?"

Shit. Shit. Shit.

It wasn't fear for his own life that made Titus turn on his heel and run like Sheol. It was knowing that everything had already gone to shit right under his nose. He prayed to the gods as he lobbed himself onto the back of his horse and raced to get back home that he wasn't too late.

~

The gods showed Titus mercy as he raced home on his horse, who galloped so fast it was as if she could fly like one of those wretched winged beasts that roamed the Wild Wood. But her speed didn't feel like enough to counteract the boiling, raging fear that threatened to swallow him whole.

If anything happened to Penelope and the baby... If anything happened to Penelope and the baby...

He threw open the back door of the house, tearing through the kitchens to the back stairs that led directly to their bedchamber.

"Milord!" he heard a servant call.

"Where is she?" he asked, not bothering to slow down, still taking the steps two by two.

"We were looking everywhere for you. They came so quickly and—"

Titus's feet stopped as abruptly as his heart. He turned slowly on the narrow steps and faced the old man standing feebly in the kitchen. "Who came?"

The old man had streaks of tears down his reddened face. Titus didn't even care that he couldn't think of his name, so he just said, "Servant. Tell me where she is."

The man's lip quivered. "They took her."

"Took who?" Terror. Sheer, unadulterated terror. That's all he could feel.

"They took my baby girl," the old man said.

Slight, slight relief and then guilt came over Titus as he stepped back into the kitchen. "Who did they take?"

"They took my Daphne," said the old man and buried his face in his dirty hands. That's when Titus realized there was blood on his shirt and hands and a bruise blooming on his face. As if he had struggled. Fought. Fought for Daphne, his daughter: a beautiful, supple young Midvarish girl. He remembered now that it was Daphne who had taken the time to remind him that Penelope loved him, despite his wife's trepidation in those first months after he had returned home. A sweet, innocent girl.

A perfect slave for the carnal pleasures of the rutting Navarian soldiers.

"Shit," he breathed. "Where is Penelope? Where is my wife?"

Heavy, fat tears fell freely down the old man's face now as his gaze shifted to the cellar doors on the other side of the kitchen. "She tried to help, she—"

But Titus didn't wait to find out whatever the old man was going to say before he threw open the ancient doors and nearly flung himself down the cold, stone steps.

"Penelope!" he called. "Can you hear me?"

There was only ringing silence in the damp, cavernous cellar that stretched out before him. He peered around shelf after shelf of ancient Melamed family wine. "Lopee! Where are you, sweetheart?"

His heart pounded harder and harder, faster and faster with every passing, silent second.

"Lopee, sweetheart. Can you hear me?"

Empty corridor after empty corridor. No sign of Penelope. No sign of any kind of struggle—the silence as unsettling as it was eerie.

And then he saw it. The ancient door on the far side of the room. The one that led to the gods knew where. An old trade route, he had always been told, abandoned centuries ago.

Except that the door was ajar.

Damn it all to Sheol.

He ran to the door and pushed it open, but it caught on something at his feet. And when he looked down to see what it was, he realized it hadn't caught on something...

But *someone*.

Someone lying in a pool of thick, dark blood. Still. Unmoving.

Her sky-blue gown stained with ugly patches of red.

And then the world stopped turning, everything—everything—shattering around him in a scream that he realized was coming from him.

It was Penelope.

And she had been murdered.

~

A ringing silence.

Deafening.

A stillness that only accompanies death.

And black. Endless, depthless black. Eternal midnight. A chasm he could never cross. A severing. Like half of him—the best half—had been ripped away, and all that remained was an ugly, gnarly, gushing wound.

Silence.

Stillness.

Screaming black.

~

Someone was calling to him, pulling at him. Someone was trying to get his attention, perhaps. He couldn't tell. He couldn't feel.

Numbness. Stillness. Silence.

There was only himself. Him and the rag doll lying limp in his arms. The bloodstained doll whose skin had already grown cold, whose plump lips had already turned blue. Only him, her, a pool of tears and blood around them, and the sobs pouring from him in wave after wave of relentless, searing pain. His life had been branded with the worst kind of pain. Loss. Worthlessness.

He couldn't breathe. His lungs seized with choking sobs, as if grief could somehow drown him.

Gods, please, let him drown in this that he might be with her forever.

Or let him wake up to find it all a dream.

A damned nightmare.

Only let him wake from this. Let him wake. Let *her* wake. *Let her wake. If there is any god with pity, show mercy and let her wake...*

He pushed her blood-matted hair from her face, pressing a soft kiss to her cold lips, his tears falling on her ashen face, breathing her name over her mouth as if he could somehow give her back her life's breath. As if he could trade—give back this vibrant, beautiful creature, this undeserved gift from whatever god had decided to show him mercy, the life she deserved, the life that should never have been taken.

A thick, sticky wetness seeped into his woven pants from the pool of her blood, but all he could think was, *It should have been me.*

It should have been me.

It should have been me.

Chapter XVII

y lords, your graces, councilors," said Ferryl, taking his seat around the large, ornate meeting table. "Thank you for coming today. There is much to discuss, so let's not delay any longer."

Adelaide sat to his left at the head of the table, her shoulders set in her signature determination, despite the fact that he knew good and well she was still sore. The wound on her side was healing. But with her pregnancy in such early weeks, there would be no way to know if any lasting damage had been done for quite some time. It would be months before they knew if their child survived. And after the attack on the way home, followed by the attack at the ball, an aching worry gnawed at Ferryl night and day. Worry for his wife. His queen.

And now for his child.

The rest of the noblemen, including Adelaide's parents, took their seats in his meeting room, a cacophony of chairs scraping across the marble floors as they settled around the table. Some of the Haravellian council had already made their way south, attending the newly-minted Har-Navarian council for the first time. The rest would be here for next month's meeting.

But as Ferryl looked around the table of familiar and unfamiliar faces, he realized one thing. Of course—of *course*—Meria had determined not to attend today. Because, of course, she had gone back to her chambers after the coronation and had hardly come out since.

Ferryl had had enough of her dramatics, to be sure. In truth, he was glad of her absence today; it was one less thing to worry about, one less thing to stew about as he faced merging two kingdoms in the midst of war. So he cleared his throat as he looked around the table and addressed everyone.

"As you are well aware, in light of the events that transpired at the coronation ball, the security at Benalle has been doubled. Michael and Amos are working hard to ensure that no one passes through these doors that has not been thoroughly vetted, so as to ensure the safety of everyone at court." Ferryl did not glance at the guard who stood at the side of the room. He did not let his eyes meet his friend's. Since Ferryl had learned about Michael and Delaney, he and Michael hadn't spoken aside from curt conversations about castle security. Michael had been thorough. Resolute. Determined to protect the castle and his queen. For that, the ice that had formed around them had begun to melt. A little.

"May we ask how Her Majesty is recovering?" asked Lord Mistar. He had always been a kind man. Quiet, to be sure, but one of the few remaining advisors who had sat on the council not only for the duration of Ferryl's father's reign, but also for the last few years of his grandfather, King Tobin's reign. Lord Mistar had always seemed genuinely concerned with the wellbeing of the king more than just how it would affect the kingdom's affairs. Perhaps he would be no different now that Ferryl was king.

It was Adelaide who answered him. "Thank you for your concern, Lord Mistar. I am recovering well."

The surety of her words seemed to put the councilor at ease. Ferryl wished they could do the same for him.

"I am glad to hear it, Majesty," Mistar said with a bow of his head.

Adelaide bowed her head in return.

"It was a terrible scare," chimed Lord Westerly. "I am sorry you had to endure such threats. It should *never* have happened."

The tone of Lord Westerly's voice, the way he emphasized his last sentence—it should *never* have happened—as if there could have been a way to prevent it…Ferryl didn't like it. Not one bit. And he wondered the reason for such an implication.

"It was an unfortunate incident," said Michael, to everyone's surprise, even Ferryl's. "But as His Majesty pointed out, measures have been taken to ensure that such an incident does not occur again. I have spoken with Officer Amos as well as the other guards, discussing the situation thoroughly. At this time, we have no reason to believe that it was anything more than a threat, not an actual attempt on Her Majesty's life."

"Much like when you were attacked on the road to Benalle?" chimed Lord Westerly.

How he knew that…when Ferryl had gone to great lengths, threatening every Navarian and Haravellian guard who had been there to keep it under wraps—to not give his people any reason to worry…

"I suppose you're implying that King Derrick is merely toying with us," Lord Westerly went on.

"That seems to be his signature style," said a Haravellian lord, and the advisors around the table nodded their agreement.

"Indeed, my lord," said the king. "Which is why I believe now is the time to change course, alter our strategy. I believe now is the time to throw King Derrick off course."

"What would you suggest, Your Majesty?" asked another of the council.

"I believe now is the time to break ground on the Temple at Benalle."

There was silence around the table as the Navarian and Haravellian lords exchanged glances. Clearly, the advising council thought him mad. Perfect, actually. Because if they thought it was a strange idea, then it was exactly what needed to be done in order to play the game with King Derrick. "The king of Midvar no doubt believes, after the events that have recently transpired in our kingdom, that we are preparing for war. And while we are, we need him to think otherwise. We need him to believe we have given up hope of vanquishing this foe."

"And how do you propose we do so?" asked Lord Westerly.

"By breaking ground on the Temple. I have gone over the plans extensively with Her Majesty," Ferryl said, nodding to Adelaide. "There is more than enough in the royal coffers to finance the war and commission the building of the temple. It will be a perfect red herring—a way to convince Derrick that our attentions are elsewhere."

"This is your brilliant plan to throw off the most cunning king in our realm?" asked Westerly.

"Are you questioning His Majesty?" asked Adelaide.

"Of course not," said Westerly. "But if I may, I'd like to propose an alternative to burying our heads in the sand."

Ferryl resisted the urge to roll his eyes. This man had an opinion about everything.

"In light of the unfortunate events that transpired at the coronation ball, and though we are all no doubt relieved to know that Her Majesty is recovering so quickly, I believe it is in our best interests to begin discussing a more direct strategy with our enemy."

"And what would you suggest?" asked Lord Mistar. Across the room, Ferryl could see worry lining Michael's brow, his steady hand trembling where it rested on the pommel of his sword.

But then Lord Westerly donned a sort of look that Ferryl couldn't quite place. Not calculation. Not conspiracy. Not triumph. But something of all of them.

It didn't sit well with him.

"I believe it is time we stop waiting for the next attack and start a more... *offensive* strategy."

Yes, Ferryl liked the idea of an offensive strategy. The problem, of course, was that there were no enemy soldiers with whom to *be* offensive.

"As you well know, His Highness Commander Prince Derwin is working hard with our generals to locate the Midvarish army," said Michael.

"I'm not talking about the enemy legions," said Lord Westerly.

There was a chilling silence around the table as the council began to understand the lord's implication.

Ferryl could see Michael seething from across the room. "Then with whom are you suggesting an offensive strategy?" Ferryl asked, knowing the answer to that question before he asked it.

Lord Westerly inclined his head in a falsely humble manner, and

Ferryl could have throttled the man for it. But the bastard had the gumption to meet Michael's eyes when he finally said, "We are harboring a traitor within our own walls."

Delaney. The bastard was speaking of Delaney. Implying that her presence at Benalle was a testament to weakness, not mercy.

A muscle feathered in Michael's jaw and in the hand now gripping the pommel of his sword. Ferryl's own blood was boiling. Michael very slowly and carefully turned his gaze to Ferryl.

The presumptuous lord had the nerve to go on saying, "And I believe it sends the wrong message that we have allowed her sanctuary here."

"What message would that be?" Michael asked, icy calculation in his tone.

"That we are too weak to deal with traitorous enemies swiftly and properly."

"All due respect, Lord Westerly," said Lord Mistar, "but I am inclined to disagree. I believe the presence of Mistress Dupree is a testament to His Majesty's goodness and mercy, not weakness."

"And are goodness and mercy traits of a king who wins wars?" asked Westerly.

Ferryl did not like that he had no answer for such a question.

He did not like it at all.

He drummed the tips of his fingers together. At his side, Adelaide said nothing, though in her face shone calculation and quiet contemplation. Always the last to speak, this wife of his. And always with a word worth speaking.

Ferryl watched the new lords around the table, wondering what they were thinking of the circus that was Ferryl's first Har-Navarian council meeting.

"Goodness and mercy are among the many the traits of a worthy man and a worthy king. I will not question His Majesty's instincts to protect the innocent, nor would I suggest you do so, either," said Michael.

Ferryl met Michael's eyes, but the guard gave nothing away besides the worry that had already hardened his features.

"Forgive me, Michael," said Westerly. "But I'm afraid, despite your long-standing position at this palace, that your opinion on this matter is hardly unbiased, as the court is well aware of your affair with the former duchess."

Michael's rage was simmering to a boil now. "Mistress Dupree is no more a show of the king's weakness than you are."

Lord Westerly breathed a cool, serpentine sort of chuckle, a sly smirk curling the corner of his mouth. "I am inclined to disagree, guard. And I am so convicted in the matter that I am prepared to do whatever it takes to protect the well-being of my kingdom."

"And what, pray tell, would that entail?" This question came from Adelaide, her words as stern as they were commanding. Ferryl schooled the grin that threatened his mouth. Ah, his queen…

Westerly cocked his head like a dog. "Your Majesty," he said. "As everyone on this council can attest, my loyalty has always been with our good kingdom. Now that we face an unknown enemy, it is of my utmost priority that we vanquish this blight swiftly and aggressively. If the king will not properly punish the former duchess for her treason against the crown, then I will be forced to take matters into my own hands."

All eyes were riveted on the lord as he continued, "As you know, my father's father worked hard to secure the Westerly name and fortune for many generations. Our wealth has become such that we have been able to generously supplement the king's pension to the legions under my governorship. My soldiers have become accustomed to a certain level of comfort from their income. It would be a pity if, upon learning of the king's decision to harbor an enemy, I were forced to withdraw that substantial income. It would ruin their lives and the lives of the families who have grown to depend on it, no doubt. I could hardly imagine such legions remaining loyal to the Crown."

"And so you would deny the king a great portion of his army during this most delicate time in our kingdom's history for the purpose of proving a point?" asked Adelaide.

Lord Westerly was at least smart enough to pretend he was intimidated. Even if only for a moment. "I ask you, Your Majesties, if you can truly say that Mistress Dupree is not a traitor to the crown."

Neither Ferryl nor Adelaide answered.

"Precisely," said the lord. "Which is why swift and final punishment should be enacted immediately so as to send a message to the world that Har-Navah is no safe harbor for traitors. And to tell the world that Midvarish enemies will not be ignored."

It was Michael whose rage could no longer be leashed, Michael who said, "And tell me, Lord Westerly, what swift and final punishment would you suggest for her?"

"The only punishment suitable for treason, my lord. The gallows, of course."

~

"Tell me you're not considering this," said Michael, standing with his arms crossed while he watched Ferryl pace the floor of his private receiving room. "Tell. Me. You're. Not. Considering. This."

Ferryl couldn't stop pacing, couldn't stop the thoughts that spiraled through his mind like a funnel cloud. The Midvarish rebels had been fed by an unknown and apparently ceaseless source for a year and a half. Maybe longer. The Navarian portion of the army was spent, tired and depleted from the rebel engagements, leaving only the Haravellian legions truly fit for war at this time. Never mind that the Midvarish soldiers were not only limitless in numbers, but had some sort of preternatural strength as well. That he should be forced to face such an army with even one less man than he originally calculated sent a wave of panic down his spine. Lord Westerly was a bastard for it, but what choice did Ferryl have now? And was he truly wrong? Delaney had technically committed treason—

"Ferryl," Michael ground through his teeth.

"Michael, I have an entire kingdom resting on my shoulders."

"Indeed," Michael said, not bothering to hide the disgust, the sheer panic quavering in his voice. "But I find it shocking that you, of all people, would even consider taking Delaney's life in exchange for this... this... power play."

Ferryl stopped his pacing so that he might look Michael in the eye. "Power play or not, he controls almost half of the Navarian legions, Michael. I cannot risk losing them. Not now."

"And what of the entire kingdom's worth of men you just inherited with the unification?"

"Even still, Westerly's men represent at least a quarter of my entire army. How can I risk that?" Ferryl resumed his pacing when Michael didn't immediately answer. "My father was a damned fool for giving this man a lordship."

"We'll find another way, Ferryl," Michael finally said, and his voice held as much terror as determination.

Ferryl turned on his heel. "What way is there?"

"I don't know. But I swear to you that I won't rest until I find a way around this."

"It's simple, isn't it? I either have men, or I don't. I either have an army with which to fight these monsters, or I don't! We cannot pull men out of thin air, Michael. We cannot! This is war, don't you see it? Nothing about it is pretty or easy. Sacrifices must be made all the time! As king, I do not have the luxury of risking my entire kingdom for the sake of one wom—"

Something like ice and storms shone in Michael's features, the unfinished word hanging in the air between them, a flash of lightning waiting for its answering thunder. "Say it, Ferryl," he growled. "Say what you were going to say."

Ferryl turned his back on Michael, but he could hear his friend stalk behind him like a caracal on the hunt. "Say it, Ferryl. For the sake of one woman, right? That's what you were going to say. How could I ever ask this of you for the sake of just one woman?" A crazed sort of laugh escaped him. "That's rich coming from you, isn't it?"

It was all Ferryl could do not to punch his friend right in the mouth for that comment. "This is not the same, and you know it."

"Is it not?" Michael asked. "I seem to recall a time when you would have forsaken your very crown for the sake of one woman. A time when you *did* put your entire kingdom at risk for the sake of one woman. And I know you well enough to know that if it ever came to it, you would do it again. Don't you dare lecture me on what is right when it comes to the sake of one woman, Ferryl!"

"And don't you dare presume to understand even an ounce of what I face, Michael."

"Admit it, Ferryl. You're terrified of losing her. Aren't you?" When Ferryl didn't answer, Michael stepped closer, his breath mingling with Ferryl's. "Admit it."

"You are on dangerous ground, speaking of the queen of Har-Na-vah in such a manner," he growled.

"But she wasn't the queen when you skirted all of your responsibilities so that you might find her. Nor was she the queen when you set off on a secret journey to Haravelle to marry her. She was just a woman. A nobody. Just like expendable, useless Delaney."

"I went to Haravelle to gain support for this war, and you know it."

"Yes, and how convenient for you that while you were there, you married the woman you love. In secret. While your entire kingdom was falling apart in your absence."

It was Ferryl who stepped closer this time. Ferryl who growled in his friend's face. "Are you blaming me for my father's death? After all the lying, the going behind my back…are you saying my father died because of me?"

Something caught in Michael's eyes. A moment—however brief—of unfathomable sorrow. "No. Not for a moment. But you know damn well, Ferryl, that you could and likely should have done things very differently when it came to *just one woman.* What's done is done, and you are married now. And while I am glad for you, glad that it turned out as it did, I fail to understand how you do not see the hypocrisy in this. That you should suggest Delaney's life—and the life of the child in her womb—are expendable for the purpose of proving a point is shocking, Ferryl. Shocking. And it's not like you."

Not like him? What *was* like him? Had he ever been faced with such a decision before?

There was desperation in Michael's voice now. Desperation and a choking sort of determination. "I love her, Ferryl. She is my life, the air I breathe. I know I should have told you. I should have been up front with you from the start. But I never thought she could be mine. I never thought…" Michael choked on his own words, shaking his head once, hard. "I swear to you nothing happened between us until you put her aside. Nothing happened until the day…" He stopped, catching his breath. "Nothing happened between us until the day your father died. I wasn't here. I was with her. I shouldn't have been, but I was. Because I love her. And I will die before I let anything happen to her. Surely you, of all people, can understand that."

Ferryl froze, unsure what to say, what to think. It was when he spotted the lone tear that fell down Michael's cheek that he said, "Of course I understand that, Michael. Of course I do. But he has my damned balls in a vice."

Incredulous ire shone in Michael's quicksilver eyes. He raised his head slowly, not bothering to wipe the tear as it lingered on his chin. "No, Ferryl. If you do this, if you murder her and the innocent life in her womb, then you never had any balls to begin with."

Ferryl slid his eyes back to Michael. How dare his friend question him? Challenge him? Him, the king of Har-Navah. Nose to nose, eye to eye, Ferryl breathed through clenched teeth, "Get out."

Michael held his steely gaze, his eyes—lined with unshed tears—narrowing ever so slightly before walking out without another word.

~

"You do understand that this is about nothing more than revenge, right?"

"Revenge for what?" Ferryl asked flatly, absolutely uninterested in having this conversation with his wife but knowing her well enough to know that there would be no avoiding it. So he laid in bed next to her, his arms folded behind his head as he stared at the ceiling through the darkness, letting her say her piece despite the fact that he still hadn't cooled down since the moment Michael walked out of his chambers.

Adelaide, wisely, had let him duke it out with his friend in peace. As she had also, wisely, let him fume alone for the rest of the day. This was the first time she had spoken to him since the council meeting.

"This is Westerly's revenge for the fact that you rejected his daughter and thereby his family's claim to the throne and crown," she said.

And damn it if she wasn't right, too.

Ferryl thought back to Lord Westerly's ridiculous daughter. To that week the duke's family had visited the castle last year, throwing their pretentious, obnoxious daughter at him like a prize to be won. Except that she was no prize. She was unbearable in every way. Lady AnnaMaria Nanette Danae Westerly of Teman. Just the thought of her name alone would grate on his nerves till Mashiach come. And now, her father, after having procured for himself the next best kind of power from King Aiken, was using his position to his advantage.

So if Westerly couldn't have his blood on the throne, then he'd have the king's balls in his hand.

What in Sheol was he supposed to do about it?

"I'm growing damn tired of having the obvious pointed out in this situation when what I could really use is a solution," he finally said.

"Perhaps, then, you should allow yourself and your closest friend some time to come up with one."

"I am already on borrowed time, Adelaide. King Derrick will not wait to retaliate again. Regardless of whether it was a taunt or an actual attempt on your life, I have no faith that he will rest on his laurels and give us all the time in the world to devise a strategy. The bottom line is: I am facing a war. A war in which I need men to fight. And the man who controls the largest portion of my army is threatening to withdraw them if I do not have a woman guilty of treason executed. I fail to see how there is much of an alternative to giving in to his demands."

"Then you will have her murdered on a technicality."

"How is treason a technicality?"

"Yes, you were technically betrothed when she conceived another man's child. And yes, that is treason. But you were never going to marry her, and you know it."

"When I thought you were dead, I was going to marry her, Adelaide. I was."

"But the point is, you didn't. And you have a written document absolving her of any fault on her part in the form of the letter you sent to her while still in Haravelle."

"What good is a written document against a power-hungry man?"

"You are king. Not he."

"And what good is a king if he has no army? What good is a king who cannot protect his people—his own *wife*— from the monsters that would destroy them?"

"Not every monster comes dressed in a greasy smile and a black cloak. Some monsters, Ferryl, are the kind we never saw coming. Some monsters are of our own making."

"Are you calling me a monster?"

She rolled to her side, placing a hand on his chest as she said emphatically, "No. Never. But there will always be those waiting to manipulate you, Ferryl. Waiting to take what is yours. Waiting to destroy you. The monster, Ferryl, is the voice that tells you that you have no choice but to listen. The true monster is the voice that whispers the lies only you can hear and only you believe."

Chapter XVIII

He hadn't realized it was so late. Honestly, if it weren't for the fact that it was completely dark outside, Michael wouldn't have believed it when the servant had inquired about him, asking if he was certain he didn't want to eat.

No, he didn't want to eat. He had absolutely no appetite whatsoever.

And hadn't since the moment he had walked out of Ferryl's chambers.

Michael had spent the remainder of the day deep in a stack of papers, sorting through plans, ledgers, letters and documents, trying—desperately searching—for any alternative to the army Ferryl was being bullied into losing. Hunting for something—anything—that would save the life of the woman he loved.

For he would be damned, damned straight to Sheol, if he ever let anyone lay a finger on her.

No, he wouldn't settle for that. Oath or no oath, king or no king, if it came to it, he would hide her away and get out of Har-Navah forever if that's what it took to save her life.

But he was hoping—praying to Providence every moment—that it wouldn't come to that. Because despite the argument, and despite the fact that he had disappointed him more greatly than ever before, Michael loved Ferryl, loved his kingdom, and wanted with all of his heart to stay and defend it against the Midvarish bastards that had threatened its peace for as long as he could remember.

So he scoured every document he could get his hands on for anything that might help him, anything that might point to an alternative to Lord Westerly's sadistic and ridiculous idea to have Delaney executed for the sole purpose of proving a point. Any caveat in the law that might defend her innocence.

So far, he had found nothing.

But the servant's appearance in his chambers had made him realize one thing: he was beyond exhausted and nothing sounded better than a good night's sleep.

Well, nothing, that is, except for one thing.

~

There was no answer when Michael knocked on Delaney's door, so he knocked again. "Delaney, it's me," he said to the door, but still he was greeted with only silence.

A thousand what-ifs raced through his mind. What if Lord Westerly had already made a move? What if Ferryl, in his wrath, had already had Delaney arrested just to spite Michael? He had been out of line telling the king of Har-Navah he had no balls. Completely out of line. What if Ferryl had already decided to retaliate?

It was with those fears pounding in his veins that he opened her door without waiting for an invitation.

But Delaney was nowhere in her sitting room. Nor was she on her balcony.

To his utter and complete relief, he found her on her bed, sprawled out under a blanket, her dress laid aside so that she was in nothing but her shift. Her hair, however, remained perfectly styled, her jewels still resting upon her breast as if she had lain down to rest and fallen asleep instead.

He smiled at the sight of her, kneeling beside her bed and pressing a kiss to her cheek while she breathed steadily, deeply. He couldn't help himself when he placed a hand on her belly and knew a sweet thrill at the answering kick he felt.

Providence, he prayed, *give me wisdom. Show me what I can do. And protect her when I cannot.*

He didn't think Ferryl would act quickly or decide what to do about Westerly's demands just yet. But then again, what did he know? Ferryl had surprised him today, shocked him, really. What if he did decide to act? And what if Michael wasn't here when it happened?

That, he knew, he could not abide. So without another thought, he stood, wrapped the blanket more securely around Delaney, and scooped her up into his arms.

He had made it all of ten steps down the palace corridors when she finally stirred, her head bumping against his chest with each step.

"Where are we going?" she asked groggily.

"To my chambers."

"Why?"

"Because you're staying with me from now on."

She didn't seem keen to protest. On the contrary, she closed her eyes and rested her head against his chest without another word.

~

He had just laid her down under the heavy blankets of his bed when she finally stirred again, her eyes heavy from deep sleep. "Is everything all right?" she asked.

"Everything is fine, beautiful," he lied. No way, *no* way in Sheol would he tell her what had been discussed today. No way he would ever let her worry for her life. He knelt to remove her jewels from her neck and fingers. Then he kissed her brow before slipping into his closet to shed his jerkin and boots.

It was only when he returned, crawled into the bed beside her, and tucked the blankets securely around them both that she continued. "Why don't I believe you?"

He only slid his eyes to hers, unsure what else to say.

"Michael. I know you. Tell me what's wrong."

He tucked a strand of hair behind her ear, thinking how sweet it was to be lying next to her, how sweet it would be to just lose himself in her body tonight, never mind the fact that he wouldn't ask that of her now—not in her condition, not this close to her time. So he only shut his eyes and breathed a sigh.

"Did something happen?" she pressed on.

"I promised you I'd be there when your time comes," he said, the excuse blooming in his mind even as he spoke it aloud. And while it was partly true that he liked the idea of having her near when her time came, he also knew that there was no way he would let her sleep anywhere out of his sight now that her very life hung in the balance of what the king decided. So he only said, "I don't want you to worry if it comes in the middle of the night. I want you to just rest as much as you can until it happens and know that I'm right here when it does."

A smile found her mouth, but even so, he could see that she knew there was more to his story. Mercifully, she didn't press the subject any more. And when she kissed his mouth, her lips soft and warm against his, he closed his eyes and let himself imagine for just a moment that the world was a simpler place.

She slept with her head on his shoulder for the rest of the night.

Chapter XIX

For the better part of three weeks, there had been nothing but darkness in front of Titus. Ringing silence. A clanging void of nothingness flowing through the very marrow of his bones, clouding his vision to nothing more than a blur of gray and ash. Every moment of those three weeks had only held a chasm, ever-widening with every aching breath, every mocking reminder that Titus was alive.

And Penelope was not.

The Navarian soldiers had yet to plunder and pillage the village as had been threatened. No, their raids had been of the clandestine style, silent prowling through village streets and country homes in the night. Stealing women and killing anyone who would get in their way. Men, they were not.

These Navarian soldiers were nothing but cowards.

The lingering, eerie silence in their wake had been enough to drive any man mad. Whispers abounded amongst the remaining servants of his household—all either male or women much too old to garner the interests of barbaric soldiers. Whispers and silent prayers. Madness.

But in the stillness of the nights, Titus could have sworn he heard something else in the darkness. A quiet sort of shuffling. He had even ventured down into the cellars one night following the distant sounds. But when they had led him to the door—*that* door, the one behind which he had found Penelope—it had been too much to bear. So he had turned around and returned to his bed, deciding that whatever he thought he was hearing was likely nothing more than the nocturnal activity of prolific rodents.

Still, the madness grew with each passing, miserable day. The madness of a household ravaged by the barbaric evil of a desperate kingdom.

But Titus? His madness was of a much deeper nature. His stemmed from the stupidity of his own mistakes, his own naïveté, the bed of his own making. His madness would never cease. Not now that the only good thing left in his life had been destroyed. Slaughtered.

She had been so light, so horrifically light when he had buried her. Her life's blood spilled, her body striped with wounds from the fight she had obviously put up. He had kissed those ashen, cold lips of hers one last time. Kissed every wound across her breast, her arms, her face. But there had been not a single wound on her abdomen. Penelope might have let herself be harmed, but she had protected their unborn child with her dying breath. And she had been buried with Titus's fat tears still wet upon her belly.

Penelope had been so brave. Always.

Much braver than he.

And that bravery had gotten her killed. Alongside the fact that Titus had been too much of a fool to deserve her. If he had only taken her with him to the bank… If he had only been smart enough to know not to leave her alone…

But he had underestimated the Navarians. Underestimated their evil. When he had been their commander, this never would have happened. Ruthless, yes. Cunning, absolutely. Sadistic and evil, not on his life. And stealing women for their own carnal needs, for a slave trade, was the sickest, most vile thing he could have ever imagined. That they had tried to take Penelope but she had escaped that fate was the only shred of consolation he could find.

But that it was coming from the Navarian soldiers under Derwin's command was perhaps the biggest shock of it all.

But what did it matter? What did it matter that the world was full of barbarians and miscreants? What did any of it matter anymore? Hadn't Titus himself been a whore for a king once? Hadn't he done whatever was asked of him without question? He had stolen an innocent child and left her for dead, for gods' sakes!

It didn't get any more base and evil than that.

So he deserved his fate. He deserved to have the one good thing in his life ripped away.

Titus deserved nothing but the fires of Sheol for his sins.

And now he knew that he would live them for the rest of his miserable life.

Even so, as he stared out the window of his bedchamber, willing himself not to lie on his bed any longer, not to roll over and smell her pillow one more time, breathe in the lingering, fading scent that was Penelope, he knew that even if he was no longer interested in serving the kings of this realm, no longer going to whore himself out for another man's interests, he had to do something. Someone had to pay for what the Navarian bastards did to his wife.

And if Commander Derwin truly was putting his seal of approval on this kind of behavior, then it was only with the blessing of their king. It shouldn't have surprised Titus when he thought about it. Knowing what he knew of Ferryl's reputation when he was prince, it shouldn't have surprised Titus that Ferryl had a penchant for debauchery. He was widely known to have capitalized on his position for all carnal forms of entertainment. Apparently, he was keen for his soldiers to enjoy such spoils, too. So if King Ferryl was resorting to that kind of evil, then two could play that game.

Ferryl wouldn't know what had hit him until it was too late.

~

"Master, it is good to see you out and about," said the old man—Daphne's father. Titus had finally learned his name.

"Prepare my horse, Sedecias. I leave at sundown."

"At sundown, milord?"

Yes, sundown. Because by cover of darkness would he ride. It would shield him as he traversed the countryside that stretched between him and his goal. And it would hide him as he arrived and exacted his revenge.

"Sundown. And do not delay."

~

Sedecias had not delayed. The horse had been ready: fed and freshly shod, keen for a ride. The other servants packed Titus a satchel of dried fruits and meats and wax-covered cheese, enough food for a long journey. He had packed a bag for himself, too, with nothing more than a change of clothes and plenty of room for spare weapons. And then he covered himself in blades and a bow, prepared for whatever he might find along the way.

Rumors abounded that the soldiers of Midvar were preparing to move. It was odd not knowing such information anymore, not being privy to the inner workings of two opposing armies. But not odd enough to stop him from riding right into the heart of his enemy's home and taking what mattered most to their king.

He didn't really care anymore that it was what Derrick had wanted from him, one final task as the king's bitch. He didn't really care what it did for the war, on either side.

Titus's mission was personal now. And killing Adelaide of Haravelle was going to feel really damn good.

CHAPTER XX

pring was well underway…in theory. For while it was nearly halfway through the season, the weather had still been strange. Foreboding. As if it knew of the darkness that hovered before the entire kingdom and answered with a lingering chill.

Adelaide, queen of Har-Navah, tightened her arms around herself as she sat before the looking glass in her dressing chamber, breathing deeply to quell the underlying nausea that had plagued her day and night while Talia dutifully, carefully brushed out her midnight tresses. She hadn't allowed herself one moment to hope, one moment to consider what that nausea meant. For until she felt the child quicken in her womb, nothing was sure. Nothing.

"Still have a chill, Your Majesty?" Talia asked, a merriment to her voice that seemed never-ceasing, despite everything.

"I cannot seem to shake it today," Adelaide admitted, although she didn't admit that part of the reason for the chill had nothing to do with the weather. Or the lingering clouds. Or her nausea.

No, the chill today was of a much more foreboding nature. Though why she was so unsettled, she couldn't really say.

Perhaps it was the fact that Ferryl was in the other room, dressing for the first council meeting since Lord Westerly had made his ridiculous demands on Delaney's life. Perhaps it was the fact that, despite the weeks that had passed since the last one, Ferryl had yet to decide what to do about the demands. Perhaps it was the fact that since the last council meeting, Michael hadn't breathed a word to either of them aside from what was absolutely necessary.

Or perhaps it was the fact that today was Ferryl's twenty-second birthday, and while preparations were being made for a celebration tonight, there seemed to be little to celebrate at the moment.

Yes, maybe it was all of those things that contributed to the chill going down Adelaide's spine this morning.

But for reasons she couldn't name, she knew it was something more.

"I'll go and stoke the fire," Talia said, turning on her heel to leave the dressing chamber. But it wasn't until Adelaide saw what was in the reflection of her looking glass that she understood her servant's sudden departure.

She turned on her stool to face Ferryl as he leaned on the frame of the door. Beautiful. It was the only word to describe her king. Her husband. Like a marble statue, he was so perfectly built, so precisely chiseled. She had always thought so—from the time she was old enough to pay attention to such things. But his arduous training of late had only accentuated that perfection, his form broader, his lean muscles harder than ever before.

There was an apologetic smile on his beautiful mouth. And though his tan had faded in the months of cloudiness that had plagued the usually sunny province of Benalle, it had somehow only made the blue of his eyes even more piercing.

"You are glowing, my love," he said, ambling to her.

"My dresses aren't quite fitting anymore. Talia is having to lace them rather loosely. I'm afraid I'm bordering on impropriety these days," she chuckled.

Indeed, her belly had been rounding—a fact she hadn't let herself think too much on. Maybe…maybe the child in her womb had survived that Midvarish blade. But if it hadn't…

Still, her belly had rounded enough that her dresses were a bit tight. Even her breasts had blossomed overnight, two plump apples peeking over the top of her dress. Ferryl, of course, had no objections to such developments and expressed his approval with answering kisses to each as he knelt before her, his hands resting gently on her hips.

"You look beautiful. More beautiful with each passing day."

"You are blinded by love."

He chuckled. "If love is blindness, then I have no interest in sight."

"My poet king." She smiled, kissing his brow before he rested his head on her chest. She ran her fingers through his unruly blond locks before she said, "Are you prepared for today?"

He breathed a heavy sigh, his voice reverberating through her chest as he said, "I don't know."

"Any ideas what you'll do?"

"You asked me once if I would defend Michael and Delaney at any cost. I told you yes when I thought the answer would be easy. Now that I am faced with the dilemma, I am saddened to admit that a solution has evaded me for so long. Maybe I'm not a good man or a good king."

She lifted his head from her breast so that she might meet his eyes. "You are not a good man or a good king because you are perfect,

Ferryl. You are good because you know Good. That is what counts, Ferryl."

"Perhaps I am not too late in doing what is right. But I fear I might be too late in salvaging any sort of friendship with Michael."

"He is a good man, too, Ferryl."

"I hope so. But I am very much *not* looking forward to this meeting, nonetheless."

"I am sure you will be fine."

"You speak as if you will not be there," he said.

"I won't."

"Queen Adelaide, you are ruler of this kingdom in your own right, which means your presence at council meetings is as expected as mine."

She chuckled at her suddenly authoritative husband. "I am well aware of my expectations, Ferryl. But I have other things on my agenda today."

"And what things could possibly take priority over a council meeting?"

She did her best to purse the smile that was threatening her mouth.

"Lizybet, what do you have up your sleeve?"

"Nothing, Ferryl. I just have... things to do."

Ferryl searched her face for a moment before he said, "And do these *things*, by chance, have anything to do with my birthday?"

"Perhaps," she said, biting her lip as she toyed with an embellishment on his collar.

Still on his knees before her, he inched himself closer, wrapping his solid arms around her waist. "And are you going to tell me or leave me in suspense?"

"Birthdays, as a rule, are meant to be full of surprises, are they not?"

A raised brow and then a roguish smile were his answer. "I certainly hope that at some point, such surprises include you and not a stitch of clothing more."

"That," she said, brushing her lips against his, even as she felt a blush creep up her cheeks, "is only part of your present."

"Any chance in having that part of my present early?" he asked, losing himself in her lips.

She chuckled through his kisses. "Tonight, Ferryl. After the rest of the festivities."

When his lips traveled skillfully down her neck to her newly ample breasts, she was tempted to ignore her better judgment. Somehow, she managed to pull away a little and say, "You are going to be late for your council meeting."

"I am sovereign of this kingdom. Am I late or are they just early?"

"Now you're sounding like a spoiled tyrant," she chuckled, though her breath grew short when his fingers pulled at the laces that ran down the front of her gown. And despite her paltry warnings of kingly responsibility, she did not stop him from pulling the knot loose, relishing the wake of gooseflesh his fingers left as they brushed hither and thither against her skin.

"Your Majesty," they heard from the adjacent room, shattering the spell that was working her into a thorough frenzy. "Are you ready for the meeting, Sire?"

Growling in annoyance, Ferryl rolled his eyes before saying, "I shall be there momentarily."

"Such demands on the king," Adelaide laughed.

"Don't they know it's my birthday?" he asked, continuing his worshipful kisses down her décolletage as if he had no concept of what exactly *momentarily* meant.

"I've no doubt it's the reason they're rushing to get you to your meeting. Because the sooner it commences, the sooner it will be over and the sooner we can all celebrate."

"And thank Providence for that," he said, pressing his lips to the top of each breast as if in sorrowful goodbye before reluctantly standing to his feet, extending his hand so Adelaide might stand with him. He looked truly disappointed as he helped her tighten her laces again, and she only chuckled as she adjusted his jacket, brushing off rogue lint, and straightened his hair where she had run her fingers through.

But then he surprised her when he pulled her suddenly to him and kissed her ravenously. Although it shouldn't have surprised her. Ferryl always had a way of kissing her as if it were their last—a habit to which she had no objection.

"And where will you be should I need you?" Ferryl finally asked against her lips.

"The kitchens." She smiled.

"The kitchens?" he asked with a fiendish grin. "Then this is going to be a happy birthday, indeed."

Ferryl let the memory of his wife's sweet lips linger as he walked to his meeting room, unwilling, at least for the moment, to let his worries spoil the lingering scent of honey and lavender that still clung to him. Tonight would be pleasant indeed, what with his birthday dinner and whatever surprises his wife had in store.

He sent a rush of his desire, his love, his need for her through that bond they shared. That bond he had grown to cherish—her consciousness an ever-present comfort. She responded with an answering chuckle, replete with the same desire, the same need, the same love.

Providence, that woman. He never knew a man could love a woman so deeply. Thoroughly. Ceaselessly.

As it turned out, Ferryl was indeed a tad late for the council meeting, the advisors already having found their seats, most of them agitated from however long they had been waiting. He wondered if the excuse *If only you could have seen how irresistible my wife was this morning, you'd understand my tardiness* would suffice. He opted not to find out.

Instead he found his seat, offered his excuses for Adelaide's absence, and commenced with the meeting straight away.

"We have much to discuss this morning," he said. "What with the reunification of the kingdoms, the trade agreements with the southern and western continents must be renegotiated. Medinah has called for—"

"I do hope, for Your Majesty's sake," interrupted Lord Westerly, "and of course for the sake of our good kingdom, that you have come to a decision regarding the duchess, too. The *right* decision," he added, with a hint of warning in his voice.

That. Of course. Ferryl had hoped he could at least delay the subject of Delaney a bit.

"We will abide by whatever decision His Majesty has made, as he is king," said Lord Mistar.

"Thank you, my lords," said Ferryl. He sat up, folding his hands before him on the table. "In light of everything we know, and due to the many factors that play into this decision, I have reached the only conclusion that will not weigh on my conscience. If you, Lord Westerly, truly believe that withdrawing the legions from your duchy is the best way to prove your point, then I shall have to take that risk. For I am unwilling to execute the duchess and the innocent child in her womb for the purpose of sending a message that may or may not make its point."

From the corner of his eye, Ferryl saw Michael's eyes grow wide. Ferryl could have sworn he saw a tremor of relief course through the guard.

Lord Westerly slapped the table with both hands. "She is a traitor to the Crown! How can you allow her to live and dwell amongst your good people even as she carries a bastard in her womb?"

"Tell me, Lord Westerly," said Ferryl. "Why is it that you are so keen to see her put to death? What good do you think it will do?"

"As I have said before," said Westerly through gritted teeth, "the world needs to see strength from us. Not mercy. War is not a time for mercy."

"I would argue that there is never a time when mercy is out of fashion. As I would equally argue that hanging her from the gallows would hardly send a message to the world, much less her uncle."

"Then you are a fool," said Westerly, to which several of the lords around the table nodded their tentative agreements. Bought, then. Bought by Westerly.

Bastards. All of them.

"His Majesty is right," said Lord Mistar. "King Derrick has not inquired of her once since King Aiken's funeral. She was stripped of her title and then forgotten. Her death would hardly be a blow to him."

"Of course it would," said one of Westerly's cronies. "He's arrogant enough that regardless of whether he bears any love for her, he would see her execution as intolerable."

"Be that as it may, it does not make it right," said another lord.

"This is not a matter of right and wrong," said Westerly. "This is a matter of law. A law, King Ferryl, that not even *you* are above. And the law clearly states that the punishment for treason is execution."

"But they are legally and rightfully divorced. Her treason is no longer valid," said another lord.

Westerly eagerly retorted, "On the contrary, it was committed while they were still betrothed, which means that it cannot be invalidated or acquitted. She must pay for her crimes. And the world must see it."

"We are not barbarians!" cried Lord Mistar, the most emotion Ferryl had ever seen from the old man. "That is not the way our good kingdom has ever operated. That you would demand it of King Ferryl is unacceptable, Westerly. You are treading dangerous waters, and you know it."

"I am only thinking of the good of this kingdom," said Westerly.

"You are only thinking of the good of your own power," retorted Mistar.

And then the advisors around the large table erupted, the argument reaching its peak as Ferryl finally called, "Enough!"

Reluctantly, the heated advisors fell silent.

"Your Majesty," said another of Westerly's cronies, "with all due respect, this is not a matter of right or wrong, this is a matter of national security. We cannot risk losing even one soldier. Not with the strength of our enemy still unknown. And with the recent attack again on her Her Majesty, now more than ever, we need to know that we are safe."

"Then why don't you convince your friend to let us keep his soldiers?" asked Lord Mistar.

"I cannot in good conscience," said Westerly, his tone as haughty as his teeth were yellow, "ask my men to fight for a king who would tolerate evil right under his nose. Delaney *must* be executed. Justice *must* be served."

"Then let us serve justice," said Michael, speaking up from across the room, his voice clear and keen above the cacophony of arguments that were again erupting. All eyes around the table shot to him, including Ferryl's. "You're right, Lord Westerly. King Derrick must know where he stands. And it is equally true that we cannot risk losing a single soldier. So let us serve justice in this matter."

A ringing silence around the table reverberated for an uncomfortable moment. The guard walked slowly to the table, meeting the eyes of each man around it before he said, "You want justice, then you shall have it. You want a life to be made an example, then take mine."

Westerly, the bastard, had the nerve to laugh. "You are not the traitor, guard. She is."

"No," said Michael. "It is me. I am the traitor. I am the one who should be put to death."

"Michael," said Ferryl. "This is—"

"I claim her child," Michael continued. "I claim it as my own."

Westerly laughed again, only this time, he could not hide the hint of nerves in his breathy chuckle. "Your claim is no doubt noble, my lord. But everyone knows you were not her first conquest. Everyone knows it was her father's vassal who sired the child. She practically flaunted their affair for the whole court to witness."

"No. I am the child's father. I claim it as my own. And therefore I am the traitor. I will take the rightful punishment."

"Michael," Ferryl tried again, panic stealing over him for his friend. His loyal, faithful friend who would give his own life for the woman he loved. When he knew—knew without needing a shred of evidence—that the child was not his. Ferryl knew because he knew Michael. He had always known him. And knew that he would never have touched her so long as she was betrothed to Ferryl. He had told Ferryl the truth that day of the last council meeting..

"Hang me from the gallows if you will. Only spare her life."

"There is no precedent for this," protested Westerly, his voice growing in frantic vibrato. "Even if you are the father, there is no precedent for this. She is the adulteress, therefore she is the traitor. It is her life that is forfeit."

"There is precedent," said Lord Mistar, his eyes slowly sliding to the king's. "There is precedent for the case of a treasonous act against the Crown being spared punishment."

"I'm sure you are wrong," tried Westerly.

"I am not," Mistar continued. "I bore witness to it myself. According to Navarian law, treason can only be pardoned when a member of the court is willing to lay claim to the punishment. And it has happened once before."

"When? When did it happen?" Ferryl asked, his heart thundering in his chest.

Somehow he knew the answer even before Lord Mistar finally said, "When King Aiken spared the life of your mother."

~

"Tell me...tell me what you know, Mistar. And leave nothing out," Ferryl ground through his teeth as he paced the now worn path on the carpet spread on the floor of his private sitting room.

Lord Mistar sat before the king, the two of them alone as he said, "I was sworn by oath never to tell. Your father, he had us all swear our silence. But in light of Westerly's demands, in light of what has happened today, I feel I am right to break the oath, as it is time you know the truth, King Ferryl."

"What truth?" he asked, his breath, his heartbeat threatening to fail. "What truth, Mistar?"

"Derwin, he is not—"

Those words. The same words he had heard before. From his father.

Derwin, he is not—

His father had tried to tell him what Mistar was about to reveal. But then his mother had interrupted...

"He is not your father's son, Ferryl."

He might as well have been pushed out the window behind him, for surely he was falling, falling down a cliff, not into the open ocean, but into an abyss of all the lies, all the secrets his mother had kept. And apparently his father, too.

"Whose son is he?" Ferryl ground through his teeth.

Mistar seemed reluctant to answer, to reveal that truth.

"Whose son, Mistar?"

Mistar fidgeted with his fingers before finally meeting Ferryl's eyes. "Derwin is the bastard son of King Derrick of Midvar."

Chapter XXI

he world must have stopped. Surely the world had stopped. For surely—surely—Ferryl had heard wrong. Surely his mother had not done the unthinkable.

Surely Derwin—Ferryl's own brother—was not the son of the enemy.

"I am so sorry this was kept from you, Ferryl. There were so many times when I wanted to tell you," said Lord Mistar. "Especially after you returned from Haravelle. Your mother's behavior, the way you seemed so frustrated by it. I felt like you needed to know. But I had promised, sworn and…"

"Does he know? Does Derrick know?"

"No. No one knows except the Queen Mother, your father, myself, and now you. The other members of the council who knew of it have all died off over the years."

"How did it happen?"

Mistar's eyes were heavy, misty when he finally said, "When she could no longer hide it, when her growing body betrayed her indiscretion, only then did Aiken confirm what he had suspected. For Derrick had visited only a few months prior, a diplomatic visit with his father to discuss the final removal of the Midvarish garrisons in Benalle City.

And Aiken had suspected then what we had all suspected—that your mother loved the visiting Midvarish king. Except that he was a prince then, his father still ruling Midvar with a ruthlessness that had not been seen in several centuries.

"When she turned out to be carrying Derrick's child, it was a terrible shock to us all. To your father most especially. I've never seen him more hurt, Ferryl. Devastated. I believe he loved your mother. I believe he wanted her love in return. And while he thought he might have had it when you were born, all hopes of keeping it were ripped from him when Derwin was conceived.

"The council found out about her treachery and, in light of their love for our good king, called for her execution. It was treason, after all. Treason to commit adultery against the Crown.

"Only, your father wouldn't allow it. He wouldn't allow her death. So he vouched for her. He spared her life—the only man who could have.

"And in doing so, the council was sworn to secrecy. No one was to know that Derwin wasn't his. Not even you. Or Derwin. The secret died with the council. And with your father.

"But anyone with half a wit about them could see it, if they looked closely enough. Derwin looks just like his father—his unnatural height, his auburn curls, even his smirk. He acts much like him in many regards as well. But mercifully, he was reared by a good man. A loving man. And I believe that love is what shaped your brother into the man he is. A good man. Ill-tempered at times, yes. But good.

"And that in and of itself is a testament to the kind of man your father was, Ferryl. He never treated Derwin differently, less than. Never hinted at a preference for you over him. He loved you both equally until the day he died.

"And it is by this precedent that Delaney's life can be spared. For the sole reason that Michael has officially claimed her child."

Ferryl met the lord's eyes again. "But Michael is just a guard. He is neither a nobleman nor even a member of the court. How can his claim save her?"

"Come now, Ferryl," said Mistar, with a hint of a grin in the reprimand. "He has always been more to you than just a guard. Perhaps now is the time to make it official. And between you and me, I would not leave it at that."

"What do you mean?" Ferryl asked, still trying to process everything.

"I mean that you're the king. Do not let a bastard like Westerly make you forget it."

~

"Can someone please explain why we have been sitting here without explanation for the past half hour?" asked Lord Westerly as Ferryl and Lord Mistar returned to their seats around the meeting table. "What could Lord Mistar have had to say that he could not deign to say in front of the king's council?"

"Not everything, Lord Westerly, is of your concern," said Ferryl. "Suffice it to say that in light of new information, I am hereby declaring Mistress Delaney Dupree acquitted of any and all claims against her and free of the burden of punishment."

"On what grounds?" stormed Westerly.

"On the grounds that her child has been officially claimed by a member of the royal court and thereby spared of the associated punishments," said Lord Mistar, to which Ferryl nodded.

Michael darted shocked eyes to Ferryl, who gave his friend a reassuring nod.

"A member of the court?" Westerly balked. "He is not a mem—"

"Furthermore," said Ferryl, "I am hereby stripping you, Lord Westerly, of all titles and associated rights."

"You cannot do that!" Westerly shouted, standing to his feet.

"On the contrary, my lord, I can. And I should have from the beginning, for I too, believe in sending messages. So hear this message, Westerly. The king of Har-Navah will not kowtow to bullies or those who would manipulate the Crown for their own gain."

"Then you will lose every single man under my jurisdiction," said Westerly.

"They are no longer under your jurisdiction. They are now under Her Grace, Duchess Delaney Dupree's jurisdiction, as I am officially appointing her Duchess of Teman. And in addition to the pension you have enjoyed as the former Lord of Teman, which will generously finance the armies under the new duchess, I am allotting the monies set aside for the building of the Temple at Benalle to supplement the entire army's income, thereby negating any losses your men might have suffered in your absence.

"Furthermore, I have decided, in light of his unwavering loyalty to the Crown, to appoint Officer Michael as Lord Chancellor, second only to me in command, and an official member of the royal family."

All eyes around the council table were wide in shock. But none more so than Michael's. It was hard to tell, but Ferryl could have sworn he saw a tear fall down Michael's cheek.

Ferryl only nodded once to his friend before he went on. "So you see, Mister Westerly, that I am a king keen to deliver strong messages to the true enemies of this kingdom, no matter on what side of the border they might sit."

Chapter XXII

erryl, are you sure?" Michael asked, his hands trembling as they rested on the meeting table. The council had only just cleared the room, but Michael had asked Ferryl to stay behind.

"I am positive," the king said with a smile. "And I am sorry it took me so long to do what is right. I owe you an apology. I—"

"No, Ferryl," Michael said. "You were right. We could not have afforded to lose the soldiers. It's a risk we cannot take. I've run the numbers. I've worked through every possible scenario, and no matter how it turns out, we would not win a war losing that many men. We need them. And I'm sorry I ever made you consider otherwise."

"Michael," Ferryl said. "I should never have asked such a thing of you, to give up the woman you love. If the roles had been reversed, I never would have—"

"But it wouldn't have been the same had the roles been reversed," Michael countered. "Because you are king, not me. There is more to this than my own agenda. And I'm so sorry I ever made you question my loyalty. You are my friend, Ferryl. But you are foremost my king. You need to know that I will abide by whatever decision you make."

"And I am glad to say that you are my friend, Michael. And while what is right is not always easy, it is worth it if it means keeping friends like you."

"But the temple, Ferryl. You've been so proud of it, all the plans, the—"

"I'll leave that to my sons, of which I plan on having many. My job, it seems, is to secure a time of peace for this realm. I cannot do that if I'm too much of a coward to stand up for those who cannot defend themselves."

Michael wiped a tear from his eye. "A duchess, Ferryl?" And in her own right, not a fabricated title given to her by birth for nothing other than her father's gain. No, a true title. A true claim. Power in her own right.

Ferryl chuckled. "You fell in love with a duchess. You might as well marry one, Lord Michael."

It was a laugh that caught in his throat as Michael said, "I'll never be able to thank you enough for this, Ferryl."

~

Michael felt as if he were flying as he ran down the corridors of Benalle Palace, keen to tell Delaney everything that had happened. To tell her that she was a duchess. In her own right. To tell her of the king's goodness. Keen to hold her in his arms and just feel—for the first time in a long time—peace.

He skidded to a halt in front of his chamber doors, doing his best to wipe the stupid smile from his mouth lest he give it all away in one fell swoop. He burst through the door, fully expecting to find her in his sitting room, perhaps reading or even napping in the chair, as she had been prone to do lately, the final weeks and days of her pregnancy taking a toll on her energy.

But she was nowhere to be found.

"Delaney?" he called.

He heard what he thought was a whimper from his bedchamber and tore across the room to get to her as soon as possible.

Whimper indeed.

He found her lying in his bed, sweat pouring from her brow despite the chill in the spring air, her face scrunched in a grimace as she gripped the sheets around her.

"Delaney!" he cried again, his heart stopping and starting again at the sight of her. He knelt beside the bed, unsure what to do, what to even say.

"Michael," she breathed, letting go of the sheets that she might clutch her stomach. "It's time."

Chapter XXIII

Another day, another meeting he was not invited to. Of course. Because being nephew to the now abdicated king of Haravelle apparently meant even less in the new kingdom than it had meant in his old. Because apparently blood and birthright were of little significance to this new king and his miraculous queen.

Haughty bastards, the both of them.

Lord Adam shuffled his feet, his hands shoved in his pockets as he begrudgingly made his way down the corridors of Benalle Palace. He might as well have been a ghost, so few people even acknowledged him these days. He had only come with Ferryl and Adelaide to Navah as a show of support upon learning of the loss of King Aiken. His parents—King Aaron's brother and sister-in-law—had stayed behind in Haravelle as regents. Never—never in all his wildest dreams—would he have imagined that upon coming here, his aunt and uncle would abdicate their thrones and just hand over their power, their entire kingdom to Ferryl and Adelaide.

It was shocking.

Not to mention quite possibly the stupidest thing he had ever heard.

Not because now that Adelaide had been found and his uncle was no longer king, Adam was no longer heir to the throne of Haravelle (all right, that was partly why it was stupid), but because what business did Ferryl and Adelaide have ruling such a kingdom? The most powerful kingdom in all the realm, to be precise!

It was all unfair. And it was all stupid.

But the council meeting upon which he had been eavesdropping had been equally stupid, a bunch of poppycocks arguing about rightful punishment for treason or some such nonsense. No more discussion of the attack at the coronation ball. As if it hadn't mattered. As if all that planning, all that trouble to find and smuggle in a Midvarish rebel for the purpose of making it look like King Derrick had made the first move and attempted to take the life of the queen, as if all of that didn't matter anymore. *Oh, someone tried to kill the queen? Oh, no problem, let's try to figure out how to build a rutting temple.*

Idiot. Ferryl was a complete and total imbecile.

Of course, of *course*, Adam had made sure the damned rebel had understood that the wound was not to be mortal. He wasn't so wicked that he would actually attempt to arrange the assassination of his cousin, his own blood. But it was damn important that the attack was enough to scare the Sheol out of King Ferryl. And Queen Adelaide. And hopefully get them to do something stupid like attack King Derrick without proper preparation.

But Ferryl had done no such thing. Instead, he had been planning to build a gods-damned temple.

A temple.

To Providence.

Gods above, King Ferryl of rutting Har-Navah was the world's biggest fool.

Adam had given up on getting any useful information through the secret door that connected the meeting room to a private antechamber which remained woefully unguarded most of the time. And now he was back to his usual begrudging pastime—pacing the halls, hoping to learn something, anything of use from the gossiping, prattling court at Benalle. Which was too easy, considering just how little anyone even acknowledged his presence here.

So it was convenient, then, that no sooner had he entered the halls than he spotted Ferryl and some crusty old lord shuffling by, both of them too wrapped up in themselves to notice a useless Haravellian lord right beside them.

So Adam followed them... all the way to the king's private receiving room where he loitered outside the doors as if he were waiting on an audience with the king, never mind he had nothing to say to the arrogant bastard.

Still, the king's idiot guards were trusting enough that they didn't question his presence.

Fools.

But his attention was soon captured not by the lack of concern on the part of the guards, but on the bits and pieces he could hear coming from *inside* the receiving room.

Something about someone's son.

But whose son? And why would such a conversation merit such secrecy?

Bastard son, he heard. And then, *King Derrick of Midvar.*

Wait.

Did King Derrick have a bastard son? Somewhere in this palace? But who?

Adam's mind raced with the possibilities. Who could the Midvarish king have sired? And who could it be that it would require such secrecy? Ferryl?

No, it couldn't have been Ferryl. Ferryl was much too naïve to be the son of Derrick of Midvar.

So who, then?

Michael? Why would it matter if Michael were a bastard?

Then again, perhaps it mattered not because of who was sired, but because of who was the mother.

And Adam could think of only one woman for whom it would be a scandal to bear Derrick's son…

Treason to commit adultery against the crown, he heard through the doors.

So Queen Meria had borne a bastard with Derrick. Which meant that there was only one possibility of whom it could be. A prince with auburn curls and a pompous smile.

Commander Prince Derwin. Son of King Derrick of Midvar.

Had Queen Meria chosen such a name just to spite her husband? She sounded awfully arrogant to have pulled such a stunt. Lord Adam found he liked the wretched queen all the more for it.

But this… Knowing Derwin was the bastard son of King Derrick, enemy number one.

How many people had such information? Judging by the secrecy of this meeting, it sounded like not even Ferryl had been privy to it until now.

Did Derrick know? And what would he do if he did?

The gods only knew.

But Adam knew one thing for certain: whoever brought such information to King Derrick wouldn't be overlooked. Wouldn't be forgotten. He would be heralded. Praised. And likely rewarded. Handsomely.

An opportunity he couldn't pass up. Which was why Adam didn't tarry in the halls to be found by the king. He marched himself straight to his chambers, packed a bag, marched to the stables, called for the saddling of his horse, and set off for the kingdom to the east without a backward glance.

Because no longer would Lord Adam of Haravelle, rightful and blessedly *male* heir to the throne of Haravelle, be overlooked by those who did not know his value.

If the court of King Ferryl of Har-Navah was intent to make him a ghost of the past, then surely the court of King Derrick of Midvar would welcome the messenger of perhaps the most damning information of this entire war with open, joyous arms.

He could not ride fast enough.

Chapter XXIV

By cover of darkness. That had been his plan. To arrive in the night like a wraith that he might slaughter the one thing that mattered most to the young king who would be his enemy for the rest of his life.

But when Titus had arrived in Benalle City by the morning light, stopping off at a tavern to pass the time while he waited, waited, waited for nightfall, his patience had grown painfully thin. In fact, he hadn't made it through more than two ales before he slapped a couple of bekas on the counter and marched himself back out of the sorry excuse for a tavern. Darkness be damned.

He would slaughter that bitch queen in broad daylight.

And enjoy every damned minute of it.

Maybe that's why he hadn't been able to kill Adelaide of Haravelle the first time, all those years ago when she was just a child. Maybe the gods had been smiling on him, biding their time until today. Because then—then he would have only carried regret and remorse with him. If he would have slaughtered her then, he would not have been able to run far enough from it.

But now.

Now, he would enjoy every cry, relish every drop of blood.

Now, today, he would delight in the chance to take his revenge on the man who, whether intentionally or not, had commissioned the murder of his wife. If only he could be there to watch Ferryl suffer the way he had. If only he could be there to watch as Ferryl held his mangled, bloodied wife in his arms. Felt the sticky warmth of her blood as it pooled around him. Wept, mourned into her hair, trailing trembling fingers down her cooling cheeks.

He wouldn't see it with his own eyes. He'd be long gone by then. But the satisfaction of knowing that Ferryl would feel even an iota of the pain Titus had known would be enough.

Titus rode up the cobblestone streets of Benalle City to the palace with his shoulders back. He didn't hide. These fools had no idea he had been a traitor anyway. They had never figured out that he had been secretly working for King Derrick the whole time he called himself the Commander of the Navarian Army. So why hide? Why not mock them even more and take their precious princess right out from under their noses?

It was all too, too perfect.

~

Smiles, that's what the fool guards gave him as he walked the path to the castle entrance. Smiles and nods of greeting.

"Your Excellency!" one of them said—one of the boys *he* had trained to become a man. "Well met!"

Titus didn't answer; he only nodded his head at the fool and marched on.

Benalle Palace was exactly as he had left it last year. Bright, open, breezy. The only difference was the unnerving chill in the air. It was mid-spring, but there was still no heat from the sun.

That was the first odd thing Titus noticed.

Lengths of the bluest silk were being hung from every pillar and chandelier and flowers were stuffed into every alcove, crowding every surface possible. A celebration, then. But for what?

"Such a lovely shade of blue," he heard one of the courtiers prattle.

Another responded, her cheeks flushed with a demure smile, "It matches perfectly with His Majesty's eyes, doesn't it?"

No doubt one of Ferryl's many whores.

So the celebration was for the king, then. Which meant that the queen was likely somewhere helping plan the festivities. This was already too easy.

He listened carefully to the bustling court of nobility and servants alike as they decorated and chatted, careful to keep his features schooled in disinterest lest someone notice his eavesdropping as he strolled aimlessly down the corridors.

"No, not there," said one servant to the next. "Put the flowers in the center, like this."

"There is no need to set the tables yet, James. Dinner is not until tonight and I'll not have a speck of dust on the flatware."

"Has someone started mulling the wine?"

Information and plenty of it. But all of it useless.

He strolled on, his hands clasped casually behind his back.

Past the grand ballroom, set with a long table that met another at a perpendicular angle—a great "T" in the center of the room, covered completely with the whitest linens and lined with perfectly spaced seats. A banquet set for a king.

Oh, tonight, there would be celebration indeed. His own.

Too bad Titus couldn't commission the room just for himself to enjoy. It was a shame all that work would be put to waste.

He chuckled to himself, knowing he was being a complete and total ass. A wolf on the prowl. And he relished every damned minute of it.

There had been another woman once—long before he ever met Penelope. Before his parents had died of the sickness that had plagued the lands. A gorgeous Navarian woman with blonde hair and legs for days. Hania, that was her name. And he had loved her fiercely for the entirety of the summer before he signed his life away to the king of Midvar.

She had known him well. Better, perhaps, than anyone else had ever known him. Even Penelope. And it was she who had always said that Titus had two sides.

"You like to think yourself a bastard," she had said one day, lying beside him in the hayloft above her father's barn, her blonde hair cascading down her bare breasts as she traced idle patterns on his chest. "But I know the truth, Titus Melamed."

"And what truth is that?" he had asked.

"That you are nothing more than a sheep in wolf's clothing."

"And how can you be so sure?"

"Because there is no wolf in the world who could love the way you love me." Titus had had no response to such a statement. He had never admitted to Hania that he had loved her deeply. Fiercely. Wholly. And had he been a better man, he might have stayed.

But he hadn't stayed. He had received word that summer that his parents had taken ill of the sickness that had killed too many. And so he had departed for home—for Midvar.

He had never even said goodbye.

But her words had never left him. *You are nothing more than a sheep in wolf's clothing.*

As if he were somehow good disguised as evil.

But he knew the truth. The truth was that he was wholly evil, wholly wicked. He was just damned, damned good at pretending otherwise.

And the fact that he could stroll through the court at Benalle Palace without so much as a second glance from even one of the guards was testament to that truth.

The fact that he had thought of Hania—a ghost of a past long-since forgotten, a dream long-since abandoned, washed up with the rest of the foolish things he had done—was the second strange thing he noticed about today.

And when he overheard something about "queen" and "kitchens," he strolled without fear, without remorse, down the black-and-white corridors of Benalle until he found himself on the threshold of the vast, hot kitchens below the castle.

And there, standing with her back to him, her black hair falling down her back in glossy curls crowned with a delicate gold circlet, her slender waist accentuated by a gown fit for a monarch, was his prey.

Chapter XXV

ods, she was beautiful.

He had forgotten how beautiful Adelaide of Haravelle was. She had only been a child the last time he had seen her. But she had been beautiful then, too, with hair like silken midnight and skin like velvet and ivory and cream. The blessing of some forgotten god, no doubt.

He stood at the threshold, watching her for a moment. So immersed in her work was she that he remained unnoticed. And so he studied her—this woman that would soon meet her end by his blade. There was something oddly familiar about her. In some ways, she reminded him of that inept stable girl Ferryl had insisted on hiring all those years ago. But of course, that was absurd.

But there was something else odd about her. A glow of sorts. She stood at a long table, pouring and mixing ingredients. A queen at work in the kitchens. Strange.

Where were the rest of the servants? The cooks?

Upstairs, preparing for the celebration that was taking place, no doubt.

Yes, this day was too perfect for words.

But suddenly and without warning, it hit him. That feeling. The same feeling he had had all those years ago when she was a child and he had been the most ambitious, the most ruthless, the most cunning general of the Midvarish army, one who called himself a Navarian commander.

He had forgotten it until now. Completely forgotten what he had felt that day.

But here, inexplicably, it was back. And not just back. But stronger. Infinitely stronger.

Like a fortress. Impenetrable. Formidable.

Protection.

Adelaide of Haravelle, Queen of Har-Navah was surrounded, fortified, held by an invisible force of the strongest kind of protection Titus had ever known.

Was it a spell? Some sort of magic? He had always known the Navarians and Haravellians had been stubbornly resistant to the idea of magic—a point which had played rather nicely into the hands of King Derrick. But had they figured it out? Had they learned that magic was very much real?

No, that couldn't be possible. Because they hadn't believed it fifteen years ago when she was a child.

He had felt the same protection then, too. Only not nearly as strongly.

It was the third strange thing about today.

But if it wasn't magic that surrounded her, protected her, then what? What was it?

Whatever it was, it was remarkable. Titus could feel its power as if it were a storm. A hurricane. It nearly choked the breath right out of him.

Which she must have noticed, because she turned to face him, and Titus was struck by the emerald in her eyes, by the look on her face. Struck to his core, dumbfounded and shaken.

Never, never in his life, had he questioned himself. Never had he second-guessed his instincts.

But here before him, the queen's eyes a battlefield, he knew no words.

Because in her eyes, it wasn't fear. It was—

"So you've returned for me," she said, staring into the steel-gray eyes of the man before her. The familiarity of them was almost haunting. A ghost of her past, returned to claim her once more.

Adelaide had known it. Somehow, she had known it for some time. And even this morning, she had felt it. Known that he was coming.

Today was the day she would be taken once more.

The man stood stock-still, his face strangely familiar and yet hauntingly dark. His eyes were rimmed with red, his skin sallow, his shoulders heavy with invisible burden. Drunk? Riddled with grief?

Perhaps both.

The silence hung between them, thick with unspoken truths.

But she would not flinch. Neither would he.

The distant sounds of returning servants began to fill the space between them. He had seconds to make a move before they saw him, seconds before they caught him in the middle of his treachery. She could run now. She could escape her fate.

Or she could face it.

In the briefest of moments—a flash so subtle, so quick she might have missed it—his silver eyes shone with wild, uninhibited rage.

And then he lunged for her, his strong arms a fortress of granite and sinew as he held her to him so tightly that there would be no chance of escape.

The last thing she remembered was a black cloth covering her face, her nose and mouth, and then a strange smell before the world became a blur of darkness and stars.

Chapter XXVI

ands trembling with rage and grief and disbelief pounded on the doors to Queen Mother Meria's chambers. "I don't care if you are indecent, I am coming in there," Ferryl raged before bursting through the door.

Meria sat on her chair before her window, the same way Ferryl had found her upon his return home weeks ago. This time, at the very least, her curtains were open. But still she wore her drab gowns—this one black and sadly out of fashion—and limping hairstyles. And her ashen face and sunken mouth were identical to the expression she'd had then.

He wanted to rage and scream and throttle her for all the lies, for all the secrets, for all she had done in the name of her own damned selfishness. He wanted to throttle her for daring to cry, to feign mourning his father.

"Your secret is out, Meria," he growled. No, he would not call her *Mother* any longer. This woman was not his mother. She was... she was nothing more than a monster.

Her black eyes met his, but she said not a word.

"I know the truth," he went on.

By the look in her eyes, he knew she was wondering: *which* truth?

Which secret? How many more did this woman bear? How many more lies?

"Tell me, how soon after you married my father did you decide to betray him? Was it immediately? Or was it by surprise that the charms of Prince Derrick of Midvar turned your head? Either way, my father—the best king this kingdom has ever known—was forced to pretend that the son of his enemy was his own. My father was forced to let the son of his enemy live and dwell among us for what? The hope that you'd love him again? I never knew my father to be a fool. I never knew he could be so stupid. But he was a fool, wasn't he? A fool to think that a lying bitch like you could ever love him."

"Ferryl," she breathed, thick tears falling fast down her gray cheeks. "Son."

"Don't you dare call me that," he growled. "I am not your son. And you are not my mother. You are dead to me, do you hear me? Dead. And so help me, I will see you pay for all your treachery. For all your scheming. Your lies."

She lifted her head, feigned dignity settling on her shoulders as tears spilled freely. "What is to become of me?"

"You can rot in Sheol for everything you've done," Ferryl spat. He stepped closer to her, his breath hot as it hit her face. "And until that blessed day, you can rot in the dungeons, for all I care."

Before Ferryl was even halfway out of her chambers, he called for the guards to shackle the woman he had called mother. Shackle her and carry her away to the deepest, darkest cell in the dungeon.

~

He needed her. He needed his wife. He needed to just see her emerald eyes and let them calm him. Let her nearness become a balm before he came apart into a thousand, broken, wretched pieces. He called to her through their bond, a tug on the perdurable, shimmering strand between them, birthday preparations be damned.

But he felt no answer.

"Brother?" he heard, and Ferryl whirled on his heel to find Derwin at the other end of the corridor through which he had been marching, a look of concerned confusion on his face—which was utterly unlike his usually hot-headed little brother.

Half brother.

Damn the world to Sheol.

"Are you all right?" Derwin tried again, walking toward Ferryl. "You look like you're ready to burn the castle down to nothing but ashes."

"Maybe I am," he scowled, wondering what to admit. Wondering what to tell Derwin. Wondering what his fiery little brother would say if he knew the truth. He deserved to know the truth.

But did he *need* to know it?

"What's happened? I left a meeting with my generals only to hear that you stripped Lord Westerly of his privileges and gave Delaney a duchy, or something like that." A smile threatened his mouth. "What's going on, Ferryl?"

Ferryl finally found the gumption to meet his brother's eyes. "It has been a trying day, and it's not even midday. I need a do-over, that's all."

"For what it's worth," Derwin said, clasping his hand on Ferryl's shoulder, "I'm glad you sacked the old bastard. I've hated him ever since he came sniffing around here trying to marry you off to his daughter. Did I ever tell you that Mother tried to get me to marry her after you rejected her?"

"What? No." How very little Ferryl had ever known of Derwin's personal life. How very close to the chest his brother had played his cards.

So much like his father. His *true* father.

Bile burned in the back of Ferryl's throat. Could he trust Derwin? Would Derwin turn into the same kind of monster as his father, the rutting king of Midvar?

"Ferryl, is something else the matter?"

"What? Oh, no. I just... Where is Adelaide?"

"I don't know. I haven't seen her. But listen to me, the generals are preparing for departure soon. I would like to begin dispatching the legions. Secretly, of course. Small bands of no more than fifty men at a time. We're going to work our way eastward and infiltrate the damned king of Midvar right under his nose. With your blessing, of course."

The damned king of Midvar. What would Derwin say of the man if he knew the truth? Ferryl shuddered at the idea of someone as cunning as Derwin swearing fealty to someone as ruthless as Derrick of Midvar.

But in truth, wouldn't that make Derwin the heir to the Midvarish throne?

And wouldn't that make Derwin Ferryl's sworn enemy?

Providence, where was the wine when he needed it?

"Ferryl? Do I have your permission to—"

"Yes, yes. Of course. Dispatch the legions. Let's finish this. I'm tired of talking about it."

A satisfied smile curled Derwin's mouth. "I'm glad to hear you say it."

Ferryl turned on his heel and marched away without another word.

~

"Avigail," Ferryl called when he spotted his mother-in-law coming from the back of the palace near the entrance to the servants' quarters. "Oh good. Have you seen Adelaide? Is she still in the kitchens?"

"No, I haven't seen her," said the former Haravellian queen, decked in a surprisingly simple gown and apron. "I was just coming to look for you and see where she had gotten off to. She must have left in a hurry."

"In a hurry? What do you mean?"

"I mean she left the batter half-mixed on the table. I assumed she needed something. Or perhaps you had called her away for something. I heard the meeting was—"

"But you haven't seen her?" Ferryl interjected, feeling a sudden, inexplicable wave of nausea come over him. He pulled on the bond between them again.

And again felt nothing.

"No," said Avigail. "I was running late this morning, so I didn't get to the kitchens as early as we had planned. But when I arrived, she was already gone."

He pulled again on the bond between them.

No, not pulled. Yanked.

Adelaide. Where are you, my love? You have us in a state.

But he neither heard nor felt a reply. Something like knee-wobbling panic stole over him.

Avigail must have spotted it. "Ferryl, sweetheart," she said, stepping to him that she might place a calming hand on his arm. "What's wrong?"

"I don't...I don't know where she is."

"I'm sure she's around here somewhere, darling. There is no need to panic. Perhaps she is in the ballroom with the servants."

"Yes. Perhaps," he said absently. But he knew the truth. He knew it in his bones. Her haunting silence screamed it at him.

~

"Where is Amos?" Ferryl asked the nearest guard.

"He is in his office, Your Majesty," said the guard, a bow slung at his side.

"Find him at once. Do not delay."

"Yes, Your Majesty," said the guard before he trotted away.

"I'm sure there is no need to call on the guards, Ferryl. Adelaide is likely—"

"Yes, I'm sure she is fine, Avigail," Ferryl lied. "But in light of the events at the coronation ball, I am unwilling to take risks where my wife is concerned. I'm sure you understand."

"Of course, Ferryl," she replied, and at the quiet understanding in her tone, he felt like an ass. Of course she understood. She of all people in the world would understand.

"Ferryl," she said, her voice warm and calming as she placed her hands on his shoulders. He hadn't even realized she had stepped in front of him as they stood in front of the entrance to the ballroom. "Breathe, my son. She is fine, I am sure of it. The magic within you is much more powerful than you know."

The magic within him? What magic? He hadn't felt anything—anything at all—since his coronation day. "Wh—?"

"Your Majesty," said a young page, cutting him off. "I was told to find you straight away. Lord Michael has asked me to inform you that he is—"

"Where is Michael?" Ferryl interrupted.

"He is with Mistress Dupree, Your Majesty," said the page.

"Tell him I need him."

"I will, Your Majesty, but I don't think he is—"

"I don't care what he is doing. Tell him I need him. Now."

The page boy trembled as he took his bow and left with a quiet, "Yes, Your Majesty."

He tugged again on the bond. Hard. Still, there was only deafening silence.

Another bout of nausea assailed him.

"Ferryl, darling, maybe you should sit down," said Avigail, ushering Ferryl to the nearest seat.

It was Leala who strode up next. "What's going on? Where's Adelaide?"

"We're not sure," said Avigail, a solid hand on Ferryl's shoulder. "We're just trying to find her now."

"I thought she was supposed to be in the kitchens baking a—I mean working on a surprise for Ferryl," said Leala.

"She was. She is not there now," said Ferryl.

"Who's not there?" they heard, turning to see Derwin walk up.

"Adelaide. Ferryl can't seem to find her," said Leala.

Derwin slung a heavy arm around his wife's shoulder. "Have you checked the kitchens? She—"

"Yes, we've checked the kitchens," Ferryl spat, irritated to have to keep repeating himself. He tried to still his thoughts, tried to quiet the raging fear that was drowning everything out louder and louder. Tried to listen for a sign, a flicker, anything to tell him his greatest fear hadn't come true.

But still, there was nothing coming from her end of the bond between them.

It was then, in his peripheral vision, that he saw them.

Moths.

Dark færies.

Black and swarming. By the hundreds.

As if this day hadn't been shitty enough on its own. He wondered if anyone else could see them.

"How about your chambers?" Leala offered. "She's been tired lately. Perhaps she went for a nap or—"

"Check them if you like," Ferryl said.

"Why in Sheol don't *you?*" Derwin growled.

"Derwin," Avigail placated.

"No, let him. This is what he's good at, isn't it? Acting like an ass at the least opportune moment," said Ferryl.

"Ferryl," Avigail said, a question and surprise in her tone.

Ferryl dared to meet Derwin's eyes for a moment, only to find disgust in them. He couldn't hold them for long before he turned to

Leala. But she...Leala's eyes held something else entirely. Not disgust. Not even disappointment. It was... it was...

"Where is she, Ferryl?" Leala asked.

"I think we've already established that—"

But Leala cut Derwin off with a hand to his chest. "No. Where is Adelaide, Ferryl?"

Ferryl turned his gaze away. For to admit that he knew she wasn't here would be to admit—

"You know where she is, don't you? Or rather, you know where she is not," said Leala.

"What in Sheol are you talking about?" Derwin asked.

"She's gone, isn't she?" Leala continued. "She's gone, and you know it."

"How could he know such a thing?" Derwin scoffed.

Ferryl slid his eyes to Avigail, where a thin line of silver tears threatened to fall. It struck him then how much his wife looked like her mother. The same cascade of inky tresses, the same alabaster skin. But where Adelaide's eyes were as green as emeralds, Avigail's eyes were like molten gold and starlight.

An ache tore at his heart. He looked back to Leala. Bold, clever Leala who had figured out what no one else had.

"He knows because he can read her thoughts. And she can read his. And he can't hear her anymore."

Chapter XXVII

ichael wiped away the sweat pouring down his brow and took a shuddering breath, thinking himself pathetically weak for being so panicked when she—sweet, beloved Delaney—was really the one to be worried about.

He had sent for Mary. Several times, actually. But no one had returned with her. He was about ready to go and find the old healer himself when Delaney cried out in agony again.

He hated, absolutely *hated* how helpless he felt as he knelt beside the bed, holding her clammy hand tightly, willing her to breathe, breathe, breathe as she worked through the pain that seemed to be coming in waves every few minutes.

Her time, indeed.

Providence above, how any woman had survived the pain, much less the fear of childbirth was a mystery he would never be able to unravel so long as he lived. It was a wonder any woman ever wanted children. Much less more than one.

A warrior, that's what Delaney was, pure and simple. A warrior of the bravest and most valiant nature to face such a feat without tears, without panic. She just endured. Pain after agonizing pain.

If he thought he had loved her before, he knew now that he had only scratched the surface of the kind of abiding love he could hold for this woman before him.

He wiped her sweat-dampened brow with a cool cloth as the most recent pain mercifully began to subside.

"Where is Mary?" she asked, her voice strained and raspy.

"I've sent for her," he answered, helplessly.

Damn it, where was Mary?

"We need her here, Michael. The baby is coming soon," Delaney said, and though he saw that she tried to hide it, he could hear the rising panic in her voice. And how right she was. For if Mary didn't arrive soon, what would happen? Would he have to deliver the baby himself? And how could he possibly manage such a feat? He had no clue what to do. What if he hurt her? What if he hurt the baby?

Damn you, Mary. Where are you?

"I'm going to go and find her," he said, rising to his feet, swallowing down the panic that was threatening to engulf him.

A clammy hand gripped his own. "Don't leave me, Michael. Please."

And how could he refuse those eyes of hers, those lashes that went on for miles? He knelt again beside her and kissed her cheek in solidarity. "I won't leave you. I promise. Only let me go and speak with one of the guards. I cannot imagine what is keeping her."

She only nodded, another pain coming on. She shut her eyes tightly, managing to wave him away before the pain became too much.

Michael couldn't run fast enough to the door.

"What is your name?" he asked when he tore through it and found a young, new guard standing by.

"Peter, my lord," the guard said, bowing at the waist.

"Peter," Michael repeated. "I need you to do something very important for me."

"Of course, Lord Chancellor," said the boy, his eyes lighting up with eager anticipation that the king's second-in-command should need his help. Word in this castle apparently traveled fast.

"I need you to go and find the healer. Mary is her name. Do you know her?"

"I know of her, my lord, yes."

"Do you know where to find her?"

"At the back of the palace, my lord. In the rooms just above the kitchens."

"Good. Go and fetch her now, do you hear me? Do not delay. This is of utmost importance."

"Of course, my lord," Peter said, bowing again before scurrying off.

Michael did not like that the fate of the unborn child in Delaney's womb—*his* unborn child, because if she (if indeed, she was a girl) hadn't been before, she most certainly was now that he had claimed her before the whole of the council—rested in the hands of one very young, untested guard. He did not like it one bit.

A young page, the one he had sent an hour ago to find Ferryl, ran down the corridor towards him as if on a mission.

"Boy!" Michael called. "Where is the king?"

"He has asked for you, my lord," the boy said, clearly nervous. "He wants you to meet him at once."

"Did you tell him I need him?" he asked, exasperated.

"He did not give me the option, my lord."

Did not give him the option?

"Boy, I cannot see the king right now. I need…" Damn it all, he needed too many things. A healer, for one. Help. A damned vat of the hardest whiskey possible.

A whimpering cry jerked his attention back to his bedchamber. Without another word, he left the pageboy to wonder what could possibly be going on.

~

"The bed, Michael," she said as he tore into the room. "It's all wet."

A crashing wave of panic rushed over him. "What—what does it mean? Are you all right?"

"It's my waters, Michael. It means the baby will be here soon. Where is Mary?"

"She is coming," he lied again. "She'll be here."

Delaney let out another agonized cry, this one so great that Michael fell to his knees beside her, gripping her hand, supporting her back as she leaned into her belly, gritting her teeth as she held her breath.

"She's coming, Michael. I can feel her. You're going to have to do this."

Do what? Oh Providence above, what was he supposed to do?

"Get some fresh cloths," she managed between ragged breaths. "And a blanket to wrap the baby."

Thank Providence Delaney had had so many younger sisters, that she had witnessed her mother giving birth so many times. Otherwise, what would he have done but stood like a fool beside her bed? He wasn't doing much more than that as it was.

Still, he obeyed her commands and had cloths and a blanket ready at the foot of the bed.

But he wasn't prepared when she pulled at the hem of her skirts, revealing her bare legs, clammy with sweat, her delicate underthings. And when he had to pull them off himself—

He would remain forever grateful in that moment that she couldn't read his thoughts. That she couldn't know what an animal he must have been that even in her agony, even in the stress of the moment, all he could think of was how beautiful she was, how much he wanted her, how ironic it was that the first time he should remove said delicate underthings would be in such a moment.

It was enough that he couldn't help the hysterical little yelp of a laugh or the small tear that escaped him.

She, mercifully, was too wrapped up in another one of her pains to notice.

So he wiped the ridiculous tear away, steeled himself to man up again, and gripped her hand as she leaned into the pains, her face and arms red with the strain.

"I can feel her, Michael!" she cried, her voice colored with hysteria.

And Michael looked down to find that he could see the baby. He could *see* it.

The baby was almost here.

So when the baby finally emerged, when one agonizing push after another had finally subsided and he held the baby in his arms, it was Michael who wept. Michael who couldn't help the tears that escaped him as he held the beautiful little miracle in his arms.

A girl, of course.

He laughed at the sweet, exhilarating bliss of it.

~

It took him a full minute to even register what he held in his arms. A child. *Their* child. And Providence above, she was the most beautiful thing he had ever laid eyes on. So he pressed a kiss to her tiny, delicate, velvety little brow and wept for sheer joy.

It was then, of course, that Mary bustled into the room, flustered and fussing over the scene before her.

"Heavens, child, look at you!" Mary cried.

Michael mechanically handed the baby to Mary, who looked her over for only a moment before handing her back to Michael. She patted his hand as he took her.

"You did this, son? You helped Delaney by yourself?"

He could only nod and look at Delaney, who gave him a sweet, exhausted smile.

"Is the baby all right, Mary?" Delaney asked.

"She's perfect. You're a natural, honey. You both are."

"She?" Delaney asked.

"It's a girl," Michael said, laughing at the notion that he hadn't thought to tell her the sex of her own child.

"Oh," was all Delaney could manage.

Michael let Mary take the baby from his arms again, absently registering the old woman as she fussed with twine and a small blade, but too distracted by just how gorgeous Delaney looked to pay much attention to what the healer was doing. The love of his life lay with hair tangled around her sweat-dampened face, her skin glowing like the light from the first stars at dusk. He couldn't help but to press a kiss to her brow, tuck a strand of hair behind her ear, find her lips, and kiss them softly. To his utter and complete delight, Delaney returned the kiss intently, placing her hands on either side of his face and meeting his eyes when it was over with a kind of gratitude he knew he would not soon forget. A moment later, Mary brought a tight little bundle of blankets to Delaney, placing the baby in her mother's arms for the very first time.

Delaney let out a little sob that might have been a laugh as she held the little miracle close, pressing her cheek to her tiny little brow. She kissed the baby's nose and fished for her tiny hands, pressing kisses to each of her miniature fingers, as if she couldn't get to know her daughter fast enough.

Michael only smiled as he crawled onto the bed beside Delaney and watched the scene unfold. And when Delaney had finally satiated her need to coddle and fawn over her new little gift and sleep finally found the exhausted new mother, Michael found he couldn't resist it either and soon fell asleep beside the two most precious girls in his life.

It was only a small noise. But it had been enough to stir her, so Delaney looked around Michael's bedchamber. Mary was approaching from his sitting room.

"Just returning to check on you, honey," Mary said kindly.

"I didn't realize you had left," said Delaney groggily.

Mary patted her hand. "I left about an hour ago. You three were sleeping so soundly that I didn't want to disturb you. I decided I'd come back for the baby later."

Come back for the baby? Wh—

"How are you feeling, honey?" Mary asked, interrupting Delaney's thoughts.

"Oh. I'm all right. Tired, I guess."

"Any pain?"

"Not too bad, I suppose."

Delaney stole a glance at Michael, who slept soundly beside her on his bed, one arm slung protectively over her and the baby. She couldn't resist smiling.

But then the baby stirred in her arms with soft little coos and a precious little grimace as she practiced opening her perfect little rosebud mouth. A chuckle of delight escaped Delaney.

"She's absolutely beautiful, honey. It will be so nice to have a baby in the castle again. It has been so long."

The conversation stirred Michael, who stretched a bit before sitting up beside Delaney and kissing her temple before asking her how she felt.

"I feel fine, actually. Just tired," Delaney admitted. "And a little hungry."

"Why don't I send for some food and the wet nurse? That way you can get a proper rest with a full belly," said Mary.

"The wet nurse? What for?" Delaney asked.

"The baby will be hungry, too, of course," Mary said. "I'll send for her at once so that—"

"I don't want a wet nurse," Delaney protested.

"And let a proper lady of the court nurse her own child? What's to become of this world?" Mary laughed.

"But I want to feed her," Delaney said, looking to Michael for support. He placed a solid, warm hand at the small of her back.

"Whyever would you want to do that, child?"

Because she couldn't stand the idea of anyone else holding her. Feeding her. Because she didn't give a damn about what was or wasn't proper for a woman of the court. She wasn't a woman of the court. She was a nobody. And this nobody had every intention of nursing her own infant, thank you very much. "Because she's my daughter."

Mary raised a skeptical brow. "Do you know what you're doing?"

"I saw my mother nurse my little sister, Dinah." Because she had insisted. Her father had scoffed, claiming only country maids and gypsies nursed their own children, not duchesses. But her mother hadn't cared. Perhaps she knew Dinah would be the last baby she would hold. Perhaps she knew that she wouldn't survive another one. And she hadn't. She had never even gotten to hold Dysis when she was born. But Delaney had never forgotten the pure contentment that had poured from her mother every time she brought Dinah to her breast. It was one of the few times she remembered her mother smiling.

So by Providence, she would nurse her own child. And no one and nothing would stop her.

Michael rubbed his hand up and down her back, and when she met his eyes, she found only pride in them. It gave her the gumption to say, "I'll call you if I need your help, Mary. Thank you."

Mary only bowed her head and left the room again without another word.

"I think you may be the strongest, bravest person I know," Michael said.

"I very much doubt that."

"I don't," he said, kissing her softly. They were soon distracted by another annoyed little coo from the baby, at which they both chuckled. Apparently, Delaney wasn't the only one hungry.

Delaney began unlacing the top of her shift.

"I'll send for something to eat," Michael said, moving to get up from the bed.

"You don't have to leave. I'm not embarrassed."

Michael chuckled. "After having witnessed you give birth, I can say without hesitation that I am not embarrassed either, beautiful. But food does sound good, doesn't it?"

Delaney smiled. Yes, it sounded wonderful.

"Michael," she said, placing a hand on his arm before he could get away. "Thank you. For everything. I don't know what I would have done without you."

He tucked a strand of hair behind her ear. "Allowing me to be here, allowing me to help, Delaney, you have given me a sweeter gift than I ever thought possible. I am the one who is in your debt."

She smiled contentedly as Michael made his way to his closet, emerging a few minutes later wearing a fresh shirt and having freshly his combed hair. He winked at Delaney before disappearing into the sitting room beyond.

So she turned her attention to the little one in her arms, unable to stifle the wide grin that turned her mouth. She brought the baby to her lips, pressing a kiss to her impossibly soft cheeks, running a delicate hand over the soft, downy hair that covered her tiny head.

"I love you so much, my darling. Do you have any idea?"

Another little coo, this one accompanied with a cry.

"All right, all right," she chuckled. "You shall have your feast, my little princess."

So she brought the baby to her breast, thinking herself either as brave as Michael seemed to think or the world's biggest fool. For she soon realized she had absolutely no idea what she was doing. Whatsoever.

To her utter surprise, however, the baby seemed to be an expert at procuring her dinner, for she soon latched to her mother's breast with a tenacity that both shocked and delighted Delaney. She giggled with mirth at the strength with which she suckled and kissed her baby's brow once more.

"Yes, my darling. I love you very, very much."

Chapter XXVIII

e could hear them: his brother, his sister-in-law, his wife's parents. They bustled around his sitting room, their voices frustrated.

"What in Sheol is wrong with him? Why is he acting like this?"

"He can't hear her, Derwin. He can't feel her thoughts. He thinks she's—"

"Bullshit. That's what it is. Bullshit. No one can hear thoughts. He's just being an insufferable coward, that's what. He needs to get off his ass and find his wife before something actually happens to her!"

"Do you believe he can hear her thoughts, Your Majesty?"

"I've suspected it for a while. I've heard of such magic before. But it's rare. Powerful. If he cannot hear her anymore—"

"Magic or not, it doesn't excuse him holing himself up in his chambers when he could be out looking for her himself. He's acting just like Mother!"

Ferryl had had enough. Enough of Derwin's ranting. Enough of hearing them postulate as to his wife's whereabouts when he knew the truth. So he stood, swatted at the swarm of moths-that-were-not-moths that surrounded him, taunted him, teased him, and opened his bedchamber door.

Sudden silence greeted him on the other side.

"Finally decided to do something?" Derwin chided.

Ferryl glared at this brother who was not the son of his father, wondering what he would ever say if his true parentage ever came out. What Ferryl would tell him.

A knock sounded at the doors. All eyes turned to see a guard enter and bow. "Lord Michael, Your Majesty." Michael entered behind the guard, apology in his features.

"Michael," Derwin said. "Where have you been? We've called for you several times."

"I apologize for my absence," he answered.

"Is everything all right?" Leala asked, stepping toward him.

"Yes, everything is fine. I just—Delaney, she... she had the baby."

"Oh, Michael," said Avigail.

Leala hugged Michael tightly. "That's wonderful, Michael. Just wonderful."

"How is she?" Avigail asked.

"She and the baby are well, Your Majesty. Thank you for asking." Michael bowed his head in gratitude. "I am sorry I was unable to come when you called, Ferryl. I hope you—"

"I understand, Michael," Ferryl said, waving off his friend.

"There is nothing you could do anyway," said Derwin, crossing one leg over the other as he sat back in his chair. "Ferryl is apparently content to sit on his ass."

Ferryl scowled at his mouthy brother. *Half* brother.

"Do about what?" Michael asked. "What is wrong? And where are all the servants? Shouldn't the celebration start soon?"

"The celebration has been canceled," Leala said grimly.

"What? Why? It's your birthday, Ferryl," said Michael.

No one seemed to want to answer. Certainly not Ferryl. The room was painfully quiet for a moment before King Aaron finally spoke up. "We cannot find our daughter, Michael."

"Cannot *find* her?" Michael asked, as if such a question were absurd.

"She has been missing since this morning," Leala went on. "No one seems to have seen her."

"Wasn't she supposed to be in the kitchens?" Michael asked.

"Yes. And by the looks of things, she was. For a time, anyway. But she left. Apparently in a hurry."

"Left. Or was taken." The words that came out of Ferryl's mouth tasted bitter on his lips.

"But who would…?"

"I don't have to know *who* to know where they were from," Ferryl replied grimly. "Shouldn't we have seen this coming? Perhaps Westerly was right. Perhaps I've been too naïve when it comes to King Derrick. I thought the guards were better than this. I thought—"

"They *are* better than this," Michael retorted, startled. His whole body rebelled against the notion of it being their fault. "Our guards are the best in the realm. If someone took her, they did so with inside knowledge of their rotations. There is no way, especially now that security has been doubled, that someone could have taken the queen in plain sight."

"An insider…" Derwin agreed. "Or a wraith. I've seen those Midvarish soldier bastards myself. They are not normal. They have this… this ability to…"

"Appear out of nowhere. And disappear just the same," Ferryl finished.

An understanding Ferryl couldn't place shone in Michael's eyes.

Understanding... and fear. But he seemed keen to help. "Tell me what is being done, and I will see to it that steps are taken to—"

It was Derwin who spoke up. "I've sent out several detachments of soldiers into the city. They have been instructed to leave no stone unturned. And security at the castle has been increased tenfold. The castle, too, is still being searched."

"What can I do?" Michael asked Derwin.

The Commander Prince stood, and the full measure of his power seemed to stand with him. "I am sending the first of the advance guard out at dawn. The regiment will begin advancement after that. We are moving forward with the plan to infiltrate Midvar. However, in light of the fact that our queen is missing, and since we know damn well they are the culprits, we no longer have the luxury of taking our time about the infiltration. I have instructed my men to slaughter any Midvarish men they find along the way—soldiers or rebels or just damned sympathizers. I know of your new duties, but in light of what has happened to our queen, I am asking you, Michael, to lead the first battalion. I need you as one of my captains."

"Me, Derwin?" Michael asked. "I—"

"You were trained under Commander Titus, same as I. Everyone knew you were his favorite, and for good reason. You are smart, Michael. And you are the best archer in the kingdom. You saved our queen's life once. I am asking you to do it again. We need you to lead the charge, to help find our queen. Your battalion leaves in three days."

Ferryl could see it in Michael's eyes—the determination, the unending ocean of loyalty that colored his very being. But there was something else now. A trepidation, however small. A downright fear. And Ferryl had a pretty good idea where that fear originated.

For the sake of just one woman. Those words he had once said to his friend—had once chastised him with. King Ferryl, unable to feel the sweet rush of his wife's soul tethered to his, wondered now what either of them would do for the sake of just one woman.

Michael, ever the valiant soldier, squared his shoulders, met Derwin's gaze, and said, "Whatever is needed of me, I will gladly do."

And it was then that Ferryl knew Michael was a better man than he.

~

"I'll never understand you," Derwin said, lingering behind in Ferryl's chambers long after everyone else had departed. It was well into the night, the stars shining brightly in the first clear sky in months. Mocking him.

"Why aren't you out there looking for her, Ferryl?"

"Because there is nothing to find."

"And how in Sheol do you know that?"

"Because I just know," Ferryl said flatly, absently, pulling on the bond between them just once more. Knowing he would feel nothing, just as he had felt nothing since this morning. The silence had been a telling haunt. A taunt.

"If it were my wife, I wouldn't rest until I found her. Nothing— not even the fires of Sheol—would stop me until she was safe in my arms again."

"Well, then I guess you're a better man than I," Ferryl hissed as he stared out his windows across the plains that stretched before him to the moonlit ocean that lapped lazily along the cliff's edge.

"I never thought I was. All my life I knew you were the better man. And I was glad it would be you that would reign and not me. I was glad of it because you've always been a good man, Ferryl. A good man like Father. But now..."

"But now what?" Ferryl spat, turning to face his brother. Those words...the things Derwin was saying... *A good man like Father...*they burned like bile in his throat.

"I don't understand you anymore. Something has changed in you since returning home. You're not..."

"Not what?"

"Not the man I thought you were. You're angry, Ferryl. Angry and bitter. With good reason, I'm sure. But I've never known you to be like that. That was supposed to be my job. I'm the angry second son. You're the optimistic king. You have a marriage most men would kill for. You are the ruler of the most powerful kingdom in the realm. And yet you sit in your chambers as if there is nothing you can do about what has happened. War has been waged upon you, with your wife as bait, and your reaction is to hide."

"She is not missing, Derwin."

"And how do you know that?" Derwin growled, exacerbated.

"Because I know it." In his bones, he knew it. And if the silence across their bond hadn't been enough, then the hundred dark færies that plagued him surely told him the truth. The facts he had always known somewhere deep down.

He wasn't good enough. Not for his kingdom, and certainly not for her. He didn't deserve her.

And now, she was gone forever.

Taken.

Dead.

Grief threatened to swallow him whole even as his eyes blurred with heavy tears.

"Stop this," Derwin said, grabbing Ferryl's shoulders and shaking him. "Get ahold of yourself, Ferryl. You are King of Har-Navah for Providence's sake!"

A man is only as good as the woman beside him. That was what he had once told Adelaide. And a king was only as good as the queen beside him.

Had it been an omen?

Because without her... without Adelaide...

"Damn it, Ferryl, I am leaving tomorrow! I am leaving my wife behind! I am leaving to fight this war, to end this madness, and to find *your* wife. Don't make me leave like this. Don't make me wonder what's to happen to my kingdom while I'm gone. You're not the only one with the lives of people you love at stake. Stop acting like it, and get yourself together."

"She was pregnant, Derwin. Did you know that?" To say it...to admit it...the sting of her absence worsened, a keen, sharp pain in his gut.

"All the more reason to fight! All the more reason to utilize every resource, to stop at nothing until she is found!"

"She won't be found, Derwin. She won't be found because she is de—"

The fist at his mouth came at him so fast he hadn't even realized what was happening until he wiped his lips to find blood on his fingers.

He took a second to right himself, his balance thrown off by the power of his brother's blow. Then he met Derwin's eyes, gleaming with cool, calculated rage. Derwin: the half-blooded warrior. Derwin: the bastard son of the king of Midvar.

Ferryl's rage brimmed to a boil.

"She is not dead," Derwin gritted through his teeth. "But you will be before I'm through with you if you don't pull your head out of your ass."

As if something snapped, Ferryl launched himself at his little brother. At the son of his greatest enemy. He did not hold back a shred of the fury in his veins, unleashing himself on the dark angel he had once called brother.

Chapter XXIX

"Pardon me," said Titus as he fumbled through the crowded streets, helping the person he had accidentally bumped into. A girl, he realized. But it wasn't until he took hold of her elbow to keep her from falling that he realized who she was.

The blonde girl. The one he had seen several times since his garrison had been stationed in Benalle City weeks ago. He had run into her once before. When she had told him her name.

Possibly the most beautiful name he had ever heard.

"Oh, Hania," he said, stupidly. He should have pretended that he couldn't remember her name, that he hadn't run the image of her unforgettable face over and over in his head for the past few weeks.

"Titus, right?" she said, smiling not only with her supple mouth, but with her liquid gold eyes, with her whole being, it seemed. He found himself bewitched by that smile.

He handed her the basket he had accidentally knocked out of her arms, clumsily replacing the apples that had also fallen.

"We keep running into each other, don't we?"

"So it seems," he said, knowing he was a fool for letting himself look at her at all. He was Midvarish. A Midvarish soldier.

And she an innocent, young, virginal Navarian woman. Girl, really. Well, if she was a girl, then he was still a boy, for surely she was close to his age.

But gods, that sun-kissed hair. Those lips. Those eyes...

"Looking for anything in particular?" she asked, gesturing to the market around them.

Vendors lined the streets selling their wares—fruits and vegetables, handmade baskets and jewelry, but no one seemed to have what he was looking for.

"Yes, actually," he said.

"What's that?" she asked, mirth and innocence coloring her singsong voice.

"Feathers."

"Feathers?"

"Pheasant, to be precise."

"You're kidding, right?"

"No, why?"

"Come with me," she said.

And for reasons he never understood, he followed her without hesitation.

She led him down the bustling, cobblestone streets of the city to the outskirts of town, following a winding path through the countryside until she turned at a sycamore, her basket swinging this way and that on her arm as she walked and munched on an apple. When she offered one to Titus, he refused.

"Where are we going, exactly?" he asked her as they trod a muddy, well-worn path.

"My family's farm. My father raises pheasants, among other fowl."

"What?"

Sure enough, no sooner had he asked it than he looked ahead and saw, or rather heard the proof of her claims. Clucks and caws, a grassless, fenced field, and there before him, amongst a few errant birds, a sea of discarded feathers.

Pheasant feathers.

Immediately, he spotted several that were perfect.

It was only as he bent to pick one up that she asked, "So what do you need feathers for?"

"Fletching."

"Fletching?"

"Arrows. The feathers on arrows." He handed her a particularly beautiful feather, colored in a perfect pattern of sienna and cream, its length and rigidity the perfect make for his handmade arrows.

"Ah," she said. "So you're an archer."

He nodded. "I prefer my own arrows to those that are supplied. So I'm constantly on the hunt for feathers, as it were."

"Well then, Titus the Soldier, it would seem that you and I were meant to meet," she said with that bewitching smile of hers.

He found himself smiling back despite himself. "Should you be helping me?"

"Why shouldn't I?"

"Well, these feathers are for my arrows. And I am your enemy, after all."

She pursed a smile that somehow made her lips even plumper, softer. "The way I see it, you've never done anything to me, have you? And I've never done anything to you. Why should we be enemies just because our kings can't seem to get along?"

That, he realized, was probably the most logical thing he had ever heard. And consequently, he had no argument.

"Will you show me?" she went on.

"Show you what?"

"How to wield a bow? I've never shot one before."

"It's not appropriate for ladies," he answered quickly, thinking he had already spent enough time with the beautiful Navarian stranger.

She stepped closer, plucking another feather from his hand, her delicate fingers sending a thrill straight to his gut as they brushed against his. She said, "Well then, lucky for you, I'm no lady."

He cleared his throat in an attempt to clear his head. "Then what are you?"

"A nobody. A nobody who wants to know everything, see everything, do everything. And I'll start with shooting a bow, if you don't mind."

She plucked a few more feathers from the ground before marching off towards the surrounding woods. Again, he found himself following her as if she were a flickering candle and he a hapless moth in the darkness.

"Now where are we going?" he asked, struggling to keep up with her. She obviously knew this terrain well; this land that was so very different from the rolling hills of his home in Midvar. Perhaps she would be a useful way to spend his spare time, after all. That's what he would tell his captain, anyway, when he found out that Titus was traipsing about the countryside with a Navarian girl instead of busying himself with his actual job of keeping would-be rebellions from forming in the city. The Navarians, it seemed, were not fans of the Midvarish occupation of the city. Not that Titus could blame them. But those rebellions that popped up nearly every day were a damned nuisance.

"We'll need a place to shoot that bow of yours, won't we? I figure we could start out here."

~

Teaching a gorgeous young woman how to shoot a bow ended up being a rather delightful way to pass the time. Titus stood close behind her. Dangerously close. He could smell the soap in her hair, the remnants of her perfume as his arms wrapped around hers, helping her properly hold the bow, of course.

"Use three fingers, like this," he said, placing her delicate, soft fingers on the string. "The arrow rests between these two fingers."

"There is a lot more to shooting a bow than I had assumed," she said, never once complaining.

He huffed a laugh in her ear as he said, "Hold your elbow a little higher. Yes, perfect. And rest your finger on your lips."

"Like this?" she asked.

Yes, like that. Perfect, damn it. He had very much wanted to correct her if only for the excuse to touch her mouth.

"Exactly. It will help you aim. A guide, you see."

"Oh yes, I see," she replied. She kept those golden eyes keen and sharp on the tree across the forest. Had she been a soldier in training, she would have been his favorite.

"Now the secret is, when you release the arrow, don't be afraid of the string. Let it go gently in one fluid movement. Like this," he said, pulling the string back with her hand under his, his other arm stretched alongside hers to grip the bow.

When he released the arrow, he paid no attention to where it might land, too distracted by the keen determination in Hania's young eyes as she studied all he had taught her.

"You're very good," she said, and it was only when he turned to survey the tree they had marked that he realized he had hit the target with deadly perfection.

"Now you give it a try," he said.

"On my own?"

"Why not?"

The look in her eyes was positively wicked as she nocked another arrow from his quiver and replicated every instruction he had given her with perfection. She released the arrow in one fluid motion, and Titus watched as her arrow hit very close to his own.

"You're a natural," he said, awestruck. And not just by her accuracy with a bow.

"I have a very good teacher," she said with a flirtatious smile.

"I've never taught anyone that before," he admitted.

"You're an excellent marksman."

"The captain says I'm the best he's ever seen. I don't know if that's true, though."

"Well you're the best I've ever seen, so that has to count for something."

"Have you ever even seen another archer before?"

"No, but what does that have to do with anything?"

Titus couldn't help laughing.

"What a pair we would make!" she went on. "Can you imagine it? We could tear up the world, you and I. Two soldiers of fortune, forging a path across the lands with nothing more than quivers on our backs and bows in our hands. Nothing could stop us!"

"How you talk," he said. "Is that your dream? To be a soldier of fortune?"

She laughed. "Oh I have many, many dreams, Titus the Soldier. Too many to count."

"Tell me one of them," he said. But he regretted the question the moment he saw the look on her face—the wonder and innocence, so mesmerizing and beautiful.

"I want to see everything. I want to travel the world. I want to die knowing I'd lived." She took another arrow from his quiver, nocking it in the bow. "And I want to love deeply, wholly, irresistibly. And I want to be loved the same in return."

He couldn't help the incredulous laugh that escaped his nose.

"What? Don't you believe in love?"

"No," he admitted. "Love is for dreamers. Not soldiers. And certainly not me."

"Don't you plan to marry someday?" she asked, pulling back the bowstring, her eyes keen on the target across the forest.

A shrug. "Soldiers, as a rule, don't make very good husbands."

She released the arrow. Another excellent hit, just off the bullseye.

"Well, I have every intention of marrying a man I cannot resist. And who, consequently, cannot resist me, either." At her declaration, he didn't miss the kiss of color that found her cheeks, her delicate neck. She did not meet his eyes as she bent to retrieve another arrow.

"Is that what you believe love is? Something you cannot resist?"

"I certainly hope so," she replied, pulling back the bowstring again. This time, she hit the bullseye with the kind of precision most seasoned archers take years to achieve.

"And what is it that you want, Titus?" she asked.

"Nothing, I suppose."

"Don't you have a dream?" she asked, lowering her bow and turning to face him.

He shrugged. A dream? Hardly. At eighteen years old, he had hardly taken the time to consider dreaming anything extraordinary for his life. He barely took the time to consider much more than each day as they came. Still, though, he realized there was something he wanted. Something he hoped for. "I suppose all I really want is to matter. To do something important."

Her eyes held his with tenacity, with a sincerity that nearly knocked the breath out of him.

"Well then, you shall, Titus the Soldier. You shall do something that will change the world forever."

~

Why in Sheol he was thinking—no, dreaming—remembering Hania at such a time, he would never understand. His days, his thoughts had been plagued with Penelope. With longing for her.

Missing her touch, her scent, her nearness, the peace of sleeping beside her, holding her in his arms. Every passing day had brought more of the ache for her that wouldn't quit.

But the nights, for some reason, were for Hania. For the girl of his youth: his first love. Every night for the past four nights he had dreamt of her. Of meeting her. Of their days spent in the forest near Benalle City when he was nothing more than a boy given a man's arsenal of weaponry and told to defend the interests of his king and she an innocent young farmer's daughter with big dreams and an even bigger heart.

She plagued his dreams with a kind of persistence that unnerved him.

But the fact that she was beginning to plague his thoughts, too...

The memory of her words, of that way she had of piercing right to his soul—*You shall do something that will change the world forever.*

How very, very wrong she had been.

Unless by changing the world forever, she had meant murdering an innocent queen for the sake of revenge. In that case, she had been absolutely correct.

And he *would* murder her. Just as soon as he found the right place, the right time.

For now, though, he very much needed a drink. A very, very strong drink.

How convenient, then, that he, his horse, and his stolen wagon with his still unconscious contraband had come across a tavern a few days' ride outside the city. A tavern he knew just happened to patronize Midvarish sympathizers. He strapped the horse to a post outside the ramshackle building and dismounted, trusting that even if the powerful herbs he had given the queen wore off, the locks on the wagon would keep her securely inside.

And a drink sounded damn good.

The tavern was full. Shockingly full. Men of all ages and ranks filled it to the brim—at tables that peppered the center of the room, in shoddy booths that lined the perimeter, at stools that lined a cedar bar that stretched along the back. Some soldiers slipped in and out with that unsettling, phantom-like way they had of slipping in and out of spaces. A common man when they needed to be, an asp slithering through the grasses when it was convenient. Titus, half-blood that he was, had never possessed that distinctively Midvarish ability. Oh, Midvarish blood flowed through his veins, to be sure. But his paternal grandmother had been Haravellian. And it was rumored that his own mother had come to this continent with her family when she was only a baby. For all intents and purposes, Titus was a mutt with a little extra helping of that supposed preternatural blood. But what he lacked in preternatural ability, he made up for tenfold in ruthlessness, which was what, consequently, kept prying eyes from scrutinizing him too much.

Titus had never really known how many of his Midvarish brothers were truly pure-blooded and how many just claimed it, for even just a drop of Midvarish blood made a man... stronger than he should be. He had never seen it for himself in the twenty-plus years had been serving the king of Midvar, but the rumors claimed that the men with the purest of blood could shift in and out of some *other* form. Wraiths, monsters that prowled in the darkness. Demons incarnate.

He didn't know if it was true. He didn't want to know. Because if it was...

He shuddered to think of what a beast like that could do to a man. Men. He shuddered to think what kind of havoc... no, *slaughter* they could wreak.

There were two kinds of soldiers in the world, he supposed. The kind that fought with valor for glory and for honor. Soldiers like the boys he had trained in Navah all those years ago. Boys like young Michael Aman. Valiant. Brave. Eager. Strong, if a bit naïve.

And then there were the kind of soldiers that fought for annihilation. Soldiers like the ones he had fought alongside in Midvar even longer ago. And if Derrick of Midvar truly had ilk up his sleeve the likes of which he had heard about, if the demon soldier rumors were true, Titus was fairly certain that not even someone as brave and honorable as Michael Aman could face one and live to tell about it.

No one, thank the gods, had figured out that Titus wasn't born from a pure-blooded family, because he had made sure his reputation had preceded him from the time he joined King Darius's ranks. It was that determination alone that had earned him the rank of general in Derrick's army by the time he was twenty-six.

But it hadn't just been the lure of notoriety and wealth beyond imagination that had convinced him to leave Midvar and take up the post as feigned Commander of the Navarian army. It had also been the fact that he couldn't stand being around the Midvarish soldiers, couldn't stand the way they could slip in and out of a room unnoticed. It wasn't natural. And whether or not it was the blessing of some ancient, god-infused bloodline or not, he didn't give a damn. He had never liked spending much time with arrogant, self-serving Midvarish soldiers.

But today, mercifully, most of the soldiers weren't tapping into their god-like abilities. Today, they were just men. Drunken men, from the looks of it. And in most of the soldiers' laps sat women. Sometimes two or more. More women than Titus had ever seen in such a remote, ramshackle kind of place.

Beautiful women. All of them young, supple, well endowed.

The keep of this tavern must have been wealthy indeed if he could afford such women for such a remote place. It was shocking, really.

Not so shocking, however, was the look in most of the girls' eyes. Not satisfaction wrought by the bekas and shekels that surely lined their pockets. No, their eyes held something else. Something far more devastating.

In their eyes, Titus saw nothing but hopelessness.

Oh, how well he knew the feeling.

But stranger still was that the tavern wasn't just full of Midvarish soldiers. No, peppered in the mix here and there were Navarian soldiers, their black-and-white uniforms in stark contrast to the crimson and black of Midvar. What in Sheol?

"Can I get you something to drink?" asked one of the girls who had ambled over to him, a tray resting on her hip. She was young, probably no older than eighteen or nineteen, with auburn hair that fell in a perfectly straight river of the shiniest silk down her shoulders and remarkably plump breasts. Her skin was tan, her limbs elegant and svelte. She was so tall she met Titus eye to eye.

Strange, then, to see a Midvarish girl here in the heart of Navah. Har-Navah. Whatever the Sheol they were calling it these days.

"Whiskey. And make it a double."

"Of course, milord. Is that all you'll be needing right now?"

It was the tone of her question that told Titus what other services this tavern full of young women offered. What with the darkened doors at the back of the hall, the men who one after another led the woman of their choice through them, looks of unabashed hunger in their eyes...

Gods, the place had become a damned brothel.

His stomach turned.

Bastard or not, murderer or not, there were still some things that crossed the line. Even for Titus Melamed.

"Whiskey is fine, thank you."

"Still a whiskey man after all these years, I see," Titus heard from behind him in a voice he recognized. He whirled to see a soldier not much younger than himself standing up from a nearby table, brushing the various women from his lap, a devil-may-care grin on his stubbled mouth. "Well the fires of Sheol must have frozen over!" said the soldier. "If it isn't Titus Melamed!"

"Captain Fischer," said Titus, not bothering to stand. "It's been a long, long time."

"Yes, it has. What, fifteen, sixteen years now? Where have you been? I'd heard you retired after you finished commanding the Navarian armies." A wicked grin lit the other man's face and then he waved for Titus to join him at the full table. Some of the women around the table looked Titus in the eye, the invitation written all over them. Others didn't bother to look up, tracing their fingers through the puddles of ale on the table or fiddling with this soldier's jacket or that soldier's hair. But none of them—not a single one—looked like they wanted to be here.

Titus looked again to Fischer, who still waited for his old friend to join the table. And so the former Navarian Commander reluctantly obliged.

"I've been retired for the past eight months. I just came out of it, though," said Titus, reluctantly sitting beside a particularly curvaceous young girl who immediately took to fussing with the laces of his shirt. He swiftly yet firmly removed her hands.

"What brought you out?" asked Fischer, before drawing long on his pint.

"Personal reasons." Murderous reasons.

The buxom waitress reappeared with two ridiculously large mugs in her hands. "I figured you might need more than one," she said with a half-hearted wink. Trained. Dutiful.

"Thank you," he said, handing her a shekel.

"It's on the house, Your Excellency."

Titus looked up to see the keep standing behind the bar, raising a glass in salute. He had forgotten just how many of the Midvarish soldiers admired him. Admired him for his treachery.

He raised his glass in return and, in a few gulps, downed enough libation for three grown men.

Captain Fischer laughed merrily, slapping a heavy hand on Titus's shoulder. "It's good to see some things haven't changed, my friend. So what brings you to this part of the world? I would have imagined that only the bastard Derrick himself could have brought you out of retirement."

"I'm on a personal mission this time."

"Ah, back to your mercenary days, then?" Pride and a bit of jealousy colored Fischer's tone.

"Something like that." Titus took another healthy swig from the pewter mug.

"Well, it's damn good to see you, I'll tell you that. And here, of all places. I didn't think this sort of place was your style," Fischer laughed, toying with the laces that braided up the front of the dress worn by one of his waitresses. She giggled, a laugh that didn't meet her eyes. When she looked up and noticed Titus watching her, he could have sworn he spotted a plea in those eyes of hers.

"What the Sheol is this place? I don't remember it being so busy before," Titus said.

"It wasn't," Fischer smirked. "But King Ferryl has been so pre-occupied with looking for the Midvarish army that he hasn't stopped for one second to assume that some of us are right under his nose." He laughed mockingly and added, "They say he's a good man, King Ferryl. He's a blind fool, if you ask me."

"But surely some of their soldiers or even civilians would have said something about this place by now."

"Oh, they've made it Sheol for us. Raids. Even well-meaning cit-izens showing up with pitchforks and torches. We just make sure that none of them live to tell about it. We've done enough now to strike fear into the heart of every person for a hundred miles from here that no one will dare say a word. It's pathetic, really, how many cowards there are in this damn kingdom."

Cowards? Or sleeping giants, Titus wondered.

"But the women? Where did they all come from?" Titus asked, looking around. All of them, he realized, every single one of them was Midvarish. Their almond eyes, their tanned skin. Not just Midvarish but...

"They're pure, if that's what you're wondering. Untainted blood, the lot of them. That's how the king likes them."

"The king? What king? Ferryl?"

A snort and a laugh. "No, you idiot. *Our* king," said Fischer.

Their king.

King Derrick.

"What... Why would he—?"

"Don't tell me you don't know, Titus. You must have really holed yourself up in that manor of yours if you really didn't know."

"Didn't know what?"

"They're for us, Titus. Every damn one of them. And maybe they had been originally designed for our pleasure, but we know the truth."

"What truth? What do you mean?"

"King Derrick is no fool. He knows the lot of us will die in this war he's brewing. But he'll be damned if he lets the bloodlines lose any of their strength by losing so many men. So he's found a way around it, of course."

"What the rutting Sheol are you talking about?"

"This isn't just a pleasure house, Titus. It's a breeding ground. These women are all here because they were chosen. Chosen for their age, their beauty. But mostly for their bloodlines. And it's our job to make sure we fill each one of their bellies with healthy, pure-blooded Midvarish offspring. The king would be damn pleased to know your seed had been spread, too, Titus. Have a look around. Take your pick."

Stars. Stars and black whirled about him as he willed himself not to give away the rage that was simmering to a boil in his veins. That Derrick would pluck these women from their homes, from their lives just to—

Just like Daphne. Young, sweet Daphne. Taken right from under his nose the night Penelope had been... But no, those had been Navarian soldiers at his house. Navarian soldiers who had stolen...

Gods.

Oh, gods above.

Titus looked around again at the black-and-white uniforms that peppered the room. The same the soldier had been wearing at the bank the day Penelope was...

Looking for something, General? the soldier had said, wearing the black and white uniform of a Navarian solider.

Except that to the Navarian soldiers, he hadn't been their general. He had been their commander. And there was no such thing as Navah anymore. It was Har-Navah now. And he had seen the guards at the palace in Benalle. Seen their crisp new uniforms of black and white and... and emerald and gold. The colors of the new kingdom.

It hadn't been Navarian soldiers who had stolen Daphne and murdered Penelope. Murdered his pregnant wife.

It had been Midvarish soldiers. Midvarish bastard soldiers disguised to look like the enemy. To fool anyone who might see them—anyone ignorant of the changes in Ferryl's kingdom—into thinking that it was the enemy who had committed such unspeakable acts. The enemy who had been stealing Midvarish women for sexual slavery.

But it hadn't been Navarians at all. It hadn't been Commander Derwin or King Ferryl who had commissioned such atrocities.

It had been King Derrick.

None other than King Derrick himself who had murdered Penelope.

Titus vomited right onto the table.

Fischer, several of the other soldiers, and the women jumped from their seats. A few of the girls sprinted off toward the bar.

"He's fine," said Fischer. "He's fine. Can't hold your liquor anymore, General?" he laughed, slapping a heavy hand on Titus's back.

Titus merely stood, not saying a word as he marched through the fray. Nor did he say goodbye to his so-called friend. He couldn't get out of there fast enough.

~

The horse kept up a fairly brisk pace, considering the load it was pulling. But it wasn't fast enough for Titus. Then again, nothing and no one could have gone fast enough for Titus to get away from that damned brothel. That cesspool of the debauched thinking of King Derrick of Midvar. He had vomited once more when he was outside the tavern. Then he had hauled himself onto his horse and gotten out of there as if he were being chased by the fires of Sheol itself. He rode for the rest of the evening and well into the night before he stopped, but only because he knew the horse needed a break. It was not until he had stopped riding that he realized he was still shaking.

Shaking with rage. With fury. With a hatred the likes of which he had never entertained.

"I failed you, my love," he choked, his voice ragged, weary, and heavy from the whiskey. "I'm so sorry. I'm so sorry."

He collapsed to his knees, balling fistfuls of dirt between his fingers as he let heavy tears fall down his face, struggling through the sobs to fill his lungs with air again.

He could die from this, he realized. The pain, the sheer, utter sorrow. He could and damn well should die from it.

It would serve him right.

~

It took Titus a solid hour to regain his composure, to find a steady rhythm to his breathing and heartbeat again. In the wake of the rage, a cold burden, like a woolen blanket soaked with rain fell upon his shoulders, stifling the air as if it were made of ice and fury. It would be a long night ahead.

Therefore, a fire seemed in order.

He had just finished stoking the flames into a healthy burn when he heard a noise coming from the wagon.

Queen Adelaide was awake.

For a moment he contemplated just blindly thrusting his sword into the wagon and ending her right there, before she returned to full consciousness, because he knew damn well that if he didn't, Derrick would. Somehow, some way, King Derrick would find her. And the gods only knew what the son of a bitch would do once he got his hands on the queen.

"Please," he heard her say from within the wagon. "I just need something to eat."

Something to eat? Trapped in a wagon for four days, passed out from herbs and the first thing the queen of Har-Navah asked for when she awoke was something to eat? Not freedom, but food?

"I swear to you I will remain quiet. You won't hear a sound out of me. I won't alert anyone of my presence if you will only bring me something to eat. Anything. And water. Please, I beg you."

There was a desperation in her voice he couldn't place. It wasn't just hunger. She should hardly realize she was even hungry yet. If the herbs had knocked her out so thoroughly, she should hardly be able to register who or where she was, much less that she was hungry. And besides, how could he believe her? She'd likely scream at the top of her lungs and run for her life the moment he opened the wagon.

"I've been silent for four days, haven't I?" she asked. "I have not pounded on this wagon once."

Four days? She knew she had been in there for four days?

That meant that she had been *conscious* for four days.

Sudden, inexplicable guilt burned like bile in his throat.

"Please, I beg you. It is a matter of urgency, Commander."

Why he was on his feet, walking to the wagon with the key in hand, he did not know. But he was. And when he stuck the key in the lock and felt the click of its release, he surprised himself further. Perhaps his mind was still addled from his raging earlier.

Inside he did not find a fearful, cowering prisoner.

Inside, he found a queen with nothing but gratitude in her eyes.

He helped her from the wagon and led her to the fire he had built. She sat down in silence, her gown dusty and rumpled from four days in a wagon.

He handed her his waterskin and fished through his satchel for an apple.

She kissed his hand in response.

"Thank you, Your Excellency. You'll never know the depths of my gratitude."

She ate and drank in silence. He watched in awe from his seat on the forest floor across from her.

When she had finished the apple, he brought her some dried meat and a piece of cheese. She bowed her head in thanks before devouring both of them.

When she finished her meal, she leaned back against a tree behind her, stretching her legs for the first time in days. She closed her eyes and folded her hands neatly across her stomach as she rested.

This queen. Gods, she wasn't scared of him at all.

He, on the other hand, found that he was more frightened than he had ever been in his life.

Not just of her, her fearlessness, or her bravery in the face of certain death. No, Titus was scared of himself. Scared of what he might do. What he *could* do to this queen whose life he held in his battle-scarred hands. He fiddled with the fletching of pheasant feathers on an arrow from his quiver while he watched her rest.

Again, he heard Hania's words in his mind.

You shall do something that will change the world forever.

What if she had been right?

Gods above, what then?

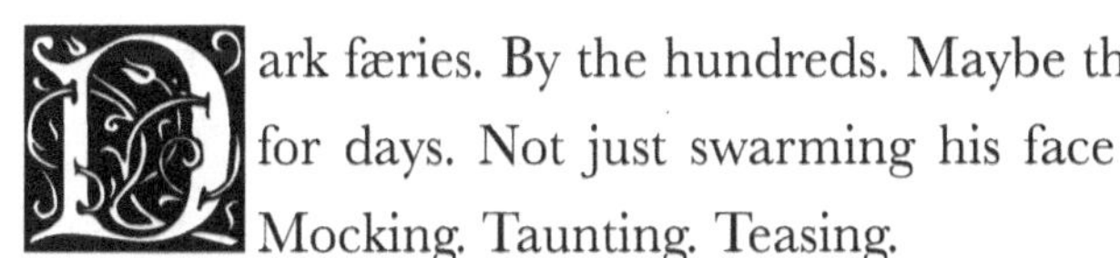

Chapter XXX

Dark færies. By the hundreds. Maybe thousands. Dark færies for days. Not just swarming his face but his whole body. Mocking. Taunting. Teasing.

Dark færies in a cloud around him—just like the cloud that had surrounded King Derrick at King Aiken's funeral. Just like the ones that had plagued him nearly a year ago after Elizabeth had left.

How had he not seen them then? How had he not realized what they were?

And worse, how was he any different than the monster king from the east? If the dark færies kept company with them both, were they really any different?

He wondered if the færies sang the same song to Derrick that they sang to him, chanting the same chorus in dissonant tones.

King Ferryl at the helm
Weakest in the realm
Coward in his very soul
Never again to be whole

Failure

Failure

Failure

A tear slid down his temple as he lay in his bed, staring at the beams of his bedchamber ceiling. The servant had just left after having freshly bandaged his leg.

"Broken," Mary had said three days ago. "And badly. I'm afraid you won't walk again if you dare to so much as move before it has had several days of rest, Your Majesty."

So Derwin had broken his leg in their scuffle. They were brothers. They had grown up together, fought their fair share of sibling battles. But never—*never*—had Derwin taken things as far as he had the other night. Never had Ferryl seen such red rage, such unleashed fury in his little brother.

Half brother.

Son of his enemy.

And when Derwin had departed with the advance guard the very next morning, he hadn't even bothered to say goodbye to Ferryl.

Good riddance.

The irony, of course, was that Ferryl was now forced to do the very thing for which Derwin had fought him in the first place. Ferryl was now forced to lie in his bed. To wait and to heal, while the kingdom engaged in what would likely end up being the bloodiest war in its history.

But he didn't give a damn. Not even a fraction of a damn.

Because if he had to face all of this: a war he didn't want to fight, a king he hated, a brother who might be his enemy, if he had to face it all without Adelaide, his Lizybet, his wife, then he could rot in this bed for all he cared.

And the kingdom could rot right along with him.

Chapter XXXI

She panicked for a moment when she woke without the baby in her arms. She had fallen asleep with it beside her, suckling her breast. She was sure of it.

Delaney sat up in the bed, pulling her shift up over her shoulder, and looked across the room, finding the reason for the baby's disappearance.

There, slumped in an armchair by his window, snoozed Michael, the baby swaddled snugly in his strong, capable arms.

Providence above, if he had any idea just how positively gorgeous he looked holding her baby in his arms...

Delaney slipped out of the bed, tiptoeing across Michael's bedchamber so as not to wake him, careful to jostle him as little as possible as she took the baby from him. But she had only just taken a seat on the bench at the foot of his bed when he stirred, mussed his hair, and yawned rather loudly.

A lazy smile curled his mouth as he looked at her. "I must have been more tired than I realized."

"I didn't even realize you had taken her," she admitted, stroking an idle finger down the delicate little cheeks exposed under the swaddling. Cheeks that had already begun to fill out, to change in just four days. Yes, motherhood was positively miraculous.

"You were sleeping, and she was stirring. I didn't want her to wake you."

"She's perfect, isn't she?" she purred, admiring her daughter in her arms.

Michael came and sat beside her. "She's absolutely gorgeous. Just like her mother."

Delaney rested her head on his shoulder as the two of them just looked at the baby.

"Have you decided on a name?" he asked, pressing a kiss to Delaney's hair.

A name. Four days old, and the poor thing still didn't have a name. Some kind of mother she was.

She shrugged. "I can't decide."

"Why not?" he chuckled.

"It's too important, a name. And I don't want to just give her any name. I want it to mean something. I want it to be a name about which I can tell her a story. A reason why she was named such."

"Do you have a family member you could name her for? Someone you admired? Your mother, perhaps?"

She had thought about that. But her baby just wasn't a Dinah. She shrugged again. "I can't seem to settle on anything that fits."

He kissed her temple. "You'll think of something, beautiful."

"Any suggestions?" she asked.

"You're asking me to name her?"

"Why not?"

A proud, if not incredulous smile spread over his face, and then he said, "Well, you could always name her for—"

There was a knock at the door just then, and Michael's attention shifted to his sitting room.

"I'll be right back," he said, standing. When he left, Delaney carefully set the baby on the bed and turned to find a robe or anything other than the shifts she had been wearing for the past couple of days. As sweet as those days had been—quiet moments with Michael and the baby, as if he were savoring every breath they took—she was very much ready to be back among the living, thank you very much.

She found one of Michael's robes in his closet, donned it, and pulled a brush through her hair before retrieving her yet-to-be-named child and appearing in the sitting room.

She found Michael with a grim set to his features.

"What's wrong?"

He met her eyes before he shook his head. "Just a note. Nothing to worry about. I've sent for dinner," he said, abruptly changing the subject.

"Oh. Thank you."

He just looked at her for a moment, his mouth relaxing into a contented smile as he finally said, "You're so beautiful, Delaney. Motherhood suits you."

What with her unwashed hair, rumpled shift, and borrowed robe, she very much doubted that.

"It's true," he said, making his way to her and pulling her to him, the baby nestled snugly between them. He kissed her softly before kissing the baby's little brow as well. "I never dreamt I'd have the privilege of loving the two most beautiful girls in the world."

"Well, you're quite the vain one, aren't you?" she laughed.

"Vain?"

"She looks just like you, doesn't she?"

He chuckled dismissively. "Right."

"I'm serious, Michael. You haven't noticed?"

"Of course not," he said, looking at the little one nestled between them.

"I didn't see it at first. But the more she fills out, the more I see it. She looks just like you."

"That's impossible." Michael shook his head, but she could see the way he looked eagerly at the baby, exploring her every feature for the proof of Delaney's claims.

"Apparently not." She shrugged.

It was true. The baby looked more like him every day, an impossibility that utterly delighted Delaney. "Maybe I should name her *Michaelina.*"

He laughed and then met her lips in a sweet kiss. No, not just sweet...a kiss that was...apologetic.

"Michael, what was in that letter?" she asked, gesturing with her eyes to the note still in his hand.

He breathed a heavy sigh.

And in that breath, her whole world froze.

"I haven't told you what's going on. I haven't wanted you to worry."

"Worry? Why, Michael? What's going on?"

He ushered her to his settee, sitting down beside her before he said, "It's about the queen, Delaney. She—" Michael rubbed the back of his neck, unable to meet her eyes.

"She what, Michael?"

"She's been taken."

"Taken? Taken where?"

"We don't know. The guards have been searching for her for four days."

"Four days!" she exclaimed.

He nodded grimly. "It's the reason Mary couldn't get to us sooner when the baby was born and why I couldn't seem to find any help. The whole castle was in an uproar at her disappearance."

"But who would have—"

The look on Michael's face answered the question before she even finished asking it. Of course she knew who had taken Queen Adelaide.

Someone from Midvar. Likely at the king's behest.

Bile burned in her throat. "Is she—?"

"At this point, we don't know anything. There is no reason to assume anything at this point. But Ferryl seems convinced that she is..."

Dead. That's what he couldn't bring himself to say. Ferryl was convinced that Adelaide was dead.

Murdered.

Delaney hardly knew what to think, what to even say, and Michael seemed to be at an equal loss.

"So this is it then, isn't it?" she finally managed. "This is war."

His answer was a solemn nod.

She looked down at the baby in her arms, at the innocence on her face. That she should be born at such a time, with the kingdom in such a state...

"What's going to happen?" she asked quietly.

"We have to find her. Derwin left a few days ago, and the first of the legions are already on the move."

"We?" she asked.

And then she understood the apology in his eyes, in his kiss.

We meant *he*. He was leaving with the legions.

Leaving her.

Of course. Of course he was leaving her. She had feared it. Suspected it. She had somehow known it all along, but like a fool, she had hoped otherwise. She had told herself that Michael was different. That he wouldn't leave her just like everyone else—

"I have remained behind to be with you and the baby for a while. But I can no longer delay."

It became hard to breathe or even to think.

Michael put his hands on her shoulders. "Delaney, it's going to be all right."

"Right," she said, standing, unable to stop the trembling that had started at her core and worked its way to her fingertips.

"Delaney—"

"Don't," she said. "Just... don't."

He stood as well, stepping closer and reaching for her.

"Don't touch me," she growled.

"Delaney, please. I swear to you, I will do everything within my power to—"

"To what?" she yelled, whirling to face him. "To come back to me? After you've risked your life and everything you have to face an enemy that is not yours? To fix a problem that is not yours to fix?"

"Delaney, that's not true at all."

She huffed a scoffing laugh.

"Listen to me, Delaney." He gingerly took the baby from her arms, setting her in a small cradle Delaney hadn't even noticed before he grabbed Delaney's shoulders. "Listen to me. I must go. I must. It is my duty as Lord Chancellor and as a subject to the Crown. But even if it weren't, Delaney, even if I hadn't sworn an oath to protect my king and my kingdom, I would still go. Because Ferryl is my friend, and so is Adelaide. I would go because if the roles were reversed—if it were you out there, taken, lost—I would hope that those I loved most would help me, that those who claimed to be my friends would stop at nothing until we found you. And Ferryl is like a brother to me, Delaney. I love him. And I will fight with him. *For* him. I will fight where he cannot. And I will use every resource within my power to bring his wife home. To bring my queen home. I will not rest until I find her."

She didn't bother to wipe the tears that fell fast down her cheeks. "Go then," she spat, turning her back to him. "Leave. Leave and die for all I care. Leave me just like—"

"Don't you do this, Delaney," he said, spinning her to face him again. "Don't you dare compare me to them. I am not your father. I am not Ravid. And I am not your mother. I am not leaving you."

"I don't know what else you call it."

"I will come back, Delaney. I will. I swear to you."

"This is war, Michael! Not a vacation. Soldiers die all the time in war."

"It's different, Delaney. It's different for me. I'm not some young man with nothing to lose, nothing to live for. I have you. I have the baby. I have a life waiting for me. I will not enter a battlefield with no regard for the sanctity of my own life. I will fight, yes. But I will fight knowing that I want to live. I will fight for those I want to live for. And I will not rest until the world is safe for us again.

"Don't you see it, Delaney? There is no life for us until this war is over. There is no world in which we can live in peace until this bastard is stopped, once and for all. I don't leave to prove anything. I leave to protect what matters. I leave to make sure that when I return, I can have the life I've dreamt of. A life with you and the baby, a family, all of us together."

"A family? Is that what we are? Because last time I checked, I'm nothing more than your shiny little plaything. You've always known you're leaving. You've always wanted to leave. Why bother marrying me, why bother with *any* of it when you were just going to leave anyway?"

"Delaney, that's not what happened at all!" he cried.

"What is it, then? What were you waiting for?"

He didn't answer. For reasons she couldn't figure out, he didn't say a word. It only fueled her rage.

"Leave, Michael. Get out of my sight. I don't want to see you again."

He grabbed her upper arms, his grip firm, impassioned. "Don't say such things."

"Why shouldn't I? You never loved me, did you? It was all just a ruse."

"That is not true, and you damn well know it."

And then he pulled her to him and kissed her. His kiss was rough, thorough, the full measure of his power and strength in his embrace. But his savagery soon waned, his grip relaxed, and his kiss gentled, the embrace of a lover, not a fighter. A deep, unspeakable need colored every move of his lips, every touch of his fingers along her back. She, too, relaxed in his embrace. She, too, pretended that he wasn't leaving her, that he was her lover and she was his and that nothing else, no shadow, stood between them. She ran her fingers through his hair with fevered need and pressed the full length of her body against him, savoring the delicious heat between them as she poured every ounce of herself into his embrace.

"I love you," he breathed against her lips, his breath ragged with a need that could only be described as hunger. "Don't you see it? I've always loved you. I would give my life for you. And I'll never leave you. Never."

But in her heart, she knew it was a lie.

Because Michael was no different from anyone else who had ever claimed to love her. Whether by betrayal or death or even just the mysterious disappearance of her sisters, everyone that had ever mattered to her had left her.

He would be no exception.

So she steeled herself, squared her shoulders, met his quicksilver eyes with a cold stare, and said flatly, "I never loved you, Michael."

And when his embrace slackened, when he slowly, disbelievingly stepped back, she didn't stop him. When he searched her, when his expression transformed from disbelief to something much, much harder, she didn't explain herself. She didn't even stop him as he disappeared through his chamber doors into the corridor beyond.

Chapter XXXII

Perhaps it was a result of the herbs he had given her, but Adelaide seemed to be getting sick at the stomach a lot on their journey across Navah. Where they were going, Titus couldn't say. Back to his home? To Midvar? Or perhaps he would continue wandering the Navarian woods with her for days on end, going in circles, backtracking like a maniac. She hadn't noticed, thank the gods. She hadn't noticed that Titus was the world's biggest coward who couldn't decide what in Sheol to do with a woman he had vowed to murder.

But still, the stomach issues... He contemplated her illness as she turned from the fire he had built at their campsite for the night and retched again.

"Are you all right?" he asked, albeit reluctantly. Why he was even asking...

She looked up, wiping her mouth on her sleeve, her face pale in the moonlight. "I think this is normal, but it's hard to be sure."

Normal? From the herbs, she meant? Or from being on a journey with a man intending to kill you? Titus failed to discern what about this situation was normal.

"My mother told me to expect some nausea, but—"

"Your mother? Wh—?"

Oh.

Oh gods.

Of course. The incessant hunger from the moment he had first let her out of her wagon days ago. The lingering stomach issues. The way she seemed so tired by the end of the day that she could collapse onto hard dirt and sleep like a babe...

"You're with child." The words were heavy, like molasses sliding down a cold spoon.

She met his eyes with that signature determination of hers. And that's when the trembling settled in again, this time coming straight from his very bones.

Queen Adelaide. With child.

A baby.

A life.

Just like the baby that was stolen from him. From Penelope. Taken when she was taken.

Titus realized he felt like retching, too. But he didn't.

Instead, he looked at the young queen again, his vision blurred by the tears that pooled in his. He stood abruptly from the fire before he let her see any more of the coward, the fool that he was.

He slept fitfully through the night, his back to the queen who carried the future of her kingdom in her womb.

~

"Where are we?" Titus asked as Hania pulled the cowl of her wet cloak

from her head and stepped into the dank barn. The rain pounded hard on the worn timbers of the roof, heavy droplets escaping and landing with a quiet thud on the straw-littered dirt beneath them.

"My favorite place," she said, and despite the dimness, he knew she wore a smile on her face.

"This *is* your favorite place?" he scoffed. Well. If nothing else, the girl had simple tastes.

She didn't say anything as she crossed the expanse of the old building, making her way to a rickety old ladder that led to the hayloft above.

Of course she started climbing it.

"Hania..."

"Will you just follow me for once without questioning everything?"

He stifled the laugh that bubbled in his belly and did as she bade, not minding the view of her slender waist, her full hips, the way her ankles peeked out here and there from under her skirts as he climbed below her. Gods, was there a more beautiful creature? Titus was certain there was not.

And being here with her in this utterly private place was dangerous, to say the least. He needed to clear his mind before he let his ideas run away with him.

They reached the top without any problem, only to find nothing but hay.

"What are we doing here?" Of course there would be hay in a hayloft. Why he had expected to find anything more, he couldn't say.

"I want to show you something."

He followed her across the questionable slats that made up the loft, the hay crunching beneath their feet as they stepped gingerly around holes and broken strips of wood. And though he certainly didn't need it, he didn't hesitate to take her hand when she offered it to help him cross a particularly harrowing stretch of rotted wood. Nor did he release her hand when the need of its assistance had expired. And when he found that she seemed to have no intention of releasing his hand, either, he understood why his heart had started a gallop that wouldn't quit.

"Here," she said, kneeling behind an intentional configuration of bales at the back of the loft, just beneath a small window where silver light streamed in. She sat down and bade him sit beside her. He did, of course, as closely as he could. She smiled and tucked herself even closer to him once they had settled.

"So why is this your favorite place?" he asked, tracing idle patterns on the top of her hand. A clover. An evergreen tree. An eight-pointed star.

"Because it's mine."

"Yours?"

"Yes. No one else comes up here."

"Obviously someone comes up here, Hania, if for no other reason than to stock it with fresh hay."

"Yes, all right, someone comes up here," she grumbled. "But my father only stocks it once a week or so. So it's mostly mine. And it's the only place I can get away from my brothers and sisters and just think."

"And what do you like to think about in this place that is mostly yours?" he asked, amusement coloring his tone.

"Dream is a better word, I suppose."

"What do you dream of?"

"Where I'd like to go. What I'd like to see. There's a whole world out there, Titus. Don't you hear it calling you?"

He closed his eyes as he clasped his hand over hers, listening for that call, whatever it was in the wind that spoke so keenly to her.

He heard only falling rain and distant rumbling thunder.

"I want to give you something," she said, interrupting his disappointment. She reached behind them and pulled out a small book from between the bales of hay.

"A book?" he asked, thumbing through the well-worn pages.

"It's my favorite." She grinned.

"I don't really like to read," he admitted, attempting to hand the book back to her.

She stopped him, pressing it back into his hands.

"You'll like this one."

"What's it about?"

"It's about a prince who falls in love with a servant in his castle."

He gave her an incredulous look, and she scowled.

"It's beautiful, Titus. It's a story of true love, of a man who would stop at nothing to be with the woman he loved."

"True love," he said flatly.

"It's real, Titus," she retorted just as flatly.

"Oh yes. Someone you cannot resist, is that right?"

She only gave him a scowling grin before snatching the book from his hand and flipping to an earmarked page, lovingly running her fingers across the words.

"Just because you don't believe in it doesn't mean love isn't real. True love endures, Titus. It endures time and distance and fear. It cannot be stopped."

"Do you really believe that?"

"Of course I do," she said. "What's the point of all this without love?"

To that, he had no retort. So instead, he asked, "And what became of this prince who fell in love with his servant?"

"She turned out not to be a servant at all, but instead a lost princess of a foreign kingdom. It was all quite beautiful, really. And when he married her, they became the king and queen that would usher in a golden age for their kingdom. The age of the Mashiach."

"The Mashiach?"

"The Promised One," she said matter-of-factly, as if everyone in the world knew of such færytales.

"And what nonsense is this that you are reading?"

"It's not nonsense!" she protested. "It's a beautiful story, and it's my favorite!"

He could see that she was frustrated by his lack of interest in the story, so he opened the worn little book and thumbed through the pages.

"Who wrote it?" he asked.

"An ancient man. Some even say he was a prophet. His name was Bedell."

Bedell. He had heard the name. But the Bedell he'd heard of was not some revered prophet. He was just a crazy old man who was rumored to traipse about spouting what he called prophecies. He wondered if they were one and the same.

"When was it written?" he asked.

"A hundred and fifty years ago," she answered.

For whatever reason, he found himself intrigued by the book and decided he would probably like to read it. Not for the sappy romance, of course, but because he wondered if it really was some sort of prophecy or just a færytale enjoyed by a young, dreaming girl.

He closed the book and set it down beside him. "I'll read it," he said.

His breath caught at the bright, endearing smile that curled her irresistible lips. "I know you'll love it."

He doubted that very much, but her smile alone had made his promise worth it.

She laughed through her nose, pressing a chaste kiss to his cheek. And suddenly all he could think about, all he could feel were those supple lips on his skin, her warm breath on his cheek, her soft hands in his.

And he wanted her. Wholly. Completely. He wanted every part of Hania, the dreamer, this beautiful creature who had danced her way into his life and his heart. His little Navarian miracle. For that's what she was—a miracle, plain and simple. One he didn't deserve for one minute. Not that he actually deserved any of this: a summer spent by the side of a girl he had never expected to meet, weeks and months learning to know the heart and spirit of someone whom he knew would color his very existence for the rest of his life.

A summer of softening to the idea that love just might be real, after all. That it might be his if he was brave enough to reach out and take it. If he was brave enough to give it in return.

And then he heard it, that call she spoke of. Ideas of a life—a life with her—danced before his eyes. The wind whispered to him, Come and see. Come and see the world. Come and taste what it has to offer. *He could taste the wind's spicy sweetness, its warmth as it tossed his hair and filled his lungs.*

And when he opened his eyes and saw that she, too, could taste it, could feel what he felt, he tilted her chin, met her eyes for a moment, and then kissed her.

To his delight, she kissed him back. And the moment her mouth opened to his and his tongue tasted hers, he was lost. And won. Wholly and completely hers. Nothing else really mattered.

So he laid her down in the straw of that old rain-dampened, cloud-dimmed loft and pulled at the laces of her simple dress. To his shock, when the knot caught and wouldn't give into his tugging, it was she who untangled it, she who loosened her bodice and kissed him more deeply, she who pulled at his shirt and lifted it over his head.

If his heart had been galloping before, it was now surely soaring like those winged beasts of the Wild Wood. And when her skin touched his, her body melting into his, he didn't care anymore that he was a Midvarish soldier with no future and nothing to offer. He didn't care anymore that she deserved better, that she was much too good for him despite the fact that she seemed intent to prove otherwise.

All he cared about, all he knew, was that there could be nothing better in all the world than to taste, even if only for a moment, this sweet simplicity she had to offer.

~

If anyone had told him when he woke that morning, eager to find out what he could get into on his day off, that he would be lying next to Hania in a damp barn, kissing her bare shoulder and listening to the sound of her soft, steady breaths as she slept peacefully beside him, he would have scoffed and said such stories were only for drunken liars and naïve dreamers.

Yet here she was, her bare shoulder beneath his lips, her body spent from making love, her golden locks falling in sweat-dampened curls around her pink cheeks. And here he was, thinking that if there were better dreams, he did not want to know them. So he kissed her shoulder again. And then her cheek. And then he tucked a strand of errant hair behind her ear and tucked her into his side a little more closely, savoring the way her breath sounded against the rain outside, the way her breasts peaked against the chill that the late summer rain had brought to the wind, wishing that time would just stop, that this moment would never end. Wishing that for one moment—for one damned moment—he could convince himself that he deserved something so beautiful.

But in truth, he knew he did not.

He rested a hand along her jaw, stroking her cheek with his thumb when she stirred.

"How long have I been asleep?" she asked, her eyes lazy from her nap.

"Not long," he answered, opting to kiss her lips in lieu of further explanation.

She smiled lazily for a moment. But then, in typical Hania fashion, her brows furrowed and she cocked her head to the side. "What is it that troubles you, Titus the Soldier?"

He only shook his head, tracing idle patterns on her taut stomach in lieu of meeting her eyes.

"I know you, Titus. There is something weighing on your mind."

Yes, she knew him. It sometimes drove him mad how well she understood him.

"Is it because your battalion is leaving soon?" she asked.

And once again, she proved that she knew him better than he knew himself. He only met her eyes.

"I don't regret anything, Titus."

I don't want to leave you. I don't want to lose you. I should never have followed you that day, or else none of this would have happened.

He tried and failed to say what was brimming in his heart.

"You like to think yourself a bastard," she said. "But I know the truth, Titus Melamed."

"And what truth is that?"

"That you are nothing more than a sheep in wolf's clothing."

A chuckle followed a shake of his head. But when he met her eyes, he could only ask, "And how can you be so sure?"

She touched his cheek and said, "Because there is no wolf who could love the way you love me." He swallowed hard, wishing he had the courage to tell her the truth.

She kissed him deeply, thoroughly, before she added, "All I know is I love you. And I wouldn't change anything about this summer."

"Why?" he finally managed. "Why would someone like you love someone like me?"

She smiled, taking his face in her hands. "Why wouldn't I fall in love with a good man?"

Chapter XXXIII

For the first night since being taken from Benalle Palace, Adelaide had actually slept somewhat soundly. The nausea mercifully decided to subside, and the lingering fear that at any moment she would find a dagger at her throat or a sword in her belly had somehow inexplicably waned. Oh, she had put on a brave face, to be sure. She hadn't for one moment wanted Titus to know the fear that had nearly drowned her from the moment she saw his face. But she had been petrified all the same, terrified for the sake of the future dwindling away before her.

Perhaps it was the ongoing prayer for protection, safety, and peace which she had been silently uttering since the moment she turned to find Titus Melamed, former commander of the Navarian armies staring at her in the kitchens below the palace. Perhaps it was the strange heat emanating from the amulet she wore—no, more than just heat. Magic. The unmistakable, tangible buzz of magic steady and constant around her neck. Perhaps it was that something had fundamentally changed in Titus from the way he had looked in the kitchens at Benalle to the moment she saw his face when he let her out of the wagon. But whatever it was, when she woke that morning, her back a little stiff from the hard forest ground, she felt protected. And she no longer felt afraid. Which was a good thing, she supposed, for what she was about to do…

Titus, on the other hand, seemed scared out of his mind. Why, she couldn't say. But it very likely had something to do with whatever was causing him to sleep in fits, to wrestle in his dreams, and to cry out in the middle of the night every night since they had left Benalle. Just as it likely had something to do with whatever had happened a few nights ago—the night she heard him weep and cry out apologies over and over until his voice was raw and unable to speak any longer.

She didn't dare take his bow and prowl into the forest to scour the brush for some kind of breakfast, even though, thanks to Ferryl, she was perfectly capable of wielding a weapon to procure a meal. She didn't dare try something as brash as stealing his weapon. Not yet, anyway. Not because she was afraid. No, because she might have a precious gift in her womb. It was strange, to be sure—to both fight to protect the life she hoped bloomed in her womb and simultaneously fear whether that life had survived at all. But she lived in that dichotomy—in hoping and fearing and protecting all at the same time. And that hope, however precious, however minuscule, was enough that she wouldn't risk anything so foolish as stealing his weapon, no matter how hungry she got.

And Providence above, this morning she was fairly certain she could eat an entire banquet's worth of food.

So when Titus finally woke from his restless sleep—if that's what she could call it—she didn't wait for him to even sit up fully before she said, "I was thinking of finding some berries for breakfast. Would that be all right with you?"

"What?" he asked groggily, rubbing his eyes as he sat upright on his bedroll.

"Are you hungry?" she tried again.

He scratched his head before letting his arm fall heavily by his side, giving her an appraising look before he finally sighed. "I'm tired of fruit. I'm going to go and find a rabbit or grouse that we can cook over the fire."

We. Not he.

He didn't even realize how much of his guard he was letting down. She decided not to enlighten him.

"I'll stoke the fire."

And with a nod to her, that was that. Titus disappeared into the woods, leaving his royal contraband utterly alone and unbound in the woods, right next to his still-saddled horse.

So this was it, then. Her freedom. Her salvation. She could mount that horse right now, leave and never look back.

But for reasons she couldn't quite name, she stayed where she was, stoked the fire as promised, and waited dutifully for her captor to return. To her surprise, he returned rather quickly, a fat rabbit in hand. Breakfast, indeed. Her mouth watered, and her rounding belly grumbled with approval.

Titus dressed the rabbit in no time, created a spit, and set about the task of roasting their meal without a word. They ate in silence as well, and Providence help her if every morsel wasn't divine.

With her belly full and her mind equally replete with questions—something she supposed Ferryl would have called typical—Adelaide opened her mouth, daring to ask the question that had been dancing on the tip of her tongue for days.

"Why haven't you killed me yet?"

A deadly silent stare met her from across the dying fire, along with unnerving stillness. Then the man said, "Are you asking me to kill you?"

A wiser person might have shut her mouth at the tone of his question. Instead, Adelaide merely met his gaze eye for eye, and said, "I'm asking you why you haven't."

Her heart pounded so hard it was probably visible to the man who sat across from her—the man commissioned with her murder. Yes, she should keep her brazen, reckless mouth shut.

Titus looked down, fiddling with the rabbit bone in his hand.

"We've been circling these woods for the better part of a week. Backtracking, changing course. Why? Where are we going?"

"Do you have a death wish, Princess?"

Apparently she did, because she said, "Do you want to know what I think?"

"I have a feeling I'm going to find out."

"I don't think you have it in you."

Red rage smoldered in his eyes. "A word of wisdom, Princess. It is never wise to call your captor a coward."

Yes, she really should learn to keep her ridiculous mouth shut.

Maybe it was the heat emanating from her amulet—the comforting, peaceful glow that circled her soul—but for reasons she couldn't quite understand, she continued.

"I don't think you a coward at all, Commander."

Surprise showed in his eyes and then a question.

"Tell me something, Titus. How long have you served King Derrick? Did you serve him the whole time you also served my king?"

Titus didn't answer. He only looked down to his hands again.

"I have to give you credit. No one in my kingdom knows of your treachery. Not my husband. Not even Commander Prince Derwin. You're good at your job, I'll give you that. But I cannot help but wonder…why didn't you kill me when I was a little girl? Is it for the same reason you haven't killed me now?"

"Don't pretend to understand me, Princess."

"I am no princess. I am queen. Queen of Har-Navah. Queen for a reason, a prophecy your master knows and fears. But I would hazard it is for a different reason that you've not killed me."

"And what reason is that, pray tell?"

Her hands were trembling violently now, but still, she had to press on. She had to take the risk because…

"You retired last year, didn't you? Went home to your wife."

His eyes met hers, deep, black sorrow showing despite himself.

"Were you happy there?"

Something fundamental shifted in Titus at the question. She could have sworn his shoulders trembled slightly as he breathed a quiet *yes.*

"And was your wife happy to have you?"

He nodded.

"Then why did you leave?"

He didn't answer for a long moment. "I didn't want to," he finally managed, his voice rough, broken. "I would have stayed forever, but…"

She was beginning to understand the darkness that lingered in his eyes and the invisible burden that rested on his shoulders. "What happened?"

"She was taken from me. Murdered. With my child in her womb."

He looked at her again for a moment before letting his gaze drift to the tiny swell in her belly. And in that moment she understood the answers to all her questions: why he was so hesitant to kill her, why he had shared his food with her. She understood the torment in his eyes.

If for no other reason than the child who might be growing in her womb, Titus would not kill her. Not here. Not this day.

And she knew deep down why he hadn't killed her all those years ago, either.

The heat that radiated from her amulet was no coincidence. It was magic. The magic of Providence, resting on her, protecting her. The same kind of protection she had felt whenever she was near Ferryl. She wondered if he knew. Did he understand? She did now. That was why Ferryl had been called the *great protector,* even as a boy. He had been given the name because the magic of Providence had rested on him even from the time he was young.

Because he had been chosen.

And so had she.

She knew then what she had to do.

"I'm sorry, Titus. I am truly sorry for your loss. I can see in your eyes just how much you loved her. And I would guess that she loved you just as deeply, did she not?"

"For reasons I will never understand, I believe she did." He was weeping, this soldier before her, silent, heavy tears sliding down his face, and he would not meet her eyes anymore.

"Grief and love, they are birthed from the same place, are they not? They are two sides of the same coin. And love is not borne of darkness, Titus. Love is only borne from Light. From good. Do you know what that tells me? Perhaps you know it not, perhaps you see it not, but there is deep, abiding Light in you, Commander Titus. And Light is only birthed from Providence himself.

"I think the reason you haven't killed me—the true reason—is not because you are a coward... but because you are good. A man with a destiny. Chosen for such a time as this. Chosen for this moment. Because if it had been any other man commissioned with my death, he would not have had the courage you had to let me live. That same courage you have even now to keep me alive.

"It is neither fate nor coincidence by which our paths have crossed. You, Titus Melamed, have been commissioned to do something that will change the world forever."

He was shaking his head, tears still falling freely when he finally said, "You don't understand. It doesn't matter. Even if I free you now, even if I personally escort you back to Benalle Palace, he will find you. King Derrick will not rest until you are dead. And if I do not kill you, he will find someone who will. He will settle for no alternative."

She let the silence fall, heavy, thick, and damning as she absorbed his declaration. She felt the truth of it in her bones. Her only chance to help Ferryl, to save her kingdom, lay in bending to the will of a king crazed with power. She had known it all along.

"Then I must be dead," she finally managed. And there it was. The bald truth of it. The traitorous commander's eyes shot to hers before she added, "And you must be the one to do it."

Titus's breathing was the only sound that broke the stillness.

"Everyone, the world, even my husband must know it. Will you do this, Titus? Will you help me change the course of the world?"

His chest rose and fell steadily, rhythmically, as if marching to the beat of destiny. His eyes steeled to cool calculation and unyielding determination when he finally breathed, "Here is what we must do."

Chapter XXXIV

Talia had the patience of a saint, for if Ferryl had been asked to tend to a brooding king day and night, moving him from the bed to the chair, from the chair back to the bed, and even wheeling him to the privy in the chair made for him, he would certainly not have handled it with such poise.

And perhaps the most pathetic part of it all was not the indignity of letting his wife's maid see him in such a state but the fact that he knew he was brooding like a toddler. Knew and didn't care.

But he couldn't walk, per Mary's orders. He couldn't even stand. So they had fashioned a ridiculous chair for him, as if he would deign to be seen wheeled around the castle. The invalid king. The incapacitated, pathetic prince.

It only fueled his ire.

And ire, apparently, kept the færies that plagued his peripheral vision healthy and happy, breeding like rabbits. If there had been a hundred of them yesterday, there were surely doubly as many today.

Which, of course, only fueled his ire even more. Which then just made more and more of them appear until they were no longer a flickering cloud of nuisance wings, but a force unto themselves. A swarm of gloom and the ever-present reminder of his failures.

Failure to protect his wife.

Failure to protect his kingdom.

Failure to see what had been right in front of him most of his life—a lying bitch for a mother, a blind fool for a father, and a damned bastard for a brother, the son of his greatest enemy.

Failure. Failure. Failure.

He swallowed the bile burning in his throat, the retching that threatened to make an even more pathetic fool of him as he turned to Talia and said, "I want to go to the dungeons today."

"The dungeons, Your Majesty?" she asked.

Majesty. Right. Because he was so gloriously majestic these days.

"Take the back halls. I don't want to run into any courtiers today."

She curtsied as she said, "Of course, milord."

Mercifully, Talia asked no questions and did not bother to carry on the one-sided conversation she had been so keen to have the last few days. No, she wheeled the king with the broken leg down the quiet, back halls of the palace without a word. And even when she came to the many stairs leading them down to the dungeons, she faced them without incident, utilizing the clever contraption on the front of the chair that allowed them to manage obstacles with ease. Bless that woman.

Before he was ready, before he had taken a moment to collect his thoughts and figure out what he was even doing here, they arrived.

"Your Majesty," said a guard with a bow.

"I want to see my mother."

"Of course."

The guard took the embarrassing chair from Talia and directed

Ferryl down a narrow corridor and around a torch-lit corner to a set of heavy, scarred wooden doors.

The doors to the dungeons. The place where Ferryl had left his mother to rot.

The king did not bother to respond, did not bother to look any of the prisoners in the eye as they passed. He didn't even react to their whispers and murmurs.

"Is that the king?"

"Gods above, what's he doing down here?"

Gods above, indeed. While Ferryl had always been certain there were no gods above, these days, he was beginning to wonder if there was even a Providence above, either.

What kind of god, after all, could be so heartless? What kind of god would take away something—someone—he had supposedly given? That morning on the mountain in Haravelle—the color, the splendor—now seemed like a distant memory. Where was that god now when he needed him most?

"Your Majesty," said the guard, ripping Ferryl from his thoughts. He realized they had stopped. Arrived, actually, at a heavy iron-and-wood door far from the whispering prisoners. A solitary door at the end of a lonely corridor. The guard pulled the heavy key from his belt, clicked the lock open, and proceeded to wheel Ferryl inside, nodding with a bow before disappearing again, closing the door behind him.

Ferryl might as well have been a prisoner, too.

His mother's chamber was by no means small, but it could boast nothing else. Certainly not warmth. Torches peppered the stone walls, a constant dripping pitter-pattering the damp, worn floors. A small wooden desk sat in one corner, holding a pen and a few scattered sheets of parchment.

And in another corner sat the queen atop a straw bed.

A queen in a smudged, wrinkled gray dress, her graying blonde hair falling down her breast in a long, unkempt braid.

She said not a word as her eyes met Ferryl's, a long silence hanging between them as they observed one another.

Ferryl second-guessed his decision to come at all. What did he hope to learn?

"What happened to you?" The queen's voice was rough with disuse and likely fatigue, confirmed by the dark circles under her eyes and the sallowness of her skin.

"Broken leg." He wasn't about to tell her how it had been broken. He wouldn't indulge her by giving her the goings on of his life or the fact that her bastard son had been the one to break it.

But she, in that way she always had, looked at him as if she already knew what happened. And for his part, he wanted to claw her damned eyes out.

She picked at a loose thread on her threadbare blanket, and Ferryl couldn't tell if she was too proud to say anything else... or too frightened.

His blood boiled in his veins, his pulse a war drum at his temple. He balled his hands into fists, resting them on his lap as he growled, "Just tell me why. I need to know why you did this. Why did you hate her so much? Why did you send her away? When you knew how much I loved her?" If she hadn't... If she had just let Ferryl love Elizabeth, marry her, perhaps none of this would have happened. Perhaps she'd be here now. Perhaps they could have found out about her lineage another way, protecting it from those who would destroy her for it. Perhaps... "Did you hate her? Or was it me you despised? For not being the son of the man you loved?"

"Is that what you think? That I hated her? That I hated you?"

"Tell me what I am supposed to think. Tell me, because I am at a loss as to why you did any of the things you did. You cursed my father with your own magic, didn't you? Cursed him and then let him die by the hand of your lover. You stole the woman I love from me over and over again. My memories of her. When you sent her away, you even tried to kill her that day, didn't you? The day—years ago—when she should have broken in two, thrown from her horse, the perfect accident. Only it wasn't an accident, was it? You did it, didn't you? It has been your magic, *your* darkness that has haunted this family and this kingdom from the beginning."

Her lip and chin quivered as she looked at him for a long moment. "I deserve every accusation. I cannot deny any of them. You're right, Ferryl. I did all of that and more. I have deceived you, lied to you, betrayed you, hurt you, taken the most precious things from you. I don't question why you put me in here. Not for a moment. I deserve it. I deserve much worse."

Of all the things he thought she might say, of all the reactions he had expected, this was not...

"But I swear to you, Ferryl. I swear to you on my life that I did every bit of it to protect you."

"To *protect* me?" he asked through thick tears. Tears of rage and hurt, tears for every tangle in this web she had woven. "Protect me from what? You?"

"From him," she said so quietly he almost didn't hear it.

"Him?"

She met his eyes, her own grief—feigned or real, Ferryl didn't know anymore—drowning her eyes in tears as she said, "From Derrick."

"Don't you dare do this. Don't you dare try to blame him for what you did. He didn't force you to curse my father. He didn't force you to treat the woman I love like dung on your boot. He didn't force you to—"

"No, he didn't. But I knew. I knew that if he knew who she was, he would never stop until she was dead, until you were destroyed by it. I knew that if he thought your father capable, he would have slaughtered him, too."

The words battered his numb mind like hailstones. She was saying too many things. Ferryl decided to tackle them one at a time, even as his pounding heart threatened to fail.

"But he did slaughter my father. He did."

A weary nod. "He swore to me he wouldn't. And I thought that by keeping your father incapacitated, by keeping him incapable of being the strong, proud man that he was, Derrick wouldn't view him as a threat. Wouldn't see the need to..." Her voice cracked, breaking off her words with the emotion that welled up. Ferryl hardly knew what to think. "When I found your father that day, when I realized what Derrick had done, something within me broke. My husband, the man who had spared me, given me mercy after undeserved mercy, had been slaughtered right under my nose. I couldn't... couldn't..."

But whatever she couldn't, Ferryl didn't know, because Meria gave into her tears, sobbing into the thin blanket.

Ferryl thought he might be swallowed by his own grief alongside hers.

"I was a young, stupid girl who fell in love with a cunning, charming foreign prince. And I had given him everything in exchange for a few shallow promises. It wasn't until I was carrying Derwin in my womb that I realized what a fool I was. I never told him. I never told Derrick about his son. It was my only solace—to know that he never knew that he finally had an heir. And when your father forgave me anyway, when he had offered his life in exchange for mine, I hated him. For so long I hated him for not hating me. I hated him for being so damned noble. It ate me alive.

"So I kept up the pretense that I was in love with Derrick. I decided loving a bastard was better than loving a fool. But somewhere along the way I realized how stupid I had been to deny Aiken. To keep him at arm's length. By then, it was too late. I knew he could never forgive me for my callousness, my stubbornness. So I decided to do whatever I could to protect him from the monster I knew Derrick to be. That's when I started... cursing him."

She looked down, tears falling onto her lap again.

Ferryl willed himself to breathe, reeling with what she was saying. Could he even believe it? *Breathe and think.* If what she was saying was true... If she had cursed his father to protect him...

No. No, that was ridiculous. What kind of fool would think of something so asinine? So selfish?

Love—real love—was supposed to protect. Trust. Keep. Hold. Persevere. If she had really loved her husband, she would have stopped at nothing to make sure he knew it, not curse him stupid under the deluded notion that she was somehow protecting him from a greater threat. Did she think so little of Aiken that she was convinced he would be incapable of outsmarting the bastard Midvarish king?

But what of Adelaide? Elizabeth? Did she think so little of her, too?

"What did you mean when you said that if he knew who she was, he would not stop until she was dead?" he asked. "Do you mean Elizabeth? Did you know who she was the whole time? Did you know she was the lost princess?"

"I suspected it. I wasn't sure. I *couldn't* be sure because Derrick was convinced she was dead. And Titus had sworn—"

"Titus? Commander Titus? What did he have to do with any of this?"

A silent tear fell down her cheek.

His breath threatened to fail as he listened to her words.

"He worked for Derrick the whole time he was our commander," she said. "And he was the one who took Adelaide from her home when she was a child."

Ferryl's fingers dug so deeply into his palms that he was near to drawing blood. He would kill that bastard the next time he saw him. The best commander they'd ever seen had lied to and betrayed his father for years. Years. When he trusted him with his own life, with the welfare of his entire kingdom. He had taken Adelaide from her home when she was only a little girl. Left her for dead in the Wild Wood.

And then it hit him, the idea dawning like a blazing summer sunrise.

Had it been Titus that had taken Adelaide this time, too?

Who else could have strolled into this castle without so much as a single guard batting an eye? Who else but trusted, beloved Titus?

"Whether she was the Haravellian princess or not, I couldn't risk it," Meria went on. "Not where you were concerned. I couldn't risk it because I knew that whoever she was, if you loved her, she would be a target. If you loved her, Derrick would only use her against you. To break you. Destroy you. You think with your heart, Ferryl. You always have. And it's both a blessing and a curse—to be driven by emotion like that. To let it guide your impulses the way you do. So I tried to protect you. From yourself. I threw every courtier I could find at you. I tried and tried again to get you to turn your attention away from her, to marry another. Someone you could love but that wouldn't destroy you if she were taken from you. Because I knew what you felt for Elizabeth. Adelaide. I knew how deeply you cared for her. And it frightened me. For your sake.

"Derrick wrote to me with the idea to marry you off to his niece, and I seized the opportunity. I knew that she, of all the people you could marry, would be your best hope at peace. Because she, being his family, wouldn't be seen as a threat to his power.

"After I convinced Elizabeth to leave, I thought it was working. I thought you were falling in love with Delaney. And for the first time in my life, I thought I might have done something right. I even had Sir Thomas stage Elizabeth's death in the forest just so that you would stop looking for her, stop hoping for her return.

"But then Elizabeth returned. And I knew…I knew you'd never let her go again. I knew it was over. And I knew that regardless of whether we ever figured out who she truly was, you'd stop at nothing until she was your wife." More tears fell, heavy drops splattering on her skirt and her wringing hands.

"I've never been more frightened for you than when you returned from Haravelle with her on your arm. As your wife. I knew then that no matter what, the two of you had targets on your backs. Derrick would never rest until she was dead. And you were destroyed."

He was breathing, he realized. He had to be, else he could not be alive to hear this. But he couldn't imagine how he was breathing, considering the heaviness, the weight of it all threatening to swallow him whole. To steal him away into a darkness from which he would likely never emerge. Somewhere, distantly, he registered the dark færies around his head, swarming in a triumphant dance, as if they had finally gotten what they wanted. As if they had finally witnessed the last severing of hope left in Ferryl's ragged, shredded heart.

He was ready to turn around, to leave this damned dungeon, to get away from it all, when Meria said, "I would not blame you for hating me forever, Ferryl. But you couldn't possibly hate me more than I already hate myself. I have failed you. In every possible way I have failed you, failed Aiken, failed your brother. I don't...I don't expect you to forgive me. I don't even ask you to, because I don't deserve it. All I ask, Ferryl, *all* I ask is that you believe me when I say that I did all of it, every single bit of it, because I love you. Because from the moment you were born, from the moment I first held you in my arms, I knew that I would do anything in the world to protect you. That I would give my very life for you.

"And you will never know how sorry I am that you have ever had to question otherwise."

Chapter XXXV

She hadn't been able to bring herself to leave his chambers. It was improper, she knew, because he wasn't here. His garrison left with Commander Derwin days ago. Improper also because she wasn't his wife, and she knew now that she never would be. But as Delaney rocked her still-yet-to-be-named child in the cradle that she had been too stupid, too blind to notice that Michael had bought for the baby, she didn't care one iota about impropriety.

All she cared about was how much she missed Michael.

And what a fool she had been to let him leave like that.

But she knew the truth. Deep down she had always known. She might have been a fool to let him leave, to end it with him, but he was much, much better off without her. Better off without the broken, disheveled mess that was left of her heart after all that had happened. Her mother's sudden death, her father selling her to the highest bidder, Ravid using her and throwing her away, her sisters having vanished without a trace. She was a broken, stupid mess, and she knew it.

And Michael was much better off without her.

But she stayed in his chambers anyway. She stayed because at night, the only way she could sleep was by closing her eyes and taking in the last vestiges of his scent that lingered on his pillow, pretending he was still here, still kissing her goodnight with heartbreaking gentleness, still holding her until she fell asleep, still jumping up at all hours of the night at the slightest sound from the baby, tending to her as if the burden were truly his to bear. Loving her as if she were his own.

Delaney stayed in his chambers because she couldn't bring herself to leave. Not yet.

The baby had finally, mercifully dozed off, her belly full of milk, her contented little lips so full and red in a slight, perfect little pout. Delaney kissed those sweet little lips before standing and taking in the sitting room around her, feeling again the emptiness that had plagued her since the moment she had said those words. Those stupid words. That lie she had told because he was better off thinking it true.

I never loved you Michael.

She knew even now that those words would haunt her soul for the rest of her lonely life.

She walked the length of the room, realizing for the first time that some servant must have come in and cleaned out the fireplace recently, the ashes and soot gone, the burned remains of the last logs long since removed. She wondered what the servants must have thought of the hapless, pathetic former duchess who trespassed in the Lord Chancellor's chambers like a vagabond.

She ran her hands along the mantle, the marble cool to the touch, smooth and perfect. Then she ran her hands along the adjacent bookshelves that lined the wall and the worn, loved tomes that filled every shelf. Leather-bound volumes, most of them tall, thick, important-looking.

But it was a small book that caught her eye. So small, in fact, that it looked out of place amongst the formidable tomes that surrounded it. The spine was so worn, so broken in that the title was no longer legible. She pulled it out, realizing immediately that the book was old. Centuries old, likely.

And deeply, deeply loved. For surely it had been read hundreds of times. Strange, she realized, because she didn't remember Michael ever mentioning a book, let alone one that he would have read enough for it to be in such a condition.

She thumbed through the brittle pages, earmarked here and there, opening to a page somewhere in the middle of the book. A page with passages underlined and starred, the ink faded with time.

"This is love. Don't you see it? And love is not so easily broken."

The prince crossed the room, taking her hands in his.

"Love or not, we cannot be. Not like this," she insisted, but she did not pull away.

"Why not?" he asked. "Why shouldn't we love each other?"

"Because I am a servant. And you are a prince."

"No, my love. You are a woman, and I am a man. What else should love need but two willing hearts?"

"A willing heart does not change anything."

"That's where you're wrong. A heart bent on love, a heart that has tasted its sweetness can never go back. A heart that loves is the strongest there is. Love changes everything."

A servant who loved a prince. A prince who loved a servant. Was this a book about...Ferryl and Adelaide? But how could that be? How could a book written— she checked the front pages to find that it had been penned almost two hundred years ago! How could a book written so long ago be about them? And why did Michael have it?

There was a knock on the door then, and that's when Delaney realized her heart was pounding. She quickly shut the little book, returning it to its place on the shelf. But something caught her eye as it floated to the ground: a piece of paper that must have fallen from the book. Worn with time but not with handling, its folds still crisp and precise. She opened it to find a single sentence:

Love changes everything, Titus. ~H

Titus? Meaning Commander Titus? But why would Michael have an old, nearly ancient book with a letter to Titus, of all people, inside? And who was H?

Another knock ripped her attention from the mysterious note, which she tucked in her bodice before finally daring to say, "Come in."

It was a servant, thank Providence. Not a guard. Or Ferryl, ready to kick her out for her treachery. Just a servant who bowed and said, "A letter, my lady. For his lordship."

Delaney crossed the room, taking the letter with a nod of her head. "Thank you."

The servant bowed and disappeared without another word as Delaney looked down at the parchment, folded and closed with a seal she didn't recognize. It wasn't a caracal or a noble crest but scales. Scales and wheat. A simple seal. Something more like... like a merchant's seal.

Michael's father was a merchant, wasn't he? What if this was a letter from him? What if... what if he was writing to tell Michael that his mother had fallen ill? Michael would want to know. Michael would need to know. And he would need to know it long before he returned from the battlefield... whenever that would be.

She tapped the letter on her palm, a nervous gesture as she weighed the pros and cons of reading Michael's personal correspondence. *It would be wrong. It would certainly be improper.*

But she didn't care one iota about impropriety.

Delaney opened the seal and unfolded the letter.

Inside, she didn't find news of Michael's mother's illness.

She found news of his father's death.

Despite the fact that it had only been a week since he left Benalle, Michael was already exhausted. Weary. Bone tired. And at twenty-three years old, he found the notion absurd. He shouldn't be anywhere near tiring, especially considering his battalion hadn't seen so much as a hint of action. Just endless, endless traveling eastward. Toward Midvar.

But he knew the reason for his weariness had little to do with the physical and nearly everything to do with the gaping hole in his soul. The bleeding, festering wound left in the wake of the knife that was

Delaney's last sentence to him.

I never loved you, Michael.

As long as he lived, he would never forget those words.

"Captain," said a soldier, riding up beside him along the wide, endless road that cut through the eastern Har-Navarian plains.

"Hmm," Michael replied, tearing himself from his thoughts.

"We were thinking we might stop here for the night. There's a grove just there and—"

"That's fine," Michael said flatly. Frankly, he didn't really give a damn if they slept in the open fields. But a grove of trees seemed a wise enough choice in this vast, unforgiving terrain. It was a smattering of groves and a few sprigs of brown grass that separated this place from being a brutal desert. And he hated it.

The soldier nodded and rode away without another word, and it was only then that Michael realized he hadn't taken the time to get to know the names of a single one of the soldiers under his command.

Some captain he was.

The grove of trees his soldiers had commissioned as their resting spot for the night proved more than adequate, and before Michael had so much as dismounted his horse, a few of the men were already building fires and claiming their spots for the night.

He found a tree that was close enough that he wouldn't look as if the last thing he wanted was to talk or interact with anyone and yet far enough away that it would afford him just such a luxury. So he uncoiled his bedroll and plopped himself down, fishing out a piece of jerky and an apple before drawing long on his waterskin.

The food tasted like ash in his mouth. Fitting, he decided, considering the wasteland through which they were currently trekking. So instead of attempting to swallow down any more of it, he just leaned back against the trunk of the tree and closed his eyes.

That, however, proved to be problematic, considering that the moment his eyes shut, all he could see was her face, her glossy auburn curls, her long lashes. She seemed so very real, this Delaney in his head. As if he could reach out and touch her, feel her, hold her. As if he could taste her skin, her lips. As if she were right here.

Damn it.

He opened his eyes and willed himself to think about something else. Something that wouldn't continue ripping apart his very soul, chunk by bloody chunk.

"I thought you might like some dinner, sir."

Michael tore himself from his misery to see a soldier—the same one who had suggested this grove for the night—offering him a metal plate filled with roasted meat and some cheese. It smelled delicious.

"Thank you, soldier," Michael replied, taking the plate, his appetite suddenly screaming at him.

"It's Ilias, sir."

"What?"

"Officer Ilias Yadin, sir."

"Oh," Michael said. "Yes, of course."

"It's an honor to be under your command, sir," said Ilias, and it was then Michael realized the solider was young. Not more than sixteen or seventeen. He seemed genuinely in awe of Michael.

How many of the soldiers knew of his rank as Lord Chancellor? How many of them thought him to be some great leader, some worthy nobleman, instead of the broken, pathetic nobody that he was?

He shrugged his soldiers. "You're too generous, Officer Yadin."

"Just Ilias, sir."

"I'm not a sir."

"My apologies, my lord. I wasn't sure which title I should—"

"Michael is fine. Just Michael."

The young soldier's eyes widened to the size of full moons as he swallowed down his shock. "Michael, then," he managed. "I was wondering, Michael... sir." He cleared his throat and shook his head quickly, diving with sloppy speed into what was brimming on his tongue. "Michael... if you wouldn't mind teaching us a little of what you know while we're together. I don't know that another opportunity like this will come along, and it would be an honor if—"

"Teach you? Teach you what?"

"Your skills, sir. Michael... my lord. I mean... Your skills with a bow."

"My skills with a bow?" Michael asked incredulously.

"Yes sir," Ilias nodded. "Everyone's talking about it. They say there's never been a better archer in the kingdom. Not since Commander Titus."

Michael snorted a laugh. "I'm not that good, soldier, rest assured."

"I don't think any of the soldiers under your command would agree. You're famous."

"Famous?"

"You were a castle guard. A castle guard who was appointed as second-in-command to the king, a rank even higher than Commander Prince Derwin. They say your time in training was legendary. That no one could best you, sir. It would be an honor if—"

"Well *they* are grossly overestimating my skills, believe me." Michael took a bite of the drumstick on his plate, the meat perfectly salted and fall-off-the-bone tender. He stifled the urge to groan his satisfaction. And then he realized that this little conversation with the eager, young—albeit laughably uninformed—soldier had been the first time since leaving home that he hadn't thought of Delaney. Or the baby he so terribly missed. So he looked up to Ilias and said, "I'd be glad to show you what I know."

A smile spread wide across his mouth as Ilias said, "Oh, thank you, sir. Lord Michael... sir. Thank you so much!"

And as he scurried off, no doubt to tell his friends of his good luck, Michael wondered when it was that he had stopped being young and eager like Ilias, when it was the world had stopped feeling rife with possibility and started feeling like a giant puddle of quicksand waiting to devour every dream.

He didn't have to think long to answer that question.

Chapter XXXVI

Training, it turned out, was little more than a gaggle of young, untested soldiers pestering Michael for tips and advice as they continued their journey on horseback through the plains of Har-Navah, scouring every village and community for any sign of the purloined queen, for any traces of Midvarish activity, ever eastward, on and on towards Midvar. But at night, when the battalion would stop to rest, the young men would seize the last vestiges of sunlight to pester Michael into shooting at makeshift targets until his arms ached, all the while ooohing and aaahing at his skills as if he were some prodigy, some genius with a quiver at his back and a bow in his hands. He resisted the urge to laugh for the sole reason that he had no desire to make them feel any less than they already did.

But if nothing else, it was a welcome reprieve from the darkness that tugged at him every time he was left to his own devices, and Michael soon found himself wishing he could train the soldiers every hour of the night for no other reason than to keep his mind from wandering back to the girl he loved. The girl he thought had loved him. Thought... and been terribly, terribly mistaken.

Somewhere in the dark recesses of his logical mind, he mused that Delaney might very well have been lying to him. That she might have only said those words—those damned words—as a matter of self-preservation. Some part of him understood the kind of broken-ness that would lead a person to lie for the sole reason that she had no other weapons in her arsenal.

But that part of him—the part that wanted to forgive and forget, the part that wanted to give her a second chance—was a quiet, paltry little whisper compared to the truth that screamed at him at all hours of the day. Whether she had meant it or not, she had said it.

And now it could never be taken back.

Words, he knew too well, were like a hot branding iron, their pain not easily forgotten, their scars brutal and eternal. He knew too well because he had felt that kind of pain before. Known it in his soul—the day his own father had branded his arm.

He absently ran his fingers along the scar that ran the length of his forearm as he laid on his bedroll that night, staring up at the shimmering stars, the unobstructed view of the heavens in the eastern countryside. The scar had healed into a nasty, gnarly cord, like a rope of flesh and sinew just under his skin.

"You're not worth it," his father had growled as he pressed the brand to Michael's young arm. "You're not worth trying to love."

For the rest of his life, Michael would never forget the rage in his father's eyes. The hatred. He would never forget how much it had hurt. And he had sworn to himself that day that he would never let himself be hurt like that again.

He supposed that had been why he had fallen in love with Delaney so easily, so completely. Because he could see the same pain branded in her eyes. The wounds of a father ran deep, the troubled waters of a bottomless river. And somewhere along the way, he had given his soul completely to her. He had trusted her with it—the first time he had ever been able to trust anyone with such a piece of himself. He had trusted her because he had understood her, and she him.

That is, until the moment she had spoken those words which had rendered his soul useless, his heart without a beat. Words that had sounded too much like his own father, words that played over and again in his head through the night. Every sleepless, fitful night.

~

"Where do you suppose they could be, sir?" Ilias asked as their horses trotted side by side the next afternoon. "The Midvarish army. Where do you suppose they're hiding?"

"Providence only knows," Michael muttered, frustrated by their lack of finding anything so far. Derwin had been right; this army was like a damned ghost. And their ability to remain illogically clandestine was wearing on Michael's already worn nerves. He urged his horse a little faster, keeping his eyes peeled for any signs—a broken twig, tracks... anything.

Ilias kept up easily. "I have a theory, sir," he said.

"Oh?"

"They say it's an army of wraiths. That they can appear and disappear into thin air. But such a thing isn't really possible, is it? Not even with magic."

No. No it wasn't possible. Or it shouldn't be, anyway. But Michael knew from what Delaney had told him that not only was it possible, it was a reality. Ilias prattled on. "What if the reason we've not found them is because we're looking in the wrong place?"

Michael inclined his head toward the young soldier. "What are you implying?"

"What if the reason we can't find any evidence of them on the ground is because they're not *on* the ground... but *under* it?"

"Underground? An underground army?" What a ridiculous notion. How could the Midvarish king have possibly commissioned the building of an underground cave large enough to house his entire legion? That would take... years. And years. Decades. Or more. It would have had to start long before Derrick was even on the throne of Midvar.

"I know it sounds crazy, sir. But I can't seem to find any other logical explanation. The commander has been looking for almost a year, hasn't he?"

Providence, had it already been that long?

"Think about it, sir. How else are they crossing the border unharmed?"

"What do you mean?" Michael asked.

"The Wild Wood, sir. It is huge. It takes up nearly the entire length of the border between the old country and Midvar, save for a small passage in the northern territory that is heavily guarded by both Har-Navarian soldiers and Midvarish soldiers. If droves of the enemy's men were crossing there, we'd know it. The only alternative is through the Wild Wood. And *no one* passes through the Wild Wood and survives. Not even the Midvarish."

"Maybe they can." Adelaide had gone through. Gone through and survived.

"They can't, sir. All due respect, of course. But they can't. I would know."

"What do you mean?"

"I was with Commander Derwin last year, sir. When he went to the borderlands. There was a skirmish near the edge of the Wild Wood. A few of our men got into it with a few of the rebels. The Navarian soldiers drove the men into the woods, not realizing they were about to cross into the Wild Wood. But their horses knew. They faltered just on the edge. But the rebels, their horses didn't stop.

"The soldiers wouldn't talk about what they saw then. But I could see it in their eyes, in the way their hands never quit shaking after that.

"It was a massacre, sir. And for the day that we lingered before departing, the air stank of carrion and the skies were peppered with circling birds."

A massacre. Yes, that's what he had always heard, that no one survived the Wild Wood.

No one except Adelaide. His queen.

A chill shuddered down his spine.

~

The small village through which they had passed that afternoon had afforded the soldiers a chance to spend the bekas and shekels that were apparently burning holes in their pockets, for by the time sunset beckoned and the soldiers had settled again for the night, not a single one of them had bothered to pester Michael for archery lessons, too immersed in the amber bottles they had purchased for themselves, and the embellished stories they shared of the women they had patronized for the afternoon.

And considering that Michael had no desire to get drunk with a bunch of eager boys, to lose his inhibitions and start spilling the contents of his tattered soul to a bunch of strangers, he had declined their eager invitation to join them for cards and boozing, opting instead to prowl the terrain in the little time he had left before nightfall. Exploring, he found, was not quite as successful at distracting him from thinking about Delaney, but it would suffice.

The terrain had begun to change in the last week, the vast plains now peppered with rocky formations here and there. Not mountains. Not by a long shot. More like small crags and caves, as if Providence had accidentally dropped a few huge boulders here, leaving them when he realized that if nothing else, they made for interesting landscaping.

Interesting indeed.

Haunting was more like it, for Michael couldn't shake the foreboding that spider-walked along his skin as he prowled the quiet field, still and graying from the sinking sun. It was a particular formation of stone and vines that caught his eye, its rounded shape and sinking holes reminding him of a huge, gray skull—as if this were a valley of bones. The bones of giants slain in a great battle.

The crack of a branch and the hoot of an owl had him jumping a foot in the air, his heart pounding in his throat.

Sheol, he needed to quit letting his imagination get the better of him. He was becoming as skittish as a girl.

He rounded the skull-like formation, intrigued by it for reasons he couldn't name, his hand resting on the hilt of his sword, his quiver a comforting weight at his back.

Nothing. There was nothing out here but a fool with a wild imagination.

But then he heard it—a sound. So small, so faint he might have missed it had it not been for the utter stillness of the night, the lack of wind or even breeze. It sounded like—well, he couldn't place it. But it wasn't... natural. It didn't fit with the sounds of night. Crickets. The flutter of bat wings. The hoot of an owl. No, it was nothing like that which he heard now. It was more like... well, it was more like... like a snort, if he was being honest.

Strange. It was unsettling enough that he decided it was time to get back to camp before he completely lost any vestige of sunlight... or sanity.

It was then that he spotted it—an opening at the back of the rock formation.

A cave.

And like a damned fool, he stepped inside.

There was little more than what he might have expected to find in such a cave, still visible thanks to the little swath of sunlight that remained from the setting sun. Cobwebs. Insects. Dust and debris. But there in the dirt he realized there was something else. Something that didn't belong.

Tracks. Human tracks. Boot tracks.

And not just his own, but tracks that led farther *in.*

To what, he wondered?

Curiosity, of course, got the better of him, and he decided he had to know, especially considering his conversation with Ilias that afternoon. It wasn't a deep cave. Not terribly deep, anyway. But deep enough that even the waning sunlight couldn't reach the back of it. So he let his hands be his guide, feeling gingerly along the rough-hewn walls of stone, hoping against hope that his hands didn't find some sort of venomous creature waiting to devour him.

The darkness was complete now, the silence eerie and ominous. But then he heard it again—a snort. A deep, rumbling snort. Like... like a hog. Or a boar.

What in Sheol...?

He ran smack into a solid stone, rubbing at his head as he stumbled a step back. But he reached out again, his hands gingerly patting along the solid stone that must have been in front of him, his eyes beginning to adjust to the darkness. Then he felt it—a weakness in the stone. He pushed on it. It opened easily. Too easily. A door, then.

And he stepped across a rocky threshold, led by a swath of muted golden light to realize...

He had found a tunnel.

Chapter XXXVII

She had felt so sure of herself this morning when she told the servant of her intentions. The servant had merely shrugged her off with a "Whatever you think, miss." Delaney had ignored the girl's flippancy, thinking—no, knowing in her gut that she was doing the right thing. But now, as the carriage approached the pathway lined by cypress trees and thick with budding vegetation, she wasn't so sure anymore.

What business of hers was this?

None, she realized. Michael's father's death was none of her business.

But Delaney was here now. It would be silly to turn back.

So when the footman extended his hand to help her from the carriage, she took it and swallowed down her second guesses.

At the sound of a sweet little coo, Delaney bent her head to press a kiss to the brow of the little one wrapped at her breast. "I'm nervous, too," she whispered, wondering how someone so tiny could instill so much peace just by being near. It gave her the gumption to take the final steps to the house.

The journey to Michael's family home had been an easy one, the quaint house not an hour's ride from the palace, situated comfortably between two green hills somewhere north and east of Benalle City. It seemed like a beautiful place to grow up, what with inviting flowers and vines growing from every windowsill and iron pots of cascading blossoms guarding the doorway. Loved, that's how the house felt. Loved and warm.

Delaney took a deep breath and knocked on the door.

"Coming! Oh, I'm coming!" she heard from within, momentarily taken aback by the casualness of the greeting. In her home in Midvar, never would a servant have called from within. A butler would have ambled unhurriedly to the door, opened it with his shoulders back and his chin high and simply said, "Yes?"

But it wasn't a servant who answered the door. It was Michael's mother. Even having never met the woman, she would have known she was Michael's mother from a mile away—the same high cheekbones, the same proud set to her shoulders, even the same abiding kindness to her eyes. Only where Michael's hair was a chestnut brown, hers was blonde, so blonde it was almost white, pulled up partially like a young woman might wear her hair so that her curls might be on display. And she certainly had the luxurious curls to display. She was absolutely beautiful. Stunning, really. A mirror to Michael's handsome face. Even the way she carried herself screamed Michael.

"What is it, dear?" she asked.

"Are you Mrs. Aman?"

A cocked head, and then the lady asked, "Who's calling?"

"My name is Delaney. Delaney Dupree. I am a friend of your son's."

Michael's mother held Delaney's gaze for a moment before sliding her eyes—so wild and beautiful, like a lioness or a caracal in the wild—to the baby. "Are you here to tell me I'm a grandmother?"

Delaney's cheeks heated instantly, and she had to clear her throat just to recover herself. "No, my lady," she finally managed. "The child is not... she's not his. I just..."

Oh Providence, why had she come? What was she doing here?

"Yes?"

"I just...I came to tell you that Michael could not receive your letter because he is not at the palace."

"Where is he?"

"He has gone to fight for king and country."

Michael's mother didn't say anything for a moment, obviously weighing Delaney's words. "And you came all the way here to tell me this in person?"

A nervous nod was all she could manage.

Michael's mother gave Delaney a weighing look. "Well, come in."

~

"I thought you should know. I thought I should tell you in person. I would want to know—if it were my son, I would want to know why he hadn't responded," Delaney said, fumbling with the handle on her cup of tea where she sat across from Michael's mother in the quaint little kitchen. A stream of sunshine shone in through the window, casting a pool of golden light on the scarred wooden table at which they sat, the dust motes dancing like glittering stars. The warm shaft of afternoon light illuminated Michael's mother's golden locks so that they looked like wildfire scattered about her face. Nuzzled closely, the baby slept soundly in Delaney's arms.

The older woman sipped her tea, her expression betraying nothing of her thoughts. "You're right. I do want to know." She let silence yawn between them, appraising Delaney with eyes that seemed to see too much. At last she added, "It is a dear *friend* indeed who would make such a journey just to tell me of my son's whereabouts."

Delaney nodded solemnly. "He is a dear friend to me, Mrs. Aman." Or was... before she ruined everything.

"Hania," she said.

"What?"

"You may call me Hania."

Hania. She wondered if Michael had ever told her his mother's name. She was sure he hadn't. It was quite possibly the most beautiful name she had ever heard.

"I know that you two haven't spoken in some time," Delaney went on, feeling the need to explain for Michael's sake. To set things right for him. Maybe she had made a mess of what was between them. But maybe she could make things right with his mother. "I know it is none of my business and certainly not my place to intrude, I thought you should know anyway, in case... in case..."

"In case something happens to him."

Delaney only nodded, pushing aside the thought—the picture of Michael, brave and valiant on the battlefield, covered in mud and blood, his sword brandished as he fought his way through a sea of Midvarish soldiers...

"I see," Hania said. She looked down, fiddling with the handle of her teacup as if she, too, could see that picture of Michael. As if it haunted her just as much.

In that quiet moment, Delaney understand the sorrow in Hania's eyes. It was the same sorrow she knew too well—that of losing someone you loved more than your own life. Hania and Michael had not spoken in years, though Michael had made it clear to Delaney that it was not for lack of loving his mother, but rather fear of the retribution from his father. Hania had lost her son to circumstance. And that pain still shone, keen and sharp in her wise eyes. The same pain Delaney had known upon losing her mother, upon losing touch with her sisters, upon losing Michael...

"Perhaps it is not my place... But maybe you'll forgive my impertinence when I tell you that I know he loves you very much. And misses you terribly."

Hania looked up from her tea, holding Delaney's gaze. "He told you this?"

Delaney nodded. "He speaks of you often. And fondly."

Silver lined Hania's piercing eyes, but where Delaney might have given into it, might have let those tears fall freely, Hania merely squared her shoulders, letting a lone tear fall down her cheek before she said, "I love him more than my own life. I would have given anything for things to have been different. For him to have had a father who could have loved him. But I knew..." she said, her voice finally quavering, "his only chance would be if he had a father at all. I knew his only chance would be if no one knew the truth."

"What truth?" Delaney asked, tilting her head to one side.

Hania breathed a laugh, but there was no humor in it. "This world does not look kindly on the bastard born, my dear."

The bastard born? What was she talking about? "Bastard? Who is a bastard?" Delaney asked, clutching her daughter just a little more closely. Her bastard daughter.

Hania met Delaney's eyes suddenly, an even deeper kind of sadness darkening her own when she said, "I should have known he wouldn't tell you. Of course he wouldn't have. It's not his secret to tell, is it?"

"What secret? I don't understand. Michael's father died, didn't he? I received the letter."

"Michael is a bastard, Delaney. My husband was not his true father."

If her heart had been a raging river a moment ago, the mighty waters had come to a dead halt now, the words settling into her mind like one heavy rock at a time, thrown into the shocked stillness and sinking one by one into its depths.

Hania seemed oblivious to Delaney's shock. "My son, he…of course not. No, he would never tell anyone because he would want to protect me from the shame of bearing a bastard. I just wanted him to have a chance, you see? I wanted him to have a fighting chance at making something of himself. So I married a man I did not love not long after Michael was conceived. But my husband…he was unfair to Michael. I think he envied the fact that Michael had a mind of his own, and maybe even envied Michael's courage. So when my husband demanded that Michael should be sent away to train for the king's army, I knew it was best. For all of us. No matter how much it broke my heart."

Awe washed over Delaney. Awe for the woman before her. She

who had sacrificed her own happiness for the sake of her son, who had chosen to stay with her husband, to live in her own personal Sheol so that her son could have something better. Just so that her son did not have to face the world without a father. To face the world as a bastard.

The courage it took. The selflessness. The strength.

Delaney wondered if she would have been so brave. She wondered if she would ever be so brave. She looked down again to the child in her arms, longing even more for Michael. If she could just see him one more time. If she could just tell him the truth. If she had only been brave enough before to trust him. To trust his love.

"Where is Michael's father now?" she heard herself ask.

"He died a long time ago. Michael never knew him."

She could see it, so plainly she could see the place Hania kept in her heart for Michael's father. The love she still bore, even after all these years. A solemn tear fell down Delaney's cheek, falling onto the baby's brow. The little one stirred at that, a soft coo coming from her pouty red lips.

Hania turned her attention to the baby, smiling warmly and wiping a tear from her cheek. "Tell me about that baby of yours. She is quite beautiful."

Delaney couldn't help it. She smiled proudly as Hania went on. "What is her name?"

Her name. It was as if Delaney had been waiting all along for someone to give her a sign, someone to point her to a name that mattered, to name her child after someone special, someone brave, someone beautiful. So looked up and simply said, "Hania. Her name is Hania."

The elder Hania didn't say anything for a moment, merely holding Delaney's eyes with an expression that Delaney couldn't place before returning her gaze to the child. Delaney wondered what she might be thinking. What she might assume, considering the child shared her name.

"You say she is not Michael's."

Delaney only shook her head, hating the lie. Yes, the child was his, wasn't she? Perhaps he hadn't sired her. But he had loved her. Taken her in. Given her what no other man ever would.

"How do you explain those eyes, then? Those eyes that are my son's?"

"I cannot," Delaney admitted.

Hania gave her a weighing look and then said, "May I ask who is her father?"

She breathed a small sigh. "A man I thought I loved. And one whom I thought loved me. It turned out he loved little more than the healthy sum he was promised upon siring my child."

"He was paid to sire your child?" Hania asked in disbelief.

Delaney nodded solemnly, heat crawling up her cheeks and down her neck. She hated this part of her story. She hated the stupidity that had gotten her here. She would never regret Hania. Never. But she regretted the girl she had been and the naïveté that had led her here. To this place. Holding a bastard in her arms. Pleading the case for a man she had pushed away. Wishing, longing for a life she would never have again.

"Why?"

"Why?" Delaney asked, returning to the present.

"Why would anyone be paid to sire your child?"

"So that a pure-blooded Midvarish child might sit on the throne of Navah."

"You are from Midvar?"

"I am the firstborn daughter of a duke."

Delaney could plainly see it all dawning on Hania, the pieces of the puzzle coming together, because she finally said, "Are you the duchess? The duchess that was betrothed to our King Ferryl?"

"I am she," Delaney admitted quietly.

Silence. And then, "And instead of marrying the prince, you fell in love with my son."

Delaney darted her eyes to the woman across the table, the baby stirring in her arms. She patted the younger Hania, bouncing her softly. How? How could Michael's mother know it? Was it that obvious?

Hania laughed dismissively, her wild curls bobbing as she did. "There are not many *friends* who would make such a journey to come to me today."

Delaney only looked down, embarrassment kissing her heated cheeks.

"Does my son share your affection?"

Delaney sighed. "Once, I suppose. But that was before..."

"Before what?"

"Before I ruined everything."

A weighing silence fell between them before the elder Hania said, "So I am to understand that you came all the way here to plead my son's case, to let me know that he still loves me, still wants me in his life, and yet you hold none of the same hope for yourself?"

"I—"

"You took great risk coming here today," Hania went on. "Not knowing me. Not knowing how I might react to your presence or your declarations of my son's continued affection for me. Yet here you are. Bold and brave and selfless. And yet you hold no hope. You hold your child in your arms and let the story in your eyes tell your truths for you. You let your past dictate your future, just as I once did. You let someone else write your story for you, don't you? Perhaps it's your father or your mother. Or perhaps it's the coward who sired that baby of yours. Either way, you've put yourself on the line for my son and fail to see the selflessness of that act alone. Fail to see the valor of it. The sheer love in it."

Delaney did not know what to say. Did not know how to respond. Hania seemed undaunted, a lioness gilded in golden light as she continued her speech.

"My dear," Hania continued, "I know my son. And when his mind is made up, there is little that will change it. That you should fear a mistake on your part has ended his affection for you tells me one of two things: either my son never loved you, or you never understood the depths of it."

Chapter XXXVIII

nything else, Your Majesty?"

Ferryl turned his attention to the servant who stood eagerly by his side, tearing his gaze from the sunset that painted the sky and the churning ocean in violent shades of crimson, gold, and pink.

"No, Talia. That will be all. Thank you."

Talia smiled weakly before also turning her gaze to the glorious sunset which had cast the whole of Ferryl's receiving chamber in warm shades of vanilla. Her skin glowed in the golden light, the rays catching strands of her black hair, illuminating them like diamonds.

She looked too much like Adelaide. Ferryl turned away from her again.

"I know how often you think of her," she said, her voice a quiet breeze. "I can see it in your eyes." She sighed heavily. "I miss her, too, Your Majesty. But I believe—with all my heart, I believe that she is out there somewhere. And she will turn the tide of this war."

How he wished it were true. How he wished he could have even an ounce of the spirit, the faith of this woman who so faithfully served him, stood by his side while he fell apart into a thousand færy-ridden pieces. She hadn't had to. As Adelaide's lady's maid, she could have refused to help Ferryl. But she had insisted. And frankly, Ferryl had been glad, for Talia was the only servant who didn't feel the need to pity him all the time. The only servant in the whole of Benalle Palace who hadn't treated him like a child, never mind that he had been acting like one.

There was something about these Haravellian women in his life. They were like rocks. Solid. Steady. Unyielding. Strong.

Even Avigail hadn't been afraid, not like Ferryl. Since the moment they had realized Adelaide was missing, Avigail had been the one to say that Providence had a plan, the one to remind Ferryl over and again to wait it out. Not to jump to conclusions.

But the only conclusion Ferryl could draw for certain was that Adelaide wasn't here. Where she should be.

And the worry had plagued him—drowned him a little more every day. It was too easy to believe she was dead when he could feel nothing from her.

"Shall I bring some tea?" Talia asked, gathering the rest of his dinner plates as she tore him from his thoughts.

He turned to see her behind him, standing upright to meet his gaze. But it wasn't Talia he was looking at. It was his chambers.

His dark, stale, empty chambers. Void of life. Void of conversation.

Just like he had found his mother upon his return to Navah only a few short months ago.

Bile burned in his throat. When had he become his mother? His lying, manipulating, scheming mother who had locked herself away like a prisoner? Like a widow pretending to mourn her beloved mate?

Only Ferryl's grief wasn't feigned. Not by a long shot.

But the fact that he had reacted so similarly: holing himself up in these rooms every day, not taking part in any court affairs, state dinners, or audiences with nobility… The whole damned kingdom had merged with Haravelle, and he hadn't bothered with any of the logistics, for goodness' sake! No wonder Derwin had fought him so fiercely that he had broken his leg!

He deserved it. Worse. He deserved much worse.

He deserved his wife leaving him.

Maybe she left of her own accord. How could he blame her? He was a waste of a king.

A waste of a man.

The dark færies seemed to dance in agreement around him at that.

"Your Majesty?"

"Hmm?" he grunted. "Oh. Tea. No, thank you, Talia. That will be all."

A knock tore her concerned gaze from him. She answered the door with a practiced curtsey and pulled it open to reveal a duchess standing at the threshold, her baby wrapped closely to her chest.

"Delaney," Ferryl said, moving to stand in her presence, only to remember he couldn't stand. Not with a broken leg.

A waste of a man.

The duchess smiled graciously. "May I come in?"

"Of course, of course," Ferryl said.

"Your Grace," Talia said, bowing her head as the duchess passed.

"There is no need for all of that," Delaney said as she placed a kind hand on the servant's arm.

Talia only smiled. "I will take my leave, Your Majesty, unless you have further need of me."

"No, no. That is all. Thank you, Talia."

"Good evening, Majesty, Your Grace." And with another curtsey, the servant disappeared.

Delaney huffed a laugh as she walked towards Ferryl. "I think she is the only servant in the whole of Benalle who still calls me that."

Ferryl's brows flicked together. "Well then, we shall have to remedy that."

She waved off his declaration as she bent to kiss his brow. "I came to see how you are feeling. Mary tells me you should be able to start walking again soon."

"I'm fine. I'm just tired of sitting."

"May I ask what happened?" she asked, gesturing to a nearby seat.

Ferryl extended his hand, nodding for her to take the seat as he replied rather curtly, "Oh, I just fell."

"It must have been a terrible fall," she said.

Yes. Falling right into the trap of a lying mother and a manipulating king. It was a terrible fall indeed.

He waved her off. "I admit I'm glad to see you. I haven't seen the baby yet, you know."

Her eyes lit up like two glittering stars, and she loosened the wrappings tied expertly around her person and turned the little one that Ferryl might inspect her.

She was beautiful. Like a perfect little doll.

And oddly enough... "Her eyes, Delaney. She has—"

"Michael's eyes. I know," she finished for him, the twinkle glittering ever brighter in her eyes.

Ferryl couldn't help but huff a laugh. He realized it was the first time he had laughed in weeks. "She's beautiful, Delaney. Absolutely perfect." He hated the guilt that washed over him. To laugh, to smile at all when Adelaide was missing…

"Would you like to hold her?"

Before he could answer, Delaney placed the tightly wrapped bundle in his arms. He might have thought to protest had he not been distracted by just how little she was. And how warm. She cooed when she breathed. A perfect little pixie with lips as red as a spring rose. Ferryl was fascinated by the minuscule person.

And that fast, his heart tore again. Another bloody piece falling away—this one for the child that might be in his wife's womb. The child he knew he might never meet.

He was surprised at the tear that fell so quickly.

"Ferryl," Delaney said softly.

"She is truly exquisite, Delaney. I'm sorry."

Her hand was warm where she placed it over his. "There is no need to apologize."

He kept his eyes glued to the tiny bundle in his arms, her eyes shut as she soundly snoozed, her lips puckering as if suckling on a phantom breast.

"She was with child. Did you know that? My Adelaide. She carried our child."

A squeeze on his hand. "I didn't know that."

"I had pictured the baby to be a strong, strapping little boy. But seeing her, seeing your little one, I realize how much I wouldn't mind a girl, either. I wouldn't mind either sex, I just wish..."

"I know," she said softly. "I know."

"No wonder Michael was so smitten with her. She was all he could talk about."

Delaney's smile did not meet her eyes, and Ferryl understood the loneliness, the fear she must have felt in his absence. He knew it well.

So he offered her the hope he could not find for himself. "He will come home to you, Delaney. He will come home safely."

She only looked down, fiddling with her thumbs as if she hadn't had her hands to spare in weeks. Maybe she hadn't.

"I'm sorry we didn't get to give you a proper crowning before he left. I thought perhaps though that you would want to wait until he returns for the ceremony."

"Ceremony? What do you mean?"

"So that the court can be there properly."

"Be there for what?"

"Your crowning, Delaney. As Duchess of Teman."

"Duchess of Teman?" she asked, shaking her head.

It took him a moment to realize there was genuine confusion on her face. "You don't know? He didn't tell you?"

But of course. Of course she didn't know. Because it had all happened so fast that day. The day of the council meeting, when the baby was born and Adelaide was—

"Ferryl, what are you talking about?"

And so he just launched into the story without thinking how it might affect her, what she might think to learn that— "Michael offered his life for you, Delaney. When some of the council called for your execution, Michael offered himself in your stead."

But when Ferryl saw the look in her eyes, when he saw the dawning realization grow wider and wider, he realized he should have thought it through, should have considered what it might be like to learn such news in such a manner.

"My *execution?*" she finally breathed. "Who called for my execution?"

And so Ferryl told her the story. From the very beginning, every moment, every word, every argument he had had with Michael. And even though he knew it made him look like an ass, he confessed to her that he had allowed himself to consider giving in to Lord Westerly's demands because he didn't know what else to do.

"But Michael wouldn't stand for it, Delaney. And so that day, that day before the council, Michael said that if they decided that your life must be forfeit, then they would take his instead."

The only thing Ferryl didn't tell Delaney was the story about Derwin. He didn't add that in all of that, he'd learned that he had a bastard for a brother.

"He... he offered his life... in exchange for mine?" she breathed.

It was Ferryl's turn to place his hand on hers, shifting carefully in his chair so as not to stir the baby in his arms. "His love for you is deeper than I understood."

Tears fell down Delaney's beautiful face, pouring in a steady stream that she didn't even bother to wipe away.

But it was something else entirely that began to blossom in her eyes. Something he hadn't expected. Especially when she said, "I want to help, Ferryl. I want to help you win this war."

"Delaney, I—" he stumbled, looking for words.

"I've realized something, Ferryl. Something that has taken me too long to see. But I see it now. We're all in this—all of us have to help. We all have to do something to stop my uncle. Before it's too late. And I want to do my part, too."

"What do you mean? You want to fight?"

"I'll fight if I have to. I'll do anything you need, only let me help you."

The eagerness, the determination in her… Ferryl hated to let her down. "I have seen your attempts to wield a sword, Delaney. Please don't take offense when I say you are hardly capable of holding your own on the battlefield."

"I can fight in other ways."

"What do you mean? Delaney, where is this coming from?"

She suddenly met his eyes, and he could see the idea blossoming there. "Let me go to him. Let me go to my uncle. I will present myself to him, and he will let me into his court. Let me be your spy, Ferryl."

"Spy? Delaney, that is too dangerous. I cannot ask you to—"

"You're not asking me. I'm volunteering. I am in a unique position, Ferryl. No one else could do this for you. He will confide in me, I know he will. I will find out my uncle's secrets for you."

"Delaney—"

"You must not be taken by surprise, Ferryl. You cannot win against the pure-blooded Midvarish that way. They're too powerful, too quick. The blood that flows through their veins is… is full of dark magic, Ferryl."

"Dark magic? In their blood? What do you—?"

"They're true, Ferryl. The stories are true. The Midvarish soldiers are not regular men. They are bred and blooded to be monsters.

Wraiths. Demons."

So it was true, then. It wasn't just some made-up notion, some færy story spread by the ignorant. The Midvarish weren't just men. They were monsters. The man he and Derwin had faced in Ramleh—he was a monster. Not just a beastly man—a creature with something otherworldly in his veins.

And that same blood flowed through Derwin's veins, too.

Bile burned in his throat.

"Please, Ferryl. Please let me help you in this way."

"But the baby, the... It's too dangerous. How will you—"

"I'll bring her with me. He would question why I came without her anyway."

"Won't he suspect? It's not as if you've kept up correspondence with your family in Midvar. Won't he realize your loyalty to Har-Navah?"

A small hurt flickered in her eyes before she said, "My uncle will not see my severing with my father as a sign of disloyalty to him. Derrick of Midvar is many things but he cannot see past his own gain and goals. If I come to him he will see it as a slap to my father. And he has always hated my father. They were only able to come to an agreement about my marriage to you because it was mutually beneficial for them."

Ferryl was at a loss for the unrelenting determination in Delaney's eyes.

"Please, Ferryl. Let me do this. Let me help you win this war."

Chapter XXXIX

e hadn't expected it to feel so cold. Empty, perhaps. Lonely. Silent. But cold? Not at all. But when Titus arrived home for the first time since losing Penelope, it had been all of that and more. Like a ceaseless winter. A sick cycle of clouds and darkness without a sliver of sunlight to warm the place.

Or perhaps that was only his heart. Cold. Empty.

Hollow.

He was still reeling from what the young queen had asked of him, still in shock at her gumption, her bravery, her sacrificial selflessness. Never in all his life had he believed in anything as deeply as she obviously believed in her kingdom, in her god. And that she had asked Titus to do the unthinkable...

He had trudged home after that and climbed into his bed intent on doing nothing but sleeping for days. He had not said a word to his servants. Not put anything into his belly save for a few swallows of wine here and there. If he withered away to nothing, all the better. For after everything that had happened, it would have been a fate he deserved.

He had left home in search of revenge, and he had returned

gutted, empty, unsure of his next path. Spent and weary. And utterly and completely afraid.

For he had no idea where to go from here.

His days consisted mostly of silence. Reading, pacing, thinking. But the silence had grown too weary, the winter that wouldn't end too much for his soul. He had left Har-Navah and come home to nothing.

So it shouldn't have surprised him that his own restlessness had brought him here. His own damned curiosity had led him to this gods-forsaken place.

And despite it all, he couldn't help but let himself wonder—had he sunk to complete madness?

The wine cellars below his manor were cold and gutted. Still and eerie. Like a cloudless, windless night without sound or movement. Just stale darkness and the lingering memories of the last time he had been here, when he had found her lifeless body, cold and blood-stained, still and silent...

Gods, what in Sheol was he doing here? He shook his head and cleared his throat. He needed a vat of whiskey, that's what he needed. Whiskey and a swift kick to the balls, apparently.

But as he turned to leave the gods-damned cellars, he heard it again. A noise. Small, faint, not unlike the noises he had heard down here before. Like...

...like scuffling feet. Or...

...or marching.

And damn him if he didn't turn on his heel and open that door. The one behind which he had found Penelope murdered and cold. The door that supposedly led to nothing.

Except now in the stillness of the night, he knew it was definitely not nothing that made those sounds.

~

Shit. He should never have come down here. He should never have stepped foot past that door. Because now, in these tunnels below his cellar, which supposedly had long-since been abandoned, Titus realized how stupid he had been. How blind. He had been wrapped up in his own life, in his own treachery as he spent the last two decades betraying the king of Navah that he hadn't even thought to consider what his own king had been up to.

But he could see it now, the lengths to which King Derrick of Midvar would go.

And at sight of the throngs of wraith-like men who slithered and wormed to and fro before him, weaving through the stalactites and stalagmites, through the underground cliffs and caves, the vast network that loomed before him, Titus finally understood the depths of his own naïveté. For while he had spent his days as King Derrick's dog, keeping the eyes of King Aiken turned away from the east, his own eyes had been equally blinded to the truth that now spread out before him.

King Derrick's famed army. Hidden from the world in a network of caves and tunnels that not even Aiken could have conceived.

Caves and tunnels that connected to Titus's own estate.

Titus Melamed had never felt more like a fool.

Chills still spider-walked down Michael's spine as his battalion pressed east. The setting sun behind them cast long shadows down the rough road, their horses and riders made to look like absurdly stretched carnival freaks, like the shadows of approaching wraiths. Which, of course, wasn't helping the incessant foreboding Michael had known since the moment he had stepped foot into that cave.

A cave full of the last thing he had ever expected to find. Not men. Not an army. But boars. Wild, raging boars, snorting and scuffing, raging beneath the earth as if populated by the demons themselves. A vast cavern full of the wildest, foulest, most aggressive beasts on the earth, all of them hungry to kill and destroy, their eyes violet in the torchlight, wild with dark magic.

Adelaide had once said that a herd of cursed winged horses roamed the Wild Wood, too destroyed from the experimental magic of Midvar to even fly, left to their own feral devices after the Midvarish were through trying to make them useful. Were the boars the alternative? Were they cursed to be even more foul than they already were by nature? If so, how could any army survive an attack by not only the Midvarish soldiers, but a herd at least a thousand strong of feral, cursed boars?

The sight had been enough that Michael wasn't in that cave more than five seconds before he had turned on his heel and run as fast as his legs could carry him. The sun had set by the time he emerged from the skull-like boulder. But he didn't care. He ran as fast as he could, stopping only to retch before he barreled back to camp.

And now, weeks later, at just the mere thought of those beasts, Michael felt the urge to vomit again.

He didn't, thank Providence. And as the boys made their way down from their horses, intent to make camp for the night in the cozy conifer forest they had found, Michael willed his mind to think of something else. Not boars. Or caves. Or potential underground armies.

And certainly not former Midvarish duchesses back in Benalle, alone and frightened with a newborn in tow.

No, he didn't need to be thinking about any of that right now.

"Sir," said Ilias, tearing Michael from his thoughts as he stepped closer to his captain.

"Hmm?" Michael asked, removing his horse's saddle. Then he realized that Ilias was not alone. "Who is this?"

"The name's Joseph, mister," the boy said, extending a dirty, calloused hand to Michael. He couldn't have been more than fifteen or sixteen, his eyes still young and his cheeks still plump with adolescence. But he stood proudly, as tall as his small frame allowed. He reeked of stale mud and dung, his face, his clothes, his hair smudged with suspect brown substances.

Michael managed to smile as he opted to breathe through his mouth. "Joseph. What can I do for you?"

"The boy here claims—" Ilias started.

"I'm no boy," Joseph interjected. "I'm a man now. Even ma says so. I'm sixteen and th' head of th' house. And I come to see what yer doin' on me land."

"Your land?" Michael asked.

"The bo—erm, *Joseph* here says we're on his property," said Ilias.

"Is that so?" Michael asked.

"Yeh. Starts just over that bend back there. We've no fence, ye see. But it's our land all the same."

Michael followed the boy's hand to where he pointed to the edge of the grove, the purported edge of his property. "I do apologize, Jo. We didn't realize, you see."

"It's Joseph."

"What?"

"Not Jo. Me name's Joseph."

The boy seemed determined that he should be called by his full name, an irritated set to his mouth at the attempt to befriend him with a less formal name.

Michael merely nodded. "Joseph, of course. We will remove our soldiers from your land immediately. I do apologize for the confusion."

"Who said anything 'bout movin' yer men?" Joseph suddenly protested.

"I'm sorry?" Michael asked.

The boy seemed irritated that Michael would have even made such a suggestion. "Ye can stay all ye like, mister. Only me mamma wanted to know if ye'd like supper. She said brave boys like you'd need to keep yer strength up if yer ever gonna kill those Midvarish bastards."

It was all Michael could do to keep from bursting into laughter.

"An' she said yer more than welcome t' sleep in the barn, though I must warn ye, that's where the pigs sleep, too. 'S not the freshest smellin' place, if ye know what I mean."

If Joseph was any indication, Michael was sure the barn was not pleasant to the olfactory organs by any stretch of the imagination.

"But 'tis warm and dry anyway. There's a storm comin', ye see."

"Your hospitality is most appreciated, Joseph. I fear that there are too many of my men to crowd into a barn for the night. But we will, however, take you up on your mother's kind offer for food. And of course, to sleep on your land for the night, if you would oblige," said Michael.

"Follow me," Joseph said, and Michael and Ilias did just that.

~

Joseph's mother's idea of feeding a battalion of hungry Har-Navarian soldiers was surprisingly generous and robust, to say the least. Whatever Michael had assumed Joseph had meant by way of food—warm bread, some cheese, perhaps—he had woefully underestimated the hospitality of the poor farming family nestled on the border of the Wild Wood.

Adina, Joseph's mother, a plump, pushy sort of woman, had fed fifty young men an assortment of hot stew, fresh, buttery bread, several cheeses, fresh fruits, and more cake than Michael had seen at the last banquet at Benalle. And heavens above, it was all delicious, the best food that had crossed their lips since departing nearly a month ago. Where she had procured such a bounty on such short notice, Michael surmised he might never know—it was enough food that Michael couldn't help but wonder if she had some sort of wealthy benefactor providing such abundance. But he was grateful nonetheless and had told her so with a bow of his head and an attempt to shake her hands, which she had turned into a full-frontal assault of a hug and a sloppy wet kiss to his cheek, followed by a plump hand patting his face while her misty eyes smiled. "Go out there and stop those bastards, won't ye?" Adina had said.

Michael could only nod. Such faith this woman had in him and his men. Such hope in her eyes at the sight of them. He hoped he didn't let her down.

Indeed, Joseph had been right about an approaching storm, for sometime deep into the night, surrounded by the cacophony of bodily noises only a brood of young, eager, well-fed soldiers can produce, Michael had found he couldn't sleep. And when rumbling thunder and distant lightning had kept him from even relaxing on the pine-needled ground, he decided a midnight stroll was in order.

The boys would be fine and relatively dry under the cover of the conifers and makeshift tents they had pitched. Michael, on the other hand, just needed to breathe air that wasn't rife with flatulence, thank you very much.

Why he headed towards the pig barn Joseph had mentioned, he wasn't sure. The air was certainly no fresher there. Still, something had pulled at him, called to him, beckoned him. Something he couldn't quite name. So he had walked through the trees to a clearing, making out the landscape with the paltry moonlight still left from the gathering clouds.

The barn sat on the edge of a plowed field, illuminated here and there by flashes of white lightning. Michael's feet carried him as if they had a mind of their own. And when he made his way inside, dodging the first fat drops of the coming storm, he wondered why he had been so drawn to it.

It was nothing more than a barn. Bales of hay. Pitchforks. Saddles. A few buckets and a water trough.

Just a barn.

He decided to explore it nonetheless.

A torch perched on the wall caught his eye, and he pulled some flint from his pocket, struck it against his sword, and lit the torch that he might better investigate the mundane place that had inexplicably drawn him. The light helped to confirm what he was already beginning to suspect—that his imagination had gotten much too big in the days since he had stumbled across the strange cave full of feral boars. It was about damn time he stopped letting his mind imagine the worst and started doing his job as captain—finding and killing the Midvarish bastards.

He had just turned to leave the empty barn when a violent clap of thunder caught him off guard. He tumbled to the ground, careful to keep his torch from landing on the straw and burning the place to the ground. Not exactly the kind of thank you he wanted to leave Adina and Joseph.

But as he was scrambling back to his feet, he noticed a handle nailed into one of the floorboards. Round and rusted with disuse, mostly disguised by rogue straw and debris, he might never have noticed it had his face not landed inches away. And sure enough, his damned imagination started running wild again. Which was why, he supposed, that he pulled on the handle.

It was stubborn at first, unwilling to give into his pulls and tugs. But it eventually gave way, revealing nothing but darkness beneath. He shone his torch down the hole to find a ladder that led down, down, down. So far down, in fact that there was no end in sight.

Only a fool would go down there.

Of course, Michael began his descent, thinking perhaps that the sting of the loss of the woman you love, coupled with the madness of a month on the road with a bunch of young men eager to kiss his ass, was the reason for such tomfoolery. Either that or he truly had lost his mind.

The ladder it turned out, didn't descend into the pits of Sheol, thank Providence. But upon further inspection, Michael realized it probably wasn't too much of a departure from what he imagined Sheol to be like—not that he spent a lot of time imagining such a place. Still, the sweltering heat, the unnerving stillness to the air, and the noises...

No, those weren't just noises. Those were screams.

He could hear them clearly now—the distant screams of... of women.

Oh shit. What was he doing down here? Genius that he was, he trudged further into what he realized was most definitely an underground tunnel. One which bore an unnerving resemblance to the one he had found under the skull rock.

Shit, indeed.

Maybe Ilias had been right.

But no, that didn't make sense at all. For if this really was a tunnel that led to an underground Midvarish army, why was he surrounded by the sounds of screaming women? And why would a tunnel replete with what he could only imagine to be torture in any way be connected to a tunnel full of feral boars?

No, no. Perhaps they were similar, these underground pathways he had found. But only in the way that he imagined everything underground to be similar, not that he'd had much in the way of opportunity to explore such places before.

No, no. Surely all the underground was like this?

The screams grew louder, no longer a distant echo as he traversed the well-worn cave but now much closer. Perhaps even on the other side of the wall.

He almost shuddered with the chills running down his spine. Whose hair-brained idea was it to come down here, again?

But if there were women being tortured here…

Before him spread a torchlit underground lair, expertly carved through the earth and obviously vast.

Michael carefully rounded a corner, his hand poised on the hilt of his sword, his breath a quiet rhythm as he peered around the wet cave wall, only to find a sight that nearly knocked him to his knees.

For there, kneeling on the ground was a young girl. Four young girls, actually. But only one of them turned so that Michael could see her profile: almond eyes set against thick, dark lashes and high cheekbones.

Her relaxed auburn curls spilled down her back as she knelt, her sturdy hands on the backs of two other girls as she whispered, "I don't think they saw us."

Frantic nods signaled the other girls' agreement.

"Listen," she continued in hushed panic. "We're going to get out of here. But you have to do exactly as I say."

And it was in that moment, when the light of his own torch shone on the girl's cheek just enough, that he saw it. The striking resemblance, the same poise, even under pressure. The same tanned skin and glossy tendrils of hair.

This girl could have been Delaney's twin.

Chapter XL

"I'm frightened, Dabria," said a tiny girl crouched close to one of the others.

"I know," said the girl Michael assumed was Dabria. The one who looked just like Delaney, if perhaps a little younger. "We're all frightened, Dysis. But it will be all right. Everything will be all right."

"Don't let the bad mans find us again," said little Dysis. And when the little girl turned her eyes to Dabria, Michael saw that she, too, looked like a tiny version of Delaney.

Something in his heart tore at the sight.

The other two girls also turned their faces enough for the truth to hit him squarely between the eyes. These girls didn't just *look* like Delaney's sisters.

They *were* Delaney's sisters. Not impeded from writing to her by an overbearing father. Unable to write to her because they had been captured.

Michael could only pray that they hadn't been subjected to whatever was cause for the screams he could still hear. But judging from the looks in their eyes, the tremor in their young hands, he imagined that they were assuredly running from something worse than he wanted to imagine.

Maybe temporary insanity had indeed come over him tonight, but Michael stepped out from behind the wall where he had been watching the Dupree girls. At the sight of him, the littlest one drew in a breath, and the other girls collectively turned to see what had given their little sister such a fright.

"Don't be afraid," Michael whispered, crouching to his feet.

"Stay away from us," said one of the other two girls, likely the next youngest of the four.

Dysis had begun to cry, Dabria holding her close to her chest, a gesture that looked so much like Delaney that Michael's breath caught in his throat. "I'm here to help you," he tried. "I think...I think I know your sister."

"Our sister?" asked the other girl. The one who hadn't spoken yet. There was a keen determination in her eyes—the same kind Michael had seen in Delaney's eyes any time she had set her mind to something. The urge to pull all four of the girls into his arms and hug them tightly was strong. He had to get them out of here, he had to...

"How do you know our sister?" the girl tried again.

"Delaney, she... She is my..." Providence, how was he supposed to explain this to them? "She was once betrothed to my king. She is my friend and..."

"Michael?" the girl asked incredulously.

Michael's gaze shot to her, and he knew for certain he was looking at a gaggle of Dupree women. Relief coupled with maddening urgency coursed through his veins. He nodded, and the sister whose name he did not know stepped towards him. It was Dabria who caught her arm.

"How do you know it's really him?" she scolded.

"He looks exactly like she described him." The younger two nodded their agreement.

"What if he's lying?" Dabria asked. "What if he's one of them?" she asked, nodding her head back down the cave, back toward the screams.

The determined sister took a moment to appraise him before she said, "He's not one of them. He's Michael. I know it. I can see it in his eyes."

"See *what* in his eyes?" Dabria scoffed.

"How much he loves her."

Michael nearly fell over at that. But he shook it off as quickly as he could. "Please, there is no time. You need to get out of here," he begged, frightened by the sounds coming from the tunnel. The sounds that were getting closer and closer and...

It was Dysis, the tiniest one, who broke free from her sister's arms and ran to Michael, nearly toppling him over when she threw herself into his arms. "Help us, Michael. Please."

He held the little girl to his chest, patting her back as he said, "It will be all right. But you must follow me. Now."

Maybe it was Dysis's bravery, or the fact that the girls were unwilling to surrender their little sister to a stranger, but the other sisters now seemed keen to follow Michael without argument, so he seized the moment and stood to his feet.

Dysis clung to him like some little monkey, her arms wrapped tightly around his neck, her legs around his torso, her little head buried in his shoulder. He held her close to his chest with one hand, his other hand resting on the hilt of his sword. Providence, Dysis even *smelled* like Delaney, and the nearness of these four Dupree girls was tugging and tearing at his already aching heart.

One of the other girls took his spare hand in hers as they walked, stalking the quiet tunnels like wildcats on the hunt. "I'm Demelza," she said.

"The kitten rescuer," he whispered, remembering the many letters Delaney had read him from the girl. The harrowing kitten rescues had given both him and Delaney many a good chuckle. He peered over Dysis's shoulder to give Demelza a reassuring smile. Her answering grin almost made him chuckle.

She squeezed his hand more tightly. "Where is my sister?"

Michael, keeping a keen eye out for anything out of the ordinary and equally keen to keep the girls calm while he smuggled them out of there, spoke in low tones while his eyes darted about the caves.

"She is at home. At Benalle. She had the baby, did you know that?"

"No, I didn't," Demelza said. "What is it?"

"It's a girl. And she's as beautiful as her mother."

Demelza smiled a sweet, young smile. "What's her name?"

But Michael didn't get to answer, didn't get to tell the girl that he had never gotten to find out the baby's name, because no sooner had she asked the question than he heard—or rather felt—someone behind him, a sword poised at the nape of his neck, foul breath like a cloud of fury behind him.

"Going somewhere with my girls?" a slithering voice asked.

Michael whirled to face the man, setting Dysis down, drawing his sword and sweeping all four Dupree girls behind him in one fluid motion. The man before him was grinning, his eyes addled with lust and likely copious amounts of booze.

Michael snarled in his face. "You won't touch them again."

"On the contrary," the man grinned, "these girls are some of my most prized possessions. I'll touch them again. And then again after that."

A feral growl escaped Michael's lips. He pushed toward the man, his sword poised on the man's neck. "Try it."

The man parried so quickly Michael nearly stumbled, thankful that his training under the commander had been thorough enough to include such things as how to fight a drunk. A strong drunk who apparently didn't care about his life or his fighting form. Providence, it was like sword fighting a sack of potatoes. Albeit strong potatoes. But clumsy, heavy, unheeding potatoes that reeked of ale. What exactly had he planned to do with the girls once he got his filthy hands on them?

Michael didn't have to think too long to figure it out, growling with disgust as he thrusted and parried, blocked and whirled about the man. He had bested him rather easily, he thought, wondering if this was one of the so-called full-blooded Midvarish men Delaney had told him about. If so, they weren't so bad. They weren't so bad at all.

But he soon realized the folly of his own thinking when, within the span of a heartbeat, the man transformed before his eyes. Not a drunken sot any longer, but a brutish, snarling giant, blooded for violence. Still, it wasn't until the man—no, the wraith—paused and spread a massive set of black, membranous wings that Michael nearly pissed his pants.

He stumbled back, one hand behind him to feel for the four girls. They were still there, thank Providence, but trembling violently. "It's all right," he whispered to them. "I won't let him hurt you."

"Michael," one of them said.

"It's all right," Michael repeated.

"Michael," he heard her say again, and only then did he realize his winged beast friend had company.

Nine friends, to be precise.

It was going to take a miracle for them to get out of this alive. So when Michael readied his sword and bent his knees that he might fight, it was absolutely a miracle for which he prayed.

Chapter XLI

It had been a pretty damn successful night, Titus thought as he pulled his last arrow from the dead soldier at his feet. No sense in wasting a good arrow, after all.

Seven girls. He had helped get seven girls out tonight. And while it was barely a dent in the number of girls still left in these tunnels, there were at least seven more girls—fifty-nine now, all told—that he had helped escape this Sheol hole over the last few weeks since discovering them right under his own manor.

But no sign of Daphne, the innocent young servant girl who had been stolen from his home the same night that Penelope had been...

But he would find her. Come Sheol itself, he would find and free Daphne if it was the last thing he ever did.

For now, Titus was tired and ready to call it a night. He would sneak down here tomorrow and start again. Rescuing these girls, he thought, although a paltry contribution, was at least something he could do to help. Fighting was certainly no longer an option, considering that he had committed treason against both the Har-Navarian king and the Midvarish king.

So he would do this; he would help get these girls out of these damned tunnels, these networked caves that housed not only the Midvarish soldiers, but the hub of their slave trade as well. Sex slaves. After all that had happened, after all that he had been made to do, Titus had determined that by the gods, by Providence, by whatever, before this war was over, he would find and kill that Midvarish king with his own two hands. Kill him for what he had done. For what he was doing. To his own people, no less.

But until that blessed day, he'd relish getting these girls out, one bloody fight at a time.

He caught a whiff of the reeking uniform he wore—the one he had stolen from a soldier a few nights ago—and nearly lost his lunch. While it did the job of getting him in and out of these caves without a second glance, no amount of washing had relieved it of its lingering reek of unwashed bodies, blood, and shit. He was ready to get home and peel the damned thing off of him.

But when he rounded the last corner of the tunnels and caught sight of the slaughter that was taking place, he realized home was a long, long way off still.

~

One soldier. It was one stupid young Har-Navarian soldier against at least ten of those wraith beasts Derrick kept hidden in these caverns. A soldier with something to prove, no doubt. Bloody imbecile. He was tempted to just let the idiot face those monsters himself and whatever fate he deserved.

He would have had he not noticed what exactly it was the soldier was defending. For there, crouched behind a boulder, trembled four young auburn-haired girls, tears pouring from their eyes.

"Please," one of them said. "Help us."

"Shh," another scolded. "He's one of them."

One of them? Those wraith pieces of shit? He most certainly was not. But when he looked down at his blood-soaked uniform—the black and crimson of Midvar—he understood her assumption.

Titus looked back toward the man defending these girls, bloodied and worn but shockingly capable of holding his own against these foul beasts. Startled, he realized that this wasn't just some random young soldier, keen to prove himself.

It was someone he knew and knew well. Someone he had trained himself when the soldier was only a boy.

It was Michael Aman.

For a split second, Titus found himself torn between helping the girls get out and helping Michael not to die. So as quickly as he could, he ushered the girls away from the fray. "This way," he said, helping them to escape undetected. They crouched behind a broken wagon as they inched toward the opening of the tunnel—the fastest route out.

He looked into the determined eyes of the oldest girl, a pure-blooded Midvarish girl, no doubt—the soldiers never took any other—and said, "If you want to live, you're going to have to listen carefully."

She met his eyes for a moment before nodding curtly.

"This tunnel," he said, pointing to his right, "is the quickest way out. You'll take it all the way to the end, and when you come to a fork, take the left, do you hear me? The left. Not the right. Take the left fork, and it will lead you down another corridor. Then take a right. You'll pass two corridors before you come to a ladder. That ladder will lead you out of here. But you must be quick, do you understand? Stop for no one and nothing. Do you understand me, girl?"

"Down that corridor, then take a left, then a right, pass two corridors and take the ladder."

"Perfect." Titus nodded. "Now get these girls and go. I have a friend who will help you on the other side, all right? She'll find you. Now go. Go!" he said, ushering the gaggle of frightened girls to their freedom.

But one of the younger ones surprised him when she stopped for a moment and gripped his arms. "Help him," she said, shifting her eyes to Michael before running to escape.

~

Gods, he shouldn't even be alive. Michael should have died about five minutes ago. But he was holding his own against these bastards, using every tool in his arsenal, every ounce of his extensive training. King Aiken hadn't been a fool; training Navarian boys to be soldiers had proven a worthwhile cause, if Michael was any indication.

Titus stayed hidden at the broken wagon behind which he had helped the girls escape, watching with awe as Michael fought off one beast after another. Good. Michael was almost…too good. As if some of that Midvarish blood flowed through his veins, too. Titus cast aside the thought, drawing his bow and nocking his arrow, still bloodied from the last Midvarish soldier he had killed. One shot. He would have one damn shot to kill these beasts. Their skin, thick and rough, was too difficult to penetrate with an arrow—even one as big as those Titus had special-made for just such an occasion. No, in his weeks down here, Titus had found that there was only one way to fell these rancid beasts quickly—one shot. Right in the eye, deep enough to go nearly clean through their head. He would have to be quick. More so, he would have to be accurate if he was going to be any help to Michael. So he pulled the bowstring, relishing the tension as it went taut in his hands. One of the soldiers charged Michael, an unearthly snarl on his black lips. Titus didn't wait for it to spot him before he let his arrow loose, flying sure and true right into the eye of the beast. Toppling dangerously, he at last fell to the ground with a thud. Michael, too engrossed in the battle, didn't bother to search from where that saving arrow had come.

Two more beasts, however, were poised to pick up where the dead one had left off, and Michael, tiring and covered in blood, was fading fast. Heart pounding, Titus released two more arrows, swift as an adder. The soldiers never saw them coming. Within moments, between the four Michael had killed and the five Titus had shot, Michael was down to only one. One who, it seemed, was enraged with his brothers' deaths and keen to exact revenge on his unlikely foe.

Michael tried to ready his sword but instead collapsed into a bloodied heap on the ground. The wraith chuckled, kneeling to snap Michael's neck.

But he didn't get a chance before Titus's arrow sank deeply into his neck. Incapacitated, he collapsed on top of Michael in a heap of black sinew and thick, inky blood, his gigantic wings sprawled over them like a blanket. Down. But not dead.

Titus jumped from his hiding place and ran to Michael's side, brandishing his bloody sword. He lifted it over his head, poised to sever the beast's head from his still-breathing body. But in a flash, too swift to be human, the beast rolled onto his back and lunged for Titus, a wicked blade angled for his gut. Titus barked a filthy curse and dodged the blade, but only just. The tip caught on his uniform, slicing through it like warm butter.

The beast growled, and horror flashed in Titus as he realized that was a smile growing on the creature's mouth.

"He'll find out what you're doing, Titus. And he'll have your head for it," he snarled, blood dripping from his lips as he struggled to say the words around the arrow protruding from his thick throat.

Titus did not wait for him to taunt any longer. He whirled, brandishing his sword, and severed the beast's head in one powerful blow.

The black skin and mangled hair toppled absurdly to the ground, spraying Titus and Michael in dark blood as it went. But from beneath the remains of the beast's body and wings, Titus could hear Michael groaning. He struggled to move the heap of pure-blooded Midvarish flesh that lay strewn over the barely breathing Har-Navarian hero. With a mighty groan, he heaved, managing to roll away the carcass and free Michael, pulling him up so that he might help him out before another round of wraiths figured out what had happened here.

Michael's head lolled sloppily, and when Titus hooked his arm under Michael's, he realized it wasn't just wraith blood that covered the younger man's body. It was his own. And a lot of it. Michael had been wounded. From the amount of blood covering his uniform, it was a mortal wound.

Shit.

Panic threatened to steal over Titus, but he willed his nerves to calm, knowing that panic would do nothing but get them both killed. He heaved Michael over his shoulder and hurried to escape the gods-forsaken tunnels.

He didn't make it two steps before he collided head first into something—no, someone—as solid and formidable as granite.

Double shit.

"What's this, soldier?" a gravelly voice asked.

Titus suddenly remembered his Midvarish uniform and thanked whatever god was watching over him as he said, "This son of a bitch has been helping girls escape for weeks. I finally caught him. I was about to dispose of the body."

The soldier grunted, inspecting Michael's limp, blood-soaked body as it lay like a rag doll over Titus's shoulder.

"He's the one that's been smuggling the girls?"

"Yes, sir," Titus said.

The other man ran an appraising look over Michael and then said, "Looks like he's still breathing."

"Barely," Titus admitted, the seconds feeling like minutes as he felt Michael's breaths grow weaker and weaker.

"We've been trying to catch that bastard for weeks, and from the looks of him, he's no grunt. Might even be ranked. Let's take him to the king, shall we? I'm sure His Majesty would love a little good news. Perhaps a fresh, young Navarian captain will remind him of his own glory."

"Excellent idea," Titus swallowed.

And so it was that Titus found himself yet again at the mercy of King Derrick of Midvar. This time, with the life of a very dear soldier and friend hanging in the balance.

Chapter XLII

"Ferryl?" he heard an adamant voice coming from his door. He angled his head, a sharp pain shooting down his neck. He was so stiff and sore. And not just the lingering, phantom pains from the fight with Derwin, but from the fact that he hadn't bothered to move in days. Hadn't shifted any more than necessary as the servants helped him move from the bed in the morning to the chair by the window all day.

Sitting.

Brooding.

Worrying.

He realized he had forgotten to respond when he heard the voice again. "I'm coming in whether you like it or not. I'm only giving you a moment in case you're not decent. But it won't be a long moment, mind you."

"Why would I be naked in my receiving chamber, Leala?" he retorted.

The princess came in without preamble. "You're capable of a lot of ridiculous things these days, Ferryl. I wouldn't put much past you."

He only gave her an annoyed grunt as she made her way across the room, this determined sister-in-law of his. He knew that whatever she had to say, he was likely not ready to hear it.

"I came to check on you," she said, a surprisingly warm hand on his shoulder as she took a seat next to him. He opted to stare out the windows that faced the valley to the north of the castle and the ocean beyond.

The princess breathed a resigned sigh. "You're worrying all of us."

Ferryl fiddled with his thumbs, steeling himself for whatever was coming. Whether gushing concern or a sound lecture, he didn't care—he could stomach neither.

"I wish you would at least try."

He gritted his teeth, turning his head away, unwilling to consider what she was asking. He knew what she wanted. The same thing everyone wanted. "You should try to walk, Your Majesty," Mary had said this morning. "It's been weeks, and your leg is on the mend. You need to try to put some weight on it." And when Ferryl had refused, Talia had picked up where Mary had left off, periodically asking him throughout the day if he wanted to try to walk. And now Leala.

No, he damn well didn't want to walk. He didn't want anything except...

"You need some fresh air. Sunshine. You've been cooped up—"

"What I *need*..." he spat. But he couldn't finish the words lingering on his tongue. He needed...

"I know, Ferryl," Leala said, clearly tempering her own outburst. "But right now—"

"I don't want to talk about it."

"Just tell me something, Ferryl," she snapped. "What good will it do to keep living as if the worst has already happened?"

It *had* already happened. It had. Adelaide was dead. As dead as the bond between them, the connection. Where it had once glittered and shone brightly, a solid, unending chain of gold and eternity, now it was little more than smoke in the wind, ashes in a wasteland. Cobwebs.

And the truth of it haunted him, gutted him every time he let his mind so much as dance around the thought.

"I swear I don't understand you sometimes, Ferryl."

"What's that supposed to mean?"

"You're not the type to sit on your ass. That's not who you are." The language was not like her and most unbecoming of a princess. Then again, he imagined being married to Derwin likely exacerbated the side of her that needed to put her foot down now and then. "You're usually the first to do something, the first to take action. But for some reason, when it comes to your wife, you fall apart the moment things don't go your way."

"I'm sorry that my love for my wife is something you fail to understand. Perhaps your marriage is different, but for me, I had every intention of spending the rest of my life *with* her, not away from her. I fail to see how it is incomprehensible that I should mourn such a loss."

"It is not incomprehensible to mourn a loss, Ferryl. The trouble is, you have no definitive proof that you've *had* such a loss aside from your adamant declaration that you can no longer feel her through the so-called bond you share."

Ferryl sucked in a breath to protest, but Leala cut him off. "And before you launch into a tirade, let me start by saying that I do not doubt your word. I have observed over the years I have known you both that you indeed share something rare and precious and that whatever it is you share was only solidified, fortified, upon your marriage. Maybe it is a bond; I don't know. What I do know is that you're not even entirely sure what it is or what it means, so you have no right to determine that the bond has been severed by her death.

"Maybe it has been. Maybe she's dead. But you've been deceived into thinking she was dead before and nearly married Delaney as a result. And while I don't think Delaney would have made such a bad queen, you certainly would have destroyed Michael in the process and ended up with a Midvarish princess for an heir.

"So let's get one thing straight, *Your Majesty,*" she growled. "I'm damn tired of sitting around brooding over dear King Ferryl and his terrible, terrible loss. The court is worried sick about you, your mother-in-law is worried sick about you—even more than she's worried for her own daughter, might I add. I'm tired of pity-pawing around you as if you're a wounded kitten. You need to pull up your bootstraps and be the king this country needs you to be. But more importantly, you need to be the husband your wife needs you to be. Because until you know she's dead, Ferryl—until you're holding her lifeless body in your arms—you have no right, no damn right, to act like this!"

Leala had worked herself into such a frenzy that she paused, sucking in a breath and allowing her shoulders to relax at last. Ferryl only gawked.

Providence, Derwin had married more than his match. He was privately grateful that his hot-headed brother had managed to marry someone who could more than handle him.

Half-brother, that is. Did that make Leala his half-sister-in-law? Was there such a thing?

"Derwin and I did not part well. Did I tell you that?" Leala's sudden change in tone ripped Ferryl from his useless train of thought. Ferryl looked back to his sister-in-law, surprised at the remorse he saw in her usually bright, cunning eyes.

"We were in the midst of a longstanding argument that I refused to resolve, even the morning he left. It has haunted me every moment since, the selfishness of it. The stupidity."

"What happened?" Ferryl asked when he saw the silver sheen of tears line her eyes.

"He wants children. He wants a whole brood of them."

"And you don't?"

"I do," she corrected. "I just didn't want them right now. Not with..."

The war looming. Providence, how well he understood the sentiment. The agony that had flooded his soul at the realization of Adelaide's disappearance had only increased tenfold when he thought of the child in her womb. Their child. The child of the promise. The prophecies. It was with heavy tears and with fear closing his throat and choking his breath that he had shaken his fist at Providence over and over, had begged to understand any of it.

"I cannot blame you, Leala. You were right to wait until—"

"No, I wasn't. Derwin was right. He was right all along. And I didn't see it until he was gone. I was too stubborn to see it."

"To see what?"

"I kept waiting, Ferryl. I kept waiting for life to fall into some sort of normalcy before we thought about children. I kept telling him we couldn't be parents right now, that it didn't make any sense, not with him about to go off to war. And he kept insisting that there would never be a time when it made sense." A fat tear fell down her soft cheek as she looked down to her fiddling hands. "It wasn't until he left, until his absence was an ache in my heart, that I realized how selfish I had been."

She shook her head before lifting her eyes to meet Ferryl's. "Ferryl, I would rather be a widow with his child in my womb than let my husband die with no legacy to leave behind. I'd rather have his child than be left with nothing. I'd rather stop waiting for life to make sense before I started living it.

"And that's what I'm afraid you're doing, Ferryl. Waiting until you *know* your wife is all right before doing what needs to be done to *ensure* that she is. I'm afraid you're missing out on what it is you could be learning because you're afraid of what might happen if you face the truth.

"She might be dead, Ferryl. You're right. But we don't know for certain that she is. And Derwin might die out there. But he's not dead yet. Don't do Adelaide the dishonor of wasting your life away out of fear of the unknown.

"I would rather face the worst knowing that I had lived my life to the fullest with the man I love than let him die drowning in my fears. And while we're in this place, Ferryl, where the unknown lurks before us, where there are more questions than answers, give Adelaide the honor of living your life the way she would want you to live it. Don't waste away to a shadow. You shared a dream once—you and your Lizybet. Don't give up on it before you've even given it a chance to fly."

~

The day was brighter than he expected, the sun a shock of light and heat on his skin after weeks and weeks inside the castle. But the halls of the palace had not warmed as quickly as had the air outside, for while it still felt like the last vestiges of winter clung to the air in his chamber, outside, spring had made her long overdue debut.

And the cheery afternoon only mocked him.

Still, he knew Leala had been right. And Talia. And Mary. And damn it, even Avigail had tried to encourage him to walk. One thing was for sure: despite his lack of a wife, Ferryl was most certainly not lacking in suffocating feminine concern. He had finally decided to go outside for the sole reason that he couldn't stand their hovering another second.

Mounting Erel, on the other hand, had proven a more difficult task than he had assumed. Yes, Mary had definitely been right. He could walk now, though he imagined he looked more like a newborn fawn than a king on these weak, wobbly legs of his. And it didn't help that he had a limp. But at least he could stand to piss without needing help to the privy any longer. And even though he had surely looked like a raging sot, he had finally, mercifully, managed to mount Erel with nothing else but the help of a stool.

So he rode his horse, letting the briny sea air and the smells of fresh grasses and spring blooms fill his nostrils and clear his mind. Before he even realized where he was going, he found himself there, at that place. The one place he wasn't sure he'd be able to face without her.

The Secret Place.

Moss clung to the granite stones that formed the little outcropping nestled in the hill. Vines slithered and slunk over the surface, a network of the new growth of a season right before his eyes. He went to dismount Erel, only to realize that he hadn't the strength in his leg to support his weight in the stirrup. So he dismounted on the opposite leg, an awkward move, and fell to his rear with a thud, cursing Derwin under his breath.

He made it to his feet again, gritting his teeth against the stiffness of his muscles, ignoring the gnawing in the back of his mind that reminded him that if the war came to Benalle today, he'd be dead in under a minute.

He plopped himself down in a spot just under the rock and plucked a long stem of grass on which to chew, thinking of how many times he had made that very move when he brought Elizabeth here as children.

"You're not a horse, Ferryl. Why do you insist on chewing on the grass?" she would ask.

"Do you question everything I do, Lizybet?" he would quip.

"Only the ridiculous things."

Ferryl laughed out loud at the memory. Providence, how he missed her. She never let him get away with stupidity. She always called him out when he was being a fool.

And as he pulled the grass from his mouth, twirling it between his fingers, he understood how very much more he needed her now than ever before.

"You know, if you'd open your eyes, you might find she's not nearly as far away as she seems."

Ferryl spun around so quickly that a pain shot down his lame leg. The source of the voice was a stooped old man in a homespun shirt and trousers, whirling his own blade of grass between his fingers. "I've always liked the taste of it, too. Helps me think." The old man put the grass between his back teeth and promptly began to chew in much the same manner as Ferryl.

"Who are you?" Ferryl asked.

The old man shrugged. "You used to know, I thought. Now I'm not so sure."

"I've met you before?"

"If you don't even remember it, I wonder if I made an impact," he chuckled. The old man's hair, as thin as cobwebs and equally as light, fluttered in the breeze, tossing hither and thither as it kissed his cheeks and shoulders. His brow, riddled with wiry and unkempt hairs, resembled two legs of a spider wiggling above his eyes. In fact, the man so very much resembled an aging, gray arachnid that Ferryl had to wonder if he were even human.

"You haven't been here in a long time, Ferryl. Any reason?"

The question made Ferryl wonder if he had met the man sometime here at the Secret Place and just didn't remember—a lingering side effect of the curse his mother had put on his memory last year, perhaps? There was something achingly familiar about him. Something Ferryl couldn't quite put a finger on.

He decided to answer the question instead of asking his own. "My wife and I have been so busy with…everything. I suppose we haven't had time."

The old man nodded, his old lips set in a thin line, his watery gray eyes appraising. "You haven't had time for many things, I fear."

True. Very true. But what things was the old man referring to?

The old man took a seat on a stone across from Ferryl, the grass on which he was chewing bobbing against his lips as he spoke. "You fancy yourself a great failure these days, don't you, son?"

Ferryl huffed a laugh. "And then some," he replied sardonically, mentally nodding to the healthy colony of black færies that skittered about his head. They seemed to enjoy his misery even more than he.

The man nodded again. "Even the færies have forgotten their purpose, haven't they?"

"You can see them? I... I didn't think anyone could see them but me."

He tried to grab one, tried to inspect them further. But they were fast...too fast for him to catch. Like a young spring lizard on the trunk of a tree.

"Who are you that you should know so much about me, anyway?" Ferryl asked, turning his attention away from the flittering nuisance cloud of færies.

"I know a great deal more about you than you realize, I would hazard," said the old man, a kind of patience to his voice that put Ferryl at ease, despite the fact that he was having a rather personal conversation with a complete stranger. "But you know, Ferryl, you never fail a test with Providence. You just take it over and again until you pass." The old man let the words sink in, let a quiet moment pass before he said, "You see it's not what's in here that matters so much." He pointed a gnarled old finger to his brow. "It's when it gets in here that it counts." He moved the gnarled finger to his chest, pointing to his heart. "And sometimes, that short little journey is the longest one we take."

"I don't understand what you mean."

"Obviously. Or we wouldn't be having this conversation," he said, humor coloring his wizened eyes. And that's when Ferryl spotted them—a pair of færies sitting on the old man's shoulder. Bright færies, their wings glistening in the mottled sunlight. They seemed to be staring right at Ferryl and smiling. Hand in hand, the two færies bowed to him. Bowed. Each wore a circlet of dandelion fluff atop their heads. A king and queen, then? Did færies have kings and queens?

"You keep thinking you're failing," the old man went on. "You keep thinking that life has to look a certain way in order to be right. And most of all, you keep thinking you can't do it without her. Don't you see it, Ferryl?"

"See what?"

"You're putting it all on yourself. When the truth is, it's got nothing to do with you."

"Who's it to do with, then?"

"Providence, of course," the old man said matter-of-factly, as if Ferryl were the only soul in the world not privy to such knowledge. "The sooner you understand who this is really about, the sooner you can go about your business."

"What business? What do you mean?"

"The prophecy, Ferryl. The task that has been appointed to you."

Exasperated, Ferryl said, "And how is it that I am supposed to go about the business of prophecy fulfillment when the other half of the prophecy I am supposed to be fulfilling is dead?"

The færies perched on the old man's shoulder didn't take flight at Ferryl's tirade. That's when Ferryl realized they couldn't—their wings were shredded.

"Since when is it for you to determine when and how Providence does things? Mighty arrogant, don't you think?"

"Arrogant? *Arrogant?*" Ferryl spat. "My wife is dead! Murdered! And you have the nerve to call me arrogant?" He moved to get up, but his leg wasn't quite capable of standing as quickly as he'd like. He fumbled, pushing all of his weight onto his good leg as he shifted awkwardly.

"Sit down, Ferryl," the old man said, and his sudden authoritative tone was such a shock that Ferryl did exactly as the old man bade. "You were chosen, you know. Or have you forgotten?"

Ferryl only nodded. How many times had he heard it? And how many times lately had he wondered if Providence hadn't made a mistake? He looked again to the two færies sitting on the old man's shoulder—broken færies, incapable of flying. And he a broken king, incapable of walking, much less ruling.

Maybe Providence liked using broken things.

"You've let your own bitterness get in the way," said the oddly familiar old man. "You've let that root grow, and if you don't look out, you'll be facing a mighty oak of hate, of bitterness, of bile that will not so easily be uprooted."

"What am I supposed to do?" Ferryl asked. "How am I supposed to do this without her?"

"She is your wife, Ferryl. And a wife is a gift. But she is not a right. You've made her your god, Ferryl. You've worshiped her above everything else in your life. And you've let the sting of her absence burn away at your heart until nothing but bitterness remains. It will destroy you, Ferryl. If you keep this up, it will destroy you and everything you hold dear."

"The prophet, Bedell—he said our destinies were entwined. They were meant to be lived out together," Ferryl protested.

"Entwined, Ferryl. Not inextricable. Not one and the same. Your destinies are like these spring vines," he said, pointing to the growth that hung over Ferryl's head. "Woven together, bound and beautiful. But each vine is its own entity. It is how they work together, how their separate threads weave a greater tapestry, that makes them beautiful. It is in their separateness that they become one. And it is a miracle, Ferryl, that only the magic of Providence could divine. You are your own person, and Adelaide her own as well. Your love is a balm and gift, but it is not the point. It is only a byproduct and a benefit. Stop putting the burden on yourself to do what only Providence can do. Learn to trust what could be instead of what is. Only then will your heart learn what your head already knows. Only then will you learn to listen to the right voices. Your heart, Ferryl, is plagued by lies. Like moths, they swarm you. Devour you. Burden you. It comes to this: which voice are you going to listen to? The lies? Or the truth?"

Like moths, he had said, and Ferryl fixated on the thought. Were the færies nothing more than…a product of his own thinking? As if they had heard him, as if even his thoughts could give them pause, the dark færies…Ferryl could have sworn there were fewer of them.

And that's when he realized it, the warmth around him. Not just from the spring day but from….magic. Yes, magic. Palpable. Strong. A present magic that buzzed through the air, through his very veins.

The old man stood from the perch on which he rested, a smile on his wrinkled mouth. He merely nodded before he said, "Yes, it's magic, son. It's time you started giving it room again. Your story isn't over. Not yet."

And then he turned on his heel, a deft move for such a feeble old man. And whether he walked away or simply vanished, Ferryl couldn't be sure, too captivated by the color, the light that he saw. Violent colors, impossible colors. Light so resplendent, so radiant it nearly blinded him. Had it been there all along?

Somewhere in his mind he realized it must have been. He had just been unable to see it.

And that's when it hit him.

He had met the man before.

Chapter XLIII

he færies followed him home.

On his shoulder.

Or maybe Ferryl was hallucinating. He hadn't decided yet. But the tiny creatures with broken wings had seemed determined to follow him after he had left the Secret Place and clumsily mounted Erel for the ride home. They had leapt—*leapt,* not flown—from the shoulder of the old man to Ferryl's. Bowing again, Ferryl knew with one look from their tiny, light-filled eyes that they wanted to come with him. So he had obliged.

For a heartbeat, he wondered what the servants and courtiers would think of him strolling through the castle corridors with two færies on his shoulder. But no one had noticed. No one had even pretended *not* to notice. Just like the dark færies that had been plaguing him for months, the people of his court were oblivious to the light færies that now accompanied him.

And as for those dark færies…

Well, they had scattered. The moment the old man had stood, the moment that light, that color had swirled about Ferryl, the dark færies had scattered like rats in torchlight.

And now, sitting in his private chambers, the færies perched on the sill of the largest window, Ferryl watched them, their music a soothing rhapsody. It shouldn't have surprised him—the fact that he could see them when no one else could was surely an indication that there was something…different about him. But when those færies *spoke* to him…

Ferryl picked his heart up out of his ass and listened.

"You are not alone, Your Majesty," said the male, his skin peppered with minuscule scars. Battle scars, a mirror to the shreds he had for wings. His silver-white hair shone like moonflame in the candlelight, a streak of black coming from his brow, as if something terrible had happened to him and his body had reacted violently. Then again, whatever had happened to his wings…

His wife—companion, mate, whatever she was—had a twin set of wings, shredded all the way to her tiny back. But where the male's wings looked like they had met a jagged blade, hers looked like they had met flame—the tatters swaying like melted wax from her shoulders.

"What happened to you?" Ferryl heard himself ask before he thought better of it.

It was the female who answered. "The Darkness, King Ferryl. And it will happen to all of Eloah's creation before this is over if we don't work together."

Eloah. He remembered the name—an ancient name. Before the humans had called him Providence, the lesser creatures had called him Eloah.

The living god.

"No offense, but how exactly can you help against humans?" *Much less those Midvarish demons*, he thought, but didn't add.

Ferryl could have sworn the male's eyes shone with a wicked

gleam when he looked to the female. "My name is Melekfa," he said. "The king of the færies. This is Malkah, Queen of the Light. We'd like to show you why we came all this way to find you."

~

Mother of all things holy.

If this was the magic of Providence, Ferryl couldn't imagine how any living creature could survive. And from such tiny creatures! Ferryl's heart pounded as he watched the færy king and færy queen conjure what could only be described as a hurricane above them. The clouds, green with menace, swirled in a vortex of wind and rain, his face already wet with the spray. He dodged a bolt of lightning—*lightning*—in his chambers and finally managed to say, "Yes, I think that could be helpful."

Ferryl's own magic seemed to dance in his veins, and for a heartbeat he wondered—what was *he* capable of? What sort of magic had he been gifted with? He had never tested it. Never even considered it. The storm swirled above him, a maelstrom capable of devouring man and beast alike, yet contained within his receiving chamber. Was he capable of such feats? Such miracles? Had Providence bestowed upon him the same kind of miraculous power?

His mind immediately began to calculate what this sort of thing could do to turn the tide of any battle…

"Let us help you, Your Majesty," said Melekfa, tearing Ferryl from his thoughts. "Let us help you turn this war."

"Ferryl," he said. "My friends call me Ferryl."

Malkah, the queen, grinned. "Ferryl. You are a good king. And your people are looking to you now. We would be honored to join you in this war."

"We?" he asked. "Are there more of you?"

Malkah grinned again. Broader. "Many more."

"My mate gave everything to summon all of the færies of the Light," said Melekfa, his eyes turning to Malkah's for a moment—and at the love, the hint of sorrow there, Ferryl wondered what exactly had happened to the færies. What was their story; what had they sacrificed? What had they faced that they should seem so determined, so hopeful, despite their broken wings?

Melekfa went on. "We have known for some time of the imminent danger awaiting us from the east. It is not only a danger for humans, but for all of Eloah's creation. So we have summoned our kind to join you. We were once, in the ancient days, the wielders of the weather, as you call it. We would like to be so again."

Thoughts, a thousand of them, swirled around in his mind. How to alert Derwin. How to prepare. What his armies would need.

"Leave the logistics to us," Malkah said, as if she could read his thoughts. "I can assure you, your people and your men will be safe."

Thunder cracked above them, startling Ferryl.

"Sorry," said Malkah, breathing a small laugh before she snuffed out the storm with a thought.

Safe. Right.

There was nothing safe about the magic of Providence. Ferryl prayed he'd never forget it.

"Will you accept our help?" asked Melekfa.

Ferryl looked again at the tiny king who somehow seemed larger than he. Larger than life.

And for the first time since losing his wife, Ferryl remembered the sweet taste of hope.

~

The færies hadn't stayed, though Ferryl had offered them a place to sleep for the night. Instead they had merely bowed and said they would return to him soon. Love—that's what had shone so brightly in their eyes. An endless love for each other. It had made Ferryl's heart ache all the more for his own wife. His mate.

He watched them disappear like a speck in the sky through the great wall of windows before he turned to face the vast chamber he had shared with his wife—the chamber that had once been his father's. But the king of Navah had not shared his bed with his queen as Ferryl shared with Adelaide. No, his father had borne the breadth of this room alone, as Ferryl did now.

He wondered how his father had fared so long without companionship.

Or perhaps his father had found it somewhere. Perhaps his father had had a mistress none of them had known about. Someone. Ferryl hoped Aiken had had someone with whom to bear the burdens of a kingdom. Providence knew Ferryl was missing his own someone tremendously, wherever she was. Whatever had happened to her.

Absently, Ferryl pulled on the bond he shared with his wife.

Perhaps his heart hoped more than he realized. Perhaps he hadn't completely abandoned the idea that she might be alive.

It was terrifying to hope. Terrifying to give his heart the space to think that she might be alive, when most of the world wanted her dead. When the king to the east had spent his life making sure of it.

But he realized he did still hope, even if ever so faintly.

He hoped for his wife.

He hoped for his kingdom.

He hoped for the child that might have survived in her womb.

He pulled a little harder on that bond, and this time, he could have sworn he felt a glimmer on the other side.

Chapter XLIV

One more hill. There was one more hill before the castle came into view. How well she knew it. How many times as a girl had she crossed that very hill in a carriage with her father, mother, and sisters? How many times had she naïvely looked forward to visiting the grand castle in the heart of her kingdom despite the man who sat on the throne?

The weeks on horseback had been tiring, but nothing exhausted Delaney more than the thought of what lay before her. When she and Talia had crossed the border days ago through the Northern Pass—that tiny sliver of land that wasn't crowded with a cursed forest—her stomach had been in her throat the whole time. But the soldiers that guarded the border hadn't questioned their story. They had taken one look at Delaney—with her signature auburn curls and dark skin—and believed her lie. The tale she had spun of running from the maddened Har-Navarian king who had lost his mind when he lost his wife. They had bought every line without question.

Easy.

It had been too easy to get back into Midvar after all the ways she had failed her father, failed her king.

The first black spire broke the horizon over the hill, and Delaney pulled on the reins of her horse, taking a moment to wrap her arms tightly around the bundle at her breast.

"Is the baby all right?" Talia asked, also bringing her horse to a stop.

"She's fine," Delaney muttered, too spellbound by that damning spire. The sheer blackness of it wickedly pointed to the sky like a beacon of darkness.

"You all right?" Talia pressed on.

Delaney tore her attention from her uncle's castle—Goleath Palace—and looked to her companion.

"From this moment forward, we cannot make mistakes," she said, the words a damning omen. "My uncle is shrewd and cunning and cruel. We must stick to the plan, or we will not only forfeit our kingdom, but our lives. Do you understand, Talia?"

Queen Adelaide's servant nodded her head, her black hair pulled back against her neck in a loose braid. The gray at her temples seemed muted in the Midvarish sunlight, but her green eyes shone like emeralds.

"We're going to succeed, Delaney. I know we are."

Delaney only nodded, nudging her horse back into a trot and praying to Michael's god—praying to Providence himself that Talia was right.

Titus had argued and argued with her. Yelled, even. But Adelaide of Haravelle, Queen of Har-Navah, had stood her ground, insisting on her plan. Insisting it would work. He had taken her north to a band of refugees who were escaping to the coast, parting with her weeks ago, half angry, half dumbstruck. She had merely waved him off, letting him think she was running—hiding until all of this was over. As he had begged her to do.

Now, standing before that damning, black castle, its spindly spires like talons clawing the clouds, willing her trembling hands to still, she wondered if Titus hadn't been right. Was she getting into waters much deeper than she had imagined?

Guards patrolled every entrance. Soldiers blooded with a brutality that emanated from the very marrow of their bones. But she had been tracking the slaves that were being quietly traded from the northern seas for weeks—had come across them when she had sneaked across the border at the Northern Pass. And she knew where they were going. It seemed as good a plan as any—to become a caracal in the darkness, awaiting her moment to pounce.

So she walked silently, the homespun fabric of the ragged excuse for a dress she had stolen yesterday scratching her skin. She had forgotten what it felt like—the fabric. The silks and velvets and fine linens she had worn in the months since becoming a queen had spoiled her.

She watched in silence as the guard herded the newest shipment of slaves toward the castle, waiting for her moment to sneak in. To become one of them.

To destroy.

It would work. It had to work.

She was the dead queen.

She was the daughter of the promise.

She would not fail.

Adelaide of Haravelle placed loving hands over the small swell of her belly and seamlessly merged into the crowd of slaves awaiting their doom.

376

378

ACKNOWLEDGMENTS

o one told me what it would be like to write novels. That three in, I'm still wondering where to begin when it comes to acknowledging what goes into these puppies.

So let me start with the heroes.

Arielle.

Once again, you've shown me that not all heroes wield swords (although I'm pretty sure you do). Some heroes wield red pens, sassy comments, and obsessive attention to detail. Couple that with your insatiable curiosity, endearing positivity, and oddly comforting way of telling me I'm wrong in the best way possible, and you, my friend, are my personal hero. Thank you for putting up with my neurotic conversations. Thank you for pep-talking me through Messenger and commenting on things you like in my books. Thank you for telling me when I need to fix things and doing so with grace. I wouldn't have the courage to publish without knowing I have you.

Nathalie, I love hearing your feedback. You're one of those rare people who does what they say they're going to do, who gives feedback that matters, and who makes me feel like my books are worth something. I wish we didn't live a world apart, but one of these days, I'm going to meet you face to face and thank you for the confidence you didn't know you had given me.

Elena, you're my timeless friend. My forever. And you make me feel like the next Rowling. Thanks for loving these characters as much as I do. Thanks for fangirling their story arcs with me, and thank you for always asking me about my books. You'll never know how much it means.

Lance, one of these days I'm going to find a way to tell you how much you mean to me. Until then, read these love stories and know that you're the one who taught me what love is. I'll love you until the end. You're my sun, my moon, my starlit sky. Without you, I dwell in darkness.

Virgil, you've shown me what heroes look like and you make me want to be a better person. I love you, Baby Bear. You encourage me daily. And when you come home with yet another paper you've written on your "author mom," you make my heart soar. I want to be just like you when I grow up.

Addie, you're a queen. To the marrow of your bones. Never apologize for that, little one. You're destined for greatness and you've inspired every strong female I've ever written—and you're only six. The world won't be ready for you. Come at them anyway.

To my family who probably won't read this because you don't read fiction... It's okay. I get it. I don't read political books, so we'll call it even. I love you all, nonetheless. I'm thankful for the crazy, reckless, wild people you are. You've inspired my worlds in more ways than one.

To the reader who holds this book in your hands—what can I possibly say? It blows my mind that you're reading this at all. That you've come this far on the journey with me. There are many more to come, and I hope they inspire. I hope they ignite. I hope they encourage. But most of all, I hope they let you dream a little bigger, hope a little harder, and love a little louder. Thank you for journeying into Har-Navah with me.

And lastly, to Eloah. I keep hoping I'll find a way to put you into words. These pages are my latest attempt. May they show the world a glimpse of what I've seen.

Also.........

Dear reader, I know you're probably a tiny bit pissed off at me at the moment. After all, this is not just a cliffhanger. This is a throw-me-off-the-cliff-and-leave-me-for-dead ending. I get it. I hate those, too.

In my defense, this was actually only the first half of the last book. That's right, the original "last book" was about 200,000 words and probably close to 1000 print pages. And since that would have been about a, oh... $50 paperback, I decided to split it up into two books.

Yep. It was solely for financial reasons that I split this book up. To save you money. I'm sorry. But I'm not. But I am. But I'm really not.

Don't worry.

The next book is GLORIOUS.

But there's a bonus book coming, too. You're going to learn the story of Melekfa and Malkah, those broken færies that visited Ferryl. So hang tight. It will all be worth it, I promise.

Confidently,

About the Chalam Færytales

Want to know more?
Visit **ChalamFaerytales.com**

~

The Chalam Færytales Series:
Book I - The Promised One
Book II - The Purloined Prophecy
Book III - The Parallax
Book IV - Coming Fall 2019

THE LAIR

Join us for exclusive content, giveaways,
and interaction with Morgan. This is the place to be to learn about
the next books in the series first!

Facebook.com/groups/MGFVIPLair

Curating the Magic

Looking for your next binge? Want to stay up to date with the best in fantasy books, movies, artists, and artisans?
Join us at **EpicFaerytales.com**
+
Facebook.com/EpicFaerytales

Plus, join our Facebook Group:
Facebook.com/groups/FantasyBooksandMovies

WRITER. MUSICIAN. ARTIST.

In case you're unaware, Morgan is much more than an author. You can find exclusive art, original music, and so much more
at her website:
MorganGFarris.com

The Store

@ Morgan G Farris

ABOUT THE AUTHOR

So let's just be real here... My name is Morgan and I'm a chronic over-achiever and avid binger of *The Office*. When I watch *Lord of the Rings*, I watch the extended versions, and they're still not long enough. I won arguments in elementary school by out-quoting everyone with my vast knowledge of *The Princess Bride*. So yeah, I'm kind of a big deal.* I used to have a mohawk‡. And once I had purple bangs‡. But I try not to let that dictate my current fashion choices, which are just as confused, I confess. Bless.

In my spare time, I write. A lot. Songs, stories, articles, novels... It's just this thing in me that I have to get out. The book you're reading, part of *The Chalam Færytales*, is sort of a magnum opus of all the things that have been stirring in me from the time I was a kid—musing about the existence of humanity, pondering the wonder of God and the ongoing work of redemption... you know, kid stuff. I'm real proud of it (that's my Texanese coming out. Fight me.) I'd be honored if you left a review of it somewhere on the interwebs. (Consequently, I'm convinced that novel writing is just an acceptable form of psychosis, but it's definitely a beast within me that roars to be freed. So I pet it and feed it and let it dictate my fingers on the keyboard without regrets.)

But even if you don't ever read another one of my novels or listen to one of my songs, I can't thank you enough for reading this one. I hope I can bring a little magic to your world in some way.

The art in me manifests in various forms—from my books, to my music, to my digital art and even the occasional article. I get confused about what I should call myself: author or musician or songwriter or graphic designer or armchair theologian. I think it's probably safe to say I'm just an artist at heart exploring the magic around us. Thanks for exploring with me!

*This is sarcasm.

‡This is not sarcasm.

OTHER PLACES TO FIND MORGAN:

» **Facebook.com/MorganGFarris**

» **Instagram @MorganGFarris**

» **Twitter @MorganGFarris**

» **YouTube @MorganGFarris**

» **MorganGFarris.com**

THE PARALLAX (THE CHALAM FÆRYTALES, BOOK III)